NINE INCHES

NINE INCHES

Bateman

WINDSOR
PARAGON

First published 2011
by Headline Publishing Group
This Large Print edition published 2012
by AudioGO Ltd
by arrangement with
Headline Publishing Group

Hardcover   ISBN: 978 1 445 89097 5
Softcover   ISBN: 978 1 445 89098 2

British Library Cataloguing in Publication Data available

Printed and bound in Great Britain by
MPG Books Group Limited

For my brother David

1

It was a dark and stormy night.

Or it might have been, for all the light getting into the office. I was three floors up, and the only hint of an outside world came from a skylight overshadowed on two sides by newer, taller buildings that blocked out ninety-nine per cent of whatever vague sunlight was managing to break through the otherwise solid grey of a Belfast spring afternoon. Somewhere in the far distance there were bagpipes, rehearsing for marching season. And pneumatic drills, tearing up footpaths, providing ammunition for marching season. We had moved on, and then put it all into reverse. It was like married life; we never knew if we were coming or going.

I had a nice desk, a laptop, a lamp, a phone and a family bag of Smarties. I was sorted for E's.

I was trying to remember the last time the phone had rang, or if it should be *rung*, when the intercom buzzer sounded and a garbled voice said, 'Starkey? Can I come up?'

In a better, more prosperous world, I might have had a security camera to tell me who it was, but as it was, I had to rely on my investigative skills to find out.

'Who are you and what do you want?'

There was an audible sigh. 'It's Jack Caramac.'

'Jack Caramac off the radio?'

'Yes.'

'Do you have an appointment?'

'*Yes.*'

'Just let me check.'

I drummed my fingers on the desk. After a couple of months I said, 'Jack Caramac, is it?'

'Yes.'

'Is it raining out there?'

'Yes.'

'Do you have an umbrella?'

'No.'

I said, 'Jack Caramac, Jack Caramac, Jack Caramac . . . oh yes, Jack Caramac. Your appointment is for three fifteen.'

'Yes.'

'It's only three ten.'

'Let me up, Starkey, you bollocks, or I'll take my business elsewhere.'

'Smoothie,' I said, and pressed the buzzer.

Jack Caramac—not his real name, incidentally, in case you're a moron—had, as they say, a good face for radio. If you took a bag of Comber spuds and sucked the goodness out of them and refilled them with Polyfilla so tight that it leaked out of their pores, then you'd have an idea of Jack's complexion. I have no idea if potatoes have pores, but that's neither here nor over there, where a man who ran naturally to fat but who felt compelled by his listeners to try every diet under the sun was squeezing through my door. He ballooned, he deflated, he ballooned, he deflated; his skin now had the elasticity of bamboo. As he lumbered into the office, it was clear that he'd recently hit the wall on his latest attempt. As he shook my hand and smiled, there was evidence of Crunchie between three of his capped front teeth.

He sat and said, 'Jesus, get a lift, I'm all out of puff.'

2

'Exactly why I have stairs,' I said. 'It sorts the wheat from the chavs.'

He had on a black sports jacket, black trousers, a black shirt open at the neck. It all looked designer expensive. But it was a bit pointless. People would just say he was a well-dressed fat bloke. He looked around very briefly and said, 'What a dive. I can't believe you have an office above a butcher's shop.'

I shrugged. 'It's cheap, and the sausages are amazing.'

He looked at me. 'Same old Dan,' he said.

'Same old Jack,' I said.

I'd known Jack Caramac for twenty years. In fact, since before he was Jack Caramac. He was a journalist once. So was I. I'd covered hard news, and tough stories, and put the boot in often, but always with a smile; I'd also been a columnist, which had brought me a certain amount of fame, and infamy. In some ways I was the print equivalent of what Jack had decided was the better career for him: for the past fifteen he'd hosted a call-in show on Cityscape FM, Belfast's most popular commercial radio station. But there was a crucial difference: my journalism was never about me; Jack's show was all about him, and exploiting the misery or mental imbalance of others. By and large, the kind of people who phone radio shows are the last people in the world you'd want to spend any time with: they are the loudmouths, the bigoted, the numbskulls and the egotists; they are the moaners, the blinkered and the self-righteous. They are the religious maniacs, the cynics, the warmongers and the apologists. They are also usually more to be pitied than scorned. It was not an accusation you could place at the large feet of Jack Caramac.

3

Though he was the living embodiment of all of these personality disorders, somehow his whole became something more profound than its constituent parts; nobody particularly liked him, but everyone wanted to listen to him. In the business he was known as the biggest cunt this side of Cuntsville, and he loved it. I used to think I rubbed people up the wrong way, but Jack took the biscuit. In fact, he took the whole tin, and usually between meals.

'Never thought you'd end up like this,' he said.

'Like what?'

He flapped his flappy hands around my pride and joy and said, '*This*. Man, *Belfast Confidential* used to be a licence to print money. Where did it all go wrong?'

'Who says it went wrong? I sold up, and now I'm a gentleman of leisure, taking on whatever jobs interest me.'

'This wouldn't be the same *Belfast Confidential* you sold for one pound because it owed a million quid?'

'They covered my debt, and I was a pound up on where I was when I went in. This day and age, who can complain about that? Anyway, did you just call round to rain on my parade, or is there something I can do you for?'

'Well,' he said.

'Well,' I said.

'I heard you were out of the journalism racket, and into like . . . investigating. Like a private eye.'

'I'm nothing like a private eye. I offer a boutique, bespoke service for important people with difficult problems.'

'Dan, no offence, but that sounds a bit wanky.'

'It's my specialist subject. I was, as you know, one of this country's leading journalists. That's still what I do, except I don't publish unless my client requires it. I enquire. I get answers. Then you tell me how you want me to deal with those answers. That can mean referring them to the forces of law and order, or using my public relations expertise to spin them into something positive. You know, on Facebake, or Twitter, maybe the *Ulster Tatler*, all the new media.' I cleared my throat. 'Have I sold you on me yet?'

'Only because I've nowhere else to fucking go.'

I smiled. He smiled.

'I'd make you a coffee, but the kettle's broke. I can send down for some mince if you like.'

'You're a funny man, Dan. But I don't need funny. I need help.'

'You were kind of vague on the phone.'

'I don't like phones.'

'You spend your whole life answering them.'

'That's different. That's work.'

'Oh yeah. The shock-jocking.'

'I'm not a shock jock.'

'As I am not a private eye.'

'I'm the people's champion.'

I raised an eyebrow.

'The problem,' he said, 'is that one of my people is threatening me.'

'So isn't that par for the course?'

'This is different. Usually it's just the nutters being annoying, but this time . . . this time they actually did something. They took my kid.'

'*Took?*'

'Yeah. I think so.'

'You *think* . . . ? Jack?'

5

'He's frickin' four, he can't exactly tell me, can he? But he was gone for about an hour. And when he came back, he'd a note in his pocket.'

'What kind of a note?'

Jack slipped his hand into his jacket and pulled out a piece of paper. He set it on my desk and pushed it across.

'Is that blood?' I asked.

'Jam,' said Jack.

The note said: *Shut the fuck up*.

2

I had been riding high, and then suddenly I wasn't. *Belfast Confidential*, the crusading news/vacuous celebrity magazine I inherited from my late friend Mouse, had given me a glimpse of the good life, and then the bitch of an economy had snatched it away. My tendency to burn bridges hadn't helped. Print media was dead and everything on the web was free; nobody was prepared to pay for what I did best, which was putting a spanner in the works. I was trying to reinvent myself, and Patricia thought she would give me a hand by chucking me out of house and home. Thirty-three minutes after I left, she'd changed her Facebook status to *single*. I would have changed mine to *couldn't give a fuck* if there had been a fucking button that allowed me not to give a fucking fuck.

Now here she was crossing the Lisburn Road, barely a hundred yards from my office, and entering the Shipyard, my city's most prestigious restaurant, looking fantastic for forty-two. Patricia, not the restaurant. She wore her hair long, dyed brown, and her clothes tight. Even the contempt of familiarity couldn't prevent me giving her the kind of once-over I normally reserved for strangers. She looked hot, and she knew she looked hot. She was bad to the bone.

I said, 'Are you going somewhere later?'

'No, I'm having dinner with you.'

'Oh. Right. It's not exactly dinner, it's only gone five. Is there a mid-afternoon equivalent of brunch? Not quite dinner.'

'High tea? Does it matter?' She smiled. I tapped my upper teeth and nodded at her own. 'Lippy?' she asked.

'No more than usual.'

She rubbed at her teeth. There was nothing there, but that wasn't the point. She would be wondering if everyone she'd spoken to since she left home had noticed her mistake. Of course she wouldn't have called it a mistake. She'd have called it a faux pas. She had developed certain airs and graces while the money was good at *Belfast Confidential*, and now that it was gone, she was still trying to hold on to them.

'Better?' she asked.

I pointed to a different tooth. She rubbed some more. In marriage, it is the small victories that are important, particularly as the larger ones are hard to come by.

And we were still married. Just about.

She said, 'So to what do I owe the honour? Last time we ate somewhere as plush as this . . . come to think of it, we've never eaten somewhere as plush as this.'

7

'A small celebration.'

She raised an eyebrow. Before I could continue, a waiter arrived at our table and asked if he could get us a drink.

I said, 'White wine, please.'

He said, 'Perhaps a Chardonnay or a Sauvignon Blanc?'

I said, 'Don't confuse me with science. White wine, and something for the mother.'

He kind of half laughed, in that patronising way waiters do, forgetting for the moment that they are fucking waiters. Patricia ordered a Smirnoff vodka and Diet Coke and said, 'I hate it when you do that,' as soon as he'd left.

'Do what?'

'The smart-alecky belittling thing.'

'You used to love it.'

'In fact, no. I just used to have a greater cringe threshold. So what are we celebrating?'

'I have a client.'

'Really?'

'Really.'

'Well, that's good. And you thought of me?'

'Well, I thought you'd be interested. And a problem shared is a problem halved.'

'Why would I want half a problem?'

'Because I always appreciate your input. And I want you to understand what I'm trying to do here with this business, and bear that in mind when it comes to me paying my share of the upkeep on our house, which I am currently struggling to do.'

'That's not my problem.'

'You threw me out.'

'Only because you're a useless waste of space.'

'Well clearly not any more. I have a client.'

8

The waiter returned with our drinks. He asked if we'd had a chance to peruse the menus.

I said, 'It says soup of the day without specifying what it is.'

The waiter's eyes flitted down to my shoes and back up. 'It's quail eggs and shark fin with ginseng,' he said. He cleared his throat and lowered his voice. 'It's eighteen pounds fifty-six.'

I nodded. 'Is that with a bap or without a bap?'

'With,' he said.

'We'll have the soup, as a main course.' I smiled across at Patricia. 'She's worth it,' I said.

Patricia smiled. He turned away. I called him back.

'Sir?'

'Just one thing. Is the bread Ormo?'

Patricia shook her head. The waiter was only about eighteen and hadn't the foggiest notion of the old advert I was joking about.

When he'd gone, Patricia said, 'Ordering for me? You've never done that in your life before. I think I like it.'

I sipped my wine. She mixed her vodka and gulped.

'So,' she said, 'what's the nature of your problem?'

'Jack Caramac.'

'As in . . . ?'

'The very same. Someone kidnapped his four-year-old son. But only for an hour or so. Sent him back with a note suggesting he shut the fuck up. The father, not the son.'

'About what?'

'He has no idea.'

Trish nodded, and for a moment concentrated

on the tablecloth. More than a decade ago, during one of our regular splits, she had become pregnant to a ginger man, and had a gingerish son. We got back together, and I grew to love him, and then because I got involved in more foolishness, he died. For me, the sense of loss had faded with the years, but the guilt never would. Trish had no guilt, and professed not to have blame. But she had. It was bleeding obvious.

'Has he gone to the police?' she asked.

'Of course not. He spends half his show ripping into them; he's not going to go crawling to them for help.'

'So he came to you?'

'He came to me.'

'As a kind of last resort.'

'As the next best option.'

'So what're you going to do?'

'What do you think I'm going to do? Investigate. First thing tomorrow.'

Our eyes met over our drinks. There had been a lot of water under the bridge, not to mention alcohol. We had always been connected, and we always would be. There had been love and loss and love again, and there had always been lust. Things would come around; they always did. We knew exactly how to push each other's buttons, in a bad way and a good way.

'Investigate to what end?' Patricia asked. 'I mean, I know you'll probably find who's responsible, but then what?'

'Then the ball's back in Jack's court.'

'Won't that be . . . unsatisfying? It's like doing all the foreplay and then someone else comes in for the money shot.'

10

Our eyes met.

'Where did you even *hear* that term?'

'Oh, these long lonely nights, what's a girl to do?'

'Well the last few months of our relationship, Scrabble seemed to be the answer.'

The soup came, and maybe later we would as well.

It wouldn't mean anything. It would be another pull on the auld roundabout and we would only know where we truly were with us when it stopped.

She said, 'I'm glad you're doing this, really. You need a new start.'

'Professionally,' I said.

After a suitable pause, she nodded.

'Don't be getting yourself into anything too dangerous.'

'I don't plan to.'

'Jack Caramac, he's a pain in the arse, a lot of people would want to harm him. But it's not good when kids get involved.'

'I know. I'll find out what's going on. More importantly, this soup tastes like cack.'

'It surely does.'

'And it's probably worth mentioning now that Jack would only employ me on a results-based basis.'

'You're telling me in a not very roundabout way that I'm paying for this cack-based soup.'

''Fraid so.'

We nodded at each other over our bowls.

None of this was a surprise to her.

I said, 'How many years is it since we last did a runner?'

She said, 'Too many. But in these heels?'

'Definitely,' I said.

11

3

Of course, it ended in tears, and she fled my apartment leaving only a flurry of curses and a bra in her wake. I was alone once more, a porn-again single man.

I spent the rest of the night quietly sipping in the *Bob Shaw*. It was only around the corner from my new home. The pub was artsy enough to be interesting, and with an old enough clientele that you didn't feel like a child molester if you glanced appreciatively at someone. It was in the heart of what had recently been christened the Cathedral Quarter, which was kind of Belfast's Left Bank without being particularly left, or featuring a bank. There were gay bars, galleries, coffee shops and bijou theatres. All in all a much greater variety of upmarket establishments from which to request protection money. The city was transformed, but it always had two fingers in the past.

I was home for eleven thirty, inebriated. The apartment was on the second floor of a new complex at St Anne's Square. It had started out neat and I did my best to keep it that way. Patricia had been impressed both by the decor and furnishings and the fact that I could afford it. I told her I'd got a good deal on the rent and when it came to the fixtures my latent good taste had flourished since our separation. Neither was quite true. In the dog days of *Belfast Confidential*, I'd squirrelled away a certain amount of cash rather than waste it paying bills, and that had served as a down payment on this show apartment, which came interior-designed and furnished to the hilt by someone who actually did have taste. I was two months behind on the mortgage.

The square was designed around a piazza, with chic cafés where you could sit outside during any one of our three days of summer. On one corner there was a Ramada Hotel, on the other the MAC, a flourishing new arts centre. Most nights the area was pleasantly busy. I like to sit in my duffel coat on my veranda, sip a whiskey and listen to the chat drift up from below. I've never liked silence, and hearing drunk people talk shite has always been quite comforting. Belfast is so much more relaxing now than in the old days, when the city centre, encased in a ring of steel, was so quiet that you could hear a pin drop—usually having fallen out of a shoddy Libyan hand grenade.

I refilled my glass, and took my laptop outside. I plugged in earphones and began to download podcasts of the past two weeks' worth of Jack Caramac. I was guessing that whatever had annoyed someone enough to want to kidnap his four-year-old must have happened in the very recent past. I wasn't sure exactly what I was listening for. It was just a case of letting it all soak in. Jack's show was a mixture of the serious and the trivial: one minute teenage suicide, the next an earnest debate about the correct thickness of pancakes. People spoke passionately. Jack was good. Cheeky like your best mate, as sympathetic as a bereaved relative, and an attack dog when riled. I wasn't just looking for the major topics that attracted hundreds of calls, but the little ones too, the insignificant items that failed to ignite the holy grail of audience participation and were very quickly cut off. I'd been a journalist for long enough to know that very often it was the odd throwaway line rather than some major accusation that most annoyed people. You could quite happily libel someone as a nut job, but if you said he supported Glentoran rather than Linfield, he'd start screaming blue murder.

I woke shivering at just after three a.m. I'd the beginnings of a headache. While I slept, someone had thrown a pizza crust at me. It was resting on my shoulder. It did not taste unpleasant. When I was done, I took the glass and the laptop inside. I took the time and trouble to wash the glass. I dried it and put it away. I went into my bedroom. The sheets still smelt of Patricia. I lay on top, and sighed.

*   *   *

Cityscape FM operates out of an industrial park on the Boucher Road. It's a single-storey building with lots of post-Ceasefire glass. I parked and entered without having to be buzzed in. Considering that Jack Caramac had so recently been threatened, security was kind of lax. There was a good-looking blonde girl on the front desk. She wore a badge that said her name was Cameron Coyle. She smiled pleasantly and asked how she could help me. She appeared not to notice the twinkle in my eye as I replied, or else dismissed it as a cataract. I was getting to that age. I told her I was here to see Jack, and she took my name and told me to take a seat, he was still on air. It was being piped in, so I knew that. He was talking about dementia, but soon segued smoothly into poo bags for dogs.

I said, 'David or Diaz?'

'Excuse me?'

'Are you named after Cameron Diaz or David Cameron?'

'Who's David Cameron?'

'Fair point.'

She answered a call. She was pleasant but firm.

When she hung up, I pointed at the speaker and said, 'What's he like to work for?'

'Jack? Jack's the best.'

'I mean, really.'

She smiled. I smiled. I was interested in how loyal his people were, or how pussy-whipped. I put that thought out of my head straight away and said, 'We're old muckers, I know what he's like.'

'He's been very good to me.'

She smiled and nodded and answered some more calls. Ten minutes later, another attractive blonde came through swing doors and asked if I was Dan and told me to follow her. I did so willingly. She led me into a surprisingly small studio. Jack had his feet up on the desk, half a sausage roll in his mouth and the other half in crumbs down his shirt. He gave me the thumbs-up and indicated for me to sit down. He had a pair of earphones around his neck, and through the glass I could see someone in the next studio reading the news, which was coming through loud and clear.

Jack wiped his mouth and said, 'How's it going?'

'It's going fine.'

'Get anywhere?'

'How do you mean?'

'With the case.'

'Jack, I've hardly fucking started. Give me a chance.'

He started to say something, but then held up

a finger and slipped his headphones back on. He turned to the next studio, where a new presenter had come in. They had a couple of minutes of on-air banter, and then Jack said his goodbyes. A green light above him switched to red.

'So what are you thinking?' he asked.

'I'm thinking I need your call records for the past two weeks. I presume they're all logged.'

'Yes, of course. But there's thousands of them. Tens of.'

'I appreciate that. I'd like them all, though. It's not just about the people you expose or humiliate on air, though they're important. It's just as likely to be someone who has a grudge because they didn't make it.'

'There are data-protection issues, Dan. We can't just release—'

'Am I working for you or the station? Who'll be writing the cheque?'

'Cheque! You're so old-fashioned, buddy. The station, obviously.'

'Then as an employee, I'm entitled to look at the call records.'

'You sure about that?'

I raised an eyebrow.

'Okay,' he said, 'fair enough. I'll organise it.'

'Good. And I'm also thinking I'll need to talk to the witness.'

'Witness? You mean Jimmy?'

'The boy, aye.'

'Dan, fucksake. He's only a tot, he can hardly talk.'

'Maybe he could draw me a picture.'

'He's *four*.'

'Four-year-olds can draw.'

16

'Yes, Dan, but he's not some kind of fucking autistic savant. It will involve crayons and scrawling. Is this your master plan?'

'You asked me to do a job, Jack, let me do it. Did I mention I know a child psychologist who'd be willing to talk to him?'

Jack blinked at me. 'Talk how? What would he do?'

'She. She'd beat him around the head with a space hopper. What do you think she'd do, Jack? Let her have a word, eh? See what she can tease out. If you're serious about this, then you need to help me.'

He looked uncomfortable. 'It's just, I'm not sure Tracey would approve.' Tracey. Wife of twenty years. Formidable. 'She doesn't believe in that kind of thing. Thinks it'll go on his record, all that, you know?'

'Don't tell her, then.' He made a face. 'Jack. Help me here. Is your boy in school?'

'Pre-school.'

'Who picks him up?'

'I do. In about half an hour.'

'See? Perfect?'

His eyes narrowed. 'This is my boy. I love him. I was careless and someone nabbed him. I thank God every day that I got him back. This is serious stuff, Dan, and I need to be able to trust you. Don't let me down.'

'Me?'

'*You.*' He heaved himself up out of his comfy chair. 'Okay. Let's do this. But you had better not be yanking my fucking chain.'

'Perish the thought,' I said.

17

4

We took Jack's Jag. 'Child seat,' he explained. It was this year's model. We drove to the Royal Victoria Hospital.

'Do you know something?' Jack asked, nodding ahead towards the huge, sprawling jumble of hospital buildings that dominated the skyline. 'The RVH was the first building in the world to install air-conditioning.'

'Really,' I said.

'Oh yes. Nineteen oh six. The engineers at the Sirocco Works, just down the road there, pioneered it. Doing this show, I learn a lot of useless shite.'

With its setting in the heart of Republican west Belfast, it could be argued that some of the locals had themselves spent years since installing air-conditioning for free all over the city.

I have always found the RVH a dark and depressing place. The only thing bright about it today was the sight of Leontia Law standing waiting patiently for us by the front gates. She was wearing a knee-length leather skirt and brown boots that met it halfway. Her hair was short and she wore no make-up. She had on a doctor's white coat.

As Jack drew up, I got out of the passenger seat and opened the back door for her. She slipped her coat off, folded it over her arm and slid in. I went with her.

Jack glanced back and said, 'No.'

'No?'

'You sit up front with me. Or she does. If you both sit in the back, I'll look like your chauffeur.'

18

'Jack, who cares? And by the way, could you put your cap on?'

He didn't smile. I got out and rejoined him. He nosed the Jag into traffic while I made the introductions. He started telling her about the air-conditioning, but she said she knew.

'Worked there long?' he asked.

'Two years,' she said. 'I'm actually in the Royal Belfast Hospital for Sick Children; it's kind of tacked on to the other side.'

Jack nodded in the mirror. 'I don't want you upsetting my boy.'

'Of course not,' said Dr Law.

'But the truth will out,' I said.

Jack's eyes flitted across.

*   *   *

The Cabbage Patch Nursery was based in a large Edwardian house festooned with security cameras, just off the Malone Road. Malone was money. Malone was class. Probably no child in the entire nursery had ever been near a real live cabbage patch.

'You've moved up in the world,' I said.

Jack said, 'Perhaps it's you who's moved down.'

Unlike at Cityscape, there was an elaborate security system to negotiate. So we waited in the car while Jack went for Jimmy.

Dr Leontia said, 'Are you sure this is wise?'

'Of course it is,' I said.

'You're a frickin' chancer,' she said.

'It has been known.'

Jimmy came back on Dad's shoulders. Cherub-faced, full of chat. Jack introduced us

19

as his old friends Dan and Lenny. Jimmy wasn't the slightest bit interested. He wiggled a plastic dinosaur in his dad's face as he was strapped into his chair and said, 'Dino wants ice cream.'

It seemed like a plan.

On the drive to McDonald's, Leontia made small talk with him. They seemed to hit it off. He lent her Dino for all of five seconds.

As we waited at lights, Jack said, 'You never have kids, Dan?'

'Kids? No.'

'Then you won't know what they mean to you. I don't care about the hair on my head. But if anyone harms a single hair on his . . .'

'Don't worry,' I said. 'He'll be fine.'

I was thinking mostly about the hair on Jack's head. We'd worked together for years, and I'd a fairly clear recollection that his mane had been rapidly receding. Now it grew luxurious and thick. Weave was the way, these days.

Jimmy demanded the drive-thru, but Lenny wanted the chance to talk one on one with him, so she quelled his protests with a promise of the largest ice cream he could eat, unstrapped him and walked him in, though not before he'd shaken his head and said that Daddy had said he wasn't allowed to go off with strangers. Daddy reassured him that it was okay this time because she was Daddy's friend. Satisfied, he toddled off, hand in hand with her.

Kids are such fricking suckers.

Jack and I stayed in the car. He shook his head at the packed restaurant before us. 'Fuck me, it's half twelve on a Tuesday; where do all these fucking kids come from?' When I didn't respond, he said,

'Do you think he'll be all right with her?'

'Relax. She's a specialist.'

'She looks young to be a specialist.'

'Cops and doctors both, Jack.'

'Christ, I know. It would sicken you.' He drummed his fingers on the wheel. Then he rubbed at his brow. 'Do you know what haunts me, Dan? Do you remember where I trained as a reporter?'

'Down in Bangor, wasn't it?'

'Aye. Family-owned paper. Not many of those around now. But the owner's wife, this nice old dear, she got to write a column every week. Kind of about nature, and literature and poetry. She lived out in the country, and she found this baby badger . . .'

'A cub.'

'I know what it is, Dan. Anyway, she found this baby cub badger, abandoned, or I think maybe dogs killed its mum, and she raised it herself. From a wee tiny thing to a bouncin' big badger, and she wrote about it every week, and published photos, and it was like house-trained and one of the family and it was so sweet, it was like a fucking Disney picture. People loved it. Kids came to visit.'

He fell silent. After a bit, I said, 'Your point?'

'My point, one morning she came down to let it in, 'cos like it still went out foraging or whatever the fuck badgers do at night, but it always came home for breakfast and a snooze. But you know what one of her loyal and lovely readers had done? Battered it to a pulp and left it lying dead in her porch. And do you know why?'

'No.'

'Because that's what people are like. Evil.'

I sighed. 'Yeah, I probably knew that.'

21

'And that's what worries me, that they'll do something to Jimmy just because they can. Children, they're your fucking weak spot.'

'What does Tracey think about it?' Jack drummed his fingers again. He studied the passing traffic. 'You haven't told her, have you?'

'I told her about the note, but not how serious I thought it was. Didn't want to worry her. I mean, what if it's just one of the local kids having a laugh? Feel pretty bloody stupid then, won't I? You'll get to the bottom of it, though, Dan, won't you? You were always the best at sniffing shit out.'

For all the good it did me.

Ahead, Dr Leontia and Jimmy were just emerging. He had ice cream plastered across his face. So did Lenny. They were giggling.

'There's nothing you want to tell me, Jack, some reason someone's after you that you haven't mentioned? Better I know now.'

'Swear to God. How can I shut the fuck up if I don't know what to shut the fuck up about? I talk all day on national radio. It's what I do. I can't just zip it, you know, unilaterally.' He swivelled as the back door opened and his mood lifted instantly. 'Look at you!' Leontia lifted Jimmy into his chair. 'Ice cream everywhere!'

He reached back with a handy wipe and proceeded to rub.

'Well,' I said, giving Lenny a wink, 'what did you manage to wring out of the wee bugger?'

'*Starkey.*'

'Sorry, Jack.'

'That he was taken into a car and driven around.'

'The bastard!' shouted Jack.

'Make and model, licence plate?'

'Yeah, right. It was silver.'

'Description of suspect?'

'If I find him,' Jack snapped, 'I'll fuckin' kill him.'

'Wasn't a he,' said Dr Leontia.

*   *   *

From McDonald's, it was quicker to drop us back at my car and for me to take Lenny on. She apologised for finding out so little, but Jack was over the moon.

'I got bugger-all squared out of him, so this is a result. Isn't it, Dan?'

'Certainly is. Narrows it down to half the world's population and its most favourite car colour. Case more or less closed.'

But it was something, and something is always better than nothing. I drove Lenny back to her work. I slipped her a twenty. She slipped it back.

'Just doing a friend a favour.'

'Nice touch with the doctor's coat,' I said.

'I feel a bit bad,' she said.

'Balls,' I said. 'You have four kids, you know as much about child psychology as anyone.'

'Well, if you insist. Will you be in later?'

'Never know your luck.'

I winked, and Leontia shut the door and hurried in to start her shift in the *Bob Shaw*.

5

It was gone three on an April afternoon, a light rain falling. It was mild. Mild is the best we ever get. All our weather is varying degrees of mild. And not just the weather. Our mountains are mildly high. Our rivers never rage. Our wildest creature is a badger. A badger would roll a cigarette for you if you asked it nicely. As a people, it is our very mildness that prevents us from dealing with the very few nutters who screw up our country. In Northern Irish terms, *shut the fuck up* was pretty fucking mild.

The Malone Road is mild, and inoffensive. Malone and the various Deramores and Bladons that lead off it. The area is dominated by the Royal Belfast Academical Institution's playing fields, by Methodist College, by people with more sports cars than they know what to do with. Malone is home to millionaire pop stars, celebrity chefs, heiresses and politicians. Home to Jack Caramac. A million and a half for a house in any provincial city isn't bad going. Jack's was north of that. Red brick, mature trees, rolling grounds.

I parked just around the corner, but in a position where I could just about see the lower half of his lengthy driveway. Ten minutes after I arrived, Jack drove out. I gave it a couple of minutes before starting up and driving in. There were still two other cars sitting on the gravelled forecourt, a BMW and a Mercedes. I was hoping to catch his wife, Tracey. I knew her of old. Jack spent so much time projecting his personality and opinions on the radio that when he was off air he didn't have a huge amount left to say for himself; even with his child momentarily kidnapped, he had been vague on the exact circumstances, on the detail I needed to move forward. Jimmy was missing for a while, nobody seemed to notice, then suddenly he was back with the note. Tracey at least should be able to give me a little more detail. She wouldn't be able to help

24

herself. She was a motormouth.

I rang the doorbell. It played 'Lady in Red'. For a *long* time. I wanted to smash it with a hammer. But I had no hammer. It would keep. After an eternity, a girl, probably no more than nineteen, twenty, opened up; she had Jimmy in her arms.

I said, 'Hiya, Jimbo, long time no see.' He gazed at me without any semblance of recognition. So I said, 'Is Tracey in?'

'No.'

I said, 'Oh. I was hoping to catch her. You're . . . ?'

'I am nanny.'

'Is that your name or your occupation?'

Nanny the nanny wasn't absolutely impossible.

'I am nanny.'

Okay, it was going to be one of those ones. Her face was pale and expressionless. She was in tracksuit bottoms, a buttoned bally jersey and slippers. Every few seconds she gave Jimmy a little jiggle with her arm. There wasn't a lot to pin her accent on, but it was probably somewhere west of Carnlough and east of Krakow.

I said, 'I'm Dan—I'm working for Jack. About what happened to Jimmy . . . him disappearing?'

'Not my fault.'

'I didn't say . . . Do you mind if I come in and have a wee word with you? I need—'

'No come in. Come back when they are here.'

'It's just a couple of questions.' I delved into my jacket and took out one of my business cards 'That's me, that's my name.'

She looked at it, nodded and handed it back. 'It is card. Anyone can have card. You could be serial killer.'

25

'Well if business doesn't pick up . . .' I stopped that one almost as soon as I started. Talking to someone with only a basic understanding of English is like speaking to a moron. I said, 'You haven't noticed anyone hanging around, maybe checking the place out?'

'Yes,' she said. 'You.'

'I mean—'

'Come back another time. No thank you. Nice day.'

She closed the door. I stood there, mildly damp. I was not unused to rejection.

*   *   *

I walked back down the drive, past my car and out on to the main road. As a reporter, I had spent many unhappy hours knocking on doors asking questions. You get kicked back all the time. Reporters make Jehovah's Witnesses look popular, and they're a bunch of bloodless cunts. At least *then* I could legitimise my enquiries with a nice laminated NUJ badge. Now I was just being nosy, with only a dodgy business card out of a cheap machine to back me up. But it had to be done. Once in a very long while you hit paydirt.

To the left of Jack's, there was a half-built house leveraged into what appeared to be a patch of ground that was too small for it. Certainly the outer edges of the building butted up against the perimeter trees and hedges of its neighbours. There was no sign of workmen, or large construction equipment; a cement mixer sat neglected, with weeds growing up around its base. Across the city there were many similar developments destined

26

never to be finished. The world economy was in the shitter. Everyone had a different theory about who to blame. With my luck, I was surprised nobody had pinned it on me yet.

To the right, there was another large dwelling, considerably older than Jack's, with a hint of neglect about it. Opposite was a row of six more recently constructed townhouses: I had a vague memory of the fine old house that had been knocked down to make way for them. *C'est la vie.*

I decided to try the townhouses first. My eyes were immediately drawn to the one on the far left with the silver car in its short driveway. I knocked on the door. An elderly man with wispy hair answered. I showed him my card. It seemed to confuse him. It seemed to confuse many people. But he was friendly enough. He lived alone. The car was his. He hadn't noticed anyone lurking. Nobody was at home in the next four. The final door was opened before I knocked. A young woman, maybe thirty, in tight jeans and a white shirt with her hair tied back and sunglasses pushed up, was coming out in a hurry.

She said, 'Oh!' nearly bumping into me. 'Sorry!'

Make-up perfect, lovely smile.

I gave her my card and asked if she'd heard that someone had tried to lure a child into a car across the road. It was close enough to the truth. She made a horrified face and said, 'Here . . . ? Oh my God! Where?'

I pointed to Jack's house. 'Their four-year-old. He's fine, but it could have been worse.'

'Wee boy?' She was nodding across the road. 'I see him running about their garden, and seen him out on the road a couple of times. Walked him back in once; it's a busy road. They have like a young girl, teenager, walks him up and down in a stroller sometimes?'

'Nanny,' I said.

'Yeah, she's a strange one. I tried to talk to her once about the boy wandering and she didn't want to know.'

'She's foreign,' I said.

'Yeah, I know, but still.'

'So you haven't seen anything unusual?'

'Not that I can think of. Sorry, I'm in a bit of a rush.'

'No problem. Sure, keep the card; if you think of anything, give me a bell. Or just give me a bell.'

She kind of half laughed, and looked at my card anew. 'Dan Starkey? I know that name.' She studied my face. 'Didn't you used to be big in newspapers?'

'I'm still big,' I said. 'It's the newspapers that got small. Tabloid, mostly.'

She nodded uncomprehendingly. 'So what's this? Like a wee retirement job?'

'No,' I said.

6

Lenny was gone by half one. Some nights the *Bob Shaw* has a late licence, some nights not. They aren't always the same nights. She uses this to confuse her husband so that we can grab some time together at my place. It works for me, and it seems to work for her. We call it the Happy Hour.

I took a Bushmills out on to the veranda and

28

watched her wend her way through the drunks. She had a taxi pre-booked to pick her up outside the bar. It always came at the same time, and so did we.

I woke shivering at four, and there was another pizza crust, this time in my lap. I was turning into late-night sport for someone. I went inside and cranked up the heat and poured another whiskey and listened to some more Jack Caramac and sat with a notebook, making lists of callers' names and what they were whining about. Later, I managed a couple of hours' sleep and then a shower and shave before wandering across the city centre and up Great Victoria Street, on to the Lisburn Road and my office. I could have worked from home, but it was too easy. It seemed important to make the effort to get out.

I was in position by ten. I had coffee from Arizona, a few doors down, and a Kit Kat from Nestlé. I read the papers online and then moved on to Facebook. I had discovered, by bumping into them in Starbucks two weeks earlier, that Patricia was meeting one of her work colleagues for coffee. She swore that there was nothing in it, but they looked shifty enough for me to suspect the worst. We were separated, though not legally. We—and when I say *we*, I mean *I*—had always played fast and loose with the marriage vows, but nevertheless, this was a knife to the heart. His name was Richard McIntosh. I shook his hand and passed idle chit-chat for all of thirty seconds before pretending I had to take an urgent call and fleeing. In years gone by, fists would have flown and I would have ended up in Casualty feeling miserable, so I was quite proud of the way I dealt with her treachery. I was older, more mature. When I got home, I went

29

online to find out what I could, but there wasn't much beyond a couple of photos on Google Images of him playing rugby for a work team. He wasn't even on Facebook. So I created an account for him, uploaded his photo and set about asking random strangers from around Belfast to be his friend. People rarely say no to such requests, so before very long I'd acquired more than one hundred and fifty new mates for him. Then, working tirelessly, I went through the photo collections of many of these new friends, adding pithy comments on his behalf. Things like: *love the chins, fatty*; *see you're keeping incest in the family*; *those are fucking big ears, Dumbo*, and *yer ma's yer da*. The level of abuse that appeared on his wall in response was quite incredible. Every time he was removed from a list of friends, I found him another. According to Patricia, her strictly platonic friend Richard had been punched twice in the face by random strangers in the past few days while out and about in the city. It was such rewarding work.

The buzzer sounded at eleven. A vaguely familiar voice said, 'Hi, I'm from Cityscape FM. Jack asked me to pop round with an envelope for you.'

'Oh right, come on up.'

I was hoping it was Cameron, but it wasn't. It was the other one. I tried not to look too disappointed. She was equally gorgeous. She had on a black Puffa jacket and purple jeans. Her hair was dirty blonde and short. I put my hand out and told her I hadn't caught her name yesterday.

'Evelyn. Evelyn Boyd. I'm Jack's producer.'

'Oh right—I thought you were just like one of those dizzy blonde girls who ran around doing things.'

She gave me a look and said, 'No.'

I smiled. 'Have a seat.'

'I have to—'

'Kettle's broken, but I can offer you one quarter of a Kit Kat.'

'No, really, I—'

'Is this them?' I nodded at the envelope she still held in her hand.

'Oh. Yes.'

She handed it over.

I said, 'Thanks for bringing them. You didn't have to come up.'

'Yes I did. You don't appear to have a letter box.'

'Good point. My mail gets left with the butcher downstairs. When I pick it up, it's usually bloodstained. It adds a certain frisson.'

She smiled hesitantly. 'I should be—'

'No, seriously, take the weight off. Not that you . . . I mean, I wanted to have a word anyway. Jack said it would be okay.'

'Did he?'

'Absolutely. He said you were the first and last line of defence between him and the great unwashed.'

She sat. She smiled. 'Really?'

I nodded. He hadn't, but he should have. It's good to appreciate. I was appreciating now. If I was ten years younger. And she was ten years older.

'I take it he's told you what this is about? The threat, his kid.'

Evelyn nodded. 'He's very worried.'

'You must talk to a lot of cranks.' She held my gaze for a moment before nodding. 'How do you sort them out? You let some of them on air purely for entertainment purposes?'

'Course we do.'

'And what about those who don't make it; do they not just get crankier?'

'We try to be kind. We just say there's such a high volume of calls that we've run out of time. And actually, it's usually true.'

'Do any of them ever turn up at the station, try to confront Jack?'

'Rarely. We don't really advertise the address; we have a post office box number. Of course if people want to find us, they generally will, but most of our callers haven't . . . the wherewithal, if you know what I mean.'

'What about when he's out and about? Does he get approached much, maybe threatened, asked for autographs? You know, like John Lennon?'

'Not really, no. Jack's a radio man, so his face isn't that widely known. It's one reason he avoids doing TV, so he can preserve that anonymity. Again, you can Google him and get as many pictures as you want, but he hasn't got that kind of recognisability that goes with genuine fame. He can get about pretty much unmolested.'

'What about in the station itself?'

'How do you mean?'

'Would he have enemies there?'

'Enemies?'

'Someone who might want to give him a scare, put the frighteners on him?'

'No, of course not.'

'A jealous presenter with an eye on his slot. A chairman who resents paying him so much. A blonde who's been sleeping with him and hates the fact that he won't leave his wife.'

Evelyn raised an eyebrow. 'Of course other presenters are jealous of him; he's got the number one show, best time slot, highest paid. But they're also aware he keeps them in work, because he's the only one making the station any money.'

'The golden goose who lays the . . . what about that?'

'What about what?'

'Is he getting laid? A woman scorned and all that.'

'No. Absolutely not. And I'd know.'

'Fair enough. Had to ask. How would you know?'

'Because I'm with him from the moment he walks into the station until the moment he walks out. And the rest of the time he's with his wife.'

'Sure about that?'

'No reason to believe otherwise.'

'Trudy.'

'Tracey.'

'That's what I said. You know her well?'

'No. A bit. She comes to station functions. Jack has a New Year's party. She's . . . okay. Protective.'

'Possessive?'

'Protective.

'And older.'

'Older?'

'Than the general age of blondes you'd find working in a radio station.' Before she could respond to that, I followed it up sharply with: 'Jack has a certain reputation. For being awkward. Hard to work with. Egotistical. Mean. Given to rages. In fact, people say he's a bit of a cunt.'

Evelyn's eyes widened. 'I don't like that word.'

'I'm sorry. No wish to offend. Is wanker any better?'

33

'I'm not sure I like your tone, Mr Starkey.'

'Please, nobody calls me Mr Starkey.'

'I'm not sure I like your tone, Mr Starkey.'

We stared each other out. I quite liked her, but sometimes people have to be pushed and prodded, even the attractive ones.

'He's a star. All he wants is to be treated like one.'

'Fair enough,' I said. 'So you're doing him too.'

'That's just . . . ridiculous. I'm engaged, if you must know.'

'Couldn't be true then, fair enough.'

She stood up. I stood up too.

'I better fly,' she said.

'Good luck with that. And thanks for the info.' I tapped the envelope. 'I've been friends with Jack for twenty years, so don't take anything I say about him personally. We like to wind each other up.'

'Is that why he told me you were a sad alco who needed a break?'

'He's *such* a bitch.'

She smiled. I smiled.

I said, 'I'm heading out myself. Can I give you a lift back to the station?'

'No, I'm fine, thank you, I've the car with me.'

'The silver one?' I asked.

She looked suitably surprised. 'How'd you know?'

'I know many things,' I said, cryptically.

She stood her ground. 'No, really, how do you know?'

'Relax, it was an educated guess. Last year, sixty per cent of new cars bought in the UK, including that part of Ireland that will always be British, were silver. I have an endless amount of such trivia in my head.'

'But why would you even say that? I might have been up all night worrying about how you would know.'

I shrugged. 'I'm very good at keeping women up all night,' I said.

She gave me a tight smile. 'Hard to believe,' she said.

7

'Hey!'

I had just locked the front door of the office and was turning away when the voice stopped me and I turned to find the butcher from the butcher's standing in his doorway, mid-fifties, stripy apron matching his stripy awning. Bald head, toothy grin, sawdust on his loafers.

'Catch!'

He threw something and I caught it, a reflex action. In Belfast you should *never* catch things people throw at you. This was a white plastic bag, nipped with a tiny ribbon of harder red plastic at the top. Within: what I hoped were cold thick sausages.

'Oh—thanks. I . . . ?'

'You're new, upstairs.'

'Yeah. Six weeks.'

He'd served me twice in the shop, but I suppose one customer looks pretty much like another.

'A private eye.'

'No, I . . .'

'That's your commission.'

I blinked at him. I lived in a city more familiar with decommission.

'I don't under . . . ?'

'Yer man Jack Caramac off the radio was in the shop yesterday, hanging around waiting to be recognised. When nobody did, he said who he was and that you'd recommended us. He was angling for free sausages. I don't give free sausages to no one.'

'You just gave . . .'

'Like I say, commission. Eventually he bought some, and he must've liked them 'cos he was raving about them on his show this morning, gave us a name check'n all. Been busier than usual all day. So cheers.'

He gave me a wink.

I said, 'Cheers, mate, and thanks for the sausages.'

*   *   *

I've always had a soft spot for the Shankill Road, even though it's hard as nails. One and a half miles of arterial road through a twenty-five-thousand-strong Unionist working-class ghetto. It's one of the few places you can still buy a pasty, rather than a panini or a panacotta without them looking at you like you're a fucking space cadet. The Shankill bore the brunt of, and equally was responsible for, some of the worst violence of the Troubles. Paramilitaries ruled it, and they still do, only they've transmogrified from Loyalist freedom fighters financing their struggle through robbery, drugs, protection and murder into gangsters who finance their lifestyles through robbery, drugs, protection and murder. They justify their continued existence in the face of widespread peace by occasionally rolling out their flags and yelling about their loyalty to the Queen and the imminent danger of a Republican uprising. Republicans usually oblige by shooting someone. It is the gangster equivalent of fixing the market. It works equally well for both sides.

I turned off the West Link and spent fifteen minutes driving around reacquainting myself with the area. It used to be one giant slum, rows and rows of crummy terraces designed to squeeze in as many workers from the old linen mills as inhumanely possible. They're gone now, the mills flattened and the houses bulldozed to make way for wider streets and modern, neat grey-brick houses, nearly every one of which now boasts a satellite dish. It gives the impression of a vastly improved lifestyle. But it's just another PR job, stone cladding over rising damp. Community workers will tell you that it is still one of the most socially disadvantaged areas in Europe—the very same community workers who aren't long out of pokey themselves for helping to make it one of the most socially disadvantaged areas in Europe.

Shankill Road PSNI Station is actually just off the Shankill Road in the inaptly named Snugville Street. It is known locally as Comanche Station. In the dark days its inhabitants always preferred to fight fire with fire. Not exactly taking no prisoners, but taking them and then beating their heads till they talked. These days you have to be a bit more circumspect, but for all the softly-softly edicts about community policing coming out of HQ, on the Shankill you still need to be able to kick arse or you're dead in the water, often literally. In other parts of Belfast, beat bobbies patrol the streets on *bicycles*. If you tried that on the Shankill, you'd be on stabilisers for life.

In the old days, if something happened, you could just wander into Comanche Station and get the facts first hand; you could hang out, exchange info and gossip. Now you have to call the press office at HQ, and they get back to you with a sanitised version of a sanitised version; it's depressing and half the reason I knocked straight news journalism on the head. Back then, the station was as dark and doomy as Mordor. Now it looks more like the regional office of a moderately successful insurance company.

I drove past and turned back on to the Shankill and parked. There's a café a few doors up from West Kirk Presbyterian Church. I went in and ordered a pot of tea and three German biscuits. I studied my notes for ten minutes and glanced at my watch. Then he came in, and he wasn't alone.

'Maxi,' I said, 'how're you doing?'

'Starkey,' he said, 'long time no see.'

In my prime, I never would have called him by his first name. Maxi McDowell was a thirty-year veteran, a desk sergeant nobody dared cross, inside or outside of the station. He was the only cop in north and west Belfast who didn't bother to hide the fact that he was a cop when he arrived for work; who parked his own car outside his own station and never worried that someone would try and blow it up, either with him in it or not. They knew it would only make him angry. Of all the contacts I had had in Comanche Station, he was the only one still working. Just about.

'My last week,' he said, 'and then I get to put my size twelves up for good. That's why I've brought DS Hood. Gary Hood.'

I nodded at him. 'Good name,' I said.

Hood gave me a wan smile. He was clean cut, early thirties, smart suit.

'Heard them all before,' he said.

'He's a good man,' said Maxi, 'though obviously I won't say that to his face.'

Maxi poured tea for the both of them. Then he picked up a biscuit and admired it. 'I wonder how many of these I've had down the years? It's all fucking energy bars now, isn't it?'

Hood said, 'What's this about? Journalists are supposed to go through—'

'Easy, tiger,' said Maxi. 'I told you, Dan's an old friend. Or enemy. I can't quite remember which.'

'Somewhere in the middle,' I suggested.

'Yeah. That sounds about right. Pain in the hole you were, Starkey, but you always stood your ground. And your round, as I recall. So. You were kind of vague on the phone about what you're into these days.'

'Well, it is kind of vague.'

'Then tell me about Jack Caramac; what's that fucker gotten himself into? I remember him when he was plain old Jack Cairnduff. He was a shite reporter then and he hasn't improved much since. Done well for himself, mind, have to give him that.'

'He's being threatened. Him and his kid. For obvious reasons he doesn't want to go through you lot. I'm just trying to work out who it might be, and why.'

'I would think the *why* is fricking obvious. He's

an annoying fat prick.'

'Yeah, well, it's the nature of his show. I've been going through the transcripts, and the one that sticks out is this young fella, Bobby Murray.'

'Bobby Murray,' said Hood, shaking his head.

'Bobby Murray,' said Maxi, 'deserves everything he gets. And then some. He should consider himself lucky he only lost the one leg.'

'Ah well,' I said, 'he's somebody's son.'

Maxi rolled his eyes. 'Jesus, don't get me started on that old bag! Thirty years of shite I've put up with, and she's the one driving me to retirement. Never out of the shop, complaining about this, that and everything to do with her wee fucking sunbeam.'

Bobby Murray himself wasn't that important. He was fourteen, mixed up in the usual kid things, but with a Shankill twist. He hung out with his gang, he drank, took drugs, he dealt a little, he fell out with his supplier, his supplier was in the UVF, he got threatened, he was told to leave the area, he refused, he got beaten up and told to leave again, he stayed, so they kneecapped him. Blood poisoning set in, he lost a leg. It's a common enough story. The Shankill Limp is a familiar sight all over the city.

There are a hundred Bobbys on the Shankill, but they don't all have a mother like Jean Murray. He wasn't quite the apple of her eye, but he wasn't entirely rotten either. She wanted to know why in this supposed peacetime the members of the UVF whom 'everyone' knew were responsible for her son's shooting hadn't been picked up by the police, why they were still allowed to walk the streets. When she didn't get satisfactory answers, she decided her only course of action was publicity, and there was no better conduit than that self-proclaimed people's champion, Jack Caramac.

Most of the things Jack talks about usually enjoy a two- or three-day run, but this one seemed to prick the public's imagination, and his own. He interviewed her on the phone, he brought her into the studio, he kept it going, and going, and going, for months, switching between lambasting the police for doing nothing and the UVF for exercising gun law over the poor downtrodden people. After a while it seemed that Jean had become the Shankill correspondent of the Jack Caramac show; and maybe she grew to like it a little too much.

'Tell you what,' Maxi said, 'I wish Jack Caramac *would* shut the fuck up. He hasn't a clue what he's talking about. He calls us all the names of the day, so he does, and we have to sit here and take it. Dan, you can't just fly in and round up the usual suspects these days; you need evidence, you need multiple witnesses, you need the weapon, the DNA. These guys, if they do something, they're power-hosed, bleached and lawyered up before you can even type *search warrant*. And yes, she may know exactly who did it, but do you think her wee Bobby's gonna stand up in court and point them out? You honestly think he'd live that long? Besides, with his record for dishonesty, he wouldn't have a fucking leg to stand on. So to speak.'

'And the thing that pisses us off,' said Hood, pointing half a biscuit at me for emphasis, 'is that Jack Caramac knows all this damn well. He's just stirring the pot for badness.'

We talked on for another twenty minutes, but pretty quickly it got back to Maxi reminiscing about

41

the good old bad old days. I'd heard it all before, and so, clearly, had Hood. He began checking the text messages on his phone. When I eventually steered Maxi back round to the matter at hand, he gave me a couple of names of people I should talk to and then we left Hood to settle the bill—which he didn't look too enamoured with—and dandered back towards my car.

'How's the missus, Dan?' Maxi asked.

'Fine and dandy,' I said.

'That bad?'

I gave him my shrug and said: 'Can't imagine you retired. What're you going to do with yourself?'

'I'm going to sit on my arse and do bugger-all.' He laughed. 'The wife's picked out a wee place up the coast; we'll be up there by the weekend. Always been a city boy, but it's all changed round here. Maybe get myself a fishing rod. Or maybe get my hands on some Semtex, catch them in half the time.'

I hadn't actually heard anyone say Semtex in years.

'Go for it,' I said. 'What about yer man?' I thumbed back towards the café. 'Child protégé?'

'Ah, he's not a bad kid, Dan. When he joined, he was as straight as a Methodist hymn book and I got about as much joy out of him. But he's learning, and I think he'll be okay. I'll text you his mobile number. Keep him in the picture, and you never know.' Maxi thrust his hands into his pockets and gave a slight shake of his head. 'I didn't think you had much time for Jack Caramac.'

'I don't. But it's a job, and there's the kid involved. Hate that.'

'Aye. Fair enough. I remember your wee one.'

42

I nodded.

We arrived at my car. It was a Range Rover, black, and had once been pretty sleek. It was another smuggled-away reward from *Belfast Confidential*'s glory days. Maxi's eyes roved over the empty tax disc holder. He kicked lightly at a tyre. I'm sure he noticed the lack of tread. He smiled back at me.

'Dan—word of advice. I know you've been out of it for a while, but don't be fooled into thinking this peace shite means anything up here. Our pals in the balaclavas, maybe they were fighting for something once, but they're doing it for themselves now, and they're not even that bothered about the balaclavas any more. They always were a bunch of fucking animals, but in the old days they wouldn't have dared touch a journalist; now they'll fucking torch you as soon as look at you. So if you start asking questions, prepare for the worst.'

'Bear it in mind,' I said.

8

Dewey Street is just a few twists and turns away from Comanche Station. Jean Murray's Housing Executive semi featured brand-new double glazing, with wire-mesh security grilles and scorch marks up the brickwork. There was one security camera facing down above the front door, and another covering the tiny garden. There were probably others around the back. As I parked outside, I saw a couple of kids sitting on a wall opposite. Teenagers. One skateboard between them. Cropped hair, neck chains, trackies, trainers, sullen looks. I nodded over and they nodded back. When I walked up to the front door and rang the bell, one of them shouted, 'Whaddya want with that cunt?'

I said, 'A cunt's a useful thing.'

They were still thinking about that when a man's gruff and tobacco-thick voice said over the intercom, 'What?'

I said, 'Hi, ahm, my name's Dan Starkey . . . I'm working for the Jack Caramac show. Would it be possible to talk to Jean Murray?'

'You're talking to her.'

'Oh.' I'd heard her on the radio and knew her voice was deep, but this was much further down the scale. 'Sorry, the speaker . . . Anyway, could I have a word?'

'What about?'

'I'd really prefer to do it without the neighbours listening in.'

After a moment she said, 'How do I know you're not sent from them to shut me up?'

'Ahm, you don't.'

'You have ID from the station?'

'Sorry, don't have any. Jack's employing me privately.'

'So how do I know?'

'You don't. Don't I look trustworthy?'

I beamed up at the camera. Something that was halfway between a snort and a laugh came out of the box, and thirty seconds later I heard a single bolt being drawn back and the front door opened. Jean Murray was standing there, cropped red hair, freckled, housecoat, slippers, fag hanging out of her mouth.

'Sorry, I've a stupid cold, my voice has gone.'

44

I said, 'Shouldn't you have better, bigger deadbolts than that?'

'Aye, you would think that, but they tell me if a petrol bomb comes through the windies, you're not going to want to spend ten minutes trying to get out of the house. It's half a dozen of one, about four of the other. Come on in.' She stood to one side, and I moved past her. She stepped back into the doorway and glowered at the kids across the road. 'Why don't youse go and play outside your own house?' she yelled.

'Fuck off, tout!' one shouted back.

'Fuck off yourselves!' Jean yelled and slammed the door shut.

*   *   *

Jean showed me into a front room. Although it was still early afternoon, she had three lamps on to counteract the filtering effect of the security grilles. There was a large TV with an untidy pile of DVDs beside it. A leather sofa and chair with what looked like cigarette burns and dotted with used tissues. A hearth with a lit gas fire, and above it half a dozen framed photos of a boy, taking him from a rotund baby on to primary school, cherub-faced and smiling, and then one for each year of secondary school. These later ones showed the biggest changes—from slightly chubby in a neat uniform with a tidy hairstyle to beanpole, ragged tie, greasy hair and acne. You could see it in his eyes, too: from innocence to defiance.

'This Bobby?' I asked.

'Robert. Yes.'

'Where is he now?'

'Shooting people.' She thumbed above her. 'On the Xbox upstairs. You'd think he'd have had enough of guns, but he's at it all day. Zombies, mostly.'

'Not at school?'

'Well his attendance was random at the best of times, but he hasn't been back since . . . all this shite started.'

'I understand you're a single parent, but was there a Mr Murray?'

'Not that it's any of your business, but Mr Murray skedaddled years ago. Do you want a cup of tea?'

'No. No. Thank you.'

She sat on the single chair. She lit another cigarette. 'Suppose you've come to break the news; Jack's throwing the towel in as well? Fucking typical.'

'No. Jack's as . . . committed as ever. It's more a private thing. Jack's being threatened; it may well be over this. He's asked me to look into it.'

'Threatened? Fuck, he should try living here, I get it every day. Scared to leave the house, so I am. Thank Christ for internet Tesco or we'd starve to death. Threatened how?'

I told her about Jimmy, about him being kidnapped for an hour and the jammy note.

'The fuckers,' she spat.

'So what I'm really trying to do is find out who might be doing this, so maybe if I can get them for threatening Jack, that'll take some of the heat off you and your boy as well?'

'You really think?'

'Well it might help to—'

'Ah, you're pissin' up the wrong tree there, mate.

46

I'm sorry if they're hassling yer man because of my boy, but you know, at least he can do something about it. He has the money for people like you. He can move house if he has to. He can look after himself. What am I gonna do? I'm on my own here. You know how many times the house has been attacked? 'Cos I don't. Lost track. They've burned my wheelie bins, my car, tried to burn me out, smashed the windies I don't know how many times. And they're going to keep doing it till they get him, get him dead. That's all they want. Dead or out of the country, that's what they want.'

'You wouldn't consider moving?'

'Where the fuck to? *England?*' She cackled. She stubbed out her fag and lit another. Her fingers were as yellow as her teeth. 'You think I have the money for that? Anyway, this is our home. Why should we be chased out by a pack a hellions? Nah, fuck 'em, we're here to stay. If we go anywhere, it'll be out in a fuckin' bax, so it will.'

I said, 'What about Bobby? How's he coping with it? Can't be easy losing a leg like—'

'Never mind the fuckin' leg, it's his fuckin' attitude is driving me up the wall. And he had that before they shot him. Teenagers should be locked up until they get some sense into their fucking heads. You tell them one thing, they do the other. One minute they're your best friend, the next they're screaming their head off at you. Caught him taking money from my purse the other day and scalped the fucking hide off him. Wouldn't even make ye a fuckin' cup of tea.'

I nodded. 'So can I have a word with him?'

'What for?'

'It's just useful to get stuff straight from the

horse's mouth.'

'No point, he says nuthin' about nuthin'. Anyways, we all know who's behind it. Those Miller boys are bad fuckin' news, so they are.'

There was no arguing with that.

When I'd been covering the Troubles, the Millers would still have been in short trousers, but they were all grown up now, and had risen through the ranks of the UVF to the point where they now ran 1st Battalion, which covers the whole Shankill area. Thomas 'Windy' Miller and his brother Rab still had a boss, a brigadier general, who was supposed to keep them in line. They were supposed to sit down regularly and agree common policies with him and the six other battalion commanders, the so-called brigade staff, but they were still pretty much a law unto themselves. The perceived wisdom was that it was better to keep them within the organisation and try and exert some measure of control over them, rather than force them out and give them a reason to form their own paramilitary group where they would answer to no one. Through thirty years of the Troubles, Loyalist paramilitaries had killed twice as many of their own men through internecine strife than they had their Republican enemies. Nobody wanted to see that kind of open civil war on the Shankill again. That was the real reason the high command left them alone, and why the police themselves never came down too hard on them. In the larger scheme of things, Bobby Murray's missing leg meant *nothing*.

'They're, ugh, not really the sort of guys you should be messing with,' I said.

'So everyone keeps telling me, but why the fuck not? Who are they to tell me and my boy to get out? Who are they to fuckin' cut my boy's leg off? They're too big for their fuckin' boots, that's what I say. You know something? I saw that fucking Windy Miller in the fruit shop down the road, and I went right up to him and said what the fuck do you think you're doing pickin' on my wee lad, he's only fucking fourteen, and do you know what he did? He got out of there as quick as he fuckin' could, he ran away, so he did. Big man issuing commands to hammer my wee lad, but couldn't even stand up to me in a frickin' fruit shop. Big man. Big fucking man.'

She extinguished her half-smoked cigarette and tried to light another one, but her hand was shaking too much. She had a tear in her eye. She stood and went to the bottom of the stairs that opened directly into her living room.

'Bobby!' she guldered. When there was no response, she amped it up. 'BOBBY!'

'*What?*'

'There's a man here to see you!'

'What about?'

'He's trying to help. Will you come down and talk to him.'

'NO!'

'Bobby! He's come special to see you.'

'No! Tell him to fuck off!'

Jean raised her eyebrows at me, and came back into the room. 'See what I mean? Apparently you're to fuck off. The language of him! Sorry, he's just at that age.'

'Not a problem,' I said. I stood up. 'Listen, thanks for seeing me. It can't be easy.'

'I don't think it's supposed to be easy. Not for the likes of us.'

49

There was nothing I could really say to that. I reached into my jacket and took out one of my business cards. I flicked it between my fingers for a moment and then handed it to her. She studied it.

'It just says *Starkey*. What exactly do you do?'

'Mostly I interfere in difficult situations and set off a chain of events completely beyond my control.'

Jean managed a smile. 'You sound like a fuckin' laxative.'

'Got me in one,' I said.

It was scary how close to the truth she was.

I said, 'Give us a bell if you think of anything that might help, or there's anything else I can do.'

I moved past her out into the hall and reached for the door lock.

'Dan, is it?'

I turned back to her. 'Aye.'

'My wee fella, he's no angel, but he's not the worst kid in the world. He doesn't deserve this, doesn't deserve any of it. And I'm not going to let them get away with it. Jack Caramac or no fuckin' Jack Caramac.'

*   *   *

As I approached the car, I saw that *PEDOFIAL* had been scratched into the paintwork in very large letters.

The two boys were lolling on the wall opposite.

'You do this?' I asked.

'Nah,' said one.

'And even if we did, what're you going to do about it, *pedo*?'

I shook my head. I opened the door and climbed

50

in. I started the engine and pulled out. I stopped beside them and rolled down the window.

'For your information,' I said, 'that's not how you spell paedophile. And even if I was one, I still wouldn't fuck youse, youse fucking gormless inbreds.'

And then I drove on.

9

Patricia's house—*my* house, that is—is on Cypress Avenue. We were united in the bidding for it for different reasons—she thought it was the nicest part of the city, and I knew it had inspired the Van Morrison song. Now that we had split, the song was tainted for ever. Another big fat fucking mark against her, that.

The house itself is a red-brick Victorian with dodgy slates and an infestation of woodlice. It is cold and draughty and costs a fortune to heat, which it never quite does. There are too many rooms for too few people. There are four guest bedrooms. We never had that many friends. We were a tight little unit, Trish and I, when the times were good. But with the first sign of trouble I was out on my arse, and I was now forced to stand outside the front door and ring the bell, as if I didn't even have a key. It crossed my mind that she might have changed the locks, but I didn't have the heart to check. Because it's such a big house, if you're caught on the wrong side when the bell rings, you usually miss whoever's there. I knew this, and waited. It was gone four in the afternoon. When

51

she eventually opened the door, she was wearing a dressing gown. A black silk one I had bought her for Christmas and which I'd never yet seen her in.

I complimented it and her. And then added, 'You're home from work early.'

'You said you were calling. In fact you're the one who's early.'

'I'm not looking for a fight,' I said.

'Then stop trying to pick one.'

'I wasn't. How's your lover?'

'Oh fuck off.'

I held my hands up. 'Okay. Truce. You know what I'm here for.' She nodded and stepped aside. As I passed her I said, 'Did he slip out the back way?'

She said, 'No, he's still tied to the bed.'

I smiled. She did not.

I followed her up the stairs to my study. I'd never done much studying there, but it was where I kept my music. There was a lot of vinyl and several hundred CDs already packed in cardboard boxes.

She said, 'I don't know why you don't just toss all that shit out. I mean, you can download it for nothing.'

'It's not the same.'

'Yes it is,' she said.

'You'll never understand. That's why we don't work.'

'Really. I thought it was because you're such an arse.'

'Takes one to know one. Though, nice arse.'

'You noticed.'

'I couldn't not, the way you waggled it in my face coming up.'

'That's just the way I walk.'

'You should get that checked out.'

'Maybe I am.'

She gave me a smile. I didn't give it back.

I was flicking through the CDs, taking them out randomly and checking that she hadn't removed the discs from within.

She said, 'How's the case?'

'It's not a case. It's a job.'

'How's the *job*, then, pedant?'

It was the second time I'd been called something similar in the last half-hour. I shrugged.

She sat on one of the boxes and said, 'Tell me. I'm interested.'

I gave her a long look. When she didn't crack a smile, I said, 'Jack's been championing this woman and kid from the Shankill the UVF are trying to chase out.'

'Jean Murray.'

'You know her?'

'No, dummy, I've been listening to his show since you mentioned you were working for him.'

'I'm not working for him. He's one of my customers.'

She sighed. She said, 'Well, despite you being an arse, I *am* interested. She's hard as nails, isn't she? And brave to the point of stupidity.'

'Yep,' I said.

'So you're thinking she and the kid are tied into the threat Jack got?'

'It's a possibility. I went out to see them. Not a great situation.'

'Why did you feel the need to go and see them? Didn't it all come out on the show?'

'Not really, no. She keeps saying it, and God knows Jack keeps saying it too, that they know who's responsible, but they won't let her name them on the radio. Too worried about getting sued. The show's not quite live, there's like a twenty-second delay to allow them to yank something if it gets dodgy. Anyway, you know I always prefer to get it straight from the horse's mouth.'

'And sometimes you get taken for a ride.'

'Nature of the business.'

'And what business would that be?'

I looked at her. 'I'm not a private eye.'

'No you're not, Dan. You're a PA.'

'P . . .'

'Private arse. And you'll get it kicked if you start messing around on the Shankill. You know that.'

'It's a distinct possibility.'

'So why do it? There'll be other customers; you just have to be patient.'

'Trish. I need the money. *We* need the money. Unless you want to sell swanky Cypress Avenue here, then maybe I could afford to be a bit choosier.'

She smiled. 'That'll be the day,' she said.

*   *   *

I put the last box in the car. She stood at the door and watched.

She said, 'Somebody's written on your car. Unless you're advertising.'

'Ten minutes on the Shankill and my reputation's in ruins.'

'Darlin' . . .' she began.

I put my hand up. 'Enough already.'

'So what're you going to do now?'

'A pie and a pint had crossed my mind.'

'I mean about the case.'

'It's not a case.'

'Dan . . .'

'I'm going to ruminate, that's what I'm going to do. But before that, if you don't mind.' I came up the steps. She stood against the frame, and there was a very slight arch to her back, as if she was expecting a kiss. 'Do you mind if I use the bog before I go? Been on the road all day.'

She moved to the side, and I hurried past and up the stairs. I turned at the top towards the bathroom, but kept on going until I got to her bedroom. I had to check if that fucker was tied to the bed.

10

Visiting Trish was just a time-killer, with the remote possibility of no-holds-barred sex, while I waited for my anointed appointment with Boogie Wilson, publican, poet, and brigadier general of the Ulster Volunteer Force. Only two of these professions featured on his business card. He had come by the name Boogie not because he was scary in any way, although he was, in many ways, but because as a teenager in the seventies he had briefly been Northern Ireland disco-dancing champion. He always seemed inordinately proud of that. His poetry was widely regarded as 'shite', but he hadn't had a bad review yet. Boogie always said he had a soft spot for me because I'd been instrumental in the permanent removal of his rival for the top position in the organisation, Billy 'Dainty' McCoubrey, nearly twenty years previously. Any time I'd met him since, he had been friendly, a great story-teller and liberal with the free drinks. You just had to keep at the back, or indeed front, of your mind that he was the leader of possibly the most vicious terror organisation in Europe.

Boogie Wilson's pub is on the Newtownards Road in east Belfast. It is called, for some reason, the *Red Hand*, and if you sit at the right table, and crick your neck in a particular way when you look out of the window, you can gaze through a decorative arch above the road outside, celebrating the Battle of the Boyne in 1690, and see the massive twin cranes Samson and Goliath, permanent tombstone reminders of the shipyard that had once seemed to employ every Protestant in Northern Ireland. The gable wall of the *Red Hand* is completely covered in a mural showing the men of the Ulster Rifles falling at the Somme in 1916. Inside there are framed posters, photos and newspaper clippings depicting the rise of the UVF in the mid-sixties and its hooded men armed to the teeth on various manoeuvres; there are pictures of POWs from inside the Maze, paintings by prisoners, photographs of visiting Hollywood stars calling in for a little local colour and to perfect their accent for an upcoming movie. You can buy T-shirts emblazoned with *Proud to Be a Prod*, UVF badges, scarves, jigsaws, *No Surrender* hoodies, flutes, twirling batons, and Oranjeboom lager imported from the homeland of the Duke of Orange.

The thing is, I'd been in the pub a little over a year previously on a different story, and there'd been none of this. It had just been an ordinary spit-and-sawdust bar, albeit the only one in town you

56

could still smoke in because the inspectors were too scared to tell Boogie otherwise. The decor had been strictly seventies, and the menu consisted of a box of crisps and some salted KP nuts. Now you could order à la carte.

Boogie shook my hand, and I said, 'What the fuck is going on with this place? It's like Disneyland designed by a Kick the Pope band.'

Boogie did me the honour of giving an embarrassed grin, and said, 'Ach, Dan, you gotta move with the times. We're celebrating our Ulster-Scots heritage, so we are. We got a grant from the tourist board to do it up. Most of our drinkers now come off the tour buses. Tourists or Italians doing their PhDs on fucking post-Troubles stress. Isn't it great? And it's a licence to print money.'

'You used to do that anyway,' I said.

Boogie put a finger to his lips. 'Shhhh . . . I still do.' He gave me a wink. He probably wasn't joking. He showed me to a table and then went behind the bar. 'A pint, is it?'

'No thanks, I'm driving.'

'Latte?'

'Seriously?'

'We use only the finest beans, Fairtrade, hand-picked by Somalians, then smuggled in to avoid the VAT.'

I took that on board, and asked for a Diet Coke. It came via a spray and tasted like rusty water. It probably wasn't made by Coca-Cola. In fact, it probably was rusty water.

Boogie made himself a latte and brought it across. He was in his sixties now, almost completely bald, muscled still but a little overweight. He wore a white shirt open at the neck and a thin gold chain. His sleeves were rolled up, purposefully revealing his many and varied UVF tattoos.

I said, 'So the bar business is booming.'

He said, 'Aye.'

'And how is the poetry business?'

'Cut-throat.'

'And what about the business of saving Ulster from the Republican hordes?'

'Ongoing.' He shook his head. 'Every year, every year on Remembrance Day, I issue a proclamation solemnly declaring that it is time for us to lay down the arms we haven't already laid down and for us to disband. Every year I get roundly ignored by the rank and file. So I soldier on, trying to keep a lid on it.'

He gave me a wan smile. I nodded with fake sympathy. It was a bit like me and Trish, constantly fantasising about peace but locked in a perpetual state of war, except he seemed to enjoy more of the benefits.

I took a sip of rust. 'And what about the Miller boys leaning on some poor wee woman and her one-legged son on the Shankill?'

'Is that why you're here? I thought it was to do with Jack Caramac?'

'It is, I think.'

I mentioned the threat to little Jimmy.

'Really? A note in his wee pocket? I'm not convinced either of the Millers can actually write. Anyway, it seems a bit anaemic for them, if you know what I mean?'

'I know. But I thought that seeing how it was Jack, and the publicity that might come with it, they probably didn't want to go the traditional route, something a bit more subtle.'

'Aye. Right. Bollocks. Sure they love the publicity. It's what the half of them is in it for. It used to be they modelled ourselves on *The Godfather*—now it's all gone *Sopranos*, you know what I mean? They lack class.'

'I hear what you're saying, Boogie.'

'What's it with the Murray woman anyway? If she just shut her bake, she wouldn't get half the hassle. She goes blabbing to the likes of Caramac, she's just pouring petrol on the fire, you know? She's her own worst enemy. I've people in the Housing Executive, so I know she's been offered houses outside the Shankill and she's refused them. She's an obstinate, mouthy cow and she's up against the likes of the Millers? Come on. I mean, how many legs does the boy have to lose before she realises she can't beat them? You know how it is, Dan, they can't be seen to look weak.'

'I know that, but Jesus, there must be some way of sorting it.'

'Dan, it's their problem, they need to deal with it. It's not a good time to rock the boat. I notice you didn't take this direct.'

'Well, different generation. I thought maybe you . . .'

'Could have a quiet word?'

'Or have them shot or something.'

'As if I would be involved in any of that! But tell you what, seeing as how I probably owe you one, I'll do you a deal.'

'I don't really . . .'

'Hear me out. You're well in with Caramac, right?'

'He's a client.'

59

'He's a useless waste of space, but he has the ears of the nation.'

'A certain section of.'

'You get me a mention for my new poetry collection and I'll see what I can do about the Millers. And when I say a mention, I don't mean him tearing into it and saying who do I think I am publishing poetry when I'm responsible for this and that, and then every man jack phoning in to rip me to shreds. And I don't mean him reading them out in a silly fucking voice and taking the piss. You get me a serious mention, then I'll see what I can do about getting the heat taken off the auld doll, and maybe that'll ease up the pressure on Jack and his wee lad. What you say?'

I looked at him. I took a sip. 'Sounds good to me,' I said. 'What's your book called?'

'*Love and Rockets*,' said Boogie.

11

I parked in Jack's driveway, behind eight luxury vehicles. Mine was quite luxurious too, but it was the only one with *PEDOFIAL* etched on the side. I took a copy of *Love and Rockets* from the glove compartment and slipped it into my jacket. I locked the car and walked up the gravelled drive to the front door. I rang the bell and Tracey answered. Short black hair and eyeliner, turbo tan, fag in one hand, cocktail in the other, and a crowned smile beneath enhanced lips. There was music of a sort in the background, some kind of jazz cack.

She said, 'Dan Starkey! Long time no . . . Come

on in and join the party . . .' She came forward and kissed one cheek and then the other. 'Do you wanna cocktail?'

'No thanks, Tracey, I'm driving.'

'Leave it, we'll get you a taxi later.'

'Okay,' I said.

She sniggered. 'Were you always this easy?'

'Yes,' I said.

I followed her down a well-lit hall into a large open-plan kitchen. There were about a dozen or more middle-aged well-offs sweating in the heat from a green Aga. I said *hello-hello-hello-hello* as Tracey led me through to where Jack was setting up the drinks.

'Hey, Danny.' He grinned corpulently, holding up a glass. He turned to gaze into a large, mostly empty green-tinged vessel. 'We had a vat of it made up earlier, but they've drunk me outta house and home.' He poured the remnants into the glass and held it out to me. 'For you, the Last of the Mojitos.' He giggled, and then repeated it louder, for everyone else to hear. He was greeted with sycophantic laughter and patronising groans. His producer Evelyn was there, grinning; an older man I half recognised had his arm protectively around her shoulders, his mouth set in what appeared to be a permanent grimace.

'What's the occasion?' I asked.

'Who needs an occasion? It's Friday, buddy, Friday.'

I sipped my drink. We were thirty years of global warming short of a highball summer, but it wasn't unpleasant.

Jack came out from behind the counter, put his arm round my shoulders and squeezed. 'Danny

61

and I,' he announced, 'started out in journalism. And now I am what I am and Danny boy here is a private eye!'

'I'm not—'

'Danny's a private detective,' Jack declared, 'a PI, a bird dog, a bloodhound, a peeper, a sleuth . . . anyone else think of . . . ?'

'Nark,' said one.

'Shamus,' said another.

'Dick,' said Evelyn.

Everyone laughed. I gave them my tight smile and said, 'Very funny, heard them all before . . .'

Jack gave me another squeeze. 'Loosen up, man! Friday night!'

He propelled me into the centre of the room, in amongst his fan club. I forced myself to make small talk and answer mindless questions about what it was like to be a private eye. I made shit up. They didn't know any different. They weren't particularly obnoxious, they were just from a different world. Maybe I had been like them when I'd had a bit of money, but I hoped not. They talked Swiss chalets and the après-ski, they talked school fees and who was a useless idiot on the board of the Lyric Theatre, who was going to Castleward for the opera and their hopes for Ireland in the Six Nations. Nobody mentioned Liverpool, nobody talked about The Clash, nobody seemed aware of exactly how many wonderful cans of Harp you could get *right now* for a fiver at Stewarts Wine Barrel.

After a while I pulled the sliding doors open and slipped out of the stultifying heat and conversation on to a sheltered patio. It was still raining, and dark now. I sipped my third bottle of imported Australian Crown lager and checked my watch. I was only really there to pass the poetry book on to Jack and kill time till Happy Hour. Ahead of me there was a long garden festooned with kids' play things: a climbing frame, a slide, a set of swings, three pedal cars and balls in various sizes. The lawn beneath the swings and around the frame was immaculate. I hadn't seen hide nor hair of little Jimmy since I'd arrived.

The doors behind me opened, giving me several bars of something that to my eternal shame I recognised as the Swingle Singers, and quickly shut again. Tracey joined me. She was on the vodka now, and her voice was thick. She said, 'Who're you hiding from out here?'

'You,' I said.

She snorted. 'Dan, you're still a geg, so you are. How's that wife of yours?'

'Absent without leave,' I said.

'Really? You mean like split up?'

'Yes, like split up.'

'So you're available?' she asked, and followed it with a throaty cackle and the flick of her lighter.

'For the right price,' I said.

Tracey grinned. 'You okay, Dan?'

'Yeah, I'm fine. Yer man seems in good form, considering.'

She inhaled, blew out and said, 'Yeah, he's okay. So what do you think of the auld castle? Smart, eh?'

'It's very nice, Tracey.'

'Be a lot nicer if that monstrosity wasn't there.' She nodded towards the hedge that separated their garden from next door and the dark outline of the partially built house beyond. Blue plastic sheets on the roof flapped in the breeze. 'Our garden used to be perfect, south-facing, sunlight till sunset, now half the light's blocked and once they start building again I won't even be able to get me tits out without them having a bird's-eye view.'

'Sure they're half out anyway,' I said.

She giggled. 'You noticed.'

'It's difficult not to.'

'Too much?'

'Absolutely not. I'm all for—'

The doors opened behind us again and we turned to see Jack coming out. 'Here's youse are,' he said, and handed me another bottle.

'Never worry about me,' said Tracey, holding up her now empty glass.

'I don't.' He winked at me and kissed her cheek. He slipped an arm around her waist. 'Get you in a mo, honey, soon as you tell me what you two are jabbering about.'

'I was just saying,' I said, 'about what good form you were in. Life and soul and all that.'

'And why not? Listening figures up, advertising up. Did you see yer man with Evelyn?' I glanced through the glass at the unhappy-looking bloke still standing with his arm around Jack's blonde producer. 'Face like a fucking Lurgan spade. Do you know him?'

'He looks vaguely . . .'

'John D. Lehane. Anyone who introduces themselves with their fucking initial in their name deserves a rocket in their arse. He owns the station.'

'Ah—right. He's your boss.'

'So he thinks. Whenever I joined it was going down the pisser, so I was able to cut this fucking cracker deal. I get such a whack off the advertising, you wouldn't believe it. He resents every bloody farthing he has to give me. He should be happy we're doing well, but oh no, all he can think about is how much he's paying me. I hate glass-half-empty people.'

'My glass is completely empty,' said Tracey.

He kissed her again. 'Don't worry, sweetheart, I'll get you one now . . .'

He began to turn, but she stopped him with a hand on his chest and said, 'No, you talk to your mate. I've some entertaining to do. I think it's time the karaoke machine came out.'

She gave us a mischievous grin and disappeared. Jack smiled after her.

'Some woman, heh?'

'Yep, you pulled a cracker there,' I said.

He lurched suddenly to one side, but just managed to steady himself against one of the wooden support pillars for the patio cover before he landed on his ear. He looked accusingly down at the patchwork flags, as if they had somehow conspired to unbalance him.

'How's the wee man?' I asked.

His brow furrowed. 'Wee . . . ?'

'Jimmy.'

'Ah—gotcha!' He cackled. 'Never worry about Jimmy, he's at his granny's.'

'I do worry. At least until I get—'

'I hate kids at parties, they're always whining for attention. I'll pick him up in the morning.' He tapped his head. 'Or the afternoon, depending on the auld noggin.'

'I meant, from the security point of—'

'Dan, I know what you mean.' He straightened against the pillar. He cleared his throat. He nodded at me. His mouth worked as he fished for the right words. He was leading up to something. It's always fun watching a drunk trying to be taken seriously. And God knows I'm an expert. 'Dan, yes, good, listen. While we're here, alone, like, I've been wanting to have a word.'

'Have several,' I said.

He contemplated that for a while, then said, 'Never mind that, I've been thinking about us . . . what we're doing. I mean, about you looking into this, Jimmy, the whole . . . kidnapping thing, and, anyway, I think maybe we overreacted, a wee bit. I've talked it through with Trace, and people at work, and, I know people too, if you know what I mean, and they're all inclined to agree that it was most likely local kids just fuckin' with us, you know what I mean? That or maybe some listener on day release, a bit mental, but no real harm done, and lesson learnt.'

'Jack, your boy was snatched. He was gone for an hour. You were very lucky.'

'We don't know that. He's four!'

'He's still three, Jack.'

'Oh pish and sticks, Dan, I know this job means a lot to you, but there's no point in turning it into something it isn't. If there was a woman in some mythical silver car, most likely she found him wandering and brought him home, y'know? *Nothing happened to him.* It's not that kind of a neighbourhood.'

'And the note?'

'Well maybe she wrote it as a warning to be more careful. Or he coulda just as easily found it lying in the street; you know what they're like, pick everything up. Anyway, Dan, I'm sorry, we panicked. It's over.'

'Over?'

'Over.' He patted his left trouser pocket, then his right. He looked momentarily confused before remembering his back pocket. He produced a folded envelope. He unfolded it and handed it over, not a hint of the sheepish about him. 'This is for your trouble.'

So that was it.

I took it. I opened it. Two hundred quid.

'That okay? I presumed you'd want it in cash.'

So, that was how it was. I slipped the envelope into my jacket and drained the rest of the bottle.

'Whatever you think, Jack. I just hope you're right. I should hit the road anyway.'

'Hey—don't be like that. Dan. Stay, buddy, we're hardly getting started.'

'Nah, gotta see a man about a horse anyway.'

'Dan, c'mon.' He punched me lightly on the shoulder. 'We go back.'

'I know we do, and it's not a problem. But seriously, I'm late already. No hard feelings, your decision.'

'You're a good man, Dan. I appreciate the help.'

I nodded, turned, and then stopped, and pulled out *Love and Rockets*.

'Would you do me a favour, though?' I asked.

'Anything,' said Jack.

12

I had five pints of Harp in the *Bob Shaw*, and a packet of Tayto cheese and onion crisps, for fresh breath and confidence. Leontia was behind the bar, and every time she served me, I gave her a winning smile.

In the old days—and I hate people cracking on about the old days, it's really fucking boring, but I've gotten to the age now where the old days are the most fascinating part of my life—publicans were sole traders surviving on luck and circumstance; then, when our war flagged, big business began to squeeze out families and install dead-eyed managers with timesheets, franchises and corporate practice. But there are still a few oddities dotted about the city. The Crown, on Great Victoria Street, is arguably our most famous pub—a replica of it was built at Denham Studios in Buckinghamshire so that James Mason could film *Odd Man Out* without having to get on the ferry—and is now operated by the National Trust. You can drink and protect your heritage at the same time, which is just *bizarre*. The *Bob Shaw* is another. I'm growing to love it. It has a slightly bohemian feel and boasts good vibes. I have a favourite chair. I even have a mild affection for the books of the man it is named after, and I fucking hate science fiction. Bob Shaw is better known now as a pub than he ever was as a writer, but I'd read his *Orbitsville* as a kid and loved it, and later kind of related to his 'Light of Other Days', a story that introduced the concept of *slow glass*, through which the past can be seen. He probably didn't mean pints of Harp, but I'd lost months to them. Thankfully, apart from a few posters of his book covers, the bar is just a bar, and not stuffed with sci-fi memorabilia.

I was quids up on my case, but annoyed and unsatisfied. Jack, on the other hand, was smug and self-satisfied. He'd engaged me on a results-based basis, but had still paid me off. Of course, he could afford it. But the way he did it, half-cut and cash in hand, made it feel less like a reward for hard work and more like a donation to charity. He had been worried enough about his own safety to seek me out in the first place. Now suddenly, with nothing apparently having changed, he had sacked me. I didn't like it. Not one bit. And then I thought that maybe the reason I didn't like it was because I was so pathetically grateful for the cash, and that it just underlined where our respective lives and careers had taken us, him with his big house and cars and local celebrity lifestyle, and me with my mortgaged-to-the-hilt flat and my baldy tyres. About the only thing we now had in common was his wife. He probably wouldn't have employed me at all if he'd known I'd given her one for Ulster, and a couple for the twenty-six counties we hadn't yet seized.

It was a long time ago, of course.

Now I was strictly a one-woman man.

Leontia set me up with another one. 'Happy Hour approaching,' she said, leaning against the bar. 'And did I mention that the hubby has taken the kids up the coast, and won't be back till tomorrow, so I can stay over?'

'No,' I said.

'Well he has,' said Leontia, 'and he won't.'

'Oh goody,' I said.

One woman at a time, I mean.

*   *   *

Previously the time constraints that went with Happy Hour had required our union to be all-consuming and explosive. Now, the removal

69

of the shackles also seemed to drain it of some of the passion; it started furiously enough, gradually became languid, and then ultimately pretty hard work. Perhaps the Malone Mojito, four bottles of Crown and six pints of Harpic didn't help, though it may have been the crisps that did the real damage. Banter over beer pumps and whispered encouragements between sweaty sheets had not revealed very much about Leontia beyond the fact that she could impersonate a child psychologist with aplomb and was in fine shape for a woman with four kids and a Labradoodle, but an entire night together gave us the opportunity to get to explore our inner beings and share our regrets, thwarted ambitions and lingering hopes.

Naturally, it was a disaster.

For a start, she complained about my taste in music. I'd the iPod shuffle on and she either kept telling me to turn it down or complained that she couldn't make out the lyrics. When 'In the Ghetto' came on, she said it was hard to believe that Elvis had been dead for so long, and I said, 'Elvis Costello is dead?' and she didn't *get it*. She had never heard of 'Less Than Zero', 'Goon Squad' or '(The Angels Wanna Wear My) Red Shoes'. I could have forgiven her his collaboration with the fricken Brodsky Quartet but still. I knocked off the shuffle and played her the best of him and she lay there making encouraging sounds and forcing a toe beat against the mattress, but her eyes were glazed with boredom and when she said, 'Do you have "Uptown Girl"?' and I said, 'The Billy Joel or Westlife version?' she thought I was being serious. Not only that, she *preferred* the Westlife version. She was lucky I didn't drag her from the bed by her ankles and hurl her through the window into the piazza below.

You don't *have* to be compatible musically, but it helps. Trish and I weren't exactly like for like, but she dipped into mine and I dipped into hers, and when we fought she knew exactly where to hurt me. She had melted, scratched and frisbeed dozens of my favourite records over the years, but the point was that she knew which ones to go for. Not the most valuable, but the ones that *meant* the most.

Leontia, it became clear, liked to talk. I don't mind that when it's two-way or interesting, but it was all in one direction. I didn't particularly want to hear about her husband and how much she loved him. I didn't need to know about everything he did for her, how good he was with the kids and how hard he worked, for with every second of bigging him up she managed to diminish herself; I had had no reservations about our fling, but the more she talked, the worse I felt for him. I had spent most of my life avoiding a conscience, but now I was developing one on behalf of someone else. Besides that, she snored like a fucking elephant.

Either way she conspired to keep me awake most of the night. In the morning, in the cold light of sobriety, we didn't quite know what to say to each other. She had on last night's make-up and revolutionary hair. She wanted to make me eggs and bacon and all we lacked were the eggs, and bacon. There was bread, but she had to pick the blue corners off it. Burning the toast wasn't the worst. She caught me staring at the tub of butter as we sat at the kitchen counter.

She said, 'What?'

I said, 'Nothing. It's nothing.'

71

'What's nothing?'

'Nothing. Just. I hate people who leave jam in the butter. And crumbs.'

She blinked and said, 'Hate's a bit strong.'

'I don't mean hate,' I said. She smiled. 'Loathe is probably a better word.'

'Does *Trish* not leave crumbs in the butter?'

Her eyes narrowed. So did mine.

'Does whatever the fuck his name is, your hubby, churn the butter himself? 'Cos it sounds like he does everything else perfectly.'

'Oh—I see now.' She put her hands on her generous hips. 'You're jealous!'

'That's right, jealous of Mr Prick Perfect.'

'Jealous.'

'Yeah, that's it. Spot on.'

'He's not perfect, I never said he was perfect.'

'I know he isn't, because otherwise you wouldn't be over here fucking me and leaving crumbs in the butter, would you?'

'As a matter of fact, you were too drunk to fuck.'

She had clearly never heard of the Dead Kennedys. I could have had my hands on it in an *instant*.

We glared at each other.

Until I said, 'Well I'm not too drunk now.'

'Okay,' she said.

*   *   *

Leontia was in the shower, I was on the balcony drinking a Diet Coke and listening to the radio. I was looking for something good, but all I found was Jack Caramac.

He was explaining to any listeners who were

just tuning in that the entire show was being devoted to one subject: last night's tragic event. And for the next eternal minute he said everything but what last night's tragic event was: he ranted about anarchy on the streets of Belfast, he railed against the intimidation of working-class people by paramilitary gangsters, and hc harangued the police for being ineffectual, for being cowards, for betraying the very people who were most in need of their help, the vulnerable, the disenfranchised, the poor and the needy, and most of all for deserting Jean Murray in her time of need.

I sat up, straighter.

'Jean Murray,' said Jack, 'a friend of this show, a friend of mine, a tireless campaigner for peace, who stood up for the youth of this city, who dared face down the hooded thugs who ply their drugs on our unprotected streets, Jean Murray who died a most horrific death last night, petrol poured through her door and set alight, screaming as she burned to death, trapped in her own home while her neighbours stood helpless, or too frightened, to do anything to help her. This show is dedicated to our Jean.'

Fuckety fuck, fuck, fuck.

13

I felt wick. I felt shite. A pot of tea and three German biscuits weren't going to help, but they were a start.

'Fuck,' said Maxi McDowell. 'We're like those fucking women knitting at the guillotine.'

Same café, same table, same company. DS Hood looked a little more relaxed. As they sat down, I said, 'What about the boy, Bobby?'

'No sign of him,' said Maxi.

'Do you think they've taken him?'

'Doubt it. The rebs, they take you and disappear you for thirty years; this lot, there's usually a corpse in the middle of the road by daylight.' He lifted the pot. 'Will I be mother?'

He poured without waiting for a response.

I said, 'I was past the house. It's a real mess. There's flowers and wreaths piling up outside.'

'Yeah,' said Maxi, 'saw that. The community are united in their grief. Bit fucking late.'

'I stopped and had a look at the cards,' said Hood. 'Not a name or address on any of them.'

'Of course not,' said Maxi. 'They're sorry, but not so sorry they're going to reveal themselves.' He opened a packet of sugar and poured it in. As he stirred, he said: 'How come you never see sugar lumps any more? It's all wee packets, isn't it? I imagine it's to do with hygiene; you don't want to be putting something in your tea some hobo might have been fingering.' He shook his head and stirred some more. Then he sighed. 'Jean was a pain in the arse, so she was, but no one deserves that.'

'Jack was saying this morning something about her screaming and the neighbours doing nothing,' I said.

'As per usual, Jack is talking shite.'

'The fire brigade say the house would have filled with smoke very quickly,' said Hood. 'That's what got her, probably in her sleep. Nobody heard any screaming. And bearing in mind it was the early hours, and that if Bobby was in bed he would have

74

been overcome, or even if he'd woken up, with his disability it would have taken him too long to get out. We're working on the theory that he wasn't in when the attack took place.'

'So where was he, then?'

'He'd hopped it,' said Maxi, and gave a wiseacre smile.

'I don't blame him,' said Hood. 'He should get out and stay out.'

'We're looking for him,' said Maxi. 'As I'm sure they are too.'

'You don't think they'll have found, like, closure, by killing Jean?'

'Yeah, right. They'll be even more determined to find him. Those boys, they're like Jack Russells. Once they get their teeth into you, they never let go.' Maxi shook his head. 'And talking of terriers, you're going to have to have a word with that *wanker* Caramac. On this morning giving us this three kinds of crap like it was our fault? He's a whiney little guttersnipe and I don't know how you can work for him.'

'I can't, as it turns out,' I said. 'He fired me.'

'Seriously? How come? Did you fuck up?'

'*No*. And I don't really know why. Anyway, I'm out.'

Maxi fixed me with a look. 'You're not really out, though, are you, Dan? In fact, knowing you as I do, I'd say you're about to get even deeper into it. It's in your nature.'

'I think not,' I said.

He was right, of course. There was no legitimate reason for me to be shooting the breeze with two cops in a Shankill greasy spoon apart from the fact that it was in my nature to poke and poke and

75

poke at something until I got a satisfactory result irrespective of whether I was being paid for it or not. Also, I could not ignore the possibility that I was at least partially responsible for Jean Murray's death. Yes, she had already been the target of a long-standing intimidation campaign, but the day after I had asked Boogie Wilson, brigadier general of the Ulster Volunteer Force, to intercede on her behalf, Jean was burned to death. That was too much of a coincidence, at least for me.

It didn't *need* to have anything to do with Jack, but if it was, and was intended as another warning to *shut the fuck up*, then they'd misjudged it badly. Even as we sat there with our tea and biscuits, he was giving it everything over the airwaves, and I suspected he'd still be at it a month down the line. Judging from the calls he was getting, and the other coverage in the local media, thousands of people across the province were genuinely upset about what had happened to Jean and were clamouring for action to be taken against those responsible.

Equally, it might have had nothing to do with my intervention, or Jack, but everything to do with a power play within the notoriously volatile command structure of the UVF. Killing Jean was the Miller boys' response to being asked by Boogie Wilson to lay off her. This is our turf, they were saying, we'll do what we want.

Whatever the reason, I was pissed off at having jumped to the most obvious conclusion, and then waded in like a bull in a china shop. Now Jean was dead, Bobby was missing and Jack was exploiting it to the hilt, riling up the public and coining it in at the same time. And I was still no closer to finding out who had kidnapped his son. The fact that Jack no longer cared was neither here nor there. *I* cared.

I looked from Maxi to Hood. 'So what *are* you doing about Jean?'

'Bugger all,' said Maxi. 'Not my department, and even if it was, I'm forty-eight hours from retirement.'

'And it *is* my department, but I'm not on it,' said Hood.

'But you know.'

'Of course I do.'

'Sharing is caring.'

'What's in it for me?'

I smiled at Maxi. 'The boy's learning,' he said.

'Well then, I'll have to make it worth his while. What would you say to, say, half a German biscuit?'

I indicated the plate. I turned it seductively. Hood studied the biscuit. Then me. He glanced at Maxi, who gave a non-committal shrug.

'The *whole* biscuit,' said Hood.

I faked a sharp intake of breath.

'And playing hardball,' I said.

'Sweet tooth,' said Hood.

I gave it some more contemplation before pushing the plate closer to him.

'Deal,' I said.

He made no attempt to pick up the biscuit. I suspected that it was in fact a symbolic biscuit. Instead he swept one hand across the table, pushing crumbs over the edge into his other hand, which he then didn't quite know what to do with. He began to rub them between his palms. He may have been trying to reduce them to the size of subatomic particles, but he only succeeded in creating a worse mess than the one he'd been trying to clear up in the first place. Eventually he scraped the residue on to the floor, cleared his throat and said: 'Well, we picked up the Millers first thing this morning, and if Jack Caramac had bothered to do any research then he'd know that. But they'll be out by this afternoon. It's not likely they set the fire themselves, is it? Someone will have seen who actually did it, and if they cared to tell us then maybe we could link it back, but we're not holding our breath.'

'She had security cameras. If they poured petrol through the front door, then they must be on tape?'

'Yeah, you would think that. Just a couple of problems there. One, cameras melt under extreme heat. Two, you might think that maybe before they melted, some of that footage was transmitted elsewhere first? Well, for that to happen, we would have been needing the cameras to work in the first place. It's the same everywhere, cameras and burglar alarms on the outside of a house, most of them are just there for show. Cheap shit that fools no one. As for the neighbours, well they're all suddenly afflicted with blindness. And our regular cast of weasels, snitches and gossips are keeping it well zipped. So we have nothing yet. Maybe we'll get there, maybe we won't. That's about it, for now. But early days. Unless, of course, you have something to contribute, you being about the last person to see her alive.'

He raised a speculative eyebrow.

'What's in it for me?' I asked.

Hood smiled knowingly. He pushed the German biscuit back across the table to me.

I studied it. After a while I picked it up. I licked it. Then I put it down on the plate and pushed it back to him.

'You think I'm going to risk my hard-won reputation for that? Wise the scone, wee lad.'

I got up, pulled on my jacket, and walked out of the café. Even as the door was closing, I could hear Maxi laughing.

14

I parked about thirty metres beyond Comanche Station. I watched McDowell and Hood saunter back up Snugville Street and into their work. They were a mismatched couple—he the burly uniformed copper who took no prisoners and inspired equal amounts of respect and fear in the local community, and he the plain-clothed, clean-cut young detective fresh on the job but whose mild accent suggested that working-class west Belfast wasn't his natural environment. I'd hung out with enough police in my time to know that there were pretty strict demarcation lines between uniformed and plain clothes, between beat cops and CID. Hanging out *socially* was virtually unknown. Of course, we weren't exactly social, and they were using me as much as I was using them, but still, there was something odd about their match-up. I suspected that Maxi had spotted Hood struggling and had decided to take him under his wing. Not so much his protégé as the runt of the litter.

I sat there for a long time. Nobody was actually blaming me for anything, but I still felt responsible. Everything in life has a knock-on effect. If a butterfly beats its wings, and all that cack. You can't go back to the butterfly and pull its wings off for daring to beat them in the first place. I *could* have just driven away, gone back to my office and waited for the next case to come through the door, or, more probably, retired to the *Bob Shaw* to contemplate love and life and lust. But I didn't. I sat on, The Clash on the iPod, watching Comanche Station, debating what to do. Maxi was right, I was already in, and all I was really waiting for was someone or something to drag me even further down a dark road.

Ahead of me, outside the entrance to the station, where there might once have been concrete barrels to deter car-bombers getting easy parking, where there might once have been huge security grilles and armed cops keeping watch out of security towers, but which was now open-plan and carefree, half a dozen men in various denims and tracksuits were gathered, smoking and yakking and waiting.

I glanced at my phone. It was three fifteen. I'd been sitting there for *two hours*. I'd left a message for Boogie Wilson not long after I'd heard about Jean, but as yet, no response. I tried the number he'd given me again, but it went to voicemail.

I switched off the music and phoned Patricia.

I said, 'When you pass a certain age, you can't sit in a car all day without having to pee about six times. I've a Diet Coke bottle I could do it in, but what if I want a number two? You never see *that* in the frickin' movies, do you?'

She said, 'What do you want? I'm at work.'

'Just wondering how you were.'

'I'm fine. What do you really want?'

'Can't I phone you for a pleasant chat? Has it really come to this?'

'Dan, I'm not here to entertain you when you're

bored.'

'Who says I'm bored? And why not?'

There was a long silence.

Eventually I said, 'It's very quiet. Are you sure you're at work?'

'Yes.'

'Can you prove it?'

'Dan, will you stop it?'

'So you can't prove it?'

'Dan, for fuck—'

'You're getting very defensive. Where are you really?'

'I'm in work, Dan. Swear to God. Who do I share an office with?'

'Uhm. Mindy?'

'Cindy. Now listen carefully. Cindy, will you assure Dan that I'm in work and not in bed with my lover?'

A woman's voice, slightly removed, said, 'Dan, this is Cindy. Trish is right here with me in work and not in bed with her lover. Today, anyway.'

Patricia giggled. So did Cindy.

'Proves nothing,' I said. 'Especially if Cindy *is* your lover.'

'That's right, Dan, now I swing both ways. Protestant *and* Catholic.'

I sighed.

She sighed.

Four more men sauntered past my car and approached the others in front of the station. It was an al fresco meeting of the Miller Support Group. The brothers were still inside being lightly grilled.

She said, 'What is it, Dan?'

'I got fired. By Jack.'

'What'd you do wrong?'

'I didn't do anything wrong, but I like that it's your natural assumption.'

'It's the voice of experience.'

'Well on this occasion I was fired because Jack reckons he got the threat thing all wrong and there was never actually a problem.'

'Dan, that doesn't sound like you were fired. That sounds like he changed his mind, like he's entitled to do. Did he pay you?'

'Yes, I suppose.'

'So, what's your problem?'

'I don't know.'

'You probably do.'

'It's the whole Jean Murray thing. You know.'

'I *don't* know. What are you talking about? What did you do to her?'

'I . . . didn't . . . Trish, you have heard the news?'

'*What* news?'

'I thought you listened to Jack's show?'

'Yes, sometimes, but I have a job as well, unlike certain people I could mention. Now what's wrong with her apart from being annoying?'

'Trish—she's dead.'

'Fuck off! I mean—seriously dead?'

'No, Trish, she's dead in a somewhat comic way. Yes. Christ.'

'Oh, Dan, I'm sorry, I thought you were . . . Dan, I really hadn't heard. What happened?'

'A fire. Petrol poured through the letter box.'

'That's terrible. *Horrible*. There was a son . . . ?'

'He's disappeared.'

We were quiet.

'What, Dan?'

She was good at reading the silences.

I said, 'The thing is, I think it might be my fault.'

'No, Dan. Don't be daft. It's the fault of whoever poured petrol into her home and set fire to it.'

'But I—'

'You're not responsible, Dan. I know you. You're always on the side of the good guys. Invariably you make matters worse before they get better, but that just goes with the territory. You went out there to bat for her, and it's not your fault if someone takes the bat off you and beats her to death with it. I mean . . . you know what I mean. You can't be faulted for having your heart in the right place and for trying to fix things when everyone else stands by doing nothing.'

'That almost sounds like a compliment.'

'Yeah, well.'

'Does that mean there's the possibility of sex?'

A pause, and then, almost whispering, she said: 'Wanker,' and hung up.

She was not, I feared, a million miles from the truth.

I switched the music back on and returned my attention to the station. The iPod shuffle brought me to 'Police and Thieves'.

＊   ＊   ＊

Twenty minutes later, a cheer went up, and what had now become a baker's dozen crowded forward to meet two men emerging from the station. One burly, in a smart suit—Windy. One stick-thin, in T-shirt and baggy shorts—Rab. I already had slightly blurry Google photos of them on my iPhone. The head-and-shoulders shots emphasised their similarities; the reality encouraged the thought that they were brothers from a different

83

mother. They were grinning and high-fiving. Their followers punched the air and sang, 'No, no, no surrender!'

They began to move en masse up the middle of the road in my direction. No need for transport home; this was their patch, their kingdom. I already had the window down and my elbow out. The temptation was to wind one up and the other in. There was always one idiot at the safari park who thought he was perfectly safe. But there was really no reason to be afraid. I was just a civilian in a nice car, no reason why they should pay any attention to me other than the *PEDOFIAL* scratched into the side they were approaching on. Even in my pomp, in my big-mouth days, and plastered, I wouldn't have considered getting out of the car and confronting them about Jean Murray.

Walk on by.

They passed, singing still. One, at the back, thumped his fist into the side panel of my car, and I jumped, but he was only beating out the rhythm. He did it with the next car, and the next. Then their chants were drowned out by the roar of a motorcycle coming up the street behind them. They turned defiantly to stop its progress, and only then saw the pillion passenger lean around the driver and raise something, and the judder of automatic gunfire rang out, spraying the Miller boys and their flock.

15

I am not unused to gunfire, but it is always a shock. Even if my inclination might once have been to spring into journalistic action, the wisdom of age now insists that I stay safe, and merely do what I was supposed to do all those years ago: observe. The pressing need for a pee vanished. I watched and listened to the panic and the screams, and then the staggered calm as the police streamed out of the station to offer first aid. Ambulance sirens filled the air, and camera crews descended. I just sat there and nobody noticed or cared, and the adrenalin that I couldn't stop from pumping through me eventually eased, and I sipped a bottle of water and stuck my tongue through the hole in a Polo. There was blood and panic and fear, but I got the impression that it wasn't really that bad. When I judged that a sufficient amount of time had passed, I slipped out of the car and mingled in with the reporters, looking for a familiar face, but my generation had moved on, and those fresh young hairless chins that hadn't even been formed when it all kicked off didn't know me from Adams. I didn't mention that I'd seen the attack. There was no point. They were just two men in dark helmets on a Kawasaki that was already in flames somewhere else in my city.

Loyalist paramilitaries are, famously, crap shots. They had once peppered a taxi carrying the leader of the IRA with machine guns, and managed to shoot him in the elbow. A quick survey confirmed that they hadn't improved much with the passage of time: the Miller boys had escaped without a scratch and were bustled away, leaving behind three hoodlums with flesh wounds that could have been treated with a pair of tweezers and a jar of Sudocrem.

The hordes of journalists surrounding Comanche Station—at last, a decent story!—were in no doubt that this was the start of something that had been brewing for a long time, a nice dirty, bloody internal feud. It was no coincidence that they were also massing around Boogie Wilson's *Red Hand*, and no surprise that they found it shuttered and the streets around about ominously quiet.

But nobody expected it to remain like that for long.

Eventually I drove away. I parked at the apartment, but didn't go in. The adrenalin was long gone, replaced by a nervous tension. The fact that there was a long tail that maybe only I could trace running from Jack employing me to an attempted massacre outside Comanche Station stopped me from settling. I walked down to the *Bob Shaw*. I sat at the bar and had a pint. I asked where Lenny was, but they said she'd called in sick. The bar got crowded. Every once in a while I checked my phone for messages, or scanned the news sites for any further developments, but nothing was happening, yet. The Shankill was barely half a mile away, but it might as well have been a hundred. There was a nice buzz. People didn't seem to care what was happening. Let them shoot themselves in their ghettos and leave us alone. Some guy got up with an acoustic guitar and sang Neil Young songs and Jeff Buckley, and I had another pint or three.

And then around nine, I got the impression someone was watching me from the other side of the bar. Mid-forties, hair receding, trim beard, sports jacket, open striped shirt. Furtive glances over the top of a pint. A few years back I would have ignored it, or enjoyed it. People recognised me. They'd come up sheepishly and say, 'Are you Dan Starkey? I read your column in the paper. Here's a story for ya . . .' and they'd tell me something boring, or a joke only they found funny, but I'd nod and laugh and take a note of it and wink and bluster and maybe have sex with them at the end of the night, if they were women. I always had an excuse for Trish about the long hours and the socialising you had to do as a journalist with a finger on the pulse, but she knew, she knew and seemed to accept it, right up to the point where she didn't. But these days I wasn't recognised much. Even if I'd still been in gainful employment, they wouldn't have known my face. People don't buy newspapers any more. Not many, anyway. But now someone was definitely keeping tabs on me.

Wise up. It's just the shooting has you on edge.

I glanced up; he looked away. He took out his phone. He texted. He ordered another pint. I ordered one too. He didn't look at me for a while. I was imagining things. Then I caught his eye again. And this time I looked away. Had I seen him before somewhere? No. And then I thought, two middle-aged men by themselves, at a bar in the artsy Cathedral Quarter, with a different gay venue springing up every month, but it must still be a hard thing for a man of a certain age to come out in strait-laced Belfast, maybe he's giving me the eye.

So I glowed for a while, only because it's nice to be appreciated, and then I caught a glimpse of myself in the mirror behind the bar and thought,

Nah, he probably isn't after my ass. The next few times I looked over, he was facing in the other direction, so I relaxed. Trish was right, I was just doing what I do, I couldn't be blamed for what bad guys did. It had been an eventful few days. Relax, enjoy your drink.

Still.

It.

Kept.

Nagging.

Next time I checked, my friend across the bar had been joined by two others, both a little younger, burlier. They were chatting. One of them caught my eye, held it for a couple of seconds, and looked away. He lifted his pint and drank half of it. He glanced back. I looked away. I studied the bar optics.

The older guy had texted his two mates, or maybe his sons or sons-in-law, to let them know where he was, and they'd duly arrived. They're on a night out, quite innocent. Chill.

Or; one to spot me, two to do the hit.

Paranoia is the most cancerous of mental processes; once it has a grip, it runs rampant. Trish was right to think the way she thought, but that didn't mean that was the way the bad guys with guns thought. That was why they were bad guys. They often acted on impulse. I had sought to interfere in their business, and now they were interfering in mine.

No, they keep looking at me because I keep looking at them.

I was thinking, I'm okay in a crowded bar.

And then: *what the fuck are you thinking that for?* They've a long history of killing people in crowded bars. They *don't care*.

The barman said, 'Do you want another pint?'

I nodded. As he poured it, I leaned forward, shielding the left side of my face with my hand by pretending to rub my cheek, and said quietly: 'Without looking, you see the three guys on the other side of the bar? One with a beard and two younger?'

'How can I see them without looking?'

'Look surreptitiously.'

He gave me my pint. I gave him some money. He brought me my change. 'I looked,' he said. 'What about them?'

'Do you recognise them?'

'No more than I recognise you.'

'I talk to you most nights, Sam.'

He said, 'I'm sure you do. But you all blend in after a while. No offence, mate, but it's just a part-time job. I pull the pints and nod at all the shite people say to me. Are they hassling you?'

'No, no, it's fine.'

No point in creating a scene. I sipped my drink. I looked at my phone. No messages from the brigadier general of the UVF or the love of my life. Deep breath. Better to be safe than sorry; slip out, lose them. But I needed an exit strategy. I'd just bought a pint, so if they were watching, and they were, they'd think I was planning on staying for at least as long as it took to drink it. From where I was standing, the doors were directly behind me. They opened and closed at regular intervals as punters popped in and out for a smoke. The toilets were at the far end of the bar, and there was another exit there, but that would mean walking right past them. I'd been drinking steadily, but remarkably I hadn't been for a pee since I'd first noticed I was under surveillance, or not as the case may be. I was busting for one now. But it would wait. No point in giving them the chance to jump me in there. Home wasn't that far away. I just had to make it there. My building had a buzzer system, and you had to know the security code to get in, through the glass door. That would foil them. I laughed, and the barman looked at me.

As the night had worn on, the *Shaw* had become even busier; the tables were full, the length of the bar was packed, and people were standing six deep in front of it. I lifted my pint and edged into the nearest group and said, 'Hey, you didn't happen to hear the Liverpool score?'

My eyes flitted over their shoulders. My guys were watching. I wanted them to know I was with friends.

'They weren't playing,' said a small, peeved-looking bald guy trying to chat up a looker. I pushed on until I was within bolting distance of the door. I said to the guy beside me, 'You didn't happen to hear the Liverpool score?'

He said something in Dutch, or Swedish.

I said, 'Liverpool?'

He said, 'What about Liverpool . . . ?'

'Would you hold my pint for a moment?' His brow furrowed. I held the pint out towards him and he shook his head and I said, 'Just take it.'

'I do not wish to take your—'

'Just . . . *fucking* take it . . .' I thrust it into his chest and it spilt on his T-shirt. I let go of it, thinking he would catch it, but he just stepped back and it fell and smashed and sprayed on the hardwood floor.

The crowd split to avoid the splash. Everyone turned to look. Behind me, the door opened and a smoker came back in.

I darted through it and it swung back shut behind me, instantly reducing the bar sounds. I turned left and started walking fast. Behind me the bar sounds came back for a moment, and then dropped away again. I heard multiple footsteps. I glanced back. There they were.

I upped my pace. There are two alleys leading off Donegall Street, both leading on to Henry Street; if I dipped into either one, it would allow me to race away out of sight and hopefully throw them off the trail enough for me to loop back round to my apartment. But I'd had more to drink than I thought; I mistook Donegall Street Place for Commercial Court, and had ducked into it and charged along it full pelt for twenty metres before I realised I'd turned into the wrong one, and was now facing a dead end. There was a high barbed-wire- and glass-topped wall straight in front of me and no other way out but the way I had come. As I stopped, my three friends turned into the entry and were briefly silhouetted.

Fuckety fuck fuck fuck.

I moved against a wall and pretended to have a pee. As they closed in, I staggered back into their path and said, 'Caught me on there, lads,' then put a finger to my lips and said, 'Don't tell anyone, eh?' and tried to push through them, but the two younger ones grabbed me, each taking an arm, and threw me back against the same wall.

The one with the beard said, 'Dan Starkey?'

'Wah? Who?'

He punched me once, hard in the stomach. I

91

would have doubled up if they hadn't held me. Beardy reached inside my half-open jacket and felt around for my wallet. He extracted it and flipped it open. He angled it and squinted. He removed a cigarette lighter from his coat and flicked it and took out my driver's licence and read out loud: 'Dan Starkey . . .'

'I stole it from Dan Starkey, look at the photo, I look nothing like—'

He hit me again.

I retched and threw.

'Fuck sake!' spat one of my captors, moving his feet from the splash.

Beardy was less squeamish. He got hold of my jacket lapels and pulled my face close.

'Starkey. I used to read your column in the paper.'

'Really? Do you want an auto—'

He hit me for a third time.

'Funny fucker, weren't you?' He took hold of my hair and pulled my drooping head back up. 'Not so funny now.'

So, I'd had the punching. Now there'd be the speech, and then the killing. I'd been this close many times.

He said, 'This is just a warning. If you ever go near my wife again, you're a fuckin' dead man. Do y'hear me?'

I heard him all right.

Heard him loud and clear.

He said, 'What the fuck are you laughing at?'

But I was going at it so hard, I couldn't stop to answer him, so they started punching me again, and then when they finally let go of me and I slipped on to the damp cobbles, they laid into me with their feet. They pounded me until they were gasping for breath, and there appeared to be none left in me. I lay there quietly and took it. It hurt like hell, but inside I was still laughing my head off.

16

I was as stiff as hell and everything ached. There was Diet Coke in the fridge and orange juice cunningly disguised as Jaffa Cakes in the cupboard. As I ate, I watched the breakfast news. There had been a number of shootings, but none of them fatal. Armed and hooded men were on the Shankill threatening anyone they felt like threatening. Politicians, police and community leaders were calling for calm. It could have been so much worse. I might have been dead.

So I was relatively happy, at least until I switched to the radio for Jack's show and heard the tail end of him saying: '. . . well it appears to be self-published, so I think we all know what that means. Do you want me to read one of them? I think I should. What about this one? "The Green, Green Hills of Down"?'

He proceeded to read it, in a deliberately high-pitched, highfalutin voice that would have rendered Wordsworth even more ludicrous.

When he was finished, he said, 'We have Michael Ridley, Professor of Poetry at Sheffield University, on the line . . . Michael, you're the expert, what do *you* make of "The Green, Green Hills of Down"?'

'Well it's—'

'It's a bit rubbish, isn't it?'

'Well I wouldn't go that far. It's, it's quite . . . I would say free form, almost stream of consciousness . . .'

'It doesn't even scan, does it?'

'Well, no . . . but poetry doesn't necessarily—'

'What do you think about self-published poetry? Anyone can do that and call themselves a poet, can't they?'

'Actually, many of our leading poets started out by—'

'Do you want me to tell you who wrote this one?'

'Well, I . . .'

'What would you say if I told you that this book of poetry was published, *self*-published by Boogie Wilson. You're in England, so you won't necessarily know that Boogie Wilson is *allegedly* the brigadier general of the Ulster Volunteer Force, one of our murderous terrorist organisations, which, incidentally and only yesterday, murdered a poor innocent woman on the Shankill Road. What do you say to that, Professor Ridley?'

'Ahm, I'd say I'm glad I live in Sheffield. But I have to—'

'Thank you, Professor,' said Jack, abruptly cutting the call. 'Now we have Noel, from Limavady, on the line—Noel, what do you think of this self-confessed terrorist spouting lines of poetry about how beautiful our countryside is?'

'Jack, mate, I think it's a bloody disgrace, so I do . . . This guy claims to represent the Protestant community, and likes to think he's an artist or a poet or something, and he's sitting at home writing his little verses while his men are out there viciously—'

I turned him off. Jack was doing what Jack did. Stirring it up. He was like me, but with an audience. He had been giving it to the Miller brothers for weeks, and now he had widened his scope to Boogie Wilson. He was, I supposed, admirably fearless, or you could call it admirably reckless. But it only strengthened my newish theory that whatever had spooked him in the first place had nothing at all to do with the UVF and everything to do with . . . something else that I had yet to determine.

I sat at the kitchen counter and sipped my Diet Coke and gingerly stretched my aching limbs while wondering what to do with myself. The *Bob Shaw* wasn't the only bar in Belfast, but it was my local, and my favourite. However, I would probably have to stay clear of it for a while. I needed to keep a clear head. Jack Caramac was annoying me. He had led me up the garden path and then paid me off, either because the original problem had been resolved or because I was getting close to some truth he no longer wished me to discover. I'm not brave, never have been. But I like poking.

*   *   *

I drove to work. There's a private lane behind the block where I usually park which is safe from traffic wardens who might notice the tax disc and the tread, and who might enquire and find out about my licence and the non-existent insurance and the fact that my car hasn't been anywhere near an MOT for several years in a row. I locked it up, then stood and looked at it. It had once been top-of-the-range but was now near the bottom; to even make it legal would cost me more than it was worth. It would be quicker and easier to just put it out of its misery, but the sad fact was that I couldn't afford anything else.

I went back down the lane and was getting my keys out for the office when the butcher said from his doorway, 'Been in a scrap?'

I was limping, a bit, and one eye was swollen. 'Yes,' I said.

He said, 'Word of warning.' And I thought: *Christ, what now?* But he nodded at my door and said, 'I was opening up, and couldn't help but notice your lock's been forced.'

I moved up to it. The door appeared firmly closed, but there was a slight splintering of the frame around the lock. I put one finger on the wood panel and pushed. The door drifted slowly inwards.

I looked at the butcher.

He said, 'I would've checked it out, but didn't want to go in without your permission. Are you going in or calling the peelers?'

'Going in,' I said.

'I'll go with you,' said the butcher, 'if you just give me a minute.'

I nodded. He darted back inside his shop, and came back with a meat cleaver. 'Just in case,' he said.

He moved past me into the doorway. 'I'll go first, if you don't mind.' He gave me a sample swing of his cleaver. 'I've probably got a bit more practice at this than you have.'

'Be my guest,' I said.

There was only a hall at ground level, then two floors of vacant offices before you got to what the estate agent had called an executive penthouse office suite and most sane people would have called an attic.

We proceeded cautiously; I more cautious than he.

'Anything valuable up there?'

'Laptop and a family bag of Twix.'

'Aye, well, I was right then, better not to phone the police if you have a laptop.'

'I don't follow.'

'Saw what you have on your car; maybe you don't want the cops checkin' out your files.'

'If you're suggesting . . .'

'Each unto their own, mate. Doesn't worry me. I met all sorts inside, so I did.'

'Inside?'

'Oh aye, before I was a butcher on the Lisburn Road, I was one on the Shankill.'

He gave another swish of his cleaver.

'You were a Shankill Butcher?'

'Coulda been, but never had the inclination.'

Just as we reached the top of the stairs, there was a noise from beyond my office door, about twenty paces ahead of us along a short hall.

'I should warn you,' I whispered, 'that I may recently have upset the UVF.'

The butcher looked surprised, but undaunted. 'More power to your elbow,' he said, and gave me a theatrical wink. 'You ready for this?'

I nodded. He gave me a broad smile, before suddenly letting rip with a blood-curdling yell and hurtling forward. The lock on my door was clearly already busted, but he kicked it in anyway and leapt through the gap.

'Gotcha now!' he cried, raising the cleaver, ready and willing to decapitate the teenager sitting in my chair, one good foot propped up on my desk, and the other resting peacefully on the other side of the room.

17

Bobby Murray was wearing a rumpled and stained white T-shirt, black jeans and one big trainer. He was shaven-headed and acne-faced, tired-eyed and haunted-looking. There was a healthy amount of defiance in there too. He didn't appear fazed at all by the butcher looming over him with a cleaver, and his lack of fear seemed to puzzle my new friend and protector.

'You know him?' the butcher asked, the cleaver still held high and ready for beheading.

'I know of him. What're you doing here, Bobby? And why's your leg over there?'

'Chafing,' said Bobby.

I nodded at the butcher. 'It's okay, I think.' He lowered his weapon, but continued to look suspiciously at the boy. I crossed the room and picked up Bobby's leg, somewhat squeamishly, and set it on my desk. 'Would you mind putting it on?' I asked. 'It's just . . . *not right* leaving it lying around.'

Bobby made a face, but swung his good leg off the tabletop, pushed his/my chair back a bit and began to fit the leg back into place. All the while the butcher was looking down at him, shaking his head.

I said, 'Well?'

'Well *what*?' the *what* pronounced with a silent *h* and with the impact of a slapped face.

'In case it has escaped your notice, you've broken into my office and busted two locks in the process. What do you *want*?'

Fully legged up again, Bobby sat upright and pulled himself closer to the desk. He used one finger to push a crumpled piece of card towards me. I peered down at my own name. Bobby sat back and folded his arms. The top of the desk was also littered with Twix wrappers and crumbs.

I picked up the card and said, 'Yes, but what are you doing here?'

'My mum said if there was trouble I should come to you, that if I went to any of my relatives I'd be found and they'd be shot too.'

'So you're not worried about me getting shot?'

Bobby shrugged.

The butcher said, 'Do you want me to turf him out?'

I sighed. I shook my head. 'No, I'll sort it myself. I appreciate the help.'

He nodded. He came forward and put his hand out. 'Name's Joe. I'm only down the stairs if you need anything.'

'Appreciate it.'

Joe gave Bobby a long hard look before turning for the door.

'Nice dress,' said Bobby, nodding at Joe's striped apron.

Joe hesitated for just a moment. He gave me a fleeting glance that included a surreptitious wink. Then he turned suddenly back, swung his arm and buried the cleaver in the desk inches from Bobby's fingers. Bobby let out a yell and threw himself back in the chair, cowering down as the butcher loomed over him.

'What was that, son?'

'Nothin' . . . nothing . . . Jesus!'

Joe let out a short laugh, jacked the cleaver out of the wood and turned back to me.

'Sorry about the desk,' he said, 'I'll send you up some sausages.'

* * *

I pushed the door closed behind Joe. It swung open again. The lock was fucked.

I turned back to Bobby and said, 'What happened to your other trainer?'

'I lost it.'

'You can walk on that thing okay?'

'It's not a thing. It's a prosthesis.'

'Is it now? Would you and your prosthesis mind getting out of my chair?'

I pulled out the less comfortable chair I keep for customers and indicated for him to sit in it. He glared at me for what was supposed to be an intimidating five seconds before slowly pulling himself up and limping round.

Satisfied, I sat in my own chair. He watched me as I gathered up the Twix wrappers, balled them and threw a perfect shot into the round file against the far wall. I then swept the crumbs into my palm and opened one of the empty drawers and poured them in. I was working on the theory that if I collected enough crumbs, eventually I could make my own Twix. It's good to have a purpose in life. I switched on the laptop, and as I waited for it to power up, I opened a different drawer and took out a large notebook and a pen and flipped back the cover and wrote Bobby Murray's name down at

100

the top of the first page. I nodded to myself. I sat back. I had no idea what I was doing, but it seemed important to look professional.

Bobby took a squashed packet of Embassy Regal out of his jeans pocket, slipped one into his mouth and then offered the box to me. I shook my head. He patted his pockets, without success.

He said, 'Do you have a light?'

I said, 'Yes.'

When I made no move, he said, 'Can I have it?'

'No. It's a non-smoking office. And you're too young to be smoking. And it's not good for your health.'

He snorted at that.

I smiled too. 'So, Bobby,' I said, 'how're you doing?'

'How do you think I'm doing?'

'You broke into the building, and then my office. That's going to be expensive.'

'I had nowhere else to go.'

'It's not just the locks, it's the door frames.' I cleared my throat. 'I'm sorry your mum got burned to death.' He stared at me. I shrugged. I doodled. The last time I'd spoken to a fourteen-year-old one-to-one I was fourteen myself. 'So, Bobby, what are we going to do with you?'

'I don't know.'

'You mentioned relatives.'

'I told you, they're not—'

'Aunts, uncles . . . ?'

'Nah.'

'What about your dad? Could you not go to him?'

'Never met him. He lives in England somewhere.'

101

'You could go there, safer.'

'I don't want to go to fucking England.'

'Okay, and watch your language.'

'Fuck off.'

'You're coming to me for help, and you're telling me to fuck off? Good thinking.'

'I'm here because my mum said, that's all. Far as I'm concerned, you're just another useless wanker.'

'It seems to be the general opinion,' I said.

'What?'

I shrugged. I doodled some more. In times of stress I draw swastikas. No particular reason, other than the fact that I have no artistic talent and they're easy to draw.

'Well I can check out your dad, if you want.'

'I don't want.'

'Just give me his name and last known whereabouts, I can put out a few feelers . . .'

'You want his name?'

'Yes. Please.'

'Johnny. Two ns. Jay oh aitch . . . en en why . . .'

I wrote it down. 'Johnny . . . ?'

'Johnny Cunt Fuck.'

I glanced up. 'Is that with a cee or a kay?'

'Whatever makes you happy.'

I put my pen down. I sat back. 'The police are looking for you.'

'Sure they are.'

'They can protect you.'

'Yeah, right.'

'Where were you when it happened?'

'Where do you think I was?'

'I don't know, that's why I'm—'

'I was up the fucking stairs with the Xbox LIVE, earphones on, shootin' zombies, and this smoke starts coming under the door and I tried to get downstairs but the fire was . . .' He trailed off. 'Since it all started, she always slept downstairs, on the couch.'

'To protect you. She was your first line of defence.' He shrugged. 'So you got out, how?'

'Back window, down the back alley.'

'So you didn't see who . . . ?'

'Course I did. When I got to the end of the street, I saw them.'

'Clearly?'

'They were just standing there, watching.'

'So you could identify them?'

'To the cops? Yeah, *right*.'

'They killed your mother, Bobby.'

'She was asking for it. She'd never shut up. I told her a million times but she kept on and on and they killed her.'

I balled the swastikas and threw them. Two out of two. I was definitely in the wrong career.

'Where have you been since it happened?'

'Here and there.'

'You have friends?'

'Course.'

'They can put you up?'

'If they could put me up, would I have had to break into this shitehole?'

'It's my office, show some respect.'

'*Sorry*, office.'

'I can call social services, they can sort you . . .'

'No.'

'*No?*'

'Been down that road before, not going.'

'Bobby, I'm sorry you're in this mess, and I've suggested various things and you've rejected every

103

one of them. What exactly do you want me to do?'

'I want you,' he replied, 'to buy me breakfast, because I'm fuckin' starving.'

18

I bought him breakfast in a café down the street and he wolfed it down: two bacon baps and hot chocolate and an apple flapjack. There was barely any chat from him. He sat with his back to the door. Whenever it opened, he didn't look round or show any interest; he knew the police were looking for him, that the Miller boys were after him, and that both sets of hunters had to have feelers out all over the city, but he appeared inured to it. He had been besieged and intimidated, he had lost a leg and now his mother; maybe he thought they'd done their worst. I suspected they hadn't. Every time the door opened, *I* jumped.

He said, 'What happened to your eye?'

'I got in a fight. It'll heal. What about your leg?'

'What do you mean what about it? It won't heal.'

'I know . . . I mean, you seem quite proficient with it.'

'I had lessons. I'm aimin' for the Paralympics.'

'Really?' He gave me the eye. I blew air out of my cheeks. I fiddled with the remnants of my fry. After a while I said, 'So?'

'So what?'

'What are your plans now?'

'You tell me.'

'What do you mean?'

'You're supposed to look after me.'

'I bought you breakfast, and you found my secret stash of Twix. It's the least I could do, after what happened, but . . .'

'You're right.'

'I'm right. I'm right *what*?'

'It's the least you could do.'

'I don't follow.'

'My mum said you would look after me.'

'Yes, I appreciate that, but just because she says something, *said* something, it doesn't mean it's magically going to happen. I met her once, for five minutes, I gave her my card. I'd never even set eyes on you till you broke into my office. I have an Xtra-vision card in my wallet, but I don't expect them to look after me if I fall on hard times.'

'I was listening to youse from the top of the stairs. You said to her, if there's anything else I can do. She took you at your word.'

'I was just being polite.'

'So you were lying to her.'

'No, it's just something you say.'

'If you didn't mean it, then it's a lie.'

'Okay. It was a lie. Happy?'

'What am I supposed to do now?'

'I don't know. It's not my problem.'

'Great. Thanks.'

'What do you want me to say?' I snapped. 'Come back to my place, put your head down till I sort something out? Come under my wing? You can be the son I never had?'

He looked at me for a long time, and there were tears in his eyes and he was straining, bloody *straining* hard to stop them coming out.

Fuckety fuck fuck fuck.

105

I am not *completely* callous. I said he could put his head down in my spare room for one night until I sorted something out for him. In response, I got a shrug. As we drove to St Anne's Square, I spelt out how it was going to work. He wasn't to mess with my stuff. He wasn't to use my phone. He wasn't to go out. No drugs. No drug deals.

He said, 'What do you think I am?'

'I know exactly what you are. The Millers weren't picking on you because you were choirboy of the year.'

'That was then.'

'So you say. I don't have to do this. If it's not good enough for you, I can stop the car now.'

'Yeah, right.'

'I'm serious.'

'Do you have an Xbox?'

'No.'

'PlayStation? Anything like . . .'

'No.'

'PC?'

'Not usually.'

'What does that mean?'

'Yes, I have a computer. Yes, you can use it, if you're careful and don't spill anything over it and don't use it inappropriately.'

'Ina . . .'

'You know what I mean. And if you're on Facebook, don't update your status to your new location, don't tell anyone where you are.'

'I'm not fuckin' stupid. And Facebook? You fuckin' jokin'?'

'Sorry, is Facebook not where it's at these days?'

He just shook his head. We rode in silence for a while.

Then he said, 'They didn't spell paedophile right.'

'I know,' I said.

*   *   *

We got to St Anne's Square and parked. Bobby nodded appreciatively as we crossed the piazza; he nodded some more when we got to the block and took the elevator up, and continued nodding as we entered my apartment. He stood just inside the door and smiled.

'I could get used to this,' he said.

'Well don't. The bathroom's straight ahead. Go take a shower, you smell of smoke and cigarettes and sweat. The spare bedroom is on the left. There may be some food in the fridge, but there's definitely Coke. Not that kind of coke. I have work to do, I have to go out again, so I'm going to leave you to it, okay?'

'Okay.'

'I can trust you?'

'Yes.'

'Though you would say that.' He made eyes. 'Okay. I'm not sure how long I'll be; make yourself at home, keep your head down, I'll sort what I can sort.'

I nodded.

He nodded.

I left. I walked down the hall and pressed the elevator button. It came, and went, but I stayed where I was. I gave it three minutes. When I let myself back into the apartment, Bobby was standing exactly where I'd left him, with his arms folded.

'Do you not fuckin' trust me or somethin'?' he barked.

I said, 'I forgot something. *Okay?* I can come back into my own fuckin' home if I fuckin' want to.'

I crossed the room and sat down at my desk and switched the computer on. I had forgotten nothing, but it seemed important to check my e-mails.

He said, 'I'm gettin' my shower now, *okay*?'

He stomped towards the bathroom.

'Bobby!'

He stopped reluctantly. '*What?*'

'Don't forget to wash behind your ears.'

'Fuck off!'

He roared in and slammed the door. The handle moved up and down several times as he tried to work out how it locked. It didn't. There were no locks on any of the doors, apart from the front. It was a design flaw, or a design *preference* depending on your point of view.

After a bit, I finally heard the shower running, and the sliding doors open and close. Five minutes later, I shut the computer, stood up and crossed to the bathroom. I opened the door. Bobby's outline was just visible through the steam.

I did what any single man with a helpless, naked fourteen-year-old boy at his mercy would do.

I stole his leg.

19

In position, Diet Coke, freshly purchased Twix, sober, keen, spare leg in the corner, I phoned Tracey. Nanny the nanny answered, and eventually I heard the click of heels on a polished wooden floor.

'He's not here,' were her first words. Followed swiftly by: 'But then you know that.'

Jack was broadcasting. She could probably hear his voice in my background, and I could certainly hear it in hers.

'I was thinking about inviting you for lunch,' I said.

'Really? Why?'

'Old times.'

'What's that noise?'

'Hammering,' I said. 'Getting some work done to the office.'

'You must be doing well.'

'Yes,' I said.

I had engaged a joiner to fix the door frame, and a locksmith to repair the locks. They both came in the form of one overweight man who charged for two. I had found him online and he had appeared within twenty minutes. He was either extremely efficient, or desperate. He had an eastern European accent and made Nanny seem like a conversationalist.

'Why now?' Tracey asked.

'It's been a long time, wanted to pick your brains, not that you have two. I thought a full and frank exchange of information might benefit us both.'

She hesitated. 'About what?'

'You know.'

'No, I don't know.' I said nothing. I waited. After a goodly while, she said, 'Are you trying to bluff me, Dan Starkey?'

'*Moi?*'

'Yes, you.' She giggled abruptly. 'You never change, do you?'

'You can't improve on perfection.'

'Course you can,' laughed Tracey. 'It's called lipo. All right, you've convinced me. Where do you fancy? Have you been to the Shipyard?'

'Tracey, the Shipyard is so last year.'

We agreed on the Cloth Ear, the bar bit of the Merchant Hotel. I hung up and sat back in my chair with my feet up and listened to some more Jack. He was calling on the people of Ulster, Belfast and the Shankill in particular to come out en masse for Jean Murray's funeral, to show their support for her stand and sacrifice, and their disdain for the gangsters who were controlling our streets. I knew they would turn out, too. Hundreds, perhaps thousands would see her off; they always did. And then they would go right back to doing what they had been doing before, which was a big fat nothing. Only Jack would keep the flame lit, using her to goad police and gangsters alike. He was a man who seemingly did not know how to *shut the fuck up*. And yet, and yet, his mood had lifted. His worries about little Jimmy had vanished. *Something* had changed. Had he in fact shut up, and I just hadn't noticed? Because the events on the Shankill had so dominated his show, I had gone for them as the source of the problem, but it could just as easily have been to do with any one of the dozens of other

110

subjects he tackled each week.

I took out my notebook and traced down the list of items he'd featured recurrently in the podcasts prior to the kidnapping of his son, and then those he had covered since the night of the cocktail party, to see if any had been abruptly dropped.

Fifteen minutes later, I had three that seemed to have disappeared: loyalty cards from major retailers that were supposed to give customers preferential treatment and discounts, but which actually cost them more; the Planning Service's failure to clamp down on those who flouted the planning laws; and the epidemic of deaths caused by addiction to the 'legal' drug mephedrone, which overlapped to a certain extent with the existing problems on the Shankill. Any one of them might have been discarded because they'd come to the end of their natural life, or because Jean Murray was so dominating the programme that there simply wasn't room. All I could do was wait for a few days to see if any of them returned as subjects once the Jean furore died down.

I closed the notebook, listened to the rest of the show, and then paid my handyman a fortune for his work. When he was gone, I sat back safe and secure and had a think about what to do about Bobby. While Jean had clearly been foolish to place so much faith in me, she was right about one thing—it definitely wasn't safe for him to be staying with his relatives. It would hardly have mattered in London or New York—those were places where you could just disappear—but Belfast is remarkably small. If Bobby went to even distant relatives, people would notice, and gossip, and word would spread. Likewise a children's home, or even if social workers found foster parents for him; it would still trickle back.

If I was going to deal with it at all, then it came down to either tracking down his father in England or sorting out the underlying problem. The only way to do that, since my approach to Boogie Wilson had backfired so spectacularly, would be to try the Miller brothers directly. As they seemed to think nothing of killing anyone who annoyed them, and they were currently involved in a potentially murderous feud with someone I had apparently allied myself with, I put that one to the back of my list of two.

So I spent the rest of the morning making phone calls to old connections, and others to new acquaintances whom I tried to dazzle with my charm. They all seemed surprised that I was actually physically making a phone call. Even when I confirmed the details of what I was after, they would ask me to send an e-mail as well to double-confirm. The world is too much with us, late and soon.

Love those beer mats.

*   *   *

The Merchant is a brand-new five-star hotel hiding in the vacated Victorian headquarters of the Ulster Bank. It has a nice Italian-style façade, but I was more impressed by the fact that in the Cloth Ear you get a bowl of nuts with your drink. I was on my second pint when Tracey clacked up.

'Started without me?'

'It's only my first,' I said. She was looking marvellous. Leather boots with high heels, plaid skirt, leather blouson, lipstick red and perfect. 'Do you want to eat five-star or will you settle for pub grub?'

'Do I look like a girl who settles?'

'There's no answer to that.'

'Actually,' she said, 'you can take a girl out of the Shankill, but you can't take the Shankill out of the girl. I'd be happy with a plate of chips and a burger, been killing myself all morning at Pilates.'

We crossed to a table. We ordered drinks. I had a third pint and she had a Californian Pinot Gris.

I said, 'I'd forgotten that's where you came from. The Shankill.'

'Yep, born and bred.'

'Ever go back?'

'You joking?'

'Family there, old friends?'

'Nope and no. We were gone by the time I was six. Thank God.'

The drinks arrived, and the same waiter took our food order. I had the burger and chips as well. I'd only recently consumed an Ulster fry. I'd be lucky if I survived through to dinner. Tracey took a sip of her wine, then leaned forward, closer, and smiled.

'So, Daniel,' she said, 'out with it.'

'Here?'

'Tell me what you're after.'

'Can't a single guy invite a married woman out for lunch without there being an ulterior motive?'

'Dan, as I recall, your whole life is an ulterior motive.'

'Fair enough. I thought a swift one here, then straight upstairs. I hear the rooms are fantastic. I could tell the other night you were gagging for it.'

'O-kay.'

She held my gaze.

'Or you could tell me straight out what's really going on with Jackie boy and the mysterious disappearing case type thingy.'

'The . . . ?'

'Tracey, I'm a little bit miffed.'

'Miffed? That's not really a Dan word.'

'I'm a bit fucked off, then.'

'With me?'

'With your worser half.'

'Worser?'

'It's for your benefit, being from the Shankill and all.'

'Fucked off about what?'

'Getting sacked before I hardly got started. I went to some trouble, I put myself in danger, certain things have happened because I started asking questions, and besides all that, it doesn't look good on my CV, getting fired off my first case. What do I tell my next one? So just tell me the truth. Why am I off it?'

'I have absolutely no idea, Dan. Is that why you lured me here?'

'You're easily lured. What's it really about? Was it someone threatening to expose his affair?'

'*What* affair?'

'No idea. Just putting it out there. Successful, charismatic guy like Jack, nothing but young blondes at Cityscape.'

I raised an eyebrow.

'You can raise all the eyebrows you want, Dan, there's nothing going on.'

'You would know?'

'I would know.'

'What then? Tracey, come on, we go back, throw

me a bone here.'

'*Here?*' She smiled. 'Dan, you weren't sacked. The problem just . . . went away. Jack said it was over, so it's over.'

'You didn't ask?'

'He always has a hundred and one things on the go, it's the nature of him. As long as my Jimmy is okay and Jack keeps me in new clothes, I don't really enquire.'

'I hear you maxed out your loyalty card.'

'*What* loyalty card?'

'You know, the one you maxed out.'

'I told you I'm a Shankill girl; Mum would rather have killed herself than ask for anything on tick. Strictly cash, darling. What are you getting at?'

'Me? Nothing. Still. Anyway. You're looking well.'

'Thank you.'

'You've obviously fully recovered.'

'Recovered?'

'Yeah, that mephedrone is lethal.'

'What are you *talking* about?'

'Or were you maybe dealing, is that where the money's coming from?'

'Is that what you're on, Dan? 'Cos you're talking shite here.'

Our meals arrived. We paused until we'd unwrapped our cutlery and poured vinegar on our chips.

I said, 'Ah, never mind me, I'm just shootin' the breeze.' I smiled winningly across the table. 'Seriously, Tracey, you are looking well. Fresh. Fragrant. You must get out in that lovely garden of yours often enough. Pity you're selling it, though.'

She shook her head. 'Okay, let's hear it.'

'You've been trying to sell it for months; everyone else is building houses on every scrap of land, why shouldn't you? You've got rolling acres of it, on the Malone Road? Must be worth a fortune, but the Planning Service isn't playing ball, so Jack's been chipping away at them on air.'

'You're suggesting my son was kidnapped by the Planning Service?'

'They can be ruthless.'

Tracey picked up her knife and fork, cut off a thin sliver of her burger and put it in her mouth. She spoke around it as she chewed.

'Dan, no offence, but do you ever think you might be in the wrong job?'

'Tracey, no offence, but did nobody never teach you not to speak with your mouth full?'

'Dan, no offence, but did nobody never teach you not to use three negatives in a sentence?'

'Tracey, no offence, but nobody isn't a negative, and from memory, you always did have a problem swallowing.'

It was kind of out before I thought it through. She looked suitably shocked. I raised my hands, peaceably.

'Sorry, I didn't mean . . .'

She pushed her chair back and stood. She picked up her napkin and dabbed carefully at her lips. She lifted her handbag.

'I knew this was a mistake. Did nobody ever tell you to grow up?'

'Frequently, yes. Sit down, Tracey. I'm sorry. I thought we were just winding each other up. Playful banter.'

'Can I tell you something, Dan?'

'Absolutely,' I said.

'I've moved on, I'm happy with Jack, and if you think there's anything mysterious going on, you're barking up the wrong tree. And one more thing?'

'Uhuh?'

'You always were a useless cunt.'

She picked up her glass and threw her wine over me. Then she strode away, clacking across the stone floor.

There were many things I could have shouted after her, witty, pithy, funny things. But I held my tongue. I'm much more mature now. She was wrong about one thing, though, you *could* take the ghetto out of the girl. A true child of the Shankill would have necked the wine and then glassed me.

20

I sat where I was, and sipped my beer, and ate some of Tracey's chips. I was happy enough, if a little damp. You see, you *think* you're just having a bit of banter, and they're right there with you, but then you go just a little bit too far and suddenly they're in tears. Part of me wanted to think that I had misjudged the reason for her joining me. What I had dismissed as drunken flirting at her cocktail party could actually have lodged in her sozzled head as a real come-on. Even after so many years she retained strong feelings for me, and why not? She had agreed to lunch so quickly, and then arrived dressed to the nines, only to discover that instead of a secret affair, I was more interested in grilling her about the case.

But most of me knew that was bollocks. She

was from the Shankill, and they breed them tough there. Something was bothering her, something she'd hoped to share with me, but I'd wound her up too far and in her nervous state she'd snapped and bolted.

Still, it suggested I might be on the right track, or *a* track, at least. When I emerged on to Waring Street, Tracey was standing at the end of the hotel, facing away from me, smoking. I walked up and she turned just as I arrived. She studied the pavement.

I said, 'Sorry, Tracey.'

She turned panda eyes up to me. She took another drag, her hand shaking. 'I can't believe you finished your fucking pint rather than come running after me.'

'I'm fond of a pint,' I said.

'You always were a bastard.'

'As I recall, it was you who finished with me.'

She threw the fag down and ground it into the footpath. 'You've a good memory,' she said. 'What is it, once bitten, twice shy?'

'It's complicated.'

'Still Trish, yeah?'

'Yep, she's the only one for me.'

'Always hated her.' She forced a weak smile. 'Sorry about that in there. It's not you. It's me. It's *him.*'

'The voice of the people?'

'Don't, please. You were right first time. Those fuckin' clippies from the station. I can fuckin' smell it off him. I thought I'd have my wee bit of revenge, but when it came to it, I couldn't.' She lit another. 'I could have had you, though, couldn't I?'

'You had me at *chips,*' I said. 'Tracey, love, something's up. Is it just the affairs?'

'*Just?*'

'You know what I mean. Jimmy.'

She held my gaze for a long time. Then she said, 'No, it's not just the affairs; there's other stuff he won't tell me about. He never has, Dan. I've never really been interested in the business end, so I can't go crying to him now if he freezes me out. It's just with Jimmy, I nearly die every time I think about what might have happened to him.'

'You were lucky.'

'I know. God, I know. And I know you understand. You lost one too.'

I looked at the passing traffic for a bit. When I turned back to her, she was lighting another.

'So tell me, what really happened? One minute he's worried to death, the next he's top of the world.'

'And I'm telling you I *don't know.*'

'Is it to do with the show?'

'You can ask me in as many different ways as you want, Dan, but I can't tell you if I really don't know.'

'Well maybe you could find out.'

She studied me. 'You mean like . . . ?'

'Yes. Snoop around. Check his calls, his computer, anything.'

'On my own husband?'

'He's screwing around behind your back.'

'I'm resigned to that.' I raised an eyebrow.

'Y'know, you're like fuckin' Roger Moore when you do that, except you're a better actor. Dan, I can't just go hoking through his stuff.'

'Why not? Listen to me.' I reached out and took her hand. Or tried to. It was meant to emphasise my point, but it was the hand with her fag in it and she burned my palm by mistake and I said, 'Fuck!' and rubbed at it.

'Sorry! Here . . . let me . . .'

She took hold of it and kissed the burn and then held it against her cheek. There were tears in her eyes. I let her hold it for a few moments, then gradually drew it away and let it drop to her shoulder.

'Tracey,' I said, 'you need to help me. I've been involved in crap like this before and my experience is this: he may look happy, he may sound happy, but if you get into something that involves your own child being kidnapped, then you are not dealing with normal people and it is unlikely to end happily. And I have worked with media people before, and as a rule of thumb, the less demanding their job, the larger their ego. He will think he can deal with this because he is Jack Caramac off the radio, with the highest listenership in Ireland, but it will mean nothing to the people who might eventually put a bolt through his head.'

'I know. I know. I know. I have thought all this. I could just up sticks, take Jimmy away, keep him safe.'

'Yes, you could.'

'Except.'

'You love Jack.'

'Yes, I do.'

I nodded some myself.

'Love's a bitch, isn't it?' I asked.

'No,' said Tracey, 'love is great.'

'That's my girl,' I said, 'metaphorically speaking.'

*　　　*　　　*

I walked back to the office with the full intention of making some calls, sat down, put my feet up on the desk and dozed off. I was out for *three hours*. I woke groggy and stiff and with a mild headache. I necked some paracetamol, drained a warm Diet Coke and tried to decide if I was sober enough yet to drive home. Only a few years back it wouldn't have mattered. I have driven while spectacularly drunk and never actually killed anyone, though I did once bounce a nun off my bonnet. She just rolled off and kept walking. She'd either taken a vow of silence or I'd broken her throat.

But times have changed. There wasn't an exact method of working out when I would be sufficiently legal; it was guesswork.

I went into the small bathroom and threw water on my face. I sucked on an emergency Polo mint. I lifted Bobby's spare leg and walked to the car. Nobody mentioned the leg. The Lisburn Road was busy enough. I drove carefully. Guessing that it was what teenagers were most likely to want to eat, I stopped to pick up a bargain bucket of KFC. I drove on home with the windows down. St Anne's Square's piazza lights were just coming on. I parked. I nodded to a neighbour on the way up, and let myself into the apartment. It was very quiet. I called Bobby's name. There was no response.

'Hey, Bobby, you here? I went to Kentucky. Do you want a leg?'

Still nothing. I went from room to room. Gone. I checked my valuables. TV, present; PC, present. There was a dirty plate in the sink and a sodden towel on the bathroom floor. I picked it up and put it over a radiator. I checked the spare bedroom— not slept in. So, he'd done a runner, or, at least, a hopper. Maybe it was no bad thing. I wasn't equipped to deal with any teenager, let alone a one-legged drug dealer whose mother had just died. I set his leg appendage down on the counter. Maybe he had spares dotted all over the city, like Scott on his way to the Pole, who didn't have legs, but supply dumps. That hadn't ended so well. But it wasn't my problem.

I looked at the KFC. If I ate anything else dripping in fat, I really would implode. I left it sitting there and went to the cupboard above the sink. A healthy dose of Black Bush was in order.

There had been a three-quarters-full bottle, but it was gone. As I discovered this, I heard a groan. It did not come from me, though it should have. I turned and surveyed the open-plan kitchen and lounge. My eyes were drawn to the veranda. The curtains were still closed from the night before, but one of them was flapping gently in the breeze.

Another groan.

I moved across to the sliding doors, pulled the curtains back and saw Bobby, naked, on his hands and knee. He was throwing up. There was my bottle of whiskey, empty, on the ground beside him.

Christ.

I opened the door and went out. His head turned very slightly.

'Sorry . . . sorry . . . sorry . . .'

I knelt beside him, reluctantly, and said, 'It's okay . . .' through gritted teeth.

'I'm not drunk . . .'

'I can see that . . . C'mon . . .'

I tried to pick him up. He was heavier than he looked. Dead weights always are. I levered him straight-ish and balanced him against my shoulder.

'Lean on me,' I said, and tried not to hum it.

I tried to shuffle him forward.

'Can't . . . can't . . . fuckin' . . . gonna . . .'

He threw up down my arm. My natural and understandable response was to step away from him, which I did, leaving him to topple in the opposite direction. He reached out for support, and I caught hold of him and pulled him back towards me, and in the same fluid movement he sprayed me again, and then fell into me, and we both fell backwards, slathered in boke, on to the cement. Horrified, and about to hurl myself, I shoved him hard, and he slithered off and cracked his head on the ground and threw up again. I lay there, simultaneously gasping for fresh breath and trying not to breathe in, and it was only a new sound from him that turned my head in concern: big, aching sobs. They were so powerful that they made the heaves of his boking seem tame.

I didn't know whether to crawl over and give him a hug, or break out the power hose.

*   *   *

I poured large amounts of coffee and Diet Coke down his ragged throat. He sat on the sofa with a basin in his lap and his head drooped, saying nothing, while I showered the stench off me. Then I gave him his leg and told him to go shower again. He attached it, and moved meekly towards the bathroom.

I stood at the kitchen counter, a towel around my waist, and just shook my head in disbelief. I had *volunteered* for this. He was nothing to do with me. I was not responsible for him or his predicament, unless you wanted to be really, really pedantic. He could sober up and he could *fuck off*.

The door bell sounded.

I remained where I was. I was harbouring a child whom ruthless terrorists were looking for. I had no way of knowing if Boogie Wilson had mentioned me to the Miller brothers or if they were even aware I existed. But only that morning I had very definitely been seen to be in Bobby's company, and had probably been spotted driving off with him, by a cleaver-wielding butcher who had strong ties to prison and the Shankill Road. It would not have taken a genius to track us back here. It was still a remote possibility, but I decided to err on the cautious side and ignore it, at least until the bell rang again and Lenny said through the door, 'Dan? Are you there? I saw your car outside. I know you're angry with me, but please let me in.'

It wasn't anger, it was relief. I opened up and she fell into my arms. She peppered me with kisses and paid particular attention to my eye, which had blackened like an overripe banana.

'I'm sorry, I'm sorry, I'm sorry,' she cried.

'It's okay,' I said, patting her back, 'it's okay.'

'No it's not, he could have killed you.'

'No he couldn't, I'm indestructible.'

More kisses. Then she held me at arm's length and said, 'I'm *so* sorry. When he said he was taking the kids up the coast, it was all a lie. He was watching me. Watching us. He followed us here. He confronted me when I got home. There was nothing I could do but admit it, and then he wouldn't let me leave or phone or anything.'

'Did he hurt you?'

'No. He wouldn't. But he wanted to hurt you.'

'Him and his pals.'

She frowned. 'He had help?'

'Did you think one man could pin me down?' I smiled. 'Don't answer that.'

'Oh baby, I'm really sorry.'

'Does he know you're here now?'

'No, of course not. He dropped me off at work. Soon as he drove off, I came here. What are we going to do?'

'I don't know,' I said.

We sat on the sofa. She leant back against my bare chest and kissed it. 'I can't give you up,' she said.

I nodded. I could see her point.

'We'll work something out,' I said.

She stroked my arm. After a little while she said, 'I saw your car. Someone has scratched *paedophile* into it, though I don't think it's spelled properly.'

'I know,' I said. 'The state of our education . . .'

Before I could finish, and with perfect timing, the bathroom door opened, and my fourteen-year-old mostly naked guest, with steam still rising from his body, limped across to the kitchen counter, lifted the KFC bargain bucket, and returned swiftly to the bathroom without once looking in our direction.

As the door closed I said, 'I can explain.'

21

In east Belfast, a taxi driver with known connections to Boogie Wilson was shot in the back of the head by a passenger and died at the wheel. On the Shankill, two associates of the Miller brothers were cornered and kneecapped by an armed gang who arrived in a minibus that was later found burned out in the shadow of the shipyard. In St Anne's Square, a fourteen-year-old with a tremendous hangover slept it off in my spare bed. In the *Bob Shaw*, a confused barmaid started the new day shift her sullen, bitter husband had insisted she switch to. On the Malone Road, I sat in my big scratched car watching Jack Caramac's opulent home, the road ahead of me busy with early-morning schools traffic, and thought about the meaning of wife.

Jack was being a bastard to Tracey, yet she stayed for love. She had promised to help me to help him. I had, undoubtedly, been a bastard in my time as well, yet Patricia had thrown me as far as she could throw me. What was so wrong with me that I wasn't worth sticking with? Or what was so wrong with Tracey that she didn't feel she could leave someone who cheated on her? Who was right? Did two rights make a wrong? Was a bird in the hand worth two in the bush? Sometimes you can ponder too much. I have this fantasy where I'm like a shark, always moving forward, while at the same time being totally aware that I'm more like a goldfish, going round and round and round in an eternal quest for crumbs. I always forget what my reality is the moment something new and shiny comes along. I get inexplicably excited and hopeful all over again, convinced that love and lust and peace and happiness are all just around the corner. I should have *There are no corners in a goldfish bowl* tattooed on to my forehead.

Focus.

Jack was on air, and Tracey was supposed to be finding out *stuff*. I had no reason to believe that she would recognise something important if she found it, but she wouldn't let me in to do it myself. I was used to trawling for information, it was part of what I did, but she was adamant. She said she would call me if she had anything to report. She had no idea I was outside. It was good to have her on my side, but not good to keep all my eggs in one basket. Not when I could be keeping an eye on Nanny the nanny as she left at the end of what must have been an overnight shift. She was wearing an anorak, zipped right up; she took a cigarette out as soon as she was halfway down the drive, but didn't light up until she actually left the property. She turned right, moved along the footpath parallel to the Caramac hedge, and on to the end of the garden of the half-built house next door. She stopped there and waited. She lit another fag. She had earphones in. Ten minutes passed, and then a silver-coloured Ford Mondeo pulled up beside her. There was a woman with blonde permed hair behind the wheel. Nanny got in, and they drove off. I followed.

It was unlikely to be *the* silver car, but if it was, and the blonde was the woman who had nabbed Jimmy, then it was a pretty bloody amateurish operation. But then writing *Shut the fuck up* on a scrap of paper was hardly the height of sophistication. Was it possible that Jack, and Jimmy, for that matter, had been taken for a ride by their own nanny? And what did it say about my half-arsed attempts to investigate the case that I hadn't grasped the bleeding obvious? Had Nanny the nanny outfoxed me by the simple expedient of not talking to me?

I started the car, and followed. Jack was still waxing lyrical. He was on health service cuts and

127

castigating the Department of Health for not providing a spokesman to be annihilated live on air. I followed the car down the full length of the Malone Road until it turned into Chlorine Gardens and wound its way round to Colenso Parade. It was an area, and street, mainly inhabited by hard-partying Queen's University students and resilient older folk. It took them a while to find a parking space. When they finally got one, I drove past them once, and then doubled back via Elaine Street and Sandhurst Gardens, just in time to see them enter a small red-brick terraced house with a black front door. Duly noted, I spent another ten minutes trying to find somewhere to park for myself. It's never hard in the movies.

I rang the bell. Nanny the nanny opened the door with a smile that faded when she saw me. She was still in her anorak.

I said, 'Hi, remember me?'

She said, 'What you want?'

'Oh, thanks for asking. I want to come in for a chat with you and your partner. Is she your partner?'

'I do not under—'

'About you and your employer, Jack Caramac, and little Jimmy, your charge? Little fella, rosy cheeks? Can we talk about him? I'll only be five minutes. Can I come in?'

'No,' she said and closed the door.

I stood there, nodding to myself for a little bit, thinking about booking lessons at the charm school and how painful it would actually be to undergo surgery to have the cheeky bone extracted. Then I rang the bell again. This time it was the blonde woman who answered. Up close, she was a good deal older than Nanny, face lined, yellow teeth, bony legs in faded jeans. Actually, I was only surmising that she had bony legs.

I said, 'Hello, I'm—'

'Fuck off!'

'If you would just give me a—'

'What don't you understand about *fuck off*? Fuck off!'

She slammed the door.

I nodded for a little while longer. But I didn't get where I was in life by taking no for an answer, so I crouched to letter-box level and pushed it open. I could see Nanny the nanny and Blondie standing together at the end of the hall.

I said, 'I only want to talk. Better you chat with me than with the police. I know what you did with little Jimmy; this isn't going to end well unless you talk to me.'

Blondie said, 'You're talking shite. Fuck away off. Or *we* call the police.'

Not wanting to confuse the police, I said, 'Go ahead.'

She took out her mobile phone and moved out of sight.

Nanny remained in the hallway. She drew on her fag.

She said, 'I haven't done anything wrong.'

But she looked like someone who knew she had and was in the early, middle and late stages of denial.

Out of sight, Blondie said, 'Don't talk to him.'

Nanny kept looking at me.

I said, 'Nobody else needs to know.'

She began to shake her head. Blondie re-emerged, took her by the arm and pulled her into the side room. A moment later, Blondie came back out and moved down the hall. She crouched down beside the letter box. We were eye to eye and mouth to mouth. She stank of onions and cigarettes.

She spoke quietly, as if not wanting Nanny to hear. 'Do you have like a card or something, I can call you later?'

I delved into my wallet and reached through the letter box. As I did, she grabbed my hand, sandwiched it between her elbow and ribcage and ground her lit cigarette into it.

I yelled and tried to pull away, but she held me tight, and she ground, and she ground and she fucking ground. I wailed like a banshee. I rammed my foot into the door and pushed hard, trying to use the leverage to rip my hand back out, but she'd too strong a grip.

Fuck, fuck, fuck, fuck, fucking FUCK!

Abruptly she let go and I tumbled back on to her flagstone path. I lay rubbing furiously at my smouldering hand while she cackled with laughter through the letter box, at least until she guldered: 'Now piss away off!'

22

I was saying, 'If God had meant men to iron . . .' but wasn't sure how to finish it.

Trish was saying, 'This is not an ironing burn. Tell me the truth.'

'I've told you the truth.'

'Please yourself.' She dabbed and I jerked and

she said, 'Will you sit still!'

'Then stop fuckin' stabbin' me, it's sore enough without you!'

'Did I ask you to come here?'

'No!'

'Then shut up and sit still.' She took a firmer grip on my hand. 'You should go to the hospital with this.'

'It's fine.'

'It's not fine. Dan, I know you, you're not being brave, you're just scared of hospitals.'

'So? You're scared of . . . commitment.'

'Hah! Don't start me, Dan, please don't start me.' She shook her head. 'Seriously, this is really deep.'

'I know. But please, just . . . you know, do what you do.'

She held my gaze, then nodded and continued her work. We were in the kitchen on bar stools on either side of a counter. It was warm and bright and smelled of fresh pastry. It most probably came from a spray. Trish could hardly boil an egg. It had once been my home, and now it wasn't. Even looking around the kitchen I could see that much of my accumulated clutter was gone. I was being spring-cleaned out of her life.

I said, 'Big house, this. I used to have one just like it.'

'You still have.'

'Plenty of space. Spare bedrooms and the like.'

'Dan, just say what you're going to say, just ask what you're going to ask, I hate it when you beat around the bush.'

'You didn't use to.'

She rolled her eyes, but there was a smile with it.

131

'Out with it.'

'How would you feel about having a lodger for a wee while?'

'*You?*'

'No. Jesus. That ship has sailed, baby. I mean, a fourteen-year-old boy.'

'A fourteen . . . ? What have you got yourself involved in now?' Her eyes narrowed. 'No, wait. Wait.' I could almost hear the cogs turning. 'Fourteen-year-old boy. *That* boy. The missing boy?'

'Ahm, yes. As it turns out, the whole Shankill Road thing seems to have been a bit of a red herring as far as Jack is concerned . . .'

'That's the case you were *fired* from?'

'Yes, but what does *fired* actually mean?'

'*Dan.*'

'You know, like sometimes you say no, when you actually mean yes?'

'No.'

'I rest my case. Anyway, it turns out that the poor old bag who got burned to death must have been demented or something, because she left me her one-legged son in her will.'

'She . . . ?'

'Well, more or less. He showed up at the office, nowhere to go and half the Shankill after him, so I put him up for the night. But, you know, it's not right, a grown man with a young boy, I mean, this day and age. You know what I mean.'

'And *so*? You want me to what, take him in? Some wee shite I don't know from Adam?'

'Yes. He's a lovely lad, once you get to know him.'

'Some wee shite who the police are looking for?'

'The police and the UVF. But really, he's cute, you'll love him.'

'Dan, why *on earth* would I want to do that?'

'Because he needs help and I'm not equipped to give it.'

'You mean you can't be arsed.'

'No, I tried, really. He's fourteen, for God's sake, he's lost his leg, he's lost his mum, he's scared, he has nowhere to go and no one to turn to. He needs someone to talk to, look after him; you can do that, you're good at that. Poor wee guy.'

She was just securing the final layer of cotton bandage around the burn. She gave it a tight pull. I yanked my hand back.

'Jesus!'

'Jesus nothing! I don't believe you, Dan Starkey. Coming round here, trying to pressure me into taking some . . .'

'I'm not trying to pressure . . .'

'. . . fucking street kid, giving me the whole fucking guilt trip. Typical, you get yourself into something, you come crying to me, *sort it out for me, Trish, please, Trish, I can't cope, Trish*, just so you can piss off back to whatever the fuck you're doing and leave me to clean up the mess. Well I'm not having it, Dan. All you ever think of is yourself. You don't for one minute think I might have a life? A job? That I don't need this? You don't even consider the fact that it might get me in trouble? That if the fucking cops don't trace him to here then maybe the UVF might, and while they're dealing with him they might just deal with me. Eh? Do you ever think of *any* of that, Dan?'

'Trish, I—'

'Shut up! I don't want to hear it. Now just go.

133

Go. You need to grow up, Dan. Sort your own problems out, all right?'

I kept my eyes on the counter and nodded. 'You're right. I'm sorry. I will go.' I held up my hand. She'd used so much gauze, and wrapped such a length of linen bandage around it, that my hand had all the dexterity of an oven glove. 'Thanks for this. Really. I appreciate it. Could you, ahm, help me on with . . . ?'

I took my jacket off the back of the stool. Trish came round and held it while I manoeuvred one arm into it, then helped to stretch the other cuff wide enough to get my injured hand through.

'Cheers,' I said. 'And sorry.'

I gave her a kiss on the cheek. I walked out into the hall. Trish followed me as far as the kitchen doorway and stood there with her arms folded. I opened the front door and was about to step out when:

'Dan!'

'What . . . ?'

'I fucking hate you!'

'Okay.'

'This is the last time, I swear to God it's the last time. Just for a couple of nights, okay? You sort it out, quick as you can, all right?'

'Are you sure?'

'No! Now away and get him before I change my mind.'

'No need,' I said. 'He's in the car.'

Her mouth dropped open. I stepped out on to the driveway before she could say anything.

Bobby was in the passenger seat. He was wearing my sunglasses, the music was booming away, he had the window down and his elbow resting on it, and he had used the car lighter to light his fag. He looked just about as happy as a pig in shite. Which, funnily enough, was exactly the opposite of . . .

*   *   *

I waited until he was in the house, and had grunted a hello at her, to tell Trish that she might need to invest in some clothes for him, and to hide whatever booze she had, and that stealing his leg might be the only way to stop him from venturing out. He didn't hear any of this because he was too busy rifling in her fridge. On the plus side, I assured her that Jack Caramac had paid me before firing me and that I'd be able to fully reimburse her as soon as his cheque hit the bank. She should keep receipts.

For some reason she did not look particularly thrilled.

I drove away, smiling.

But then I looked at my hand, resting on the steering wheel. Not only did it hurt like billy-o, it was a serious masturbation injury.

23

I drove back out to Malone and parked in my usual position. Six paracetamol and the three mini-bottles of Bladnoch lowland malt I'd half-inched from Patricia's sideboard did little to dull the pain. Actually, that's a lie. It was *my* sideboard, and *my* whisky, paid for with hard-earned Dan Starkey cash, with the exception of the whisky, which was a Christmas gift. And the sideboard, which was

135

inherited from Mouse, my old friend who'd been murdered and who'd left it in his will. Like most people who think they're funny, Mouse was not. He'd written his will when there was no immediate prospect of death, and leaving me some furniture was his idea of a cracking wheeze. My point being, *however*, that I was reduced to stealing *my own stuff*, from *my own house*.

I sat with my partial view of Jack's house and ruminated. I could just as easily have ruminated in the more comfortable surroundings of my office or the *Bob Shaw*, but sometimes it's important just to *be* somewhere that is relevant to what you're ruminating about. Also, being a journalist is all about waiting for something to happen, and it always helps to be there when it does. I was no longer a journalist, but the principles are roughly the same. As a reporter I had occasionally displayed foolhardy confidence, although never courage. In my new capacity—*I offer a boutique, bespoke service for important people with difficult problems*—it still felt like I was unfocused and fumbling around intent on getting answers to questions nobody was actually asking, and all because I had a bee in my bonnet about not being messed around. To which Patricia would say: *Get over yourself*. She would also say, and did, actually: 'If you worked in advertising and were handling the Birds Eye account, and Birds Eye decided to switch to another agency, you wouldn't camp outside their corporate headquarters because you thought there was something fishy going on. You would go looking for the next client.' There was no need for her to follow it with 'Duh!' Yet she did.

Start the engine, drive away.

My phone rang. I hoped it was Tracey. It was not.

A man said, 'Dan Starkey? Jim Dougan.'

'Hello, Jim Dougan,' I said. 'What can I do for you?'

'It's what can I do for you.'

'That's what I said.'

'No, I said what can I do for you, and you just repeated it.'

'One of us is confused,' I said, 'and it's usually me. So who's Jim Dougan when he's at home?'

'I'm not at home.'

'Please,' I said, 'or we'll be here for ever.'

'I had a message on my desk saying phone Dan Starkey at this number.'

'About what?'

'I have no idea.'

'Oh. Neither have I.'

'Oh.'

We were quiet for several moments. Eventually I filled the space with: 'Turned out nice, after all.'

'Not here,' said Jim. 'It's bucketing.'

His accent was country enough to prompt laughter if he ever attempted a eulogy.

'Where's that?' I asked, prolonging the conversation for no reason other than the fact that there was nothing else happening in my life. 'Ballymena, is it?'

He laughed. 'Way back, sure. Been in Manchester for fifteen years.'

'Really, I don't hear it.' But the penny was dropping. 'If you don't mind me asking, who was the message from?'

'Ahm. Let me see. Uhm, a Catherine Riley? I don't know her either.'

I did. One of my contacts. The penny had dropped into the one-armed bandit, and was now paying out dividends.

'Ah,' I said, 'the clouds are parting. Jim Dougan isn't your real name.'

'Yes it is.'

'Let me rephrase that: it's not the name you were born with.'

He cleared his throat. 'No.'

'James Douglas is your real name.'

There was a long pause, then he said: 'What do you want?'

'You had a baby with Jean Murray fifteen years ago.'

'Oh fuck! Is that what this is? You bastards are always . . . He's nothing to do with me . . . and I don't owe youse a fucking penny!'

He hung up.

Across the road, a lorry had arrived at the entrance to the half-built house beside Jack's. Builders jumped down and began to unload equipment. Another lorry followed behind. Maybe the economy was looking up again.

I phoned Jim Dougan back.

He said, 'Jim Dougan.'

I said, 'Dan Starkey, what can I do for you?'

He said, 'Okay, so you have my number, I can change it.'

I said, 'This probably isn't about what you think it's about.'

'Child Support Agency?'

'No, the Dan Starkey Support Group.'

'The what . . . ?'

'I'm a . . . never mind what I am and just give me a minute, this is slightly complicated. You had a child with Jean Murray . . .'

'The cow . . .'

'That is, the late Jean Murray.'

'Late? You mean like . . . ?'

'Yep.'

'I didn't know.'

'Killed in a house fire. An unfortunate accident.'

'Oh, Christ.'

'Yes, tragic, but the thing is—her son, Bobby. I know you've had nothing to do with him, but you're his father . . .'

'Allegedly.'

'. . . and he has nowhere else to go.'

'That's not my problem.'

'Well, technically it is.'

'Technically it's not. I was never married to Jean Murray. I went out with her for a few months, but I wasn't the only one. She can claim what she wants, but I'm not the father.'

'The CSA has been pursuing—'

'You can stick the CSA up your hole. I'm married *now*, I have a family *now*, I don't need this . . .'

'He looks just like you,' I said.

That stopped him for all of about ten seconds. Then: 'You don't know what I look like.'

'Yeah, I know, but he doesn't look like Jean, and she said before her untimely death that he was the spitting image of his dad.'

'Did she?'

'Yep. The dead spit.'

He was quiet for a bit.

'While I'm on,' I said, 'why would you change your name in the first place? And then why would you change it from James Douglas to Jim Dougan,

139

which is hardly changing it at all?'

'Not that it's any of your business, but I got out of that shitehole because I was in prison for a couple of things.'

'What sort of things?'

'Nothing much, low-level paramilitary stuff, but I was getting dragged in deeper and deeper, I was unemployed, I had a crap girlfriend . . .'

'The aforementioned dead Jean.'

'Yes. Okay. Jean. I decided to get out, reinvent myself, so I moved over here. And I have reinvented myself. I'm doing very well, thank you very much.'

'And the name?'

'Well, not that it's still any of your business, you don't really want anyone from your new life finding out that you've changed your name, it makes you look a bit shady. At the same time, it really is a small world, and particularly with Manchester, half of Northern Ireland comes over to see United play every other week, so there's a reasonable chance that one day I'll bump into someone from my old life, and when that happens, there might well be someone from my new life with me, so I thought I'd give myself a new name that was close enough to my old one that neither side of my life is going to realise the difference. Jim for James, Dougan for Douglas, everyone's going to think they heard their own version of the name. Okay, see where I'm coming from?'

'Absolutely,' I said. 'Glad I asked. Anyway, what about your son, Bobby? The apple of his mum's late eye.'

James or Jim took a deep breath. 'Look, I'm at work now, I can't talk about this. It's just a bit of a shock. I told her to get rid of it. She chose to have it, I washed my hands.'

'He's still your son. And he's a good kid. Smart. Sporty. He's been left without a mother. He's not looking for much. He just needs a leg up.'

'Just . . . just . . . let me think about it. I have your number, okay? All right?'

He had my number.

And I had his.

*   *   *

There was still nothing from Tracey. I called her and it went to voicemail. I tapped my oven glove on the steering wheel. I wanted to know more about Nanny the nanny and Blondie, and Tracey was my in. I checked my watch. Jack had about ten minutes left on his show. He wouldn't be back for at least half an hour. Fuck it. It was her own fault for not answering her phone. I got out of the car and walked down the slight incline, and then across the road up the drive to her front door. I rang the bell. No response. I stepped back and looked up. I caught a very slight movement at the top window on the left. I rang the bell again. Nothing. I would have shouted something through the letter box, but lately I was wary of them.

'Tracey!' I shouted. 'C'mon. I know you're up there!'

Nothing.

'Tracey! For fucksake! I'm standing here like a fucking eejit!'

Nothing.

'Right! Have it your way! Just . . . just give me a call!'

141

I stomped back down the drive. I love women, but the half of them are fuckwits.

As I waited for traffic to pass, I glanced to my right and saw two builders manoeuvring a Portaloo into place just inside the entrance to the house next door. Apropos of nothing much, I wandered up.

After watching them in the throes of gainful employment for a bit, I said, 'Yon Portaloo, is it like the Tardis, small on the outside, massive within?'

One, squat, said: 'No, it's just somewhere to shit in.'

I nodded up at the house. 'Starting work again?'

'Wasn't us last time,' said the other guy, 'but yeah. You live next door?' He nodded in the direction I'd come from.

'Yeah,' I said. 'Just worrying there's going to be a lot of noise, we have a young one.'

'Oh, right,' the squat one said. 'Well, because of the delay, they want it done pretty quick, so I think we're working nights too. You'll maybe want to have a word with the boss.'

'Who he?'

'*She*,' said the other one, with a smirk. He turned and pointed behind him, not at the half-built, but at the larger, more imposing house directly behind it. 'Speak to yer woman up there, she's the boss. At least, she gives the orders, if you know what I mean.'

'I know exactly,' I said. 'What do you call her?'

'Sir,' laughed the other one.

'Dunno, we answer to our foreman, and we see him answering to her, tugs the auld forelock, so he does.'

'Not all he's tuggin',' laughed the other one some

142

more, with a big stupid grin. 'Sorry, mate,' he said to me, 'no offence.'

'None taken,' I said.

'But she is a bit of a ride.'

He gave me a big wink.

I thanked them in my matey fashion and looked up at the other house. It was well set back from Jack's. With the shell of the new build in front of them, neither the ride nor her family would have had a view of the road where Jimmy was snatched, and therefore probably wouldn't be much help. Nevertheless, I made a mental note, adding her to the list of people to talk to when all else failed. She was right up there with the Samaritans.

24

The buzzer woke me. It was three in the afternoon. My feet were on my desk. My mouth was sour with the whisky. I would have slept through it, but the buzzer buzzing was sufficiently unusual to pique my interest. I yawned and popped a Smartie. I pressed my end of it and said, 'Lambert and Butler, Attorneys at Law.'

'Starkey? It's DS Hood, can we come up?'

That pesky officer saw *straight through me*.

'Are you making house calls now?' I asked.

He didn't respond. I pushed the buzzer and tidied my desk while they mounted the stairs. This consisted of removing sweetie papers and sweeping crumbs. The only reason I was working in a paper-free environment was that I had no cases from which to generate paper. I had a notebook in my desk drawer, so I was prepared for any eventuality, though with cops coming up to see me, I'd have to be careful in case they misinterpreted the swastikas.

Gary Hood came in first. Behind him there was another detective in plain clothes. I did not recognise him.

'Where's Maxi?' I asked. 'I thought you two travelled in pairs.'

'Maxi's back on the desk,' said Hood, 'at least until Friday. Then he's gone. This is Detective Inspector Springer.'

I shook his hand.

'Like the dog,' I said.

He had a needlessly strong grip. He was about the same age as Hood, but looked as if he'd been around a few more corners.

'He's the senior investigating officer,' said Hood.

'Mad but lovable,' I said.

'Excuse me?' said Springer.

'Springer spaniels. You would only get one as a guide dog for the blind if you wanted rid of someone. I'm sorry—have a seat. Both of you. You're lucky there's only the two of you, because I only have two seats. If there were three of you, one of you would have to stand, and that would be awkward. I should invest in a third seat.' I nodded at them. They nodded back. 'If there were four of you, it would be absolute chaos.' I sat down. They sat too. 'Senior investigating officer for what?'

'The murder of Jean Murray,' said Hood.

'Oh yes. Poor Jean.'

'What is it exactly that you do?' Springer asked.

'Good question,' I said. 'With no easy answer.'

'We believe you spoke to her shortly before her

144

death,' said Springer.

'Day before,' I said.

'Did she intimate any particular fears to you? Threats received, et cetera.'

'Intimate, no. State bluntly, yes. But you know this.' I nodded at Hood. 'You know who's responsible. She was round the station often enough telling anyone who'd care to listen.'

'Well we're interested in your take on it,' said Springer. 'Who do you think was responsible?'

'Apart from the bleeding obvious, I have no idea. Who do *you* think caused it?'

Springer ignored my question.

Hood said, 'Would you be prepared to come in and make a statement about what Jean Murray said to you, when you met her?'

'You mean about her accusing the Miller boys of shooting her son in the leg, and them threatening her and trying to burn her house down on previous occasions?'

'Yes.'

'Well, no, obviously.'

'It would help us build a case.'

'Well come back and see me when you're putting the slates on, because I'm pretty sure if I give you a statement it'll be the only one you have, which means I'm down in the foundations somewhere, which is where I'll end up if the Miller boys get wind of it.'

'You're refusing to cooperate?' Springer asked.

'Yes,' I said.

'You can be compelled to, by a court of law. You're withholding information.'

'Really?' I looked at Hood. 'Does he always talk like this? He doesn't exactly have a winning way

145

about him.'

'We're serious,' said Hood.

'You can give us a statement now, or we can take you in.'

I nodded some, and contemplated the skylight. It was more of a skydark, but that wasn't a word.

'Have you ever heard the expression, you can take a horse to water but you can't make him drink?' I asked. 'Or maybe, you can take a whore to culture but you can't make her sing?'

I put my feet back on the desk. I clasped my hands behind my head. It was supposed to give the impression of being relaxed and cool. They didn't look overly impressed. But I wasn't of a mind to care. Besides, I didn't believe they were the slightest bit interested in my statement. And almost immediately they proved it.

Springer said: 'When you were at the Murray house, did you speak to her son, Bobby?'

'Bobby with the one leg?'

'Yes.'

'No.'

'You didn't speak to him?'

'No.'

'Have you spoken with him since the fire in which his mother was killed?'

'No.'

'Do you know his whereabouts?'

'No.'

'You're sure about that?'

'I think *no* pretty much covers it.'

Springer shifted forward in his chair. 'Cards on the table here, bucko. You were seen with him.'

'*Bucko?*'

'You were spotted with him in a café just a few

146

doors down. He's hard to miss.'

'But seriously, *bucko*?'

Hood shifted forward too. 'Dan, don't mess around. We're trying to help him. You were spotted together.'

'You may think that, but it wasn't him,' I said. 'You see, I do a lot of charitable work amongst the one-legged community. I'm getting a team together for the paramilitary Paralympics. He's probably been mistaken for someone else, or vice versa, seeing as how they all have the same affliction and wear the same tracksuits and shit.'

'You should know,' Springer said, 'that at this moment the Millers are not the focus of our inquiry.'

Now *that* surprised me. 'Meaning?'

'There is certain evidence to suggest that Bobby Murray may have been complicit in the death of his mother.'

'Complicit by annoying the Millers?'

'Complicit by setting the fire himself,' said Hood.

'You're serious?'

They did appear to be.

Springer said, 'Bobby Murray not only has drugs-related convictions, but he also has one for arson. He was known not to get on with his mother; they were heard to be fighting by neighbours on the night of the fire. You could make the case.'

'You mean, *you* could make the case.' Springer kept his gaze steady on me. 'And it would be laughed out. You know that's just crazy bollocks.'

Springer raised an eyebrow. 'We want to talk to him. If you know where he is, you tell us. If you know someone who's sheltering him, you should let them know we want to talk to him. And if you do know that someone, well maybe they should think twice about leaving him alone with a box of matches.' He nodded. I nodded. 'You may consider this a courtesy visit,' he said. 'We know you know where he is. Do yourself a favour and either wire us off or bring him in.'

'Duly noted,' I said.

Springer stood, put his hands on the table and leant forward. 'I was told you had an attitude problem. I was told you used to be a big-shot reporter. That you thought you could get away with murder because you were someone. Well you're before my time. I've never heard of you. And whatever you were, you aren't now. So if I were you, *bucko*, I'd watch out for myself.'

At that, the buzzer sounded.

'Your taxi's here,' I said.

Springer made a sudden feint forward, as if to attack.

I moved an involuntary fraction. He smiled. He turned. Hood raised an eyebrow and went with him.

I sat back. The buzzer sounded again. When I pressed it, a gruff voice said, 'Mr Starkey? Can we come up?'

'That depends,' I said. 'Who are we?'

'We're here representing Jack Caramac and Cityscape FM.'

'Representing? Are you like his agent? Or his estate agent?'

'I'm his solicitor,' said the man.

And then another voice chipped in: 'And I'm from Malone Security.'

'Wow,' I said, 'it's my lucky day. Okay, you can come up. Any friends of Jack's are friends of mine. Just let me tell you the password.'

'Password?'

'Yeah, sorry, can't be too careful. Two of my security guys are about to open the front door. Just say to them, *You'll never take me alive, copper*, and they'll let you right up.'

I took my finger off the buzzer, replaced my feet on the desk and awaited developments.

25

'Come on, on, on, on in,' I said. 'It's like Piccadilly station round here this day.' I indicated the chairs. 'You're lucky there's only two of you, because I only have the two seats. If there were three of you, one of you would have to stand, and that would be awkward. I should invest in a third seat.' I nodded at them. They nodded back. 'If there were four of you,' I said, 'it would be friggin' anarchy in the UK.'

They just looked at me. I was hoping that a different audience might appreciate me better, but it was looking as if it was the material that was the problem. The fact that they were an ill-matched pair shouldn't have been a surprise, given their respective professions, but it was. Because the big, muscular man in the zip-up Puffa jacket introduced himself as Conor Wilson, from Wilson and Maguire Solicitors, and the small, bony-looking guy in the trendy black boutique hotel manager's suit said he was Paddy Barr, from Malone Security.

I sat down and said, 'No trouble downstairs?'

'Ah, no,' said Conor Wilson. 'They didn't seem very interested.'

'It's an act,' I said. 'They'll be checking out your

bona fides as we speak.'

Paddy Barr glanced at Wilson. Wilson kept his eyes on me. So I concentrated on Paddy Barr.

'Malone Security, is it?' I asked. 'At a wild guess, would that be providing security up Malone direction?'

Paddy Barr nodded. 'We provide a bespoke service . . .'

'Gotcha!'

'. . . for clients in the Malone area, yes.'

'Sorry, yes. I'm just excited to meet someone else in the bespoke trade.'

His nose had been broken at some time in the past and had mended crooked. Now that I looked at him he wasn't so much bony as wiry, an important difference. There was some evidence of scarring around his eyes. I checked out his knuckles. Two of them were missing.

I said, 'What weight did you fight at?'

'Bantam,' he said.

'Olympics?'

'Commonwealth.'

I nodded. I like my boxing.

'Gold?'

'Bronze. You?' He indicated the eye.

'The wife,' I said. 'Punches above her weight. I used to be best buds with Fat Boy McMaster, remember him?'

'Must be before my time.'

'Most everything I know seems to be before everyone's time,' I said wistfully, and shifted back to Conor Wilson. 'What about you? You remember Fat Boy? He fought Tyson for the world heavyweight title, New York, St Patrick's Day, fifteen years ago, must be.'

150

'I'm not here to discuss boxing.'

'Are you sure about that? Because we could outvote you.' Conor Wilson shook his head, slightly. There wasn't a lot of animation in him. Or personality. Or humour. There wasn't much of it in Paddy Barr either. I gave him a shrug, and sat back and clasped my hands in what I hoped was a mildly professional manner. 'Okay, folks, what can I be doing for you? Is it a case, a job, a crime that needs solving? I'm kind of busy, but if it was sufficiently interesting, I'm sure I could find a window. My rates are competitive and my service is . . .' I showed a hand to Paddy Barr. He did not take the bait. '. . . bespoke.'

'No, Mr Starkey, I am not here to offer you a job,' said the solicitor. 'I am here on behalf of my client, Mr Caramac, and his employers, Cityscape FM, to give you due notice that if you continue to harass Mr Caramac and his family, we will commence legal proceedings against you.'

'Harass?'

'We seek that you should desist from approaching our client, his wife, any of his employees; we seek that you should desist from entering his property uninvited; we seek that you should desist from loitering outside his property and accosting any members of his staff as he, she or they leave said property; we seek that you should desist from following said employees to their places of residence; we seek that you should desist from harassing said employees at said place of residence.'

'My, that's a lot of seeking,' I said, 'but I like it.'

'You like what, Mr Starkey?'

'Your turn of phrase. It's not really how humans speak, is it? *We seek that you should desist.* In a

151

letter or maybe a court order, I understand, but not face to face, one-on-one. Those are words you don't often hear out loud. I like them, but you should have just written them down and stuck them in the letter box. The desisting loses something spoken out loudy.' I nodded. 'Not that I have a letter box, but you get my drift.'

'We wished to give you the option of desisting before we formalised matters.'

I looked at Paddy Barr. 'You don't look like a man who asks many people to desist.'

'No, Mr Starkey, I prefer a more practical approach. You might almost say physical.'

'Ah,' I said. 'Let me see then if I understand this correctly. There's kind of a twin thing going on here—on one hand, I'm being threatened with legal action; on the other, I'm being threatened with what you might call a good diggin'. Is that a fair summation of what we have discussed here this afternoon?'

'Mr Starkey,' said Conor Wilson, 'this isn't a joke.'

'Well,' I said, 'it's a little bit of a joke.'

'No, sir, it is most assuredly not . . .'

'Desist,' I said.

Conor Wilson stopped. I leaned forward. I smiled from one to the other. 'You have to remember, Mr Wilson, Mr Barr, that I worked with Jack Caramac for many years, indeed before he became Jack Caramac. I know him very well, and he knows me, likewise. As reporters, he would know that if we were ever threatened with legal action or physical violence, our reaction was always to dig deeper, because it was surely a sign that there was something to hide, that we were on the right

152

path. So what I interpret from your visit here is that Jack is actually making a cry for help, that he's in some trouble but can't talk about it, that he is in fact asking me to look into this whole situation even more thoroughly.'

'Mr Starkey, that is the very opposite of—'

'Well you would say that, because you're not in on the joke. Oh, I'd say he knows exactly what he's doing.'

Conor Wilson cleared his throat. 'Mr Starkey . . .'

'Or,' I continued, because when you're on a roll, it's best to keep rolling, 'there's also the possibility that he's not sending me a coded message at all, but that he has disappeared so far up his own arse that he actually thinks that sending in you two eejits really will frighten me, in which case I'm sorry to tell you that you may seek to inform said fuckwit that I've no intention of laying off, and that in fact I've a fair mind to crank it up. So you see, whatever way you want to interpret it, the result is the same. I'm on it, I'm going to stay on it, and there's not a fucking thing you can do about it.'

Paddy Barr stood up. His hands were at his sides, but bunched into fists.

'Please,' I said, 'you were a bantam; that's about two ounces above pixieweight.'

He was all ready to come over the desk at me, but the solicitor put a hand on his arm. 'No, Paddy,' he said.

Paddy kept glaring at me, but didn't come any closer. Instead he growled, 'Funny fella.' He pointed a finger. 'Well I'm telling you, sunshine, this is a warning, so watch your back. There's plenty more where I come from.'

'Where's that, Pixie Land?'

'Funny fella,' said Paddy, 'fun-ny fella.'

Conor Wilson stood up. He said, 'Very well, Mr Starkey, we have delivered our message, you have given us your response. I appreciate that taking umbrage is a natural response when presented with such demands. But I would suggest you take a little time to think about it more thoroughly, and if you decide to change your position, then your cooperation will simply become apparent to the parties involved.'

He turned for the door. Paddy gave me a sneer and went after him.

'One thing,' I said. They stopped. '*Umbrage*. Is that where the Archers live?'

26

It was, by any standards, a remarkable half-hour: two groups of visitors, two threats of legal action and two of physical violence. And they had all come from the supposedly right side of the law—the police, a solicitor and a security guard. Clearly I was doing something right. It was intriguing on so many levels that I felt compelled to adjourn to the *Bob Shaw* to think about it.

Lenny was behind the bar. She looked surprised, and then somewhat cool. She had said she absolutely believed my explanation for having a one-legged teenager in my bathroom, but now I wasn't so sure. She had read the graffiti on my car, and then jumped to a conclusion. It stood testament to the power of advertising. She kept herself busy and away from me. On the few occasions she did pass within range and I attempted small talk, her response was smaller.

I didn't let it bother me, much. I had bigger fish to fry. I sat in the corner with a Harp. It used to be the drink of choice in Belfast because it had virtually no competitors, but the city has opened up since what passes for peace was declared, and now the auld Harp is under siege. I take seriously my responsibility to support it, sometimes above and beyond the call of duty.

I sipped and pondered. As threats went, these latest ones were genuine, but mild. Of the two, Springer and Hood's had to be taken more seriously, because they had the power to do more than just repeat the word *desist* at regular intervals. If the PSNI was trying to twist my arm, then it didn't take a huge imagination to, uhm, imagine what the Miller brothers might do if *they* got wind of my role in protecting Bobby. It was a small city, and people talked. I'd a former Shankill Butcher downstairs from my office and a possible spy in my local café. If either the cops or the Millers were serious about finding Bobby, then they wouldn't have to employ a rocket scientist to track him down to either my apartment or what Patricia fondly imagines is her house.

Bobby having a conviction for arson was somewhat worrying. I was pretty sure Springer had only mentioned it to try to get me to open up, but still, I'd handed the boy over to Trish to get me out of a hole without really thinking about how it might impact on her. She had a heart of gold and tended to think the best of people. If someone literally bumped into her on the street, it was always Trish who said sorry. Bobby could be standing over the

155

smoking embers of her house, with a can of petrol in one hand and a box of matches in the other, and she still wouldn't quite be convinced of his guilt. I, on the other hand, trusted few people, always suspected a dark side, and I was pretty sure that there was more to Bobby's fallout with the Millers than the fact that he owed them a few quid.

I phoned Trish.

I kept my voice low so that Lenny wouldn't hear, particularly the 'Hello, how's the love of my life?' bit.

'Fine,' she said.

Fine to me is a grand summer's morning, or the first pint on a stag night. Fine coming from a woman translates as *appalling*.

'How's the boy wonder?'

'Fine.'

'Is he holding you hostage and restricting you to one word?'

'No,' she said. Then she sighed. 'No, really. It's okay. I suppose. He's bored. I'm bored. You've lumbered me with this. He knows he can't go out, but there's nothing here for him to do. I can't entertain him. So, I was wondering . . . *he* was wondering . . .'

'Mmm-hmmm?'

'Well, he was asking if I could run him up to his house, just so that he can go in and get his Xbox. It's in his bedroom, sitting there doing nothing.'

'No.'

'He'd be in and out in two minutes.'

'Absolutely not.'

'Dan, he's a teenager, they're miserable at the best of times. With everything he has going on, he needs something to take his mind off it, and I'm afraid daytime television doesn't cut it.'

'Rent him a movie. Download something.'

'Dan, he wants the Xbox. Look, his mum is gone, he can't talk to his friends. Just let—'

'Trish—no. He goes near the Shankill, they'll have him in an instant.'

'Then I'll take a run up and—'

'No.'

'Are you *telling* me no?'

'Yes.'

'Then you do it for him. Dan. *Please*. I'm harbouring a fugitive, the least you can do is—'

'Okay. *All right*. Leave it with me, I'll see what I can do.'

'So you'll do it?'

'I said to leave it with me.'

'Dan, just say you'll do it.'

'Okay! Christ. *I'll do it*. Satisfied?'

'Thank you. Was that so hard?'

'Trish. Jesus.' *Calm. Deep breath*. 'Right. Okay.' I drummed my fingers on the table. 'What're you going to do about your work?'

'What do you mean?'

'You're going to take some time off?'

'Dan, I happen to be off today. But I'm going in tomorrow.'

'Are you sure that's wise?'

'It's my job, Dan. It's not a case of it being wise or not.'

'I mean, you're just going to leave him at home by himself? Couldn't you take a couple of days off, just till I get this sorted?'

'No. I don't have them to take.'

'Okay. It's up to you. I'm sure it'll be okay. We are insured, aren't we?'

'Dan, *don't*.'

'I'm just asking.'

'Tell you what, why don't you come round and babysit him? It's not like you have a job.'

'Nice one, Trish.'

'You asked for it.'

We were quiet for a bit. Lenny came past and lifted my empty glass. She didn't ask if I wanted another.

I said, 'I appreciate your candour, Inspector,' for her benefit.

'You what?' Trish asked.

'Nothing. Sorry.' I sighed. 'You okay?'

'Yes. It's just . . . strange, having him around.'

'I know.'

'Because I keep thinking . . .'

'I know.'

'Do you ever think . . . ?'

'Trish . . .'

'What he would have been like? He'd have been fourteen by now.'

'Yes, he would. I know that. A little ginger teenager.'

'He wasn't ginger.'

'He was one gene from it.'

'But not your gene, Dan.'

Dagger between the ribs.

'No. That's true.'

'I'm sorry, Dan, I didn't mean that.'

'I know that. Anyway, gotta go . . .'

'Dan, don't be like that.'

'Like what?'

'*Dan.*' I didn't say anything. After a bit she said: 'Are you okay?'

'I'm fine,' I said, and cut the line.

*　　　*　　　*

The house on Dewey Street had been boarded up
after the fire, but its defences had long since been
breached. Scorched furniture lay in the garden:
a sofa with the stuffing spilling out, a blackened
sideboard, various battered kitchen appliances.
Crime-scene tape flapped in the breeze. It was a
Housing Executive dwelling, and they would soon
be round to clear it out and make it ready for the
next young couple on the list desperate enough
for their own home that they wouldn't care that
someone had recently been murdered in it.

The front door was lying open. I stepped into
the hall, and on into the living room. It smelt
of burning rubber. Shards of broken glass and
smashed ceramics littered the floor. The fire
hadn't made it upstairs, but the smoke had, and it
still clung to everything. Jean's bedroom had been
thoroughly ransacked: drawers emptied and clothes
ripped apart; someone had taken a dump on her
bed. There were cider bottles lying around, stubs of
cigarettes and bags with residue of glue. She'd not
been dead for more than a few hours and her home
had already been colonised by vermin. Bobby's
bedroom was similarly trashed. Posters on the wall
had been torn to shreds and his clothes appeared to
have been pissed on. There was a portable TV that
wasn't considered valuable enough to steal, so its
screen had been smashed in. There was no sign of
an Xbox.

I went back downstairs and outside. I turned
to my left and knocked on the next front door.
Nobody answered. I went right, and a small man in

his sixties answered; white T-shirt, fleshy neck.

'All right, mate,' I said. 'I'm from the Housing Executive, we're going to be starting work on next door.'

'Yeah? We're puttin' in for compensation, been coughin' our guts up ever since.'

'That's not really—'

'I worked in the shipyard, thirty years, me lungs aren't good, I can't be having that.'

I nodded sympathetically. I said, 'It was a tragedy, what happened.'

'Aye,' he said.

'Have any of her relatives been to the house, clearing out? The upstairs wasn't too badly damaged.'

'There was a few here, but they were too late. Minute the peelers and the firemen left, the scavengers were in, stole everything worth stealing. I couldn't do anything about it. Fucking vultures, so they were.' He nodded beyond me, across the road. 'No respect, these young 'uns. My day they would have got a boot in the arse; these days they just boot you right back. Wee skitters.'

I looked where he had looked. 'In there? Number four?'

'Aye. Little shits.'

I thanked him. *That*'s why reporters knock on doors. Sometimes you get a break. It might mean nothing, or it could lead to a little tiny something that sends you in the right direction.

I crossed the road and knocked on number 4. A small man in his sixties answered; white T-shirt, fleshy neck. It seemed to be the style of the moment. I said I was a detective investigating thefts from the burned-out house. He asked if his

160

brother had sent me. He glared across the road, at his brother, glaring back.

'What's it to do with me?' he barked.

'I'm afraid, sir, it has to do with your sons. We have CCTV footage that shows them entering the house.'

'You've fuckin' what?'

'Security camera footage. They were in the house. Are they here?'

'Aye. They're upstairs.'

'If you could send them down? The relatives want some of the family possessions back. If they get them, that'll be the end of it; if they don't, I'm afraid I'll have to take them in. Sir?'

He was too busy glaring across the road to pay much attention to me. He gave his brother the fingers.

'Howl on,' he growled, and turned to the stairs behind him. 'Nathan! Clint! Get your arses down here now!' There was a chorus of whats and whys. 'Just get fuckin' down here!'

Nathan and Clint arrived. They looked neither sheepish nor worried. They looked at me without apparent recognition and grunted.

'He's a peeler,' said the dad, pointing at me. 'Were yousuns in Jean Murray's house?'

'Wasn't us!' both of them cried together.

'Not the fire,' I said, 'after. You stole stuff.'

Nathan shrugged. Or maybe it was Clint.

'Youse came back here with a clatter of stuff,' said the dad.

'House was fuckin' lyin' open,' said Nathan or Clint.

'Everyone else was fuckin' doin' it,' said Clint or Nathan.

The dad slapped their heads, one after the other. 'Don't fuckin' curse, show a bit of respect. Now whatever you took, go and get it.'

'Can't,' said Nathan or Clint. 'We sold it. It was shite stuff anyway, only got a couple of quid for it.'

'Who'd you sell it to?' the dad asked.

Nathan and Clint shrugged.

I said, on a hunch, 'You didn't sell the Xbox.'

Nathan and Clint looked surprised.

'How the fuck do you—' Nathan or Clint started.

Nathan or Clint shoved Nathan or Clint. 'Shut the—'

The dad slapped them both again. 'You have the Hexbox?' They both avoided his eyes. 'Right. Go and fuckin' get it.' They looked at each other. The dad barked: 'Now!'

Nathan and Clint bolted up the stairs.

I stood for a long minute with the dad. Eventually I said, 'Terrible thing,' and nodded across at Jean Murray's house.

The dad grunted. 'Never knew when to shut her bake.'

I nodded. 'Still.'

'You know, I worked in the shipyard for thirty years.'

'Really?'

'Got laid off. He didn't.' He nodded across the road. 'Not for another three years.'

His brother was in his front room, staring across.

'Close, are you?'

Before he could respond, the boys arrived back downstairs. Nathan or Clint had the Xbox in his arms. He thrust it into my hands. 'Here,' he barked. 'Satisfied?'

The Xbox was squat and black and scratched; the

twin ventilation strips were smudged and clogged with dust. The other boy pushed two controllers against my chest. They both turned and stomped back up the stairs.

'You're lucky he doesn't haul your arses down the station!' the dad yelled after them.

I thanked him for his cooperation and said it was unlikely that we would be taking any further action, but he should consider my visit an official warning. He grunted. He closed the door. I was halfway back to my car when I heard a shout:

'Hey, pedo!'

Clint and Nathan were at an open window, upstairs.

'He knows his name!' said Clint or Nathan, and they both cackled.

I turned back to the car.

'Enjoy the Xbox,' shouted Clint or Nathan. 'It doesn't work anyway, you sad fucking wanker!'

I put the Xbox in the back seat and climbed in. I drove away to a chorus of Clint and Nathan singing: 'FUCK THE POLICE! FUCK THE POLICE!'

27

I dropped the Xbox off at my usual repair shop on Botanic Avenue, and the old fella asked if I'd checked the plug, with the weariness of someone who'd dealt with me before. I lied *yes* and he told me to come back in an hour.

So with time to kill and Colenso Parade only up the road a bit, I drove there and found a parking spot handy for keeping an eye on Nanny the nanny's house. I'd bought a packet of crisps in the *Bob Shaw*, but with one hand the size of a small cushion, they were impossible to open. I was still trying to work it out when Nanny and Blondie emerged, climbed into their silver dream machine and drove off. A few minutes later, I sauntered down the alley behind the parade, counting off the houses. They all had back yards guarded by above-head-height walls. There were doors in the brickwork, but they'd been there for sixty or seventy years and there wasn't much evidence of them having enjoyed the benefit of maintenance work. The locks were rusty, the hinges loose. When I came to Nanny's, I didn't have to do much more than lean on their green door before the lock gave way. I slipped inside and closed it behind me. I stood there and listened for a wee while, before negotiating my way through an overgrown and rubbish-strewn yard to the back door. It was in better nick than the yard door, but instead of being solid, it was made up of twelve small smoked-glass panels in a wooden frame. I took my bandaged hand and punched the panel closest to the handle. It cracked well enough for me to prise the glass out in two pieces. I then reached through and unlocked the door from the inside. I opened it and entered the kitchen.

I felt quite proud of myself. The way my luck ran, I could easily have opened a vein breaking the glass and bled to death on the back doorstep. There was a pleasant buzz of adrenalin. When I was a reporter, I wouldn't have dreamed of breaking into someone's house. But now that I was whatever I was, I was beholden to no one. It felt like exactly the right thing to do. I wasn't a burglar. I was a champion of justice, which was, I'm sure, exactly how the police would look at it if they found me.

It was a two-up, two-down and sparsely furnished. There was cat food set out in a bowl in the kitchen. There was a flat-screen TV on the wall in the living room. There was a telephone stand in the hall with a small pile of mail. Most of the letters were bills addressed to Betty Spense. That would be Blondie. There was one letter addressed to a Marija Gruevski, with an unfamiliar foreign stamp. It had already been opened, so I took out three neatly hand-written pages in a language I did not recognise. I pocketed one bill, and the letter. Upstairs there was one bedroom packed to the hilt with cardboard boxes stuffed with nothing but old clothes and knick-knacks. The second had a large double bed and just about enough room for a small locker on either side of it. On the left one there was a framed photograph showing Marija with two girls of roughly similar age, smiling against a snowy background. There was nothing much of interest in her drawer. In Betty's locker there were tights, nighties and a vibrator. I took the battery out, and put the vibrator back in the drawer.

I turned at the sound of a car door slamming. If the windows had been double-glazed I wouldn't have heard it. I moved to the bedroom window and saw Betty approaching from about four cars up. I nipped smartly downstairs. I set the battery from the vibrator upright in the middle of the kitchen table. It would sow a confusion that would probably not be resolved until she tried to pleasure herself.

As the front door opened, I slipped out the back. I pulled the yard door closed behind me and returned to my car. I sat there for a while. When

Blondie or Betty didn't immediately burst out on to the street screaming that she had been burgled, I started the engine and drove back to Botanic and parked. I still had ten minutes until the hour was up, so I took out Marija's letter, picked a word out of the address in the top corner and typed it into Google on my phone. It was a town in Macedonia. I knew nothing about Macedonia, but nine minutes later I knew a lot more, although it was from Wikipedia, so it might have been cack.

The owner of the repair shop claimed to be a master of all trades. He not only did Xboxes, he did vacuum cleaners too. And refrigerators, and electric heaters, and televisions, and computers, and alarm systems, and he could rig up a satellite system that would give you all the benefits of Sky without having to pay for Sky. I, who could not wire a plug, admired him immensely. I had used him on and off over the years. He knew me as Dan, I knew him as Bill. He had once had a brother called Ben. Together they and their shop were known as Bill and Ben, the Repair Men. According to legend, Ben had been electrocuted by an electric guitar he was repairing. Ben, apparently, was not a master of all trades.

As I entered, a bell sounded above the door. Bill was behind the counter, repairing a portable typewriter. He looked up. There was no familiar smile.

'Haven't seen one of those in a while,' I said. He grunted. I followed it up with: 'So, Bill, how's the patient, could she be saved?'

He responded by moving out from behind the counter. He came past me, closed the door and locked it. He turned the *Open* sign to *Closed*. He moved back behind the counter. He shifted the typewriter to one side and fixed me with a look.

'That bad, is it?'

He said, 'How many years have I known you?'

'Many,' I said.

'Have I ever cheated you?'

'No, of course not.'

'Have I been anything but courteous?'

'No. Bill . . . ?'

'Yet you bring this *shit* in to me?'

I cleared my throat. 'I know the Xbox is overrated, but . . .'

'No,' he said simply, and reached down and lifted up what appeared to be Bobby's console. He set it down and nodded down at it. 'This is your Xbox?'

'Yes. No, in fact. I'm getting it fixed for a wee lad I know. Has he completely destroyed it?'

Bill thought for a moment, before nodding to himself. 'Dan,' he said, 'I know you've had troubles, but you seem to be a decent enough, straight-up guy. I also know you haven't the technical know-how to physically take the top off this Xbox without fatally damaging either it or yourself.'

'Sad but true,' I said.

'And *that* is the only reason I haven't gone to the police.'

'The . . .'

'If it had been anyone else, I'm telling you, I'd have had them here in a flash. You want to know why your Xbox doesn't work? You think maybe *this* has something to do with it?'

I moved closer and peered down as Bill removed the top. I expected to see the inner workings. I did not. Inside, the electronics had been removed and replaced with a small handgun, a thick wad of cash and a see-through plastic bag containing a very large amount of white powder.

28

I was through the front door almost before Patricia had opened it. And before she could say anything, I was spitting out: 'Where the fuck is fucking Peg Leg?'

'Dan . . . Jesus . . . what's got into you?'

She followed me down the hall. When he wasn't in the kitchen, I went into the lounge. When he wasn't in the lounge, I went into the living room.

'Where is he?'

I went to leave the living room, heading upstairs. Trish stood in the doorway.

'Dan. Settle down.'

'Don't tell me to . . . The little fucking—'

'*Dan.*'

I had the Xbox in my arms. I blew air out of my cheeks. I sucked it back in again. In, out, in, out.

'Right,' I said. 'Sorry. Where is he?'

'Upstairs.'

'Call him down. Please.'

'Not until you tell me what—'

'Trish. It's fine. Honestly. All will be revealed.'

'It's not fine if you're going to smack him.'

'He's fourteen, I'm not going to smack him. I'm going to punch his head off. Please. Just get him.'

She raised an eyebrow. I raised one back.

'Sure?'

'Sure.'

She turned for the stairs. I retreated back across

into the living room and set the Xbox on the coffee table. I heard her calling him. I paced. A couple of minutes later he came into the room. He had on an old pair of my football shorts and a twenty-year-old Liverpool top. His eyes immediately went to the Xbox. Patricia leant against the door frame, arms folded.

'Got your Xbox,' I said. He grunted. He moved towards it. I said, 'Why don't you plug it in, we can have a game.'

'There's a TV in my room.'

'I'll come up there, then.'

He screwed his eyes up. 'Yeah, right. I just want to play by myself.'

'Hey, son, you're here as our guest; the least you could do is have a game. Our wee family. Go on, plug it in. I got you a game. A new one. Thought you'd appreciate it. *Grand Theft Auto Remember 1690*. It's a special Belfast edition. Come on, plug it in, Bobby. *Plug it in*.'

He stood where he was.

'Dan . . . ?'

'PLUG IT IN!'

'Fuck off!' Bobby exploded. He spun on his one heel and would have fled if Patricia hadn't blocked his path. 'Get out of my fuckin' way,' he growled. His fingers bunched into fists. His head jutted forward, right up against Patricia's. 'GET OUT OF MY FUCKIN' WAY!'

He didn't know Trish. She could have made the defenders of Stalingrad look flaky. She remained resolutely in position, even as he grabbed her blouse and tried to drag her out of the way. That lasted for all of one second; then I had him by the throat. I dragged him backwards and threw him down. He landed in a heap. I stood over him.

'You ever put a hand on her again, and I'll fucking kill you. Do you hear me?' He said nothing. I crouched down. I took a hold of his hair and pulled his head up. 'Do you fucking hear me?'

Still nothing.

Patricia knelt beside me. 'Dan . . .' she said softly. 'Dan . . .'

She took hold of my hand and eased it off his hair one finger at a time. I was shaking. She got the last finger free and he slumped back to the floor.

I stood up. 'You ungrateful little shit,' I spat.

'Dan . . . Dan . . . it's okay. We all just need to calm down.'

'We need to get our fucking heads examined, taking him in, looking after . . .'

She put a calming hand on my chest, and I breathed in, out, in, out, against it.

It eased.

'Good,' said Trish. 'Now what's this all about?'

I stepped up to the coffee table. I removed the top of the Xbox. 'This is what it's about.'

Patricia moved up beside me. She looked down. She looked at me. We both turned to look at the boy.

He said, 'If you touch me again, I'm calling ChildLine.'

'If you call ChildLine, I'll break your fucking head,' I said.

'And I'll help him,' said Trish.

What a team.

*   *   *

When Bobby refused to get up off the floor, Patricia

170

asked *me* to leave the room. I did so, eventually, and under protest. I left them together for ten minutes. I stood in the garden, fuming. It was neater than I remembered. There was new furniture. I saw Trish through the French doors, on her knees beside him. I was disappointed with him, and myself. I'd known he was trouble, I had all the evidence for it, yet I'd still brought him into our lives. I had made the cardinal error of trusting him *because* he was disabled, as if that somehow made him incapable of being evil.

Trish waved me in and we took our places at the kitchen table. Between us we had the gun, the cash and the drugs, two cans of Diet Coke and a cappuccino made with a cappuccino machine for which I'd been denied visitation rights. We had one Twix. I took one leg of it, Patricia the other. Apply your own metaphor.

She said, 'No shouting, no storming off, no fighting, agreed?'

I stared at Bobby, he stared at the table. Trish gave me a look, and then a second, and then, '*Dan?*'

'Yes. *Okay*. If you insist.'

'Bobby?'

He nodded.

'He needs to say it,' I said.

'Dan, for fuck . . .' She trailed off. 'Bobby, do you agree?'

'Yes.'

'And have you anything to say about what we found in your Xbox?'

'Apart from some half-arsed excuse,' I said. 'Own it.'

'Dan?'

'Okay!'

171

'Bobby—what do you want to say?'

His eyes flitted up to Trish. She gave him an encouraging nod.

'Sorry,' he said.

'It doesn't mean anything if you don't mean it,' I said.

Patricia rolled her eyes. 'Jesus, Dan, give him—'

'Okay. *All right*. Apology accepted. Now you need to tell us about . . . *this*.' I indicated the gun. Bobby reached out for it. 'Without touching it,' I added.

'It's a nine-millimetre short-barrel Luger.'

'O . . . kay.'

'It's semi-automatic with an eight-round detachable box magazine and—'

'*Okay*,' I said. 'Bobby, I'm not really concerned about the mechanics of it; I want to know how you came to have it and why. And the same applies to the money, and the drugs. My mum used to say, if you're going to do something, do it well. You appear to be dealing on quite a remarkable scale for a fourteen-year-old.'

Bobby shook his head. 'No,' he said, 'I'm not . . . I wasn't . . . only a bit . . . just some draw and pills for me mates.'

'*This* isn't a little . . . there's enough here to start a bloody—'

'Let him talk,' said Trish.

I showed her my Twix finger.

'Okay,' I said. 'Sorry, Bobby. Continue.'

He kept his eyes on the gun.

'It's not mine,' he said.

'Oh, you're just holding on to it for someone? *Right*.'

'Dan, cut the sarcasm . . . Bobby, please,

172

everything's going to be okay . . . Just tell us . . .'

'I am *telling* youse if youse would just bloody listen. It's not mine, okay, *all right*? The Millers, they don't keep anything themselves, don't want to get caught with it, so they spread it out across the boys. I was okay just selling some dope, but they made me take all this other stuff. They just kept sending people to the house. I'd more customers than the bloody Mace on the corner, and I didn't want any of them. But I'd no choice.'

'There's always a choice,' I said.

'Jesus fuck!' Flecks of spit sprayed from the corners of his mouth. He brought his fist down hard on the table. The gun, the drugs, the cash, Trish and I all jumped. He jabbed a finger across at me. '*This is* why I hate fucking do-gooding wankers like you, *oh there's always a choice*, well it's easy for you to say that in your fucking showhouse or here on fucking Cypriot Avenue. In case you didn't notice, they shot my leg off . . . you . . . you know nothing . . . *nothing*.'

'It's Cypress Avenue,' I said. 'Like the song.'

'FUCK!' He held his hands to the sides of his skull and pressed.

'Nobody is fucking listening to me!'

He cracked his forehead down on the tabletop, *hard*.

'Don't,' said Trish. 'Please.'

'It's her favourite table,' I said.

Trish looked daggers at me, but, most unexpectedly, Bobby laughed. He banged his head again, but not as hard. And then he laughed some more.

'This is so fucking fucked up,' he said.

He rested his head on the surface. I looked at

173

Trish and raised my eyebrows. She raised her own and nodded at me to say or do something.

I said, 'Bobby. There's sixty grand here. I counted it. God knows how much the coke is worth.'

'*Yes.*'

'It's why they're after you.'

'*Yes.*'

'So why don't you just give it back to them?'

Bobby finally sat back. There was a spot of blood right in the middle of his forehead. He was looking across the table, but not at me, somewhere way beyond. When he spoke, his voice was tired, almost a monotone: 'I can't give it back, because my mum found the coke. And before I could stop her, she flushed half of it down the bog. Maybe forty grand's worth. What was I supposed to do? I couldn't just go to them and say, sorry, I've lost half your stash. So I tried to raise the money myself, but y'know . . . Christ . . . I was cutting it weaker and weaker and the Millers heard about it and thought I was ripping them off, so they did my leg and said get us the money, get us our gear, or you're fuckin' dead. One of me mates got the gun, we was going to do a post office or fucking Marks and Spencer's even though I could hardly walk and they're fucking useless anyway. But we would have done it, except me mum started all that shite on the radio, and it made it ten times worse. I couldn't even leave the house. She kept at it and kept at it, like she was daring them, so they came for me, and that would have been okay, but they didn't get me, they got my ma instead. They killed her.' He shook his head violently. He looked to Trish, and then to me, his eyes big and red. 'I don't want the Xbox back for the money or the drugs. I want it for the gun. I want it for the Millers. They killed my mum. And I'm going to fucking kill them.'

He was fourteen, for fucksake, and Patricia was in tears.

29

Never underestimate the ego of a self-published poet. Boogie Wilson, brigadier general of the Ulster Volunteer Force, safe in his east Belfast stronghold, couldn't resist the temptation to travel outside his comfort zone to read at a poetry slam event held upstairs in the Errigle Inn on the Ormeau Road with not a bodyguard in sight.

Boogie was one of dozens of poets who stepped up to the mike. Success at a slam has more to do with performance, projection and personality than actual content, and at this at least, Boogie Wilson was an old hand. He was well used to addressing large groups of people, although they generally wore balaclavas. By all accounts, he went down extremely well, although to be fair, who was going to heckle a man with such easy access to death and destruction? Afterwards, he stood his round and talked iambic pentameter with the other poets. When he was leaving at the end of the night, slightly tipsy but elated, someone stepped up to him and blew his head off. Those critics, they're lethal.

Maxi McDowell was still laughing about it when he ambled into the Singing Kettle. He sat down and poured himself a cup of tea from the waiting pot. We didn't have to regurgitate the facts. It was sufficient for me to say, 'Any wild guesses?'

'The Millers were at the movies,' said Maxi. 'They have stubs.'

'Seriously?'

'Something like that. The stupid, stupid bastard should have known better.'

'So is this a coup?'

'Could be. What'd you call that . . . y'know . . . when Hitler took out all his enemies?'

'The Night of the Long Knives.'

'That's it. They might want to be taking out every rival while they're at it, or they might be working the phones, see where people are going to stand. Either way, you're not going to be their major concern.'

'Well that must be good.'

Maxi raised his cup and sipped. He made a face and added more sugar. 'Thing is, I've known them since they were wee lads; shit, I was kicking their dad up the arse when he was a wee lad'n all. So I don't doubt I can get you in to see them, get you in safe and out safe, but with everything on their plate, they're not going to give you much time.'

Maxi was a big guy, with a corrugated forehead. He had that older-man thing of appearing to struggle for breath.

I said, 'I appreciate you coming alone.'

'You don't like him much, do you?'

'It's not him so much as his boss, Springer.'

'Springer? How do you know him?'

'They came to see me at my office.'

'About what?'

'Bobby Murray.'

Maxi nodded to himself. 'He didn't tell me that. Not that he has to. What'd you make of Springer?'

'He was doing the bad-cop thing.'

'Yeah, that would be him. Don't know him well, don't want to. Bit of a cold fish. What'd you tell him?'

'As much as I've told you.'

'That much?' Maxi smiled. 'So he tried to turn the screws.'

'Sticks and stones.'

'Yeah, I think you'll find he's only getting started.' Maxi set the cup down, and slowly turned the saucer. 'They're very keen to get your boy.'

'They were trying to say he might have set the fire himself. That's shite, right?'

'It's not impossible, Dan. Do you know where he is?' I stirred my Coke. The ice clinked. 'Okay, fair enough.'

'I'm just trying to sort it out.'

'His family paying you?'

'Nope.'

'What do they call that in America, when you do something for nothing, like a public service? Bleeding heart, is it?'

'I think you mean pro bono.'

'Really?' He smiled. 'Dan. What are you really up to?'

'What I say. Just trying to help the wee lad out.'

'It's your call, but if you really want to help him, help him out of the country, because this place is all fucked up.' He pushed his cup into the centre of the table. He raised his hand and rubbed two fingers together for the waitress to bring the bill. 'God knows, I'll be glad to be out of it.'

'How long now?'

'Hours rather than days.'

'You'll miss this place.'

'Like a hole in the head.' He laughed. 'Yeah.' And then he looked almost wistful. 'There *are* good people on the Shankill. They just don't get much of a chance to blossom.'

'Because of the Millers.'

'There have always been Millers.' He glanced up at the waitress, puzzling over the correct change, and then leaned across the table and lowered his voice. 'Dan,' he said, 'Jack Caramac is right, of course he is, it's obvious to anyone with half their head screwed on. We go softly, softly so the war won't start again. It's policy, from on high. But this much *I* know: those Millers, they don't give two figs about politics or religion; they care about their own power and they care about money. If you rip them off, if you challenge them, they will put you down. They were evil kids, and they haven't changed. Bobby Murray is just another fly caught in their web; don't you get stuck there with him, because the Millers will devour you too. If I can't talk you out of it, then fair enough, I'll get you in to see them. But don't go appealing to their better nature. They don't have one. If you go in, go in with something they value, or don't go in at all.'

30

Sucker, that's what I am. I went back to Bill and Ben, the Repair Men, and bought a reconditioned Xbox and a clatter of de-scratched games off Billy so that Bobby Murray could sit in my former home shooting zombies in the head all day while Patricia went out to work and I paced my office trying to

178

decide what I could bring to the Miller meeting, what I should be doing with the sixty thousand quid, a bag of cocaine and a revolver, while only occasionally allowing the subject of Macedonia to enter my thinking. Maxi said it would take a couple of days for the heat to fade off the Boogie Wilson killing, and only then would he be able to take me in to see them.

Trish's opinion was, 'Give them the sixty grand and the drugs; it may not be everything he owes them, but it's a start, and maybe it'll put you in their good books.'

It did seem the most obvious thing to do. Except for the fact that they had made it clear to Bobby that they wanted *everything* back, and not only that, they wanted him out of the country or dead for even daring to deal watered-down coke behind their back. So even if I did hand it to them, they'd still be angry. No, I would hold on to it. In fact, I decided to make it work for me. Nothing crazy, like putting it on a horse. But I thought that a few extra missing pounds weren't going to make any difference, and I had certain needs. Every man has them. For example, I paid for the Diet Coke and the pot of tea in the Singing Kettle. I sent off for my car tax. I purchased new tyres. And I got several quotes for a paint job to remove the hideous slander from the side of my vehicle, just like a fully fledged grown-up would. These were significant sums of money for someone who wasn't earning any, but insignificant for someone who could afford to stash sixty thousand quid with a fourteen-year-old. It did cross my mind that until the situation was resolved I could invest it in a series of guaranteed fixed-rate ISAs with tax-free returns, or even

Premium Bonds. And then I thought, maybe not.

I was still left with the problem of where to keep the cash, the drugs and the gun. Trish was doing enough for me without running the risk of her being busted for cocaine and drug money. But both my apartment and my office were too obvious: I needed somewhere unlikely, but with easy access. Until I could work it out, I packed it all back into the original Xbox and took it with me when I locked up the office.

As I turned from the door, Joe the butcher called over: 'How's business?'

'Fair to middlin'. You?'

'Same,' he said, stepping out on to the pavement. 'You ever get that boy sorted out?'

'What boy? Oh . . . the wee fella in . . . Yeah. Sure. Just my nephew. Mitching from school, that was about the height of it, but all sorted now.'

I nodded and turned away.

He said: 'Hold on.'

Under normal circumstances I would have found it hard to take seriously someone dressed in a red and white striped apron and wearing a similarly coloured hat that was something between a straw boater and a panama, but I did. Joe was from the Shankill. He'd been in prison. He had a meat cleaver in his hand. He might have betrayed Bobby already.

'Yup?'

'I was thinking some more about him.'

'Uhuh.'

He came right up until we were almost face to face. I wanted to take a step back, but resisted. He smelled of blood and sawdust. If there had been even the remote possibility of late-afternoon sun, it might have glinted off his cleaver. He lowered his voice. He said, 'I don't want to be too nosy, like, but it looked to me like it was more than just playing hooky.'

'Nah, nah, just teenager stuff, y'know . . .'

'I was thinking I might be able to help you out.'

'Help? Me?'

'Sure. You. Him. When I was a teenager, I was a bit of a handful myself, and the last couple of years I was hardly at school at all. Tell you what sorted me out . . .' He thumbed behind him. 'Dessie Martin. He had a butcher's on the Shankill. Me ma took me in there, said if you're not learning nothing in school, you can learn something here. He took me on, fourteen, an apprentice. Best thing ever happened to me. You've a trade behind you, you've always something to fall back on. Was thinking maybe the kid there, if he's getting into mischief, and he's no stomach for school, well maybe I could use him in the shop.'

It was not what I had expected at all.

'That's, uhm, really kind of you to offer. I'll certainly mention it to him.'

'Well if you don't mind me saying, that's your first mistake right there. Don't *mention* it to him. *Tell* him.'

'Okay. Right. Getcha. And would you be, you know, paying him?'

'As little as I can get away with, but yeah, sure. I had a young fella there for a while, but he didn't know his arse from his elbow, which is unfortunate when you're slicing up a pig. I pay minimum wage and as much as you can carry in sausages.'

I was wondering how long it would take Bobby to pay off half a bag of cocaine on minimum wage.

I thanked Joe again, and said I'd have a word with the boss. There was no need to explain.

*   *   *

I drove to Malone and parked across from Jack's house. I hadn't quite made my mind up about Tracey—whether she'd been caught looking for evidence and ordered to stop communicating with me, or if she'd been playing me the whole time. It wouldn't be the first or last time I'd been played by a woman. I called her phone; it said number not recognised.

As I sat there pondering, Jack drove in. Ten minutes later, the nanny formerly known as Nanny the nanny came walking down the drive. As she exited the gates, she lit up her fag and fixed in her earphones. Instead of stopping by the building site next door to wait for her lift, she kept on walking. She reached the end of the property and turned into a narrow lane running up the side of it. Any time Betty wasn't around to stub cigarettes out on me seemed like a good time to approach Marija. I got out of the car, but had to wait for a minute until the traffic allowed me to cross. By the time I got to the lane entrance she was about thirty metres ahead of me, moving up a slight incline. I called her name, but she couldn't hear me with the music. I set off after her. To my right, the building site merged into what remained of the garden of the house immediately behind Jack's, which was just visible through gaps in a high hedge. It appeared older, darker, larger. When I emerged from the lane on to Marlborough Park, Marija was just passing a red Porsche parked sideways in a driveway belonging to the same house. I called her name again, and this time she turned. Her brow furrowed, she made the connection, she shook her head and hurried up to the front door and rang the bell. She glanced back as I drew closer and waved me away. The door opened and a toddler came tottering out, and she scooped him up and disappeared inside. The door closed.

I loitered.

It's not easy, loitering. You can sit in a car and nobody much pays you any attention, but if you stand in a street or sit on a wall or hide in the branches of a tree, people tend to think the worst, particularly in this kind of upmarket neighbourhood. So I made a note of the Porsche's licence plate on my phone, and then went back down the lane. Having nothing better to do with my time, my master plan now amounted to driving round and parking within sight of the house, waiting for an opportunity to talk to Marija. It wouldn't necessarily be less suspicious, given that I was still advertising myself as a *pedo*. However, I was prepared to take the chance, and would have, if my car had been where I left it.

I'd been gone five minutes and it had vanished. There was a Range Rover there, in its place, but it was a different colour, and year, and it had an altogether more respectable *Malone Security* etched on the side.

As I approached, the doors opened. Paddy Barr got out the driver's side, and from the other, someone fully twice his size. They were wearing black jackets with *Malone Security* printed across them, one word on each side of the zip, and baseball caps, also emblazoned with *Malone*

Security.

'Youse aren't by any chance from Malone Security, are you?' I asked.

'Look who it is, it's the funny fella,' said Paddy Barr. 'This is the guy I was telling you about. Laugh riot, aren't ya, mate?'

'If you say so,' I said, and smiled, although without conviction. I nodded at the other guy. He was not only twice the size of Paddy Barr, his body appeared to be straining to get out of his uniform. He had giant hands. There was some evidence of scarring around the eyes.

'Heavyweight?' I asked.

'Cruiser,' he said.

His voice was a little high-pitched. His eyes were too small for his face. He might once have fought at cruiserweight, but he had bulked out well past it. He wasn't just muscled, he was misshapen. Steroids will do that to you. He was chewing gum; his white teeth were perfect, but false. They had probably been knocked out.

'Bantam and a cruiser, little and large.' I nodded some. 'I don't know if youse were useful in the ring, but you're pretty useless at security.'

'Go on,' said Paddy Barr, 'crack one.'

'I'm just saying, no offence like, but my car was just here a few minutes ago, and now it's gone, stolen, and you appear to have missed it completely.'

'Really?' asked the cruiser. 'What make was it?'

'Range Rover, the vehicle of warriors, just like yours. Or that may be worriers.'

'Range Rover?' Paddy Barr asked. 'That's a coincidence, we were past here a couple of minutes ago too and there was a Range Rover just like ours sitting right here. Oh no . . . *wait*, I know what happened.' He clicked his fingers, as if it was just coming back to him. 'That's right, that's right . . . this is an upmarket area, man, the neighbours round here were concerned, particularly a car with something disgusting written on the side. Know what I mean? Demanded we have it removed, and you know, the customer is always right. That wasn't yours, was it? Gee whiz, have we made a mistake?'

'Sorry, mate,' said the cruiser, 'we were just doing our job. We had it towed off to Titanic Scrap, you know them? It's company policy to have all abandoned vehicles scrapped straight away. In fact flattened; stops the scavengers stripping them for parts, important that nobody profits from it. But it was yours? That's a shame. Still, listen, maybe if you start walking now, you might get there before they start.'

'Not laughing now, are you, laughin' boy?' Paddy Barr was grinning from ear to cauliflowered ear.

I shook my head, though not in answer to him, more in a disappointed manner. He probably wasn't smart enough to tell the difference. But he was smart enough to be concerned when I took out a small notebook and pen and began to write. The cruiser, too.

'What, uh, what're you doing there, pal?' he asked.

'Like you say, *pal*, this is a pretty upmarket area, but it attracts a lot of dubious characters, so when I park my car, if I can I always make sure it's covered by security cameras.' I pointed with my pen to first one camera, above the gates of the house opposite, and then a second, high on a wall covering the approach to the house behind where we were

185

standing. 'I'm pretty sure both of those were filming my car. They'll show me parking, walking away, and within a couple of minutes they'll show you pair showing up with a tow truck and yanking my car away. No warning, no ticket, no anything, straight down to the scrapyard. Flattened, you say?'

The cruiser nodded warily.

I smirked. That could be annoying. I only did it because I knew what was coming.

'Papers are going to love this.'

'Balls,' said Paddy.

'Balls yourself. The car doesn't worry me in the slightest; your company will have to replace it. It's fully comp anyway. You two, though? Good luck with your next job.'

I tore the page from my notebook. I folded it in half. I then walked forward, passing between them, and counting each step I took out loud. When I got to twenty-three I stopped, peered over the garden wall beside me and then reached over to pick up a stone. I took the folded paper and placed it on the flat top of the wall, and set the stone on it to stop it blowing away. Then I retraced twenty-one of the twenty-three steps until I was standing back with Paddy Barr and the cruiser. I nodded with satisfaction.

Paddy Barr said, 'What *the fuck* are you doing?'

The cruiser said, 'What's on the paper?'

I raised an eyebrow.

'Are you fuckin' mental or something?' Paddy Barr asked.

'What did you write?' the cruiser demanded. 'And why did you put it on the wall?'

'I could tell you,' I said. 'But then I'd have to tickle you.'

'You fucking *what*?' asked Paddy Barr.

'Tick . . . I mean, kill you. I'd have to kill you.'

I glanced at my watch.

'What're you playing at?' the cruiser asked. His eyes darted from me to the stone and back. 'Do you want us to brain you?'

'If you brain me,' I said calmly, 'then the note will self-destruct and you'll never know. Believe me, it will really annoy you.'

His brow furrowed. He looked at Paddy Barr for support. Paddy Barr was looking at the cruiser, likewise. Then he blurted out:

'Fuck it, you keep an eye on him, I'll read the note.'

Before he could move, the cruiser said, 'Why me?'

'Why me what?'

'Why do I have to stand with him while you read the note?'

'Because I say so.'

'You're not the boss of me,' said the cruiser.

'I didn't mean to be divisive,' I said.

'You shut the fuck up,' snapped Paddy Barr. 'It's just a piece of paper. I don't know what the fuck we're even doing giving it the time of day.'

'Me neither,' I said.

The cruiser shook his head. '*I'll* read the note, you stay with him.'

He took a step towards the stone.

Paddy Barr took one too.

They looked at each other for guidance. None was forthcoming. They kept moving closer to it, while taking turns to glance back at me.

The cruiser got to it first. He crouched down and reached out; Paddy Barr knelt beside him. The cruiser's hand hovered over the stone; Paddy Barr tried to peer beneath it. They had watched as I wrote on the paper, folded the paper, walked with the paper, and then set the paper on the wall with the stone on top of it. But they were behaving like bomb disposal experts.

There was a lull of about five seconds before Paddy Barr finally knocked the stone off and grabbed the folded paper. He turned it over in his hand, unsure. Then he quickly pressed it into the cruiser's massive paws and said: 'Open it!'

The cruiser hesitated before carefully pushing up the corners. His cheeks were tight and his eyes narrowed and his shoulders hunched. He flattened the sheet out. He studied it. He checked the other side of it. He looked up at me, and then at Paddy Barr. 'What the . . . ?'

Paddy Barr grabbed it. He too looked on both sides. He spun towards me and held it up. 'What the fuck is this?'

'It's a swastika,' I said.

'I can see that! But what's it . . . ?'

'It's an ancient symbol. It has many meanings, but more recently it was hijacked by the Nazis and will for ever more be associated with unspeakable evil.'

'But . . . but . . . but . . . why did you . . . ?'

'It's a device.'

'A what?'

He held it even further away.

'If I had the talent, I could just as easily have drawn a duck. But the swastika is about my limit. Anyway, it doesn't matter. The point is not the swastika; the point is the twenty-three steps.'

The cruiser said: 'What the fuck is he *on* about?'

'I don't . . .' Paddy Barr began.

'Where you're now standing is exactly twenty-three paces away from where I'm standing.'

'So *what*?'

'Well, I guessed that both of you would be curious enough to want to find out what I was writing. Therefore I calculated, roughly, I have to say, that if I placed what I wrote under a stone at twenty-three paces from where I'm standing, that would probably give me time to do *this* . . .'

I spun on my heel and darted the few metres to their Range Rover. I jumped in, slammed and locked the driver's door and then reached across and pulled the passenger's door shut as well and locked it. The keys, as I had correctly guessed, were sitting nicely in the ignition.

I started the engine.

I was prepared for the cruiser to batter his big fists into the side window, smash it and try to drag me out through it. I was expecting Paddy Barr to throw himself across the bonnet and cling on for dear life as I sped away.

But as it happened, they just stood there, stunned.

I even drew up beside them, and moved the window down a fraction.

'Who's laughing now?' I asked Paddy Barr.

'You . . . you . . .'

'No one ever tell you not to leave the keys in the ignition? For a security company, I would have thought that was basic.'

His pointy bantam face had turned purple with rage.

'You, you, you are going to regret this . . . I will find you . . . I will find you and I will fucking kill you, Starkey . . .'

'I seriously doubt that.'

I began to roll it along. He walked with me.

'Get out of the car . . . get out of the car now!' he cried with increasing desperation.

'Don't think so.'

'Starkey . . . this is your last chance . . .'

'No, mate,' I said, 'this is *your* last chance. If you start walking now, you might just get to the scrapyard in time to save my car. If you manage to do that, then give me a call and I'll see what I can do about swapping keys at a mutually convenient time. All righty?'

I gave him a theatrical wink.

There was a tap on the opposite window. The cruiser, big eyes and wobbly lip. 'I have three children to support,' he said.

'Tough,' I said, and pressed down on the accelerator.

I was smiling.

And then laughing.

It's not often that things work out.

31

If you get out of a van that says *Plumber* on the side, it's reasonable for people to assume that you're a plumber. I applied this logic to the Malone Security van I was now driving as I pulled into the driveway of the house in Marlborough Park. For additional effect I slipped on a Malone Security baseball cap I found lying on the floor. To completely bamboozle the woman who answered the door, I said, 'Hello,

I'm from Malone Security.'

To be fair, she gave me a healthy portion of bamboozlement in return. She had dyed raven hair, matching dark eyes with plenty of eyeliner, plumped lips, gleaming teeth and cleavage like the main waterslide at Seapark. And it was all very familiar. In fact it wasn't that long since I'd had my hands on her chest. That was, in the form of a photograph, part of a session she and her husband had agreed to do for *Belfast Confidential*. Everyone in the office had also agreed that she had a wonderful chest. It stood out. It was a chest worthy of comment and appreciation. It was a *Carry On* chest in a PC society. But she was more than just a chest. She was Abagail Pike. She was a member of the Northern Ireland Assembly. Her husband was Professor Peter Pike, or 3P, or Threepike, as the tabloids sometimes called him. He was the Minister for Finance and Personnel at Stormont. He came from the Protestant heartland of Portadown, and brought with him a religious conservatism that fell just short of charismatic. He had a lot of support in that heartland. Very straight and narrow support. The fact that he still had that support was little short of a miracle, seeing as how he had once sworn never to even share the same building as 'former' terrorists, but now routinely broke bread with them. It was testament to his powers of persuasion, his rhetoric and bluster that he could perform such a volte-face and actually increase his majority at the next election. He was an austere man for austere times, and was looked upon by those who knew as a near-genius when it came to economics. Everyone expected that he would be First Minister one day. He was not a barrel of laughs. Most people thought

191

that he would indeed sort out our finances, and that it was a good thing, but that there was a fair chance that if he came to power he might try and ban enjoyable things, like skipping, which was not. Peter Pike was a big, big man, with a booming voice. He had gone hiking once and been mistaken for the long-missing sixth Mourne Mountain. He was over eight hundred metres tall and had snow on top. When he smiled at you, you immediately changed your vote. Peter and Abagail were the glamorous power couple of Northern Irish politics. That said, they didn't have a lot of competition.

It was just such a surprise to be standing in front of her. Forget for the moment the widespread bamboozlement, I was momentarily flummoxed. Of course, she did not know me from Adam. The photo shoot, which I recalled as being particularly stressful, was a few years back, but even if it had been yesterday, she probably still wouldn't have recognised me, and not only because I was out of context. There is a particular self-absorption that comes with fame, an expansion of the ego that prevents the famous from recognising anyone they do not perceive to be on their level of importance. They are not necessarily rude or obtuse, and they will chat away quite happily. They just will not listen to a damn word you say. Gail Pike was like that. Or, as Trish would say, up her own arse.

Gail beamed at me and said, 'I'll get it for you now.'

She turned from the door to a telephone stand, picked up an envelope and gave it to me. It wasn't sealed, just tucked in. I peeked inside. Cash. Five twenties. I looked up at her. She was still smiling. She raised an eyebrow.

192

'Oh, thank you,' I said. Her brow furrowed. I was surprised that it could. 'I'd also like a word, if I could?'

'With me? I'm just on my way out.'

'It'll only take a minute.'

'Is it professional or private?'

'My profession or your profession?'

'Are you trying to be smart with me?'

'No, ma'am.'

Ma'am? Behind her, Marija crossed the hall from the kitchen, with the child attached to her leg, dragging him playfully along. She glanced at me, and then did a double-take. She hurried on into the lounge.

'I mean, do you wish to speak to me in my capacity as an MLA, and you as a private citizen, or do you wish to speak to me in your capacity as a representative of Malone Security and mine as a householder who overpays you every month?'

She said it with a smile.

I gave her my smile in return. It wasn't in the same league, but it has been known to melt the hearts of confused drunken women. 'It was security I wanted to have a word with you about.'

'If it's the usual lecture about setting my alarm and informing you when I'm away on business, then I've heard it all before.'

'It's not that, Mrs Pike.'

She studied me. She must have liked the cut of my jib. She said, 'This way, then . . .'

She turned and walked into the kitchen. I followed her. The kitchen had a stone floor and an island in the middle with half a dozen bar stools around it, though they probably had a different name for them. There were toys scattered about.

From the lounge I could hear what sounded like *Scooby-Doo*.

'Mrs Pike . . .'

'Call me Gail. Excuse me while I . . .' She had her mobile phone in her hand. She glanced at it, shook her head, and quickly began to pick out a text. While she did it she said, 'That's the problem with mobiles, you're never unreachable. There.' She sent the text. 'Do you want a coffee? I've been in politics a long time; when people say it will only take a minute, it never does.'

'No—thank you, Mrs . . . Gail.'

'Please yourself.' She pressed the switch on the kettle. Her hand was bony, the skin loose, big, expensive rings. Hands and neck, you can't do much about them. I knew she was mid-forties but her tits were still toddlers. She said, over her shoulder, waiting for it to boil: 'So what's going on?'

'There was an incident a few days ago at the house immediately behind you. Jack Caramac's place?'

'Really? A burglary?'

'Someone enticed their son into a car, took him away for approximately one hour, released him unharmed.'

'That's *awful*.' She poured her coffee and turned with it. 'I didn't hear it on the news.'

'Mr Caramac wanted it kept quiet. We're just warning the neighbours, particularly those with children, to be extra careful.'

'And have they been caught?' She sat on one of the stools.

'No, ma'am.' I cleared my throat and sat opposite her. 'You haven't noticed anything or anyone unusual, out of place, suspicious in the area?'

194

'Nope, but then I'm hardly ever here. My husband's the same.'

'Professor Pike.'

'That's him. We're very busy people. If anyone's seen anything it would be Marija . . . our nanny. Do you want me to . . . ?'

'In a wee minute. Marija . . . she's not local, then?'

Gail glanced towards the living room, then leaned a little closer. 'No. She's . . . *European.*'

'And has she worked for you for long?'

'A few months.' She came even closer, leaning in. I averted my eyes. 'Why, is she . . . ?'

'No, no . . . just checking, I'm sure she's . . . just fine.' Gail sat back again. She sipped her coffee and made good solid eye contact with me over the rim of the cup. 'Do you . . . mind me asking how you came by her? An agency, or personal recommendation?'

'It was . . . I'm not sure. I think my husband handled it.'

'You're aware that she also works for the Caramacs?'

'She does? Ah—maybe I did know. I just can't recall. I deal with so many people every day . . .'

'Are you not close to the Caramacs?'

'Close? No. I wouldn't say that. They're actually quite distant, I mean physically; what with the length of our garden and the fences and hedges, we wouldn't really see them at all, especially now with the new house going up.' She set her cup down. 'If you don't mind me saying, you're asking an awful lot of questions for someone from Malone Security.'

'Just trying to be thorough, ma'am.' There

it was again. *Get a grip*. 'You don't have a CV or references from . . . Marija, is it?'

'Marija, yes. And no. Now that I think about it, maybe she came to us through the church. We do a lot of outreach work in some of the poorer countries. Yes, I'm pretty sure that's it.'

'You haven't noticed any unusual behaviour? Maybe people you don't recognise calling to see her at the house?'

'No. She's been perfect. Really.'

'Does she have a husband, boyfriend? Involved in a lesbian relationship?'

Gail almost choked on her coffee. 'Why would you think that?'

'It's just something the Caramacs mentioned. They have, ahm, suspicions. Not that there's anything wrong with it. This day and age. Just with children around . . . formative age . . . well, you know what I mean . . .'

She was watching me *very* closely. She flicked at her hair. She set her cup down. 'What's your name, Mr Malone Security?'

'My name? Paddy. Paddy Barr.'

'Well, Paddy Barr, you're very thorough. I'm impressed.'

'Just trying to keep the area safe, Mrs Pike.'

'Well keep it up, you're an absolute inspiration.' She hopped off her stool. 'Now I must fly.'

'Understood. Thanks for your help. Can you let yourself out?'

She nodded and started to turn away. Then swivelled back. 'Can I *what* . . . ?'

I slipped off my own stool. 'Only rakin',' I said.

She laughed.

I laughed.

196

She could have my vote, any time.

*   *   *

Abagail Pike issued instructions to Marija through the open living room door, then led the way out of the house. I pulled the front door closed behind me. I had to back out of the drive to allow her to get the Porsche out. When she straightened it, I waved my hand, indicating that ladies should go first. She wiggled her fingers *thanks* in the mirror as she sped away. As soon as she rounded the bend, I reversed back into the driveway. I'd made sure to leave the front door on the latch. Marija was suitably surprised, not to mention terrified, when I strode into the lounge. So surprised, not to mention terrified, that she let out a scream and dropped the baby.

But it was okay.

Babies bounce.

32

Marija was backed into the corner of the sofa with the screaming tot now held tight against her chest like a very soft human shield. She was trying to shush it as I stood over them and pointed my big hand down at her and said, 'Now I want some answers,' but she could hardly hear me over the baby, and in truth I probably wasn't that threatening. The bandages were so thick I looked like Winnie the Pooh with his hand stuck in a honey pot. Patricia would just have laughed at me. But

Marija was a stranger in a strange land, and one with a guilty conscience to boot. I could see the fear in her eyes as she peppered the top of the baby's head with kisses. As it quieted, she whispered, 'Please . . . don't . . . hurt the child . . .'

I backed up a bit. I sat on the arm of the chair opposite her. 'Your name is Marija Gruevski. You are from Macedonia. Last time I checked, Macedonia was not in the European Union. That means that unless you are an undercover brain surgeon, you are here illegally. Of all the people you could have picked to work for, you first pick Jack Caramac, then Peter and Abagail Pike. The Pikes have built their careers on being whiter than white. If they discover that you are illegal, they will have you out of this country quicker than a very quick thing. If they find out you're a lesbian *and* illegal, which they would prefer to be one and the same thing, they will probably burn you at the stake.'

'Please,' begged Marija, 'I need job . . . money . . . please.'

'Then tell me what happened with little Jimmy, Marija, what happened with Jack's boy?'

'Nothing happened. Please, I . . .'

'You *kidnapped* him.'

'No. Yes. It was not like . . . All we do . . . we go for ride in my wife's car.'

'Betty.'

'Yes. Betty. She is drunk. She love the baby, cannot have her own. She wants to keep him, for us to go away, nobody will ever find us. Maybe to my home in Skopje. She does not know what it is like, it is poor country. I earn here more as nanny than home as teacher. I tell her no, I am happy here,

198

we must take back. We fight. I am very angry. I tell her I am taking Jimmy home, and I am going to tell police. She threaten me. But I take him. I put him in garden and then hide until they find him. I did not hurt him. I am so sorry. Please.'

'You're forgetting about the note, Marija, the note, the *shut the fuck up* note. What about the note?'

'My wife write note. She drunk and angry, thought I was going to tell police. I was locked in room with Jimmy, would not let her in. She write lots of notes . . . threatening me, what she will do, what will happen, and puts them under door, but I do not see this one. Jimmy pick it up and put it in his pocket. Mr Caramac, he find, he thinks there is real kidnapper. There is not. This is the truth. Please do not tell. Do not send me home. I cannot go home. I love my wife. She will do nothing like it again. She does not drink any more. She promises.'

The tears were flowing down her cheeks. She was shaking. The tot began to wail again. He either sensed her distress, or he hadn't bounced that well.

*   *   *

I stepped outside. If I'd been a smoker, I would have lit one. Two, possibly. Her story was believable. I had the evidence of my right hand to know what Betty was capable of. Twenty years of journalism had taught me that there are very few criminal masterminds; that conspiracies are in the crossed eyes of the easily convinced beholder; that most crimes are domestic in origin; that the victim usually knows the perpetrator; that they are mainly committed with a staggering amateurishness; that

199

the great majority are fuelled by drugs or alcohol. Betty's bungled kidnap fitted in with all of this quite nicely. And I *wanted* to believe her. It would allow me to walk away. I could stamp the file *closed*, or better still, *solved*. It didn't particularly matter to me if they got away without punishment. Jack and Tracey now knew to keep a better eye on their son. Marija had been given a scare. Betty was off the drink. Little Jimmy hadn't suffered. They say kids don't remember anything before the age of six. They could have kept him for a couple of months and kicked him up the arse every morning, and he still wouldn't recall it a year down the line. There were three hundred and sixty degrees of resolution. The problem was that it was all a little bit too much like *Quincy*.

It didn't explain Jack's sudden decision to fire me. Paranoid one day, upbeat the next. It didn't explain Tracey, flirty and ready for action one minute, incommunicado the next. It didn't explain Jack sending in a solicitor to threaten me with legal action, or recruiting Malone Security to warn me off when I'd done little more than ask a few questions and hang around a bit looking gormless.

I patted my pocket and took out the envelope Abagail Pike had given me. One hundred pounds. There was something not quite right about that either. I could see why she would pay a tradesman in cash, but a security company? In the age of internet banking, or failing that, direct debit and standing orders? I'd walked up to the home of one of our leading politicians, and his wife had stuffed cash into my hand without me having to ask for it. Cash meant off the record, off the books, tax free. Marija was off the books, an illegal alien, that meant tax free. Jack had brought me in instead of going to the police; he had paid me with an envelope of cash, off the record, tax free. Jack spent every day of his working life questioning the integrity and honesty of important people. Times were hard, the economy was screwed, everyone was holding on to what they could, but it still didn't feel right for the Pikes and the Caramacs to be paying cash.

For all I knew, Marija was the greatest actress in Macedonia, or the only one. Her story might be true, in so far as she was telling me exactly what had happened with Jimmy, but I was sure there was something more lurking in the background, something whose significance she mightn't even be aware of. I needed more detail, not just about her and Betty, but the Caramacs as well, and for the hell of it, the Pikes.

I was just turning back inside when the first Malone Security Range Rover pulled into the driveway. I say *first*, because it was swiftly followed by a second and a third. Out of these vehicles six men emerged. They gathered together, and advanced.

Fuckety fuck fuck fuck.

I said, 'You'll be wanting your motor back.'

I removed the keys and tossed them forward. Nobody tried to catch them. They landed on the ground with a pleasant jangle. In their eyes it probably meant that I had just attacked them with a deadly weapon. In response they withdrew expandable batons from within their zip-up jackets, the jackets with *Malone* on one side of the zip and *Security* on the other. They then proceeded to expand them.

I said, 'Those are classified as offensive weapons under the Prevention of Crime Act 1953.'

For some reason, even though I was right, it did not deter them.

They advanced. I would have retreated into the house and locked the door against them and they could have laid siege, quite possibly for months; I could have survived on baby food and Calpol. *Could have*, if the door had not been unceremoniously slammed in my face by Marija, with the tot in her arms. Given the time frame, she would have had to press an alarm button while I was inside talking to her, but unless it was located in the back of the baby's head, I was fairly certain she hadn't. It made more sense that Malone Security had some means of keeping track of their vehicles, and that once Paddy Barr and the cruiser had reported it stolen, it was a simple matter of following the bleep.

'Is it too late to apolo—'

As ever, I was too late with the sorrys. The blows began to rain down on me, and I fell to the ground. Getting a hiding is the same virtually everywhere. Lenny's husband and his mates had adopted a similar approach, possibly because it worked. They beat me, and they beat me, and they beat me. And when their arms were sore, they rested them, and instead kicked me, and kicked me, and kicked me.

When they were finished, they picked me up and threw me into the back of the lead car, although not before they put down a plastic sheet to collect the blood. They were talking at me, but I couldn't hear them. One of them sat beside me and held me upright when I threatened to keel over. My head rested against the window. I blew misty red bubbles on to the glass. We pulled out of the driveway in

202

convoy. Through the red haze, just a few metres along from the gates, arms folded, leaning against her Porsche, stood Abagail Pike.

33

Someone who sounded a lot like Patricia was saying, 'We should get him to a hospital.'

Someone else who didn't was saying, 'There's no broken bones, and I know how to cure him.'

'You're not a doctor and he's not a ham.'

'I've performed more operations than any thirty surgeons in Ulster combined.'

'On cows.'

'Pigs, lambs, rabbits, three ostriches and a kangaroo. It's still surgery.'

'It's not surgery when you're just cutting them to shreds.'

'There's an art to it, you know.'

At last Patricia's lovely face swam into view and she said, 'Awwww, darling, you awake, how you feeling?'

And I mumbled without anything resembling words coming out.

Another face appeared over her shoulder. 'Hey, there, you okay?' asked Joe the butcher.

I grunted. My mouth was dry as bone, and my nose stuffed with blood.

A third face: Bobby Murray. He just looked at me, shook his head and turned away.

I said, '*Harp* . . .'

Patricia smiled and gently set the rim of a bottle of water against my fat lips and tilted; I coughed and spluttered and dribbled.

'There you go, easy now, babe . . .'

I was on a single bed, in a small, neat room. There was a TV in one corner, a two-ring cooker in another. There was a shower, with an open curtain, a small sofa.

'Where . . . ?'

'My humble abode,' said Joe.

'I . . . how . . . Trish . . . ?'

'Whoever did this to you dumped you outside your office. Lucky Joe was in his shop at the time, came out and got you.'

'Joe? You live . . . ?'

'Yep, on the premises, all on me ownio.'

I raised my hand. 'I'm Dan.'

'I know that.' He shook it. It hurt. 'Hope you don't mind, went through your phone and by a process of elimination found your wife's number.'

Patricia loomed over me. 'Who's Lenny?'

'What . . . who?'

'Lenny, there's a number you've been calling repeat—'

'Trish, I need some painkillers, my head . . .'

'I'll get them,' said Joe.

'About twenty calls . . .'

'Trish . . . this isn't . . .'

'I met Lenny,' said Bobby. He was back standing beside her, looking down, unreadable. 'He came to your apartment. You were working on some case, you wouldn't tell me about it.'

I nodded. It hurt. 'Just a case, Trish, just a case . . .'

I pretended to drift away.

Joe came back in with pills. He poured six into my hand.

'Six?' said Trish.

'More,' I said.

I got up on one elbow, wincing, and swallowed them down, two at a time. I lay back down.

Trish said, 'What happened?'

'What always happens?'

'You said something stupid and you got beaten up.' I nodded. It hurt. 'When are you ever going to wise up?'

It was a rhetorical question.

'Malone Security,' said Joe. 'Roared up, tossed you out, sped away. If it wasn't for their nice cars and pretty uniforms, you'd almost think we were back to the bad old days.'

'Have you come across them before?' Trish asked.

'Sure I have. They call round once in a while trying to interest me in their services. They're quite insistent. Then I show them my very large collection of butcher's knives and they reconsider.'

'Insistent in a Jehovah's Witness kind of a way?' Trish asked.

'No,' said Joe. He shook his head at me. 'I've only known you a few days, yet I've seen you with your eye closed over, your hand up like a bap, and now this. You can annoy some of the people some of the time and get away with it, but you seem to be annoying all of the people all of the time, and clearly not getting away with it.' He turned to Trish. 'How do you put up with him?'

'I don't,' she said.

He looked from her to me, and me to her. 'Well,' he said, 'I'm sure you two have things to talk about. Hey, Bobby?' Bobby grunted. 'Have you ever plunged a knife into a dead body?'

Bobby looked puzzled. 'Wuh . . . why?'

'It's not a trick question,' said Joe. 'Come on, I'll show you how it's done.'

He shepherded Bobby towards the door. Bobby went, but not before glancing at Trish and giving her a helpless kind of a shrug.

When they were gone, I said, 'I think you're bonding with him.'

Trish said, 'Shut up, you stupid bastard.'

Then she kissed me on my sore lips.

*   *   *

It's funny how sympathy and concern can turn to sarcasm and misunderstanding in the laboured blink of a swollen eye. She wanted to take me home and nurse me back to health, and I said no, I'd be better off in my own place; I didn't know what kind of a hornets' nest I'd stirred up, and why take the chance of attracting more trouble to her place, particularly when she was supposed to be sheltering Bobby from harm. I was trying to do the right thing, but she took it as a personal slight. We got to bickering, and then some yelling, which only stopped when Joe came back in with Bobby.

Joe said, 'Guess what? This young man has agreed to come in and work as my apprentice. I think he's a natural. Give it to him.' Bobby stepped forward. He handed me a large and bloody steak. 'Perfectly carved. Though if he cuts them that size for my customers, I'll be out of business in a week.'

'That's great,' I said.

'It is,' added Trish.

'It'll mean an early start,' said Joe.

'I can drop him off on the way to work.' She

grinned at Bobby. She was halfway to ruffling his hair; he took a step back; she hesitated, and then the moment was gone.

Joe looked at our faces and said, 'So what did you two lovebirds decide?'

'I want to take him to my place,' said Trish.

'I'd rather go home,' I said. 'Safer.'

'He shouldn't be alone,' said Trish. 'But he never listens to anyone but himself.'

'Then he can stay here,' said Joe. 'I can keep an eye on him.'

'No, really,' I began, 'I'll be fine . . . Anyway, you only have the one . . .'

'I'm not suggesting we share a bed, you halfwit. There's another room behind this, perfectly good bed in there. Believe me, you don't want to be moving around for a while. Besides, I've this treatment will help with the bruises, my mum used to swear by it. One part cayenne pepper, five parts Vaseline. I'll light a few candles, get you relaxed, I can rub it on you later.' He left it for fully five seconds before saying: 'You should see your face.'

Patricia burst into laughter. Bobby too.

'Youse are *so* funny,' I said.

*   *   *

When they were gone, Joe came back in and saw that I had Bobby's steak up against my eye. He asked me what I was doing. I said it helped with the swelling. He said, 'Don't be ridiculous. It's an old wives' tail. If you press anything cold against the eye, it might do some good, but that steak was until fairly recently part of a live cow. It's still warm.'

'Oh.' I held it out to him. 'You learn something

207

new every day. Do you want to fry it or something?'

'Nope. As it happens, I'm a vegetarian.'

'But you're a *butcher*.'

'Yes. And?'

'Well . . . don't vegetarians become vegetarians because . . . you know . . . they don't like animals being killed for their meat?'

'Some do. I prefer it because I think it's healthier, and when you've been up to your oxters in blood all day, the last thing you want is more meat.'

'Hitler was a vegetarian,' I said.

'Hitler,' said Joe, 'was a dick.'

I had no idea if I could trust him. The facts were the facts: from the Shankill, been to prison, and a vegetarian. Any one of those could tilt you down the wrong path in life. Now he had Patricia's phone number and from there he or whoever he passed it on to would be able to find out where she lived, and where Bobby was. But sometimes you have to take a chance, go with your instinct.

Joe moved to the bed. He sat on the end of it. He said, 'Dan Starkey, you're in trouble. I'm going to make you lentil soup. Then I will crack open a bottle of whiskey, and we will discuss your troubles. Okay?'

34

Four whiskeys in and I was starting to feel not too Craigavad. I had slept some more. It was now dark. The only light came from an ancient TV screen. The sound was turned down. There was music from an old analogue radio. It was a sixties show and the DJ was playing vinyl, so there were two different kinds of hiss coming from the speakers; three if you included the speakers themselves, which were big and heavy and lush. If I'd had a girl there, say Patricia, or Lenny, or anyone this side of human, it would have been nice and romantic. Unfortunately, I did not. I had a Shankill Butcher. It seemed to me that whatever he did, whether it was sitting where he was on a slightly ripped comfy chair, his feet up on a stained coffee table, or footering with the radio to tune the station back in, or up getting us a drink, or ice, he made sure that he was never more than an arm's length away from some kind of cleaver. There were huge big ones that could take an ox's head off with one blow, or little tiny almost ornamental ones, which might not much trouble a vole, but they were there all the same, dotted about the place, and I suspected there was a reason for them beyond simple butchery, something in his history that might come out with the whiskey, or something in his psyche, like him being violently insane. That said, it was not unpleasant, and I was not unrelaxed.

'That was a good thing you did, with the boy,' I said. I was sitting up in the bed, propped against two pillows.

He was in his chair, holding the whiskey up under his chin, staring at the radio. 'I need the help,' he said.

'Do you not have anyone else?'

'No. Did. Had to let them go.'

'Times are hard.'

'Times are harder when you catch them with their hand in the till.'

'Did you—cut off that hand?'

He laughed. 'Should have. Someone who'd worked for me for fifteen years. Getting so that you can't trust anyone.' I *hmmm-hmmmd*. 'This boy, I won't go easy on him; he messes me around, he's out.'

'That's fair enough.'

The Rolling Stones came on. 'Under My Thumb'. We tapped.

I said, 'Do you want to know about him?'

'Expect he'll tell me in his own time.'

'Not even about his leg, or lack thereof?'

'Horse's mouth, always best.'

I sipped. It was Black Bush. It had medicinal value.

'What about you? How come you're here? Living in the shop, I mean.'

'Just protecting what's mine.'

'Does it need protecting?'

'Probably not. A habit I got into in prison.'

'Prison,' I said.

'Prison,' he said.

I sipped again. Mick Jagger had become a little red rooster.

'Expect you'll tell me in your own time,' I said.

He smiled over the top of his glass. 'Ask away.'

'How long have you been out?'

'Is that not a bit arse-about-face?'

'I didn't want to just jump in with what you did. Or didn't do.'

'Oh, I did it.'

'It.'

'I shot a man. Just to watch him die.'

'Where was this, Reno?'

Joe let out a low rumble of a laugh. 'Very good.' He gave it an American drawl: 'The Outlaw Johnny

Cash. Well I tell you something, he never came to sing in our bloody prison.' He nodded to himself for a bit, maybe imagining it. Then he said: 'I did shoot a man. I was given his name and where he worked and a photocopy of a photo. Those days the police used to pass mug shots to us, point out someone and say he's a bad 'un, topped one of our lads, see what you can do boys. And we did. He was my first one, Padraig Cree, twenty-five, lived in the Ardoyne. Caught him coming out of his work, the Ormo bakery, two shots to the back of the head. There was a motorbike waiting for me. He was told to keep it running, but it kept cutting out. I jumped on the back and we just sat there, going nowhere, and then the police just happened to be passing by and saw the commotion. It's a good job they did, I think the bakers of Ormo would have lynched us. Eighteen years old, and I got twenty-five. The kicker being that it wasn't Padraig Cree I shot, it was Frederick Clarke, a good Protestant boy, whose main crime against Ulster was looking a little bit like Padraig Cree.'

For a while there was only the soft beat of an era and the TV news in a low-definition mime. The floor was of dark wood, but against it hundreds, maybe thousands of little flecks of sawdust.

I said, 'That's a bugger.'

'Aye.'

'How long did you serve?'

'Eighteen. Soon as I went in, I told my fellow defenders of Ulster—no more, I'm out. The other side—they just wanted some revenge. So every day, and every night, watching my back. You learn who your friends are by not having any friends. Old Johnny had it right, get tough or die he said, get

211

tough or die.'

'"A Boy Named Sue".'

'Killed a man at eighteen, and the smell of blood in my nostrils ever since.'

'You have family?'

'Nope. Not now. Was married for a while shortly after I got out. Didn't work out. She was my probation officer. She thought I was *institutionalised*.'

'And what did you think?'

'I thought she talked too much.'

He got up and fixed us another drink. He handed me my glass and sat again, taking a moment to get into his ideal position. He took a sip, and with the glass still at his lips said: 'So what's troubling you, son? Or what's troubling others that they want to beat on you so much?'

I took a sip. I swirled it in the glass. I said, 'I'm not sure I've worked it out enough in my head to tell you what's going on.'

'Or you don't quite trust me.'

'I . . . Well, I'm in your bed, I must trust you a little bit.'

'I hope you feel the same way in the morning.'

He gave me a long, hard look and then we both laughed at the same time. Mine sounded a little more nervous.

Joe drained his glass and stood up. 'I'm for bed,' he said. 'Early start. You need anything, give me a shout.'

I said, 'Thanks, Joe, I appreciate . . . *this*. When I've something to tell you that makes sense, I'll tell you.'

'None of my business,' he said. He moved to the door, and then paused with it half open. 'The boy,

Bobby, I know who he is.'

'Oh. Right.'

'Hard not to know,' he said. I nodded warily. 'What you're doing, that's a good thing. There's not many would.'

'It's mostly Trish,' I said.

'It's both of you. But your wife . . . ?'

'Yes, Joe?'

'She's a fine-looking woman.'

'Yes, she is.'

'Be a fool to let her go.'

'I know that,' I said.

35

I sat up in bed at exactly three thirty-three a.m. and repeated these words: *fuck fuck fuck fuck fuck fuck fuck damn fuck fuck fuck fuck fuck bollocks fuck*. I punched the mattress and the headboard, with my good hand, and cursed some more and threw a plastic bottle of Diet Coke across the room. I buried my head in my hands and rocked back and forth.

The door opened and Joe, in T-shirt and boxers, said, 'You okay?'

'Nightmare,' I said.

'Get you anything?'

I could have said yes, you could get me the huge wad of cash, the bag of drugs and the revolver I'd just realised I'd left in the boot of my now flattened car. But I didn't. I said no and thanked him. He went back to bed. I went back to swearing.

*　　　*　　　*

Sleep was not an option. I was such a loser. I had been trying to keep Bobby safe, but had only managed to dig his grave a little deeper. I lay still, with the covers thrown back, and tried to calm my breathing. I had to try and forget about what was gone, and think everything else through. It was hard. My head was full of wee sweetie mice. Every time I managed to string two ideas together, they nibbled through the strands.

Concentrate.

Settle.

Okay. I had gotten into this to find out who had kidnapped little Jimmy and why Jack was being warned off. Losing the Xbox stash didn't change that. Nanny the nanny had confessed to being involved in a half-arsed plan hatched by her partner Betty. She had thought she'd got away with it until I started pestering her. While Betty's overreaction had helped to keep me interested, it was still Jack's sudden volte-face that most intrigued me. However hard I thought about it, I couldn't see any connection between Nanny's confession and Jack's sudden buoyancy.

If Jack knew she was involved, she should have been sacked instantly, even if he preferred not to take it to the police. So his sudden good mood on the night of his party, his firing me and then attempting to shut me up through legal and physical threats, all suggested there was something else he thought I might uncover if I kept poking around. But why was that any of my concern? Why couldn't I just let it go?

Patricia said, 'You never let anything go.'

'Including you.'

'We'll pass swiftly over that one,' she said. 'You love a good grudge, so you do.'

'I like knowing the truth.'

'Maybe you should apply your passion for the truth to your personal life.'

'We'll pass swiftly over that one as well,' I said.

'Convenient. Keep your high moral standards strictly for your day job.'

I hadn't called her *because* of Joe, although he had something to do with it. I had called her because I always did. She was part of me, and always would be. She was in bed, apparently by herself. Bobby was in the next room, wired up to his Xbox. She could hear him shouting in triumph every time he splashed a wall with zombie brain. It was gone four in the morning.

'Have you banged on the wall and reminded him he's starting his apprenticeship in the morning?'

'Yep.'

'Did it work?' It was a rhetorical question. I said, 'I'll have him out of there as soon as I can, Trish.'

'Promises.'

'Soon as I straighten it with the Millers.'

'You think that's likely?'

'I can only try my best.'

'Well you have their drugs, their money and their gun. That must count for something.'

'Yes,' I said.

'What was the street value of the cocaine Mrs Murray flushed down the bog?'

'Unknown, but informed opinion has it about forty grand.'

'Oh,' said Trish.

*   *   *

215

Joe was up at dawn to accept a delivery. There was an awful lot of clanking from a huge refrigerated truck, and then lashings of ribald banter with the driver. Eventually it quietened down, and I managed a brief doze until Patricia and Bobby arrived. When I asked how easy it had been to get him up, she just rolled her eyes. He was sullen when I spoke to him, but brightened considerably when Joe strolled in. It was either Joe's sunny disposition or the fine array of knives he brought with him. Bobby was led away without a word of farewell or thanks.

Trish stood over my bed.

'How are you this morning?'

'Stiff,' I said.

'Nothing new there, then.'

She brushed her lips against mine and said, 'I'm away to work. Will you drop him home later or will I pick him up?'

'Could you pick him up? I've work to do.'

'You should sleep.'

'I'll sleep when I'm dead.'

She looked down at me and nodded. 'Do you have any idea how much of a wanker you sound like sometimes?'

'Yes,' I said.

*   *   *

My thoughts shifted back to Abagail Pike, and the way she'd been leaning on her Porsche, arms folded, as I was driven away from her home. She had either rumbled that I wasn't a Malone employee as soon as she answered the door, or I'd given myself away

216

during our conversation. The best politicians are adept at matching names to faces. Maybe the photo shoot had lodged in her memory and it had just taken a while to click. The text she'd sent while standing with me in her kitchen was to summon help. She'd pretended to drive off, but waited around the corner for the cavalry to arrive. She could just as easily have waited in the house, but by absenting herself she could rightly claim not to have been present if it ever reached the media that Malone Security had given me a beating. She was an MLA and the wife of a government minister. If she had sanctioned the beating, it was by any stretch of the imagination a risky overreaction to being asked a few questions.

I lay back in bed and scrolled through my phone until I found Neville Maxwell's number. When I was a newspaper columnist, he had worked at Stormont, and recruited me for some freelance work shepherding visiting reporters around the North in the run-up to an election that would have given us full independence. I was supposed to encourage said reporters to give positive coverage to the preferred candidate, Michael Brinn. I hadn't, and of course it had all gone pear-shaped. People had died; the fate of a nation—or at least a province—had hung in the balance.

Neville, bless him, hadn't borne a grudge. He was a civil service man, obliged to work for whoever was in power irrespective of his own political beliefs. When Brinn was exposed as a fraud, Neville had just soldiered on, as supportive and gracious towards the next man in charge as he had been to the previous. That was fifteen years ago now, and although he was retired, he still kept his finger on the pulse. He was something of a media go-to man when they wanted a precise, sober take on whatever was happening in Northern Irish politics. As I got to know him better over the years, I discovered that this presentation of himself as the statesman-like voice of reason masked the fact that he took a feverish delight in behind-the-scenes intrigue and gossip, the more malicious the better. He was a godsend for a reporter.

When he answered, he said he couldn't stay on for long, he was about to get his make-up on.

'Really? Anything you want to tell me?'

'I'm due on telly. Doing a pre-record for *Stormont Live*. Both viewers expect me to look my best. How's Patricia?'

'I hear she's fine.'

'Like that, is it?'

'As it ever was. Listen, Abagail Pike, what do you think?'

'Fine chest.'

'Apart from that.'

'I'm serious. Don't underestimate the power of the chest.'

'Neville, I'm ser—'

'I know you are, and so am I. What have you done to upset her?'

'Just curious.'

'Dan, I know you.'

'I'm working on something.'

'Will it echo in the very corridors of power?'

'Probably not.'

'Not even in some side rooms?'

'Unlikely.'

'So what's in it for me?'

'A nice lunch, maybe.'

'The Shipyard?'

'It's overrated.'

'Tell you what, as I'm kind of stuck for time, why don't you come up here and we can have a natter? There's a very fine restaurant on site, and it's subsidised to the hilt, so it won't cost a fortune. Jesus, what am I doing, I'm talking myself out of your treat!'

*　　　*　　　*

I got dressed, not without some difficulty, and slipped out. I had a brief glimpse of Joe behind the counter, and Bobby beside him, looking uncomfortable. It was probably the stripy apron and hat. It was a difficult enough look for a grown man to carry off, let alone a teenager.

I flagged down a taxi and tried not to shout out every time it hit a pothole or braked too suddenly. Of all the roads, the smoothest was the half-mile sweep from the Stormont gates up to the Parliament buildings themselves; it had been lulling politicians into a false sense of security for years.

The uniforms at the guard hut looked at me with distaste. I couldn't blame them. I had forgone a shower in favour of trying to get the bloodstains out of my shirt and jacket, without much success. My hair was all over the place. One eye was still partially closed over and I'd scrapes on my forehead, cheeks and the one hand that wasn't trussed up like an oven-ready chicken. The three middle-aged, out-of-condition guards appeared to be all the protection our government required. Even in my weakened condition, I could have seized power with a catapult. They took a long time to

219

examine my ID and to check that I really, really was expected. Then I was pointed in the right direction and left to walk alone to the grand entrance to the buildings where the fate of my country had never quite been decided. I paused only to nod respect to the statue of Carson—Edward, as opposed to Frank—glaring defiantly over the fine lawns and rolling grounds, before entering the marble foyer. I presented my ID again and was already turning instinctively for the underground canteen where I'd always chowed down in the past when I was yelled at and redirected upstairs to the members' brasserie.

Heads turned as I entered, but only because I looked a complete shambles. Neville Maxwell was neater, and tidier, but scarcely much healthier. He was all skin and bones. He had the sallow complexion of someone not long for this world, and that was with his television make-up still on. He stood to greet me. His handshake was firm, but his fingers felt as brittle as Twiglets.

The brasserie wasn't the kind of establishment where you ordered a pint of Harp. I had a glass of white, Neville a Coke. There was classical music playing in the background. Dvorak. Neville seemed to notice it at the same time as I did. We nodded at each other over our menus. Though it was long ago and far away, I had come to the conclusion that he had known exactly what he was doing back then, employing a loud-mouthed, semi-drunken reporter to shepherd an American journalist around the North; he had expected that I would put a spanner in the works, though I'm sure he couldn't have imagined exactly what the fallout would be.

'The duly elected,' I said, nodding around the

220

tables, 'saving Ulster one scallop at a time.'

'My, Dan, you sound almost cynical.'

'Moi?' I tilted my glass. 'Used to be I knew this place inside out. I've been out of the game a long time. But let's get to the subject at hand.'

'Ah yes. The wonderful Abagail Pike. She's a fine politician, but she has her knockers.'

He giggled. I giggled too. He was seventy-three years old, and I felt it. But sometimes it's great to have a mental age of twelve. We dialled it down to a smirk as the waiter arrived to take our order, and eventually we settled.

Neville sipped his Coke, then set it down and nodded across the fine linen tablecloth at me. 'Dan,' he said, 'I've been observing politicians for a long time, and they're all pretty much the same. Just look around this room. I guarantee you that with the exception of a few of the converted terrorists, every one of them shared identical traits at school—they were smart and they knew it, they held strong opinions, of course, they were great debaters, but they . . . how do I say this kindly? They . . . they were bland, overserious swots. They didn't know how to have fun or relax; their teenage years passed in a blizzard of conformity; they probably didn't lose their virginity until they were in their twenties. They were boring, church-going, terrible at sports, largely friendless and old before their time.'

'You're too kind.'

'It's the truth. They were born to do *this* and this alone. They control our lives, but they do not live in our world. This is a place where a little personality goes a very long way. So when they actually rub up against one, they are utterly flummoxed—and that's

221

where Abagail comes in. Friend or foe, they just can't cope with her. She's fast and funny and flirty, she's in their faces. I have seen politicians who can talk eloquently on extremely complicated subjects completely off the cuff for ninety minutes who still cannot manage two words to her without dissolving into puddles of sweat. In the real world she may not be the most gorgeous creature God ever created, but in these rarefied surroundings she's a Bardot, a Monroe, and she knows how to use it.'

'Even with her sisters?'

'Yes, I think so. They admire her ability as an operator. Oh, there's a little jealousy in there as well; not all of them are similarly blessed in the looks department.'

'Oh *bitchy*.'

He gave a little shrug. 'I'm old enough now to say what I want. What're they going to do, throw me out? They know I know where the bodies are buried.'

'Metaphorically speaking,' I said.

He raised an eyebrow, before adding: 'Of course.'

'Then tell me something about Abagail Pike I don't know.'

He smiled. His teeth had recently been capped, probably to meet with the requirements of HD television. Seventy-three-year-old prefluoride smoker's teeth would scare children. But they appeared over-sized in his shrinking face.

'What do you want, rumours or fact?'

'Frumours.'

'I'm told she's accidentally walked into a few doors.'

'Doors can be dangerous.'

222

'Yes, almost like getting punched in the face.'

I raised an eyebrow. 'Seriously?'

'That's the . . . frumour.'

'Anything else?'

'She has expensive tastes.'

'How expensive? Her man's supposed to have made a fortune in the private sector before he entered politics.'

'And I believe he did. He's set up a number of charities, and plenty of his money goes into them. They do a lot of work abroad.'

'You mean Pike smuggles it into offshore accounts?'

'No, I mean actual, verifiable charity work.'

'Commendable, I'm sure. But still, a minister's wage packet, his wage as a sitting member, her own . . . put that all together, it's not to be sniffed at.'

'No indeed. Not to be sniffed at.'

He touched the end of his nose as he said it and gave the smallest sniff up. At that moment the starter he'd ordered for both of us arrived. The waiter said, 'Sir, quail eggs and shark fin soup with ginseng.' It was £3.50 on the menu, but still not as cheap as the version Patricia and I had not enjoyed at the Shipyard. Neville shook out his napkin and tucked it into his shirt collar. He thanked the waiter. He then allowed his eyes to rove around the brasserie. He nodded at a couple of Assemblymen I didn't recognise. When he came back to looking at me, I think he knew my eyes hadn't left him.

'Are you sure?' I asked.

'Am I sure what, Daniel?'

'That she . . .' and I touched my own nose as subtly as I could with my bear paw of a free hand.

'I'm sure I don't know what you mean. Lovely

soup,' he said.

I tried a spoonful. Wherever you got quail eggs and shark fin soup with ginseng, it seemed it still tasted like cack.

A different waiter, passing by and noticing the depressed state of my glass, asked if we were okay for drinks. I ordered another wine. Neville raised his glass and drained it. He handed it to the waiter.

'Why don't you bring me another Coke?' he asked. 'It's really quite addictive.'

36

When we were done, Neville walked me towards the foyer. He stopped at the top of the stairs and nodded admiringly at the Italian travertine marble. It was lovely—sleek, clean, cold.

'Spent my whole working life here,' he said. 'Fifteen when I started; can't do that these days, can you? My dad fixed me up. By the time I was eighteen, I knew how a government worked, I knew what was wrong with it, and I knew when to shut up and when to speak. There's guys starting here nowadays, twenty-five years old, loaded down with degrees in this and masters in that, they can wave ten million statistics in your face, but couldn't tell you who Carson was.' He shook his head around the foyer, but it wasn't meant to be negative. 'I love this place. There's so few measure up to it. Dan, I've always done what I can to protect it, the idea of it, and I'll keep doing it until the day I die.'

He had been using the wide marble steps for more than fifty years, but old age had brought with it a need for care. He had one hand on a gleaming rail, the other thrust into his jacket pocket to hide a slight tremor I'd noticed at the table. I was on the verge of offering an arm for support, but with my luck we'd probably have ended up tumbling to our deaths. When we eventually reached the bottom, he turned towards a small alcove close to the front doors.

'You want to come down and watch me record?' he asked.

'I'm not eleven,' I said.

All the impressive bits of the building were above ground—the Great Hall, the Assembly and Senate chambers—but the door in front of him led down into the bowels of the building. There were miles of claustrophobic corridors down there where much of the real, sleeves-up, heads-down dirty work of government got done. I'd been up and down them a thousand times in my reporting days. Drink used to be freely available. I had once gotten lost in their labyrinth-like design for twenty-four hours. But she was worth it.

Neville held his hand out and I shook it. 'Thanks,' I said.

He held on to it. 'Watch yourself, Dan. I don't know what you're into, but things have changed these past few years. It's more like business now—it used to be about defending this, or attacking that; now it's about the bottom line. No morals, no principles, no prisoners. And it's impossible to keep secrets—we're such a small bloody country, everybody finds out everything, instantly, and Tweets it. It took thirty years for the Disappeared to turn up; these days they wouldn't stay hidden for thirty minutes.' He nodded at the various

Assemblymen and civil servants around us. 'The funny thing is, the terrorists, the ones who've given up their guns and gone into politics, and won't even acknowledge that this place has any legality, they're actually better politicians than those who choose it as a career. They bring passion to it.'

'If you can conveniently forget the fact that they used to blow people up,' I said.

'Let he who is without sin cast the first stone.'

But it wasn't Neville. It came from behind us. I turned.

Man mountain, black suit, sharp, handsome but dour face, grey hair swept back.

'Will I walk you down, Neville?' Professor Peter Pike asked. 'I'm on just after you.'

'Yes, of course,' Neville replied. He darted a wary glance at me. I gave him the slightest nod. 'Professor Pike . . . I don't believe you've met . . . Mr Dan Starkey.'

Pike's brow crinkled. He put his hand out. 'Dan Starkey . . . Dan Starkey . . . Didn't you used to be big in newspapers?'

'Yes,' I said.

You can never remember a good line when you really need it. Also I instinctively dislike people who employ vice-like handshakes. Also, also I instinctively dislike people who stare into your eyes when they talk to you and who prosper because of snake-oil charm. Threepike didn't have much going for him, really. I don't have to agree with a man's beliefs, but I like a man who stands by them. I've often argued with Trish about our changing times: she favours giving people a second chance, allowing them to change. I maintain that a leopard can't change its spots. She says I'm a miserable,

226

curmudgeonly old stick-in-the-mud and I say I probably am.

Threepike said, 'You look like you've been in the wars.'

'Yes,' I said.

'We were just talking about your lovely wife,' said Neville.

'Really? What's she been up to?'

'Oh you wouldn't believe it!' Neville cried. 'That woman! She's a scandal!'

'*Neville.*' Pike pretended to give the old man a punch on the arm. 'Though for all I know, you could be right. Honestly, we're like ships that pass in the night.'

'Shits,' said Neville. 'Isn't that what *Republican News* said about you? Shits that pass in the night.'

'They did,' said Pike, drily. 'They're always misquoting me. Luckily we're all friends now. Isn't that right, Dan?'

'Yes,' I said.

'Are you joining us?'

'No.'

'Come then, Neville, let's get down to yon poky little studio. I do believe you're the only one around here who knows the short cut, isn't that right?'

Pike pulled the door open and indicated for Neville to lead. As they disappeared through it, Neville gave me a wink.

I stood where I was, a little stunned by my own inept performance. I used to be able to *pin* assholes. A question with a barb, backed up to the teeth with facts that could not be denied. Or fictions that at least earned an unregimented response. I had managed a grand total of three yeses and a no. He'd caught me by surprise as I was still trying to come to terms with the gossip Neville had so undiplomatically imparted. I was in physical pain from my burning and beatings. I had all kinds of instant excuses, but I couldn't escape from the fact that in my heyday I would have laughed in the face of any or all of these handicaps. I was Dan Starkey, master of the put-down, but I had flailed, my reflexes as rusty as . . . oh, fuck it. I was . . . diminished.

I stepped out into the fresh air.

It was raining hard and winter cold.

I stepped back inside to ring a taxi. I'd switched my mobile off during lunch. But now I saw that there were three voicemails: one from Joe saying that Bobby had stormed out of the shop and disappeared; one from Patricia saying that Bobby had called her at work, and that she was having to leave to let him into the house, and she wasn't very happy about it and had I sorted anything for him yet; and a third from Maxi McDowell asking me to give him a call right away.

I did. He said, 'You're in luck. The Millers have a cancellation. They'll see you at noon tomorrow. I'll get you in and out, but you're the performer. Okay?'

'Okay,' I said.

I cut the line. I took a deep breath. I stood in the doorway and looked out over the lawns sweeping away down to the gates. The grounds were open to the public, and were dotted with joggers braving the elements and dog-walkers with extended leads sheltering under trees that had not yet sprouted leaves.

It was a little after two o'clock in the afternoon. That gave me roughly twenty-two hours to come up

228

with something that would satisfy the Millers and possibly save Bobby Murray's life.

I was not optimistic.

37

'Where's the car?' was the first thing Trish asked when she saw the taxi driving off.

'I got a flat,' was an approximation of the truth.

'So you just abandoned it?'

'Obviously.'

She showed me into the lounge and disappeared into the kitchen. She returned swiftly with a can of Harp.

'You may need it,' she said.

'What happened with the butcher?'

'Bobby got shouted at, so he walked.'

'Why was he shouted at?'

'Smoking in the cold room.'

'As you would. What does Joe say—is he done with him?'

'Nope. I think they're both quite volatile; difference is Joe doesn't sulk. He'll have him back tomorrow. He says Bobby shows a definite flair for cutting and chopping.'

'It's good to have a talent. What does Bobby say?'

'Very little.'

'Will he go back?'

'Not if he has to apologise first.'

'Is that a condition?'

'Yep.'

'From Joe?'

'From me.'

'My house, my rules?'

'Something like that.'

'Good job you never applied them to me.'

'You were beyond saving.'

I opened my Harp. 'You shouldn't give up so easy.'

'Who says I have?' Her smile. Love it. 'Will I get him?'

'If you must.'

'Go easy on him, Dan.'

'Trish, the time for going easy has passed.'

*　　*　　*

She shouted from the bottom of the stairs.

He yelled back, 'Just let me get to the end of this level.'

'No, now!'

*　　*　　*

Ten minutes later he sauntered in. He was wearing one of my T-shirts. It had the front cover of The Clash's first album on it. It was twenty-three years old, and too tight for me.

As an icebreaker I said, 'Have you heard of The Clash?'

'*Yes*. It's the muck you try to impress me with when I'm in your car.'

Patricia smirked. 'Are you *still* doing that?'

I made *let's get serious* eyes at her.

Bobby sat on the armchair, sideways, with his legs over the arm. I still hadn't quite got used to the fake one.

'Bobby . . .' I began.

'I'm not fuckin' sayin' sorry to him,' he snapped. 'There was no need to scream at me like that.'

'That's not why I'm here,' I said. 'Though I would advise it.'

'No way am I fuckin'—'

'Shhhh, Bobby, listen to me. It's not about the butcher's.'

'What then? What else have I done?'

'Nothing,' said Trish. 'You've done nothing.'

'Trish, please . . .' I said, 'let me . . .'

'Of course. Sorry. Master of diplomacy.'

She held her hands up in apology. She pretended to zip her lips. Bobby watched her, and then me.

'*What?*'

'Bobby—this situation is untenable.'

'Unwhatable?'

'*This* can't continue. Living here, working at Joe's, even staying at my apartment, you're putting us all in danger.'

'All right, fuck it.' He swung his legs off and began to haul himself up. 'I'm off, then.'

'Bobby—sit down.'

'Make your bloody mind—'

'SIT DOWN!' It roared out of me, unbidden. Trish looked shocked, but not as shocked as Bobby.

'All right, keep your hair on.' He lowered himself back down.

'Okay. *Sorry.* Look, all I'm saying is that the Millers are still after you, and it's only a matter of time before someone spots you and gives you away. That not only means that they'll come for you, but they'll punish whoever's been harbouring you. You know this, it's what they're like.'

'So?'

231

'*So?* Don't you care about anyone apart from yourself?'

'*Dan* . . .'

'Well, fuck it, the selfish little—'

'*Dan* . . . *please.*'

Bobby's mouth twisted up in contempt. 'Do you think I need you?' he spat across. 'I can walk outta here today, no problem . . .'

'Yeah, right, you're the big man, you'll be fine, for about five minutes, then they'll carve you into little tiny bits . . .'

'Fuck off!'

'You have no idea what they're capable of.'

'Do I not, do I not?' He jutted his false leg out. 'Do I fucking not?'

'Bobby, that's nothing. It's a scratch compared to . . .'

'Dan.'

'. . . what they're capable of . . .'

'Dan.'

'*What?*'

'Will you just stop . . . fucking . . . *lecturing.*'

'I was only . . .'

'Well, just . . . *stop.* Let me say something, okay?'

'Right. Yes. Okay. The floor is yours.'

I sat back. Sarcastically.

Trish took a deep breath. She let it ease out. Bobby looked at her expectantly.

'Bobby—just hear me out, okay?' He shrugged. 'Okay?'

'*Okay.*'

'Good. Now, my late husband . . . sorry, Dan, that's not quite what I mean . . . or is it?' She smiled. 'Dan, my ex-partner, may go about things in an arsey way, but he is right.'

'Thanks,' I said.

'Shut up. Bobby. *This* cannot continue. I like having you here. But I can't live like this. Every time a car goes past, thinking they're coming for you. Or coming for *me*. I lived like that for a long time with *this* eejit, and I'm not going back there. This has to be resolved. If your leg had been left to fester, then it would have killed you. At some point the surgeons had to make a call, lose the leg or lose you. Well that's the point we're at; we have to make a decision on what to do. You can't sit upstairs thinking it will all just go away. It won't. It's festering, Bobby, and very soon we'll be at the point where that decision is taken out of our hands.'

'That's what I was going to say,' I said.

'Shut up,' said Trish. She was firm, she was direct, she was the voice of reason in a way that I, even though I was saying essentially the same thing, was not. 'Bobby—who killed your mum?'

'*What?*'

'Simple question. You said you saw them.'

'She was askin' for it.'

'That's not what I asked, and you know you don't really believe that. Who was it?'

'Yeah, right. I tell you that, I'm a dead man.'

'Bobby, you're a dead man anyway.'

'No chance, no way. I tell you, everyone finds out I'm a tout, I may as well top myself. Never be able to show my face again.'

'Bobby . . .'

'I'm not a fuckin' squealer!'

'Bobby, you are fourteen, your mother is dead, you have no money, nowhere to go, you cannot walk the streets and you are not safe for anyone to be around while the Millers are after you.'

'Don't you think I know that?'

'I know you do,' said Trish, 'but if you're not prepared to name names, then we've pretty much run out of options.'

She looked at me, and gave me my cue.

'Even your dad isn't interested,' I said.

'You fucking *what* . . . ?'

'Yeah, that's right, I tracked him down. He's living a nice comfortable little life in England, with his wife, with his children. He doesn't want to know, Bobby.'

'*So?* Big deal.'

But I could see from his face, despite all the bluster, that it was a big deal.

'I tried, Bobby, but he's really not fussed. It just kind of underlines what your mum did for you. No matter what you think of her now, she stood up for you, she protected you, she died for you, for fucksake. So think about it. She's gone and she isn't coming back. Your dad isn't interested and your relatives don't want to know either; it would be like signing their own death warrant. So listen to this and have a good hard think about it: you know and I know it was the Millers who were behind it. You wanted me to fetch the Xbox so you could get the gun and go after them. Well that's not going to happen. The only way you're ever going to be able to show your face again is by helping me. If you know who it was, you tell me. I'll work out some way to connect it to the Millers. I'll do whatever the hell I can to sort this out, to allow you to walk out of that door and not have to worry about someone shooting your fucking spine out. Do you hear me? I'm not asking you to go down the station and make a statement, I know you won't do that, but I need *something* to work on.'

Beside me, Trish said: '*Please.*'

Bobby's cheeks were red and his eyes black-ringed and hollow. He was sucking one of his lips into his mouth and biting down on it. He released it and I could see blood.

'What did he say?' he asked quietly.

'What did who say?'

'My dad.'

'He was . . . he wanted to know how you were. What you're like. He's just in a difficult position with his family.'

'And what did you tell him?'

'That you were a little angel.'

'Really?'

'Really. What did you want me to tell him, the truth?'

'What does he do? For a living.'

'I don't know.'

'What does he look like?'

'I don't know.'

'You don't know much.'

'It was on the phone, Bobby, I'm sure I can find out . . .'

'Don't bother. If he's not interested, he's not interested. Fuck him.'

Bobby hauled himself out of the chair. He walked to the door. Trish and I looked at each other in confusion.

'Where are you going?' she asked.

'We're not finished here,' I said.

He stopped at the door and looked back at us.

'I lied,' he said, 'The fire at my house. I didn't fucking see who did it. I was too busy running away.'

He clumped up the stairs, and stomped along the hall into his room.

I raised an eyebrow at Trish. 'Do you think our parenting skills could do with a little polishing?' I asked.

'He's upset,' said Trish.

'He's *upset*? I'm fucking furious.'

She was going to respond, but then stopped, listening. Bobby was on the move again. We tracked him along the hall and then back down the stairs, one step at a time. Trish raised her hands in a *what do you think*? gesture. I returned it.

Bobby came back in. He had a mobile phone in his hand.

'Where did you get . . . ?' I began.

'Shhhh,' said Trish.

'I didn't see who did it. But my mates across the road did.'

'Those cheeky wee shits? They're your friends?'

'They saw it from their bedroom window. Took photos on their phone and sent them to me. Most of them look like shite, but there's one you can see a face.' He took a deep breath. 'This isn't me squealing, this is just you seeing a photograph someone else took.'

Bobby turned the phone, tapped the screen, and held it up for me to see.

It was indeed a good clear picture, with the flames in the background providing the necessary lighting.

Neville was right, it is a small world.

Mr Paddy Barr, come on down.

38

I told Trish I needed to borrow her car. She told me to get away to fuck. I rephrased it using the words *please* and *pretty please*. She said, 'Do you want me to help you change your tyre? Because that's usually why—'

'I haven't time for this, Trish. I have to get moving *now*. Come on. I can fix *this*, but I can't afford to bugger around. Lend me the car, which, technically, is my fucking car anyway.'

'Technically?'

'Purchased with my money, in my name.'

'Do you seriously want to go down that road?'

'No! So just lend it to me!'

We only stopped when Bobby came barging back into the room with his replacement Xbox in his hands and said, 'It's fucking broken.'

'What did you do to it?'

'I didn't do anything! Why do I always have to have done something?'

'Dan! Will you leave him alone? Things break!'

'I didn't do nothin'!' Bobby shouted.

'I can't believe I'm hearing this!' I yelled. 'If it's broken, go and buy another one with your earnings! Oh, that's right, you got yourself sacked!'

'Dan,' said Trish, 'if you hadn't scrimped on a second-hand one in the first place . . .'

'Scrimped! So it's my fucking fault?'

'Yes! No! Okay! Just everyone settle down!' Her shout was louder and higher-pitched than we could match, like a dog whistle for humans, annoying to the point of acquiescence. 'Okay, fine, that's better.

Bobby—is it broken beyond repair?'

'I don't know. It was in shit shape to start with.'

'Will I just throw it out, then?'

Bobby and I both laughed at the same time.

'Trish, Jesus,' I said, 'how long were we married? Don't you know *anything* about men? We never, repeat, *never* throw electrical equipment out.'

'Why would you throw it out?' Bobby asked.

'Because it's broken and beyond fixing?'

'Nothing is beyond fixing,' said Bobby.

'And even if it can't be fixed,' I said, 'you can cannibalise it for parts.'

'Dan Starkey, you can't wire a plug.'

'I can learn.'

'Christ, one minute you're bickering like a couple of kids, the next you're uniting against me. Here!' She threw her keys at me. 'Take the bloody car. And take the Xbox and either get it fixed or dump it.'

I was *this* close to high-fiving with Bobby, but he cut me off at the pass by snapping: 'My high score's on there. Try not to lose it.'

*   *   *

Trish had a Peugeot 107. Silver. It was comfortable, unremarkable, and benefited in terms of clandestine surveillance by not having *PEDOFIAL* etched on the side. I was parked in Boucher Crescent, about half a mile from Cityscape FM, and opposite the headquarters of Malone Security, hoping to catch up with Paddy Barr. It operated out of a two-storey building, glass-fronted. A receptionist's stacked blonde hair was just visible behind a high counter. There were two cars with the Malone logo outside, and others came and went. A few of the faces I vaguely recognised from my beating. I had their website up on my phone. It said they offered a bespoke service. It was definitely the cool thing to offer. They were established in 1996. They were all about protecting the community. They had thirty employees, all highly trained, without specifying where they'd received their training or what in. In another country it might have said they were ex-police or army; here, that would alienate half their clientele. There was a photo of someone called Derek Beattie, the managing director and founder. Fat face, bald head, stern look.

I phoned the invisible blonde and asked to speak to Paddy Barr. She said he was out on a job at the moment and could she take a message. I said it was urgent and asked for his mobile number. She gave it without a problem. How secure. I phoned him. He was in the middle of a conversation with the cruiser when he answered. Something about Manchester United. There was music playing, and the sounds of traffic.

He said, 'Hi.'

I said, 'I'm a Liverpool man myself.'

'Tragic, mate, tragic,' he said jovially. 'Who's this?'

'It's Dan Starkey.'

For some reason, his joviality faded. 'You . . . Where the fuck did you get this number?'

'I looked it up in the book.'

'*What* book? It's a fucking mobile.'

'*The Penguin Book of Wee Skinny Fuck Faces.*'

'What the . . .'

'Shut up, Paddy, and listen to me. I'm sending you a photo by SMS.'

'Photo? What the . . . ?'

'Take a good look at it, because I'm on the verge of sending it out to every newspaper in the land. When you've had a look, you come and see me. I'm going to be in the café, first floor, House of Fraser, Victoria Square, in thirty minutes. You come alone. You try anything smart, I've people wired to send it out anyway.'

'Send what? What are you . . . ? Do you never fucking learn? You don't mess with—'

'Paddy.' I said it quietly.

'What?'

'Just look at the photo.'

He said nothing for a bit. I could hear the Script on the radio, and the cruiser singing along.

'Why House of Fraser?'

'Because it's comfortable and offers a wide range of quality goods. Should you give a fuck? No. Just be there. And Paddy?'

'What?'

'Bring my Xbox.'

'How the fuck do you—'

I cut the line. Then I sent the photo of him outside Jean Murray's burning home.

*   *   *

He approached warily, the Xbox in a large green plastic M&S bag. His eyes roved over the customers at the other tables. He pulled out a chair and sat. He reached the games console across to me. From the weight of it, I guessed the money, drugs and gun were still safe inside.

He said, 'It doesn't work.'

'I know. Why didn't you just throw it out?'

'I was going to get it fixed. How did you know I had it?'

'Because you would have checked my car over before you had it towed. It was probably in your boot, n'est-ce pas?'

'You what?'

'Was it in the boot?'

'Yes.'

'And how much did you get for the car?'

'I told you, we had it flattened.'

'Bollocks, it's a four-year-old car, it's probably out there already, new plates, new history and you're a couple of grand to the good.' Paddy shifted uncomfortably. 'Anyway, this isn't about the car. Do you want a cup of tea?'

'What? Yeah, sure.'

'Get us one while you're up, then.'

He almost spat something back, I could see it in his eyes and the corners of his mouth, but he held himself in check. He headed for the counter.

'Paddy,' I said. He stopped, turned. 'I take it black. Like my men.'

I gave him a wink. It confused him. He wasn't the sharpest tack in the box. He came back with two teas and two buns.

'I didn't ask for buns,' I said.

'They were part of a deal,' he said. He stirred plenty of sugar into his cup. 'So. Where'd you get the photo?'

'Doesn't matter. Good, isn't it? And you'll note there's also the last four digits of a number plate in the corner. Amazing if it turned out to be your car. Though I'm sure you wouldn't be that stupid.'

'It proves nothing.'

'Really? So why're you here?'

He drummed his fingers on the table. 'What do you want? I don't have any money, I'm barely scraping by as it is.'

'I'm not interested in money, Paddy. I want information.'

'I don't know anything about anything. I just do my job, keep my head down.'

'Jobs like Jean Murray?' He shrugged. 'How do you know the Millers?'

'What Millers?'

'Don't fuck with me, Paddy. The Shankill Road UVF Millers.'

'I don't know them.'

'So who told you to burn Jean Murray's house?'

'I got a call.'

'From?'

'Just a call.'

'Paddy, do yourself a favour. The cops are being hounded. When they get hold of this, they'll throw everything at you. It's murder; you're on twenty, minimum. You think the Millers are going to ride in with a high-powered barrister and rescue you? Catch yourself on. You'll be on legal aid; some kid who looks about twelve years old and came last in his class will try and fail to defend you. The Millers know you won't squeal, because if you open your mouth they'll rip it right round till it meets the other side and your head flops back.'

'And what if they don't get hold of it?'

'Then you carry on doing what you're doing, nobody needs to see the picture or know we had a chat.'

'Why would you do that?'

'Because it's not you I'm after.'

'Who then? The Millers?'

'Maybe.'

'Are you mental?'

'Probably. But that's neither here nor there. Who called you about Jean Murray?'

Paddy stirred his coffee. 'The boss.'

'Which one of them is boss? Windy or Rab?'

'Not them. The *boss*. Of Malone.'

'Derek Beattie?'

'Aye. He phones me and tells me what he wants done.'

'Don't you ask why?'

'I don't care why. I just do what I'm told.'

'Is this a regular thing?'

'Once in a while. Not burning people out. Kneecaps and stuff. They're just extras. Like overtime.'

'Did you do Jean Murray's son?'

'No, that wasn't me. One of the other crews.'

'From Malone?' Paddy nodded. 'You're all at it?'

'Nah. It's not like that. It's . . . there are some who do . . . and some who don't. I mean, like, ninety per cent of what we do is . . . you know . . . just security, like it says on the tin, but there's some other stuff too . . . that only some of us do, you know what I mean?'

'And this all comes from Beattie?'

'Yeah.'

'And the Millers employ him to do their dirty work?'

He rubbed his hand across his jaw. There was sweat on his brow.

'Yeah, something like that.'

'What do you mean, *something like that*?'

'It's complicated.'

'It's probably not.'

243

He picked up one of the buns and bit into it. He chewed. And he chewed. He seemed to be having trouble swallowing. He took a swill of his tea.

'Look,' he said, 'I've been with Derek Beattie since I quit the boxing. You can be the best in Europe, but there's no money at bantam, and I wasn't even the best in Ireland. I was in prison for a while, but Derek took me on, took a chance. He's okay, Derek. He was in the army years back. Far as I know, he ran the company fine, we were just guarding building sites, shopping centres, you know the form. But then the last few years, the work wasn't there. I don't know all the facts, I just heard he was in debt, and then one day he's suddenly all smiles again, someone came in and invested in the company. I think the smile lasted about one day, till he found out who it was.'

'The Millers.'

'Aye. It's supposed to be this big secret, but everyone knows. They brought their own boys in. Those of us who stayed, well, you get sucked in to doing stuff. Times are hard and the money's good.'

'So good you were prepared to *murder* someone for it?'

Paddy leaned forward, over his cup, his eyes small and cold, his voice lower, conspiratorial: 'What d'you think I was in prison for in the first place?'

39

Paddy said, 'What do I do now?'

'Now you go back to work, you keep your head down, your mouth shut and you try and keep it legal. If I need your help, I may ask for it, or you may never hear from me again. Depends.'

'What about the photo?'

'It remains in play until this is done. But you've cooperated, and I'm a man of my word.'

'And what about when the Millers kill you, what happens to the photo then?'

'Then I'm afraid it gets released, so you better keep your fingers crossed.'

'That's not really fair. I'm helping you and—'

'Paddy. Fair doesn't come into it. You're a murderer. Consider yourself lucky I don't send this off the minute you walk out of here.'

That said, the minute he walked out of there, I did send it off. It went to DS Hood by SMS, identifying who Paddy was and what it showed and who took it and what their address was. I couldn't see the benefit of holding on to it, and if Hood and his boss took it seriously, they would hopefully stop hassling me over Bobby's whereabouts. Plus, I didn't trust Paddy. I was pretty sure he'd think I was bluffing about having the photo primed for release in the event of anything happening to me. He'd take his chance when he could, so the sooner he was off the streets, the better.

Paddy was a killer, but he was still just a low-level thug following orders. Satisfied that he'd given up everything he could, I told him to go and he sloped off. I sat on, finishing my tea and the other bun. I did two tours of the House of Fraser, up and down the escalators, to make sure he wasn't following me. I didn't spot him, though I did spy a couple of rather nice jerseys. Then I checked myself in the mirror and discovered that I'd turned sixty-five overnight. I returned to Victoria Square's vast and well-lit underground car park. Nevertheless, things tend to happen in car parks. Mostly in the movies, admittedly, but it feeds into your being. I was jumpy. Any movement, any noise, and my heart went off like a car alarm. I couldn't find my car. I was searching for it for fifteen minutes before I remembered I wasn't in my own, but Patricia's. By the time I located it, the only person following me about was a security guard with suspicions. Luckily, he wasn't from Malone.

Underneath the wipers: a piece of paper.

Face down, something written underneath.

I looked around me again. The security guard had vanished as soon as I beeped the alarm, but with floodlights there are still shadows; there are still pillars to shield the presence of an assassin, cars to duck down behind. I lay flat, checking for a car bomb, and under the surrounding vehicles for evidence of feet or knees.

All clear.

I thought: it'll be a swastika.

I carefully removed the paper, using the tip of my thumb and forefinger; thinking about prints.

The paper said: *Hollister—Spring Sale Now On*.

I said out loud: *Tit*.

*   *   *

I phoned Malone Security and asked for Derek Beattie. I was told I was being put through. I hung up. My plan was to follow him home and use the Xbox gun to force my way in for a chat over a cup of tea and HobNobs. I even had the HobNobs, though if I sat for much longer outside his office, I might not. As time wore on and the staff left in dribs and drabs, and the company cars with their nifty logos went too, it became clear that he wasn't going anywhere soon. The security business is necessarily around the clock; someone is always on call to deal with emergencies. They probably didn't have to stay in the office to do it, and it didn't need to be anyone as senior as Derek Beattie, but whatever way it was working, pretty soon there was only one car in the car park, and one light on in the whole building. The car was a black Jaguar of 2011 vintage. I deduced that it was his. The solitary light was on upstairs in a corner office.

I listened to the seven p.m. news on Cityscape FM. There was no fresh violence to report. It might be the calm before the storm, or there might be no storm. I started the car and drove the few hundred metres to the Malone HQ. There were no security gates to stop me entering their car park. There was, however, a security grille and a camera over the front door, which was locked. There was no reason to think that Derek would know what I looked like, or even who I was, but I didn't want to take the chance of him coming to the door and recognising me before he opened up. Instead I crossed to his car, stood by the driver's window and cracked it once with the butt of the gun. Immediately the alarm began to sound. I stepped back into the shadow of the building. After about thirty seconds the alarm stopped. I had not thought about the possibility that he could stand at his office window and click it off without having to leave the building.

I gave it another minute, then ventured out into the car park and looked up at his window. No sign of him. I returned to his car and this time put the butt through the glass; I moved sharply back under cover as the alarm erupted anew. Again it was switched off from above, but this time a light came on behind the front door, and a few moments later it opened and Derek Beattie emerged, slightly breathless, in an open-neck shirt and with his sleeves rolled up. His eyes were fixed on the car, at least until I held out the gun and said, 'Mr Beattie?'

He saw the gun, he saw me. He said, 'Don't kill me.'

'Back inside, then.'

He went into reverse. I followed. I pushed the door closed behind me and locked it. He turned and led the way upstairs into a dark outer office and then continued through it to his own.

He stood, awkwardly. I said, 'Take a seat.'

He looked at his own chair, and then at me, for approval. Not many people ever looked at me for approval for anything. It might have been the intense look in my eyes or the grim set of my jaw. But it was probably the gun. I nodded. He sat.

There was a chair opposite, for clients; smaller, less comfortable. I didn't mind. It still felt like I had the upper hand.

'So,' I said, 'how's it hangin'?'

'It . . . Fine . . .'

'Good. It's looking a bit like rain,' I said.

'Just take what you want and go. Shoot me in the leg. Or arm. I was in the military, so I know a little about first aid, I can deal with an arm or a leg until the ambulance gets here, but there's no need to kill me.'

If he'd been in the army, he'd once been fit. This was no longer the case. He was badly overweight. His chin had disappeared in a sea of fat, making it look as if he had swallowed his own neck.

He said, 'I knew this day would come, I warned them, and they said, who ever robbed a security company?'

'This isn't a robbery,' I said. 'What is there to take, apart from stationery?'

'Oh Christ,' he said. There was sweat cascading down his face. Given his weight, he was probably always pretty damp. 'Please. There's no need. I know it's all about sending messages, but I have a wife and three young kids. What's to gain? I won't say a word. Swear to God. Look, I'll show you where it is, you won't have to mess around with taking the safe or torturing me for the combination, just let me show you where it is, take what you want.'

'This isn't a robbery,' I said again. 'I just—'

'No, look, please . . . Christ . . . just come with me.'

He got up. He took it as a positive sign when I didn't immediately shoot him. He came out from behind his desk and moved crab-like to a door on his left. He paused with his hand on the knob and looked to me for approval. I nodded. It opened outwards. I stood so that I could see round the door. Inside there was a small room with a large safe. It probably weighed more than a ton. Like something you would get in a bank. A small bank. Smaller than the Allied Irish, but larger than the Piggy.

He said, 'It looks impressive, but most of its functions we don't utilise. There's a timer, but there's no need for it, we're a twenty-four-hour operation, you can't be having to hang around for seven hours when there's a customer waiting. Look—it's easy to open . . .'

He flicked switches and turned dials. He began to open the door.

I said, 'Easy there,' in case he reached inside and produced something that could Top Trump my revolver.

His hand was shaking. He said, 'Of course, of course . . .' He stood back a little, so that he was fully behind the door, and then slowly drew it back towards him.

The first thing I noticed was a little light coming on, like in a fridge. I'd never thought about that before. But it made sense.

It was good to throw some light on the subject.

Some light on the cash, which sat on shelves in the upper half, neatly stacked in a dozen columns.

'How much is there?' I asked.

'One million, two hundred and twenty-three thousand, two hundred and forty-five pounds, plus change.'

I nodded.

'And what about that?'

On the floor of the safe there were three uneven columns of six flat whitish bricks, kind of in the shape of the floats I used to use in the local pool. Each was sealed in tight transparent plastic; on the top 'floater' in each column there was something akin to an identifying logo or seal: in this case, the image of a scorpion.

'How much is the coke worth?' I asked.

'About the same.'

I said, '*Now* it's a robbery.'

40

It was just paper with a little artwork, and plant extract with a touch of refinement, but the world turned on it. We carried it all out to my car in a black bin bag. It only took the one trip, and it fitted easily in the boot. I had the gun in my jacket pocket. I signalled for him to get in.

'The boot?'

'Passenger seat.'

He was relieved. It's amazing what difference a gun and the lack of knowledge about a person's abilities and intentions can make. I liked it. I thought that maybe I should carry a gun more often. Maybe get a holster. And a tin star. So that I could chuck it in the dirt one day and say, 'This time all bets are off.' It could be a catchphrase. I could use it maybe three times in one adventure, and bring it back for the sequel. 'This time all bets are off,' I said.

'What?'

'Nothing.'

Enigmatic, too.

He reached for his seat belt.

I said, 'What are you doing? We're not going on a picnic.'

He let go of it and it snapped back. 'Sorry.'

'So you sold out to the Millers.'

He nodded ruefully. 'Worst mistake I ever

made.'

'And you can't just walk away.'

'They had me from the moment the cash hit the table. I should have known. I was just trying to save the company, my home, my family. And now it comes to this, shot dead in a car park.'

I did not correct him. Even though I had a gun, and he was up to his neck in the coke and cash business, I suspected he was a glass-half-empty kind of a guy anyway. Probably it went with the security territory. He didn't trawl for new custom by saying, sure, it'll never happen. He sowed fear and reaped the dividend.

I said, 'Do you know who I am?' He shook his head. There was perhaps a glimmer of hope in his eyes. 'I don't mean in the sense of you promise not to tell anyone if I let you live, I mean really, literally, do you know who I am or why I'm here?'

'Does it matter? I knew one of you would come for it.'

'One of who?'

'I don't know. One of whoever supplies this stuff. One of whoever wants it back or wants to muscle in. What is it they say? It's just business?' He shook his head bitterly. 'You gangsters, no disrespect intended, but you kill each other, tit for tat, tit for tat, but you never seem to disappear. Well you have it now, and you can deal with the consequences. If you're going to do me, do me now.'

I said, 'Hold your horses. I want to know how it works. The system. Do you deal direct with the Millers?'

Derek Beattie shook his head. 'Once a week they send two guys into the back office, they cut and seal, deliver to our clients.'

'And bring the money back?'

'Most pay by direct debit.'

'Direct . . . ?'

'Sure. Look, these people, they're middle class, respectable, they don't want to be standing on street corners looking for their entertainment. They don't want hoods coming to their homes dealing either. So what we do is provide security for their home, their business, that's what they pay for, they just happen to pay a bit above the going rate so that they can get their coke delivered by a nice man in a uniform. Goes into the bank by direct debit, we take it out in cash and keep it here for the Millers to collect. No cash changes hands with the clients. It's a perfect business model.'

'With the exception of Abagail Pike. I hear she's handing out envelopes of cash to your people.'

'Yes, well, she's an exception.'

'Because of who she is? Her husband?'

'She owes and she's trying to pay it off without her man finding out. Do you mind if I smoke?'

'I'd rather you didn't. How much are we talking about?'

'Abagail? Twenty grand. Plus interest.'

'And the interest probably isn't what the Nationwide is currently offering.'

'You know how these things work, you build up the addiction, give lots of credit, then you call it in, except the interest is such that she will never be able to pay it off piecemeal. She makes token payments, but she knows what the real deal is.'

And so did I, suddenly.

'Political influence,' I said.

'She has a certain amount of her own clout,' said Derek, 'but mostly I think it's the husband.

Everyone knows that for all his big talk, he's putty in her hands.'

'That's why the Millers waltz around free and you can go on collecting your direct debits.'

He said, 'I really need that cigarette.'

'No,' I said. 'Have a HobNob.'

I showed him. He demurred.

'As a last request,' he said, 'it doesn't quite have the same effect.'

'Well that's a matter of opinion. If I let you live, will you . . .'

'Yes.'

'. . . give up smoking?'

'Yes.'

'Go from coke to Diet Coke.'

'Yes. One million per cent.'

I nodded, and tried to look thoughtful.

He reached into his jacket.

'Easy,' I said.

He stopped. 'It's just my phone.'

I kept the gun on him and gave a short nod. He produced his iPhone.

'I have that model,' I said.

'If you let me live, you can have it. Everyone we deal with is on here, contacts, amounts, dates, times, even the direct debit details.'

'I could just shoot you dead and take it.'

'You don't know the password.'

'Tell me the password or I'll shoot you.'

He sighed. 'I'm damned if I do and I'm damned if I don't.'

'That you are.'

He handed me the phone. 'There you go,' he said. 'Please let me live.'

'Why don't you just send the info to my phone,

254

then you can hold on to it?'

'No. It's my work phone. *Their* phone. If you don't kill me, they certainly will. No point in hanging on to it.'

'Password?'

'I don't have one.'

'You were bluffing me.'

'Yes, sorry.'

I said, 'You have no password for your phone? You've no security on your car park, and you don't use half the functions on the safe in your office. If you don't mind me saying, you're fucking useless at security.'

'I know,' he said, nodding mournfully, 'but as it turns out, I'm a fantastic drug dealer. Go figure.'

*   *   *

I felt sorry for him, just a little tiny bit. We both knew that if I didn't kill him then the Millers would, although not before they'd wrung every last tiny bit of information out of him. You don't lose your employers the best part of two million pounds and get a written warning.

I told him to wait for a moment, then got out and opened the boot. I took three thousand in twenties out of the stash. When I dropped it into his lap, he looked surprised.

'Take it,' I said. 'Go and get your wife and kids and disappear. Different country. Start over. Put your house up, but don't come back to show people round.'

He looked at the money. He shook his head. 'I can't,' he said. 'If I run, they'll think I'm in on it.'

'And if you stay?'

'They'll think I'm in on it.'

'So run and stand a chance, or stay and get shot.'

'You're not shooting me?'

'Nope.'

'Not even a flesh wound.'

'Nope.'

'Could you just hit me with your gun then, make it look like I didn't give it up without a fight?'

'No can do,' I said.

He looked down at the money in his lap. 'I've no choice, then. The wife's going to be furious. We've just paid for Sky HD. It's a one-year contract. We'll never get out of it.'

I had sympathy in that direction.

'The fuckers will get you every which way,' I said.

41

There were lights on in Jack's house, and four cars in the drive. So they were home alone. It was a little after ten p.m. and I was aching from my various beatings, but rich beyond my wildest dreams. I had driven with meticulous care the mile across town to Malone, thinking the whole way that if I just withdrew from the case right now I could retire and *paaaaaaarty* for the rest of my life. It would be a short life, but *glorious*. But even while I was thinking it, I kept driving, safe in the knowledge that I had enough problems mainlining Harp.

I pulled into their drive, with my lights already off, and sat there in the dark. I tapped Derek Beattie's screen, and studied the names and addresses again, just to be absolutely sure—

there were one hundred and sixty properties in the greater Malone area that were served by his company; those with an asterisk were those that received a little extra sense of security for their monthly payment.

There was no asterisk beside Jack Caramac's name.

I checked my watch, and then ducked down lower in my seat. Forty-five seconds later, only a little bit late, a Malone Security car cruised slowly past. When I was sure they were gone, I got out of the car and walked up to the front door. When I rang the bell, Tracey answered. She had a silk dressing gown on and a glass of wine in her hand. She looked me up and down and said, 'Holy fuck.'

A moment later Jack was at her shoulder. He also had a glass of wine. He pointed it at me, but extended one finger.

'You were fucking told, Dan! What the hell's wrong with you?'

I said, 'We need to talk.'

I took a step forward.

They formed a united front, blocking me.

'You need to bugger off,' said Tracey.

'Ten minutes. You just need—'

'We don't need to do anything, Dan,' said Jack.

'Call them,' Tracey hissed at her husband. 'That's what we bloody pay them for.'

'Dan . . . please . . .'

'Oh for Jesus . . .' She started to turn.

'No,' I said.

She twirled back, exploding into: 'Who the fuck do you think . . . ?' before she saw that I had removed the gun from my jacket and was pointing it at her. And then she laughed. 'You've got to be

257

fucking kidding me.'

She turned again. Jack tried to haul her back, but she slapped his hand away and picked up the house phone. Jack gave me a helpless shrug.

I said, 'If she's calling Malone, that's why I'm here.'

'It's ringing,' said Tracey.

'Malone is owned by the Miller brothers.'

'Still ringing.'

'They use it to distribute cocaine to your friends and neighbours.'

'Being transferred to their out-of-hour service.'

'And I have a list of them all here.'

I held up the iPhone. While Tracey called, Jack's eyes had been widening further with each revelation.

He finally said, 'You're serious?'

I just kept holding it up. He turned and tried to pull the phone out of Tracey's hand. She struggled. He let her go. She stumbled back and fell on to the stairs behind her, spilling her wine over herself in the process. I knew her of old. Tracey would not take falling down lying down. Her mouth twisted up into a hate-fuelled scowl, and she was preparing to hurl herself at her husband when she was stopped by three little words.

'Mummy—what's wrong?'

Tracey brushed down the front of her dressing gown and twisted from her position sitting on the third step. She beamed up at little Jimmy at the top of the stairs.

'Nothing, darling,' she purred. 'Mummy and Daddy are just playing.'

'Who dat?'

He was looking at me. He looked angelic in

his Ben 10 pyjamas. The sort of kid you'd want to whack with a silver spoon.

'I'm a friend of your mummy's,' I said, stepping into the hall, smiling at him too, 'a really good friend.'

I gave Tracey a wink that said there were things I could tell Jack about our past she would not like me to tell Jack about our past. He couldn't see the wink. Little Jimmy could. But he was too dumb to know what it meant.

*   *   *

'Dan—we're seriously concerned for your mental health,' said Jack, pouring himself a Jack Daniel's, and then one for me. He brought them across. Tracey was scowling at me one moment, grinning at Jimmy on her knee the next. 'We're used to obsessive fans, but for Christ's sake, we've known you since your cider days. Let go of it, man.'

'You bring a gun into our house.' She covered her child's ears. 'Our fucking *house.*'

'But I can't say I'm not intrigued by the Millers.' Jack settled in the chair opposite. 'So I'll listen to what you have to say.'

Tracey had removed her hands from Jimmy's ears. Now she replaced them. 'And then we'll fuck you out.'

'But first, just put it away, will you? I've never seen anyone look more ridiculous with a gun. The glass is altogether more your style.'

He was trying to be nice, I think, but it was cutting in several different ways at the same time.

I kept the revolver in my hand. It was heavier than in the movies, lighter than my conscience. I

259

absolutely could shoot someone. It would just have to be the right person, someone who could change the fate of a nation, or who looked at Trish in the wrong way.

I said, 'I need to know why you sacked me.'

'Christ,' said Tracey. 'Change the record.'

'It's important,' I said. 'Jack?'

He blew air out of his cheeks. 'Dan, I think you'll find I've been pretty consistent here. I'm not shitting you. A good business deal went through. Bit of a killing.'

'Did it have to do with Jimmy being snatched?'

'No. We know what happened there.'

'The nanny.'

'So you know that much. Okay, fair enough. Well done. She made what you might call a tearful confession. Which I suppose is down to you. Maybe I owe you something a little extra.'

'You've sacked her, then?'

'No,' said Tracey. 'She's good with Jimmy. He'd be distraught.'

'She kidnapped him!'

'No. Her partner did. She's a bad egg. They've split up.'

'When did this all happen?'

'Last night,' said Jack. 'She's genuinely sorry. We've forgiven her. She won't do it again.'

I looked at Tracey and shook my head. 'She *kidnapped* your son.'

'*She* didn't,' said Tracey, 'and good staff are hard to get.'

I laughed involuntarily. 'Right, okay. Whatever you say, Tracey. Always a good judge of character.' Before she could respond, I turned to Jack. 'Did anyone from Malone ever offer you coke?'

'Absolutely not. Even if it's true, they would know better. I'm always ripping into dealers.'

'He doth protest too much.'

'I'm serious.'

'And you're a celeb in the media; it's rife with drugs.'

'Aye, Dan, that's right, Calpol and Imodium. This is Ulster, not the fucking West End.'

'Jack, give me some credit.'

He gave a little shrug. 'Okay. So there's some around. It's not *that* bad. But if the public even got a sniff of me being involved, that would be me finished. I mean, the hypocrisy of it.'

'Nobody's tried to tempt you in . . . ?'

'We made it clear,' said Tracey, 'we won't have it in the house.'

'So they did try?'

'We have parties all the time,' said Jack. 'And back in the day, maybe we dabbled a bit, but not since Jimmy. And nothing to do with Malone.'

'What about your neighbours behind, the Pikes; you have much to do with them?'

'Jesus, no,' said Jack. 'We used to get on okay, maybe a year ago, but then we had a . . . you know, falling-out.'

'Over . . . ?'

'That monstrosity next door,' Tracey spat.

'It's not that bad,' said Jack.

'It's a disaster,' said Tracey, 'and as soon as the market picks up a bit, we're out of here.'

'We'll see.'

They glared at each other. I liked it. Friction makes for revelation.

'Tell me more about the falling-out,' I said.

'Talking about hypocrites,' said Tracey, shaking

261

her head.

'Dan, if they'd just been straightforward with us, I'm sure we could have worked something out,' said Jack. 'What pissed us off was that the builders just turned up one day and started tearing their back garden up. At first we dismissed it, just some gardening work or they're putting up a garage or something, but once we saw the foundations going in we pulled them on it and they said they already had planning permission, and if we had a problem with it we should have complained at the time they applied for it.'

'And why didn't you?'

'What do you think?' snapped Tracey. 'They're supposed to inform the neighbours . . .'

'It's the *law* . . .' said Jack.

'And they're supposed to advertise it where we've a reasonable chance of seeing it . . .'

'But somehow our notification didn't arrive, and sure they advertised it, but in some community newspaper goes straight in the bin as soon as it arrives.'

'They covered themselves, though,' I ventured.

'They thought they had,' said Jack. 'I have to admit, for a while we ignored it, kind of gave up. They're in the government, who's going to turn them down? And we thought, it's a big garden, how bad can it be? But it just kept getting bigger and bigger, and taller and . . .'

'Squeezed in like a fucking cork in a wine barrel,' said Tracey.

'It just really pissed us off,' said Jack, 'not to mention that it devalued this place. So that's when we really started looking into it. I got into the Land Registry website and there was something there

262

that started me thinking. I went downtown and had a look at the plans and took one of my mates along who's an architect, and lo and behold, the cheeky fuckers were building on a tiny part of our land.'

'*Our* land,' Tracey repeated.

'Seems whoever planted the hedge between our properties did it without consulting the plans properly, so all these years a corner of our land has been on their side of it. And the great thing is, the corner they'd nicked was absolutely vital to their drainage system, and without the rights to it they'd have to knock down what they'd already built, redesign and reapply for planning. So we had them.'

'Couldn't they just use their power and influence . . . ?'

'Absolutely, and would have, but in between times there was a reshuffle up on the hill, and whereas they'd a friend running the planning office when they started, by the time I started kicking up a storm he'd been moved on and a not-so-friendly face had his feet under the table. They tried of course, and we ended up going to court.'

'We won,' said Tracey. 'They were forced to stop building.'

'Which they didn't like,' I said.

'Of course not,' said Tracey. 'But they'd one last trick up their sleeve. One day yer woman comes knocking, all sweetness and light.'

'Abagail?'

'Exactly, and I didn't like that one bit, because she waited until I was out, and Jack was in by himself, and she comes to the door with those tits of hers hanging out.'

'Didn't know where to look,' said Jack, 'or I

263

knew exactly where to look. Either way, it was embarrassing.'

'What did she . . . ?'

'She wanted to buy the corner. Actually, not the corner, just a tiny piece of it, that was all they needed. She made an offer, and I said sorry, no. It's not the size of the land, I said, it's the principle. And she was all apologetic, she said she didn't mean to try and railroad it through, it wasn't her, it was her people, she's so busy working to get the country back on its feet, she wasn't aware of what they were doing, it's all just a ghastly misunderstanding, didn't mean for us all to fall out with each other, how much she loves the show, asked me all about it and we talked about my guests, and she was suggesting things she could do to help the show, access to ministers . . .'

'Bullshit, bullshit, bullshit,' said Tracey.

'And I nodded and smiled, and she got closer and closer and her . . .' He raised an eyebrow.

Tracey laughed. 'Jack's a boob man, always has been, and they are impressive. I'd say they're the best money can buy.'

'And I was in absolutely no doubt that they were on the table,' said Jack.

'Size of them, I bet they nearly fucking were too,' Tracey cackled.

'But I've been down that road and I'm not going back.' He smiled benevolently at Tracey. 'She took me back, and she's my girl, and now she knows it.'

'Now I know it,' said Tracey, with a smile back for him, and one for me.

Sweet.

'So?'

'So I stepped away, and said the land wasn't for

264

sale, not at any price, and maybe she's not used to someone saying no to her, but she flew off the handle, called me all the names of the day and stormed out cursing and blinding. And from that day till this it's all been through her solicitors.'

'All what's been through her solicitors?'

'Selling the land, Dan.'

'I thought . . .'

'Yeah, bollocks,' laughed Jack. 'Of *course* I was going to sell; I knew it and she knew it. It was just a question of agreeing the price. Ask anyone at the station, Dan, I drive a hard bargain. I was always a crap reporter, you know that. When I joined the station I was freelance, I'd no benefits, no expenses, but I found something there that I could really do well, and they knew it soon enough too, so when it came to getting money out of them, I held out, and I held out, and now I own half the fucking place. Well, the same principle applies here. I held out until I thought I'd pretty much gotten it as high as I could. So we settled. That's what I was so happy about the other night: the money had just hit the bank, and the builders were back the next morning. Best bit of business I ever did. One hundred and twenty thousand quid.'

'And exactly how much of this green and pleasant land did they get for that?' I asked.

Jack grinned wider than the wide-mouthed frog.

'Exactly nine inches,' he said.

42

When I was a journalist, there was a terrific buzz that came with getting a good story, nailing it down, seeing it in print. *This* was definitely up there. Everything was falling into place. Jack and Tracey were not bad people, they were just slightly up themselves. I couldn't blame Jack for making a fast buck in straitened times, even if the straitened times weren't directly affecting him. It has always been the business of moneyed people to make more money. He had known exactly when to cash in. All he had lost was a little privacy in his back garden. Abagail Pike, on the other hand, was a gambler on the verge of losing everything. The only way to settle her debt to the Millers was to sell the new house and then siphon off part of the profits while hopefully keeping her husband in the dark. Where had she found the cash to pay Jack for his nine inches in the first place? Such an extravagant amount revealed how desperate her situation was. I think a large part of me knew she'd struck a deal with the Millers, and the collateral was as intangible as fear: access to power. That there was corruption and greed in government did not surprise or concern me. It had always been like that, everywhere, and always would be.

The only reason I was still involved at all was to sort out my one-legged charge. I needed to make a deal that would allow him to return to what passed for a normal life on the Shankill. With what I now had on Abagail Pike, with the cash and drugs in my car, and the info on who else the Millers were supplying across south Belfast on Derek Beattie's phone, I would never be in a better bargaining position.

And then I thought, *Jesus Christ, what the fucking fuck am I thinking?*

I'd robbed the most ruthless gangsters in the country of two million plus. I was endangering the life of my wife by harbouring a one-legged dealer who was being pursued by those very same gangsters. And I was carrying around evidence that linked virtually every well-off middle-class family in Belfast to a drug-dealing security company that made more deliveries than Domino's, and slightly cheaper. Who the hell would want to negotiate *anything* with me when it would be so much simpler just to wipe me off the face of the planet?

*   *   *

Patricia said, 'I've been worried sick.'

She was sitting at the kitchen table, empty coffee cup before her, in the *Eraserhead* glow of a flickering fluorescent light. Like many old houses, the electrics had a mind of their own.

'I'm fine,' I said, sitting down. 'Where's the boy wonder?'

'Bed. He's okay. What happened with you?'

'Nothing much.'

'Dan.'

'Swear to God.'

'*Dan*. You demanded my car, you took off like a devil, tell me.'

'It's nothing, really. Anyway, it's better you don't know.'

'I don't know what?'

'What I'm not going to tell you.'

'Dan, if it's that bad, you better tell me.'

'No. What you don't know you can't tell.'

'I won't tell.'

'Yes you will. They have ways of making you talk.'

I smiled. She did not.

'If it affects me, then I should know.'

'After I meet with them, it won't affect you.'

'Dan, how often do your master plans work out?'

'There's a first time for everything.'

'You're not going in by yourself, though. This cop guy will be there to make sure it goes through okay, won't he?'

'Yes, absolutely. Though I'm disappointed you don't think I can handle it myself.'

'Dan, I've been with you for twenty years. You can't go out for a pint of milk without having an adventure.'

'It's nice to hear you say you're with me.'

'Metaphorically speaking.'

'Of course if it doesn't work out . . .' I glanced at the table, and then up again. 'It would be good to have one last . . .'

'Don't give me those puppy-dog eyes, you chancer. The answer is no.'

'Trish, babe.'

'What part of *no* don't you understand?'

'The *no* part. Last meal of the condemned man and all that.'

'I thought you said it was going to be fine.'

'I may have exaggerated my chances.'

'Dan, our problems are not going to be helped by hopping into bed for a quick screw.'

'Damn your romantic heart, and it wouldn't be

that quick.'

'Why, have you been practising?'

'I've had no fucking alternative. Literally.'

She was smiling, but the lady wasn't for moving.

Patricia stood up, came around behind me, put her arm around my shoulders then kissed the top of my head.

'You've a big day ahead of you tomorrow,' she said. 'You should get some sleep. I'll make you up a bed on the couch, if you want.'

'Thank you, Mother,' I said.

43

Maxi McDowell reached across to open the passenger door, and I climbed in.

He said, 'Set?'

'Set.'

He was in his own car, and out of uniform. In the twenty-five years I'd known him, I'd never seen him in civvies. He did not appear diminished by them. The suit was slightly tweedy for my taste, but he filled every inch of it. He was of a generation that didn't do workouts, from an agrarian class that seemed to inherit big bones and honed muscle. He would have made for a lethal rugby player, but from what I knew of him, he was not a team player. His was his own man, and obstinate.

He drove slowly, deliberately.

'Relax,' he said.

'I am relaxed.'

I was not. I had finally been offered the last meal of the condemned man, except that it was literally a meal. A big fry-up. Patricia had picked up a bag of Joe's sausages. I'm sure they were wonderful, but I couldn't eat. Patricia scoffed hers down.

'It'll be fine,' she said.

I nodded. 'Did Bobby say anything?'

She'd been up earlier to take him to Joe's.

'He grunted a bit. He didn't eat his breakfast either.'

'Worried.'

'No. Vegetarian.'

'Since when?'

'Since he started with Joe.'

'Did they make peace?'

'Not so's you'd notice. They just got on with it.'

'Well that's good.'

On the step, she'd kissed me goodbye.

Properly.

I love her, but I hate her too. She keeps me hanging on. There is always hope, and then I do something wrong. It's as inevitable as the seasons. She knows more about me than anyone else in the entire world, and still tolerates me. Though if she'd known she was about to drive to work with two million pounds' worth of stolen cash and drugs in her boot, her kiss might not have lingered for so long. I was also kind of hoping she wouldn't reach into the glove compartment for a sweet, in case the gun fell out.

'Big day,' Maxi said. I nodded. 'Then the party later.'

'Party?' He glanced across. 'Oh, yeah. The retirement. Is it your colleagues throwing it, or the Greater Belfast Association of Hoods and Heavies?'

He smiled.

'Listen,' he said, 'the Millers, just say your piece, get in and out quick as you can. They're not the kind of people you want to hang around making small talk with.'

'But you're coming in with me?'

We had stopped at a junction. There was a car coming from the right. It was a fair distance away. He waited for it.

'No. But they'll know I'm there and not to take liberties. I'll take you in. You'll be searched, then escorted up.'

'I'd prefer you to . . .'

'No. They won't talk to you if I'm there. I'll be downstairs.'

'In reception?'

'It's an old Methodist church. There's a snooker hall on the ground floor now where their boys hang out. They're up the stairs, what used to be the church hall. It's divided into two rooms. They're in the front. No windows, two desks, big-screen telly.'

'You've been before.'

'Aye.'

'What goes on in the other room?'

'Their nefarious business.'

I studied the traffic. After a while I said, 'It's very early in the day to be using a word like *nefarious*.'

''Tis,' said Maxi.

*   *   *

The Shankill Road was early-morning busy. The former Methodist church still looked like a church. Big sandstone blocks. There was a glass-fronted noticeboard outside that would once have announced services and congregational events but

271

now advertised a snooker tournament. There were fenced-in patches of overgrown grass on either side of the doors littered with Coke cans and fag butts. If God had ever been inside, he'd long since been chucked out on his omnipotent ear. Two guys who had probably never enjoyed the benefits of gainful employment loitered in the entrance. They watched us approach. Their eyes pretty much stayed on Maxi. They recognised him, of course, and seemed disinclined to skip and jump with happiness as he drew nearer.

'Dan Starkey,' said Maxi.

They took me into the vestibule. The doors in front were open, and I could see snooker tables, and players, and hear music. Queen. Not the one they claimed to fight for. 'We Will Rock You'. I wondered if they had the correct licence to play it in public. I couldn't imagine the man from performing rights admonishing the Millers.

I was patted down. Maxi stood back. He wasn't going to be patted down by anyone.

One of the guys, in a cap-sleeve T-shirt with a cheap and chunky medallion, said, 'You want a frame while you wait, Maxi?' He nodded into the church.

'Sure.'

Maxi followed him inside without a backward glance.

I felt bereft.

The other guy, shorter, muscled, Loyalist POW tattoos, indicated for me to follow him up the stairs. They seemed impossibly steep. They were well lit, probably deliberately. As I stepped on to the short landing at the top, I happened to look down. There was a single drop of blood sitting on a linoleum tile.

It was not a good sign.

Drifting up from the snooker hall below: 'Who Wants to Live Forever?'.

That didn't help much either.

Outside the door—a small table, two chairs, two more guys. One was studying a laptop, the other reading the *Sun*. The one with the newspaper was stubbled, with a high forehead. He folded it and set it down and got up.

'Starkey?'

I nodded. He patted me down again. As he crouched to check my legs, his zip jacket fell open and I saw the butt of a gun within. As he finished, I checked the other one out. He had small, darting eyes and an unnatural curl to his hair. He didn't pay me any attention at all.

The *Sun* guy turned and knocked on the door behind. He waited for about ten seconds. When there was no response, he pushed it open and indicated for me to enter. I hesitated for a moment before stepping through. There were desks centre front and right. On the back wall a Union Jack. A painted but chipped wooden door was set halfway along. The other walls featured a large Ulster flag with its white background tinged nicotine yellow and various items of paramilitary and Loyalist regalia and memorabilia. This then was the headquarters of the 1st Battalion of the Ulster Volunteer Force, the paramilitary organisation formed to protect my people, but which had been abusing them ever since. The joint brigadiers of said battalion were facing me: Rab Miller, stick thin, navy shirt, casual blue jacket, perched on the left side of the desk; and behind it, in a black suit with black shirt, Thomas 'Windy' Miller,

273

thickset edging towards fat with a spray-on tan, leaning forward with his arms folded. The first thought that struck me was that they had taken the ten seconds between the knock and the door opening to deliberately set themselves in this pose. They supposed they were cool and polished and intimidating, like some mutant descendants of Bailey-era Krays.

I said, 'Thanks for seeing me.'

Rab said, 'Our pleasure. Dan Starkey.'

He indicated a plastic chair. I sat. I put my hands on my legs and nodded from one to the other. The only thing between them was an Apple PowerBook and a diet.

'Which one of you is Rab?' I asked.

It was an old tactic I'd used to deflate celebs in the past.

Rab ignored the question and instead asked: 'Have you ever been to China, Dan?'

'Not yet,' I said.

'In China,' he continued, 'in business meetings it's the tradition to exchange gifts.'

'I don't come bearing gifts,' I said, 'except of knowledge. And I've the feeling you're talking about Japan.'

'Well, we have a gift. Brother?' He nodded at Windy, and Windy opened a drawer and took out a plastic bag. 'Do you know someone called Patrick Barr? Paddy, I think.'

'Yes,' I said.

'Well,' said Windy, holding out the bag. 'These are his teeth.'

They did, indeed, appear to be teeth, together with a fair smattering of gum and blood and gunk.

As I looked at them, a low, pitiful groan came

from the room behind them.

'Is he in there?' I asked.

'No,' said Windy.

'He's in the Lagan. We have someone else in there. He used to run one of our companies, until he robbed us blind. Perhaps you've met him?'

I wasn't unduly surprised by how swiftly they had discovered that they had been betrayed, or by their response. They'd had a lot of years to hone their craft. The bag was tied neatly at the top. Windy swung it round once so that it landed in the palm of his hand. Hc squeezed it.

'You've some big fucking balls on you, Starkey,' said Rab.

'Thanks,' I said.

'Walking in here, facing us down, thinking that cunt down there can protect you.'

'You know,' said Windy, 'that right now he's face down on a snooker table with a cue up his arse.'

'That would appear to contravene the rules,' I said.

Windy shook his head. 'Have you even thought this through?' he asked. 'What's to stop us pulling all of *your* teeth out until you tell us where our gear is?'

'I thought I'd appeal to your sense of fair play and justice.'

'I was told you were a funny fucker,' snapped Rab.

'It's a widely held belief,' I said.

I think they were a little unsettled by my stupid grin. I have perfected the look over many years. It often makes people want to slap my face. It is not a grin that has anything to do with humour, or smugness; it is a default mechanism to hide the panic and the terror; the same mechanism often causes me to say stupid things. But sometimes, sometimes, it gives people pause for thought. They occasionally make the mistake of thinking that I am smarter than I look, or know something that they do not.

I picked at a fleck of dust on my trousers that an atomic scientist would have struggled to detect.

'Okay,' I said, 'let's be open about this. The reason I'm here is your threat to kill Bobby Murray, and your wish to interfere with his right to live a happy and peacefully hoody life here on the Shankill. I understand he owes you money, and some drugs. But really, you give a fourteen-year-old access, what do you expect. And besides—'

'Besides nothing, you fucking halfwit,' Rab snapped. 'Who do you think you're talking to?'

'Let him finish,' said Windy.

'Thank you, Windy,' I said.

'Don't call me Windy,' said Windy.

'And besides,' I continued, 'you killed his mother. That should be punishment enough.'

They just looked at me.

'What's your point, Starkey?' Rab asked.

'I have your money and I have your drugs; I'm told it's about two million worth. And yes, I'm sure you could make me tell you where it is. To tell you the truth, I usually scream the place down when I get a filling, but that's not really what this is about, is it?'

'Really?' said Windy.

'Really,' I said. 'Look, Windy, most of the time the folks on the hill don't give a fuck what you do up here, as long as you keep it local. They even turn a blind eye when you have your wee wars amongst yourselves. But when I publish the list of people you've been supplying with coke through Malone, the times, the places, the amounts, they will not tolerate that. That's attacking them in their own back patio. They won't be able to stop it getting out any more than you will, but it will give them the mandate to stop you, both of you, once and for all. Maybe you can blackmail the likes of Abagail Pike, but you can't blackmail them all. The moment I go viral with this, you won't last twenty-four hours; it'll make Wikileaks look like a bit of fucking street-corner gossip.'

Rab glanced at Windy. Windy kept his eyes on me.

'You've got it all figured out,' he said.

'Enough of it,' I said. 'Forgetting for the moment your admirable quest to protect us from the Republican hordes, I think at heart you're both just businessmen, and you can see the benefits of making a deal.'

'What kind of a deal?' Rab asked.

'You let Bobby Murray back on the Shankill, you lift all threats against him, his family and friends, and I hold off on releasing the info.'

'So we replace our threats with your threats?' Rab asked.

'Yes, if you like.'

'What about our cash, our gear?' asked Windy.

'Say I give it back to you in stages, once a month, as long as Bobby is okay.'

'Over what time period?'

'Say, six months.'

'And what happens at the end of six months, we have all our gear back? You delete the evidence?'

'Yes.'

'How would we ever be sure of that?'

'Your continued freedom would be the proof.'

'That would only be proof that you hadn't released it. So you would be expecting us to conduct our business under a constant threat?'

'You expect others to.'

Windy got up from the desk and came around to the front, and sat with half his arse on the corner opposite his brother. He folded his arms and said, 'We are the de facto leaders of the Ulster Volunteer Force. If we are beholden to you, that would make you the de facto leader of the Ulster Volunteer Force. That is impossible.'

'It's my final offer.'

'Your final offer!' Rab exploded, and launched himself off the desk, grabbing my jacket and then thrusting his fists into my chest, knocking the chair back on two legs. It teetered for a moment and then fell back. My head cracked off the wooden floor. As the stars sparkled, Rab stood over me and jabbed a finger down. 'Who the fuck do you think . . . ?'

He aimed a kick. The only reason it didn't land was because Windy pulled him back and it sailed inches wide. Rab struggled for a moment, but then relaxed as his brother whispered urgently in his ear.

I lay where I was until Windy stepped forward, reached down and grabbed my jacket. He pulled me up. The seat of my trousers stuck with sweat to the chair for a moment, before it fell back. He stood me up straight, released my jacket, and then patted the front of it, like he was a primary school teacher reassuring a fallen child.

'You'll have to forgive my brother,' he said. 'He's not used to being threatened.'

'You're forgiven,' I said.

This did not improve Rab's demeanour.

'We've heard your offer,' said Windy, 'and under the circumstances, it's not unreasonable. In the grand scheme of things, killing Bobby Murray is no longer that important to us.'

'Okay,' I said.

'But my brother and I will need to talk it through.'

'That's not unreasonable.'

'It is good for us that people believe we are ruthless, and vicious, and vengeful. And we can be. That is what we sell. But we aren't like that all the time. We are able to come to perfectly workable business agreements without recourse to threats or violence. Leave it with us, we'll let you know within twenty-four hours.'

I nodded. But I didn't move.

'*What?*' asked Rab. 'We're done here.'

'I was thinking of a goodwill gesture on your part.'

'*Our* part . . . ? Jesus!'

I nodded at the door in the wall behind them. 'Give me him. He didn't do anything wrong; he thought I was going to shoot him.'

'You?' Windy laughed. 'He gave it all away for nothing. And he's the reason you're here, dictating terms.'

'Nevertheless.'

He weighed it up for a few moments, then without reference to his brother, who was still glaring at me, crossed to the door and opened it halfway. He spoke to someone inside. I couldn't hear what he said. Then he pulled the door open a bit wider and stood back to allow the shuffling, stooped and mash-faced horror that was Derek

Beattie to stagger through. His white shirt was bright red in places, darker in others. His torture had clearly been lengthy and systematic. The former owner of Malone Security stopped, swayed, and sank to his knees. He let out a long, shivering groan and his head dropped to his chest, and huge sobs began to shake his entire body.

I moved beside him. I crouched down. 'It's okay Derek, it's all right.'

A slight movement behind him drew my eyes to the open door. At the far end of a spartan room with but one plastic chair, there was a man methodically washing blood from his hands in a sink. As I watched, he turned to lift a small towel off a handrail beside him, and I saw who it was, and knew immediately that far from the situation being resolved through a canny mix of brinksmanship and diplomacy, things were more than likely to go from bad to worse.

Drying his hands: Detective Inspector Springer.

44

Maxi was waiting at the bottom of the stairs. He did not seem unduly surprised to see me stagger into the vestibule supporting a blood-spattered and battered Derek Beattie. He came forward to help, and together we walked Derek along towards our car. As we passed the fenced-off patch of overgrown grass outside the church, I saw that the guy who had invited Maxi to play snooker was lying in there, on his back, with a hideous red weal across his face, and out for the count.

Maxi waited until we'd laid Derek across the back seat, then climbed into the front, before he looked at me and raised an eyebrow.

'Go well?'

'As can be expected. You?'

'We had a disagreement. It was resolved.'

I put my hand to my chest. My heart was thumping like billy-o.

'Thank fuck that's over,' I said. 'They want twenty-four hours to—'

Maxi held up his hand. 'I don't want to know. I've done what I can. The rest is up to you.'

'Okay. I appreciate that.'

He started the engine, indicated and pulled out. I glanced across at the church. Some of the Miller boys were trying to hoist their comrade out and over the fence, but without much success. It was like watching one of those crane games in an amusement arcade, endlessly frustrating but also ultimately disappointing when you realise that what you've won is completely worthless.

'I can drop him at the RVH,' said Maxi, nodding back, 'and you anywhere you want within reason. But I have to get to my party.'

'Wouldn't be the same without you,' I said.

We drove for a little bit in what would have been silence but for the whimpers from the back seat. Derek Beattie had lost half his teeth, his nose was broken, his fingers snapped back. But he was alive. I shuddered to think what state Paddy Barr must have been in before he was finally tossed into the Lagan.

And I was responsible for both of them. I had sent the photo of Paddy outside Jean Murray's burning home to DC Hood. Hood had shown it to his boss, DI Springer. Springer was either in the employ of the Miller brothers, or he had an interesting hobby.

'I know you don't want to hear this,' I said.

'Don't . . .'

'But you need to . . .'

'Just zip it.'

'. . . know what I saw in there.'

'I'm retired in about fifteen minutes.'

'It wasn't the Millers . . .'

'I'm not listening . . .'

'. . . who did this to him.'

He put one hand up to the closest ear and began to sing: 'Lalalalalalalalal . . .'

'They keep their hands clean . . . they employ someone else . . .'

'Lalalalalalalalala . . .'

'Someone to do their torturing, someone you know . . .'

'Lalalalalalalalala . . .'

'Detective Inspector Springer.'

Maxi threw the steering wheel to one side, forcing the car up and over the nearside kerb with a grind and a bump. The vehicle behind gave him a blast of the horn. He twisted round and gave it the fingers as it passed. Then he slapped the steering wheel.

'Fuck it, fuck it, fuck it and God damn fuck it!' He turned to me.

'No,' he said. 'No, no, no, no, no and fucking no.'

'Yes,' I said.

'*No*, I am absolutely not getting involved in this.'

'Springer's as dirty as they come.'

'I am *out*.'

'I think he murdered a guy called Paddy Barr,

282

and he's done Derek here and God knows what else or who else for them.'

'I don't *care*.'

'Yes you do.'

'I tell you I—'

'You didn't do thirty years on the front line because you didn't care.'

He waved a finger in my face. 'Don't you dare fucking give me that. I served my time. I did what was right. I can't be accountable for everything. There's always been fucking . . . fucking . . .'

'Collusion.'

'Whatever you want to call it, it was there when I joined, it'll be there long after I'm gone. You do your best, that's all you can do. And I've done it, and I'm moving on. Okay? All right?'

'Springer is killing people.'

'That's not my problem.'

'For the next ten minutes it is.'

'Then we'll wait here for the next ten minutes.'

He stared resolutely ahead.

Derek moaned. I motioned back to him. 'What about . . . ?'

'He'll keep.'

*   *   *

So we sat there until Maxi McDowell was no longer a cop.

He switched the radio on and tapped his fingers on the steering wheel along to some Radio Ulster country and western. The guy was singing about the rolling prairies and buffalo. He was from a time before the music got Shania Twained.

Maxi's shoulders were hunched up, his back

ramrod straight. He glanced across. 'This cottage in Cushendall,' he said. 'I pretend to the wife that it's not my thing, but it really is. It's in the shadow of Lurigethan Mountain, just right at the meeting point of three of the Glens of Antrim. When you look out the window, the Mull of Kintyre is there, about fifteen miles away. You know something, Dan? You breathe in the air, it's like heaven. The River Dall flows just past our place; that's where I'm going to do my fishing. I'm just going to stand there, in the water, cast my line, catch my fish, and let all of this wash off me, that's all I want to do. Do you understand?'

'Yes, of course.'

'Enough said, then.'

He glanced at his watch. He smiled. His shoulders settled down, the rigidity went out of his back. He started the engine again.

*   *   *

They took one look at Derek Beattie in Casualty and whisked him away to somewhere more serious. I gave the nurse behind the counter what he had in his wallet by way of ID, and said that was all I knew about him. I'd found him wandering on the Falls. She looked at me and said, 'I'll have to phone the police. Why don't you take a seat over there?'

We both knew I wasn't going to stay. She lifted the phone, and I lingered by the vending machine. When she glanced away, I slipped out.

I had already waved Maxi away. He was right, he'd done enough. It wasn't his problem. He was entitled to his quiet retirement. I quite fancied it myself, with the exception of the fishing. And the

284

fresh air, for that matter.

I stepped into a taxi and told the driver to take me back to my apartment. I was sore, exhausted, stressed. There was not one molecule of me that felt good about what had happened with the Millers even if, on the surface, it seemed to have gone well. They knew they weren't in a great position, and sacrificing their pursuit of Bobby for continued freedom to extort money and supply drugs, would not be much of a sacrifice. But they were still murderous gangsters used to getting their own way. When they clicked their fingers, terrible things happened.

Before I approached my apartment, I watched it for a while. When there did not appear to be any suspicious activity around it, I cautiously entered. When I got in, I found that I couldn't sit still.

I paced.

I phoned Trish and told her nothing of any substance; it was just good to hear her voice. It was not good enough for her just to hear mine. She pressed me for more details, and I gave her a few, but mostly I was evasive in a way that she did not guess I was being evasive. I wanted to ask about her car, and if the cash and drugs were safe, but there was no way to do it without arousing her suspicions. She was still in work. She had to go.

I paced some more.

I phoned Butcher Joe and asked how Bobby was getting on, and he said fine, he had the makings of a fine master butcher. I asked if there was some kind of butchers' college he could apply for, and Joe said he was already attending one.

I paced right out of the apartment and down the stairs and round the corner and pulled up a stool in the *Bob Shaw*. Lenny was working. She got me a drink but stayed mostly at the end of the bar. When she did come up and I tried to say something, she said, 'I'm married.'

I nodded, and asked for some nuts.

She got me my nuts.

A woman came in I vaguely remembered from my time on the *Telegraph*. She was with two other reporters of a more recent generation. I bought her a drink. The other two kept to themselves and we got close. When I asked a different barman for drinks, Lenny brought them over and slapped them down hard enough to spill.

'Sorry,' she said, without conviction.

My companion said, 'Charming.'

'Can't get the staff these days,' I said, loud enough.

The woman left, I sat on for a while. Lenny lurked in the kitchen. I finished my pint and stepped outside. I took a breath of fresh air and started walking. I kept looking over my shoulder. When I got home, I investigated the notion of a mid-afternoon doze, and found it pleasing. It took me a while to realise that the bell-like sound I was hearing in my dream was in fact a bell sound.

Lacking a spyhole, I moved to one side of the door and said, 'Who is it?'

'Me.'

I recognised Lenny's voice.

'Are you being held out there against your will?'

She said, 'Yes, I want to come in.'

'I mean, are you alone?'

'Of course.'

There was no way of knowing. I opened the door.

'Sorry,' she said, 'he's having me watched.'

'And now?'

'I went into the beauty parlour on the corner, and out the back.'

'Devious,' I said.

45

Love in the afternoon. Or, at least, lust.

Later she said, 'You're distracted.'

'I am.'

'A problem shared is a problem halved.'

'No, then you just have two people with problems.'

I was quoting the master. Or the mistress. No, wait, Lenny was the mistress. I was confusing myself.

'Is it to do with me?'

'No.'

She grew silent. She was probably miffed that it wasn't about her. I pulled her closer and kissed the top of her head. That seemed to settle her. Women can be gloriously complicated, and astonishingly simple. I wished to dear God that she was my problem, but she wasn't. All we had together was what we had together there and then: between the sheets. I was using her for sex. My heart lay elsewhere. She was using me for sex also, though I suspected I was getting the better part of the deal. If there had genuinely been anything between us, then I would have cared a tad more about the fact that she still shared a bed with her husband. It would annoy me to the point of wanting to mess up his world. Meanwhile the tiniest indication that

Patricia might be with someone else was enough to ruin my day, and year, and life. Whatever you cared to call my new profession, at least part of the reason why I had only had one client and had not actually sought out any work was that I spent an inordinate amount of time worrying about what Patricia was up to, and with whom. I am in love with her, and always have been. I spend half of my life screwing up our relationship and the other half trying to fix it. My greatest fear is that one day she will finally, *finally*, have had enough of me.

Lenny left around six. I lay on in bed for a little bit, with a late-afternoon sunshine coming through the thin white curtains and across the bed, providing a tantalising hint of a summer that would probably never come. I showered and dressed, and sat out on the veranda with a Bush and thumbed through Derek Beattie's phone again. I pondered. I watched young people pass through the square below on their way to some event in the MAC. I wondered what the Millers were up to. I had a flash of Springer at the sink washing blood off his hands. Maxi was right: there had always been corruption and collusion, but this was something beyond merely palming an envelope stuffed with cash or turning a blind eye. He was a killer other killers brought in to do the stuff even they couldn't bring themselves to do. They might not murder me because of what they believed would be released if I died; but that would not prevent them hurting those who were closest to me.

I phoned Trish.

'You okay?' I asked.

'Sure. Just making dinner. You want some?'

'Okay.'

We agreed on half an hour.

I phoned Lenny.

'You okay?' I asked.

'Back to work,' she said.

'Nobody followed you?'

'Nope, not that I noticed. I fooled them.'

'Okay. Good.'

'But thank you for caring. Lovebug.'

I pretended not to hear. When I finished with Lenny, I glanced at my watch, and then phoned Neville Maxwell.

He said, 'Dan, I'm just heading out to the Lyric.'

'My commiserations, and I'll only be a minute. Professor Pike, do you have a direct number for him? And I don't mean one that just bypasses the switchboard. I mean his mobile number, or one he's liable to pick up himself.'

'Yes, of course. Anything you want to tell me?'

'I have information that may bring down the government and plunge us into a bloody civil war. You know, the usual.'

Maxwell let out a low gurgle of a laugh. 'Ah, Dan, you can't live on past glories for ever, you know.'

'Bear that in mind,' I said. He gave me the number. I called it immediately. I find it's best to do things, to say things, to act on things, right away. If you pause to think about what you're doing, usually you end up not doing it. I plunged right in when he answered on the third ring. 'This is Dan Starkey. I have information that may bring down the government and plunge us all into a bloody civil war.'

Professor Pike cleared his throat. 'Dan who?' he asked.

'Starkey. I met you the other day at Stormont, with Neville Maxwell.'

'Oh . . . yes,' he said. 'What's that you're saying about . . . ?'

'Just trying to get your attention, Professor. Do you prefer Professor, or Mister, or Minister, or first-name terms?'

'It depends on who I'm speaking to, and why. Is this government business, or Assembly, or private, or . . . ?'

'This time it's personal,' I said.

He paused for a moment and then said, 'You can call me Professor. Incidentally, how did you get this number?'

'Ah, now,' I said.

He said, 'Listen, Dan, I'm just sitting down for dinner, and I make a point of trying to protect family time, it's rare enough. So what can I do for you?'

'Well, Peter, it has to do with the Miller brothers buying influence in the Assembly, mostly through the blackmail of your wife.'

'*My* . . . ? Hold on one second.' He must have held the phone against his chest, because the sound became muffled. I could just about make out him saying: 'Darling, I'm just going to take this in the other room.'

A few moments later I heard a door close, the squeak of someone sitting down in a leather chair and then a colder, harder voice, but still the Professor's, saying: 'Now just you listen to me. I don't know how you got this number or what it is you're after, but I am a government minister, I can make so much trouble for you that—'

'Cut the crap, Pete.'

Pause for intake of breath.

'How *dare* . . .!'

'Threepio, I hear you, and I say bollocks. And also I say: shut your fucking mouth and listen to me, because I can bring you both down in a fucking instant.' Silence. 'Now, you know exactly who I am, I wrote enough about you back in the day. I believe in your youth you even had a real actual cross burnt on my front lawn. But we've all grown up a lot since then. So listen to me. You may know none of this or all of this, I don't really care, it's how you react that matters to me. Your wife is being blackmailed by the Millers. She has a cocaine habit. She owes them a fortune. Until now she's been paying the interest by influencing you and the rest of your cronies in the Assembly to go easy on or give a helping hand to the Millers' many and varied business interests. But God love her, she's trying to pay it off, that's why she's building that house in your back yard.'

'You . . . you . . . you . . . Is this some kind of a sick joke?'

'Yes.'

'What?'

'No, of course it isn't. Professor, your wife's a cokehead, what do you say?'

'My, my, my . . . *wife* . . .'

'Takes it up the nose, yes. Professor, I have it all documented and ready for release to the media tomorrow. People will *love* this.'

There was a long pause. And then: 'Unless, Mr Starkey?'

'That's more like it,' I said.

I told him what I wanted.

He listened patiently. At the end of it he said, his voice now back to its confident best: 'It strikes me, Mr Starkey, that if anyone is doing any blackmailing, then it is you. You are the one now seeking to control the actions and policies of not only a government minister, but the entire government itself.'

It was a fair point. In one day I'd gone from being a private eye in denial, with no customers, to de facto brigadier general of the Ulster Volunteer Force and now the unelected leader of the Northern Ireland Assembly. You could get used to power. Power corrupts, but absolute power must be wonderful.

I said, 'Dress it up how you like, Professor, but at the end of the day, all I'm trying to do is save a boy's life.'

'Mr Starkey, I have worked all my life for this country, one way or another. I have always felt that the Good Lord was at my side, guiding me. When I made mistakes, He forgave me and pointed me in the right direction. I am ashamed of nothing in my past. But times change, and the concerns that most agitate a young man do not seem so pressing in middle age. I am in a better place now, and I believe that is reflected in the respect I command for the work that I do. Politics is all about compromise, but perhaps we have compromised too much. Much as I hate to say it, this may be just exactly what we've needed, a wake-up call. Noon tomorrow, you say? Mr Starkey?' He cleared his throat. 'Mr Starkey?'

'Sorry, I drifted off during your speech. Yes— noon tomorrow will do nicely.'

He let out the smallest, saddest laugh. 'Noon,' he repeated. 'By God, Starkey, if he's not even your kin, this Bobby Murray must be some special boy.'

'You would think that,' I said, 'but actually, he's a bit of a shit.'

46

Patricia was at the kitchen table, having dinner with Bobby. She said, 'You're late.'

'I've been busy saving Ulster.'

I took a seat. I nodded at the boy. 'Good day?' He shrugged. 'How's Joe?'

'All right.'

Trish got up and pushed the timer on the microwave. While she waited, she came up behind me and put her hands on my shoulders and kissed the top of my head. Then she said: 'You've washed your hair.'

'Yes, I have.'

'I mean, very recently.'

'Yes, indeed I have.'

'You never do that.'

'I thought I'd have a shower before I came to see you. Is that a crime?'

Her eyes narrowed. The microwave pinged. She turned to get my food. As she set the plate down before me, Bobby said, 'Did you speak to the Millers?'

'Yes. I told Patricia. Didn't you tell him?'

'I told him,' said Trish.

'I want to hear it from you. She hardly said anything.'

'I'm not *she*,' said Trish.

'There's nothing to tell,' I said. 'We had a full and frank exchange of views. We're working something out.'

'For definite?'

'I'll know tomorrow.'

'What are they like?'

'You've never met them?' Bobby shook his head. 'Depressingly ordinary. But all the scarier for it.'

'You were scared?'

'Apprehensive.'

'When can I go home?'

'Bobby, I'm not sure that *home* home is an option. One of your relatives, maybe.'

'Okay.' He nodded to himself. 'Uncle Sidney. He's less of a dick than the others. I'll maybe see him at the funeral.'

My eyes darted to Trish, and he noticed it.

'What?'

'Nothing,' I said.

'It's something. I'm going. They can't stop me going to my own mother's funeral. You can't either. I don't give a fuck who sees me. They wouldn't dare try anything there. I'm going. I'm bloody *going*.'

'*Bobby*,' said Trish.

'If I have to go in disguise or something, then I can do that. Just get me there. When is it?'

'Yesterday,' I said.

He looked absolutely stunned.

'You're fuckin' jokin'.'

'No,' I said.

'It wasn't safe for you to go,' said Trish. 'Bobby . . .' She put her hand on his. He jerked it away and jumped up. His chair toppled backwards.

'Are you fuckin' serious?'

'Bobby,' said Trish, 'please, calm down. I know it's heartbreaking, but it just wasn't an option.'

'*It just wasn't an option*,' he mimicked. 'Do you

294

think I care about that? I shoulda fuckin' been there!'

'I know that, son, but—'

'I'm not your fuckin' son! How could you do that to me? I'm sitting here playin' fuckin Xbox and they're stickin' my ma in the ground?'

'Cremated,' I said.

'Jesus Christ!'

'We didn't hear till late on, Bobby,' I said. 'Remember, nobody knows where you are.'

'I should have been there!'

'Bobby,' I said, 'they didn't want you there.'

'What the fuck are you talking about?'

He looked mad, and cornered, and distraught, all in one.

'It wasn't just about keeping *you* safe,' said Patricia. 'It was your relatives. They were concerned for their own safety.'

His eyes squeezed up. 'No, they . . .'

'Bobby,' I said, 'the Millers would have had people there watching for you; if you'd shown, there could have been a bloodbath. They thought it better . . .'

'It was *my mum*!'

Trish reached down and righted the chair. 'Please.'

He stared at it. He was trying desperately hard not to cry.

'I should have been there,' he said.

'Yes, you should,' said Trish. 'And maybe after this all dies down, you can have another service. In the meantime, we'll get the ashes; perhaps we can go and scatter them somewhere.'

'Yes,' I said. 'Anywhere you want, apart from the Shankill.'

She gave me a look.

Bobby was shaking his head. Trish tried to reach out to him again, but he brushed her away and started for the door.

'Bobby, please . . . where are you going?' Trish asked.

'What the fuck do you care? You two? Youse are both just a bunch of fuckers.'

He clumped up the stairs. A few moments later he slammed his bedroom door.

Trish said: 'He may have a point.'

*   *   *

She got us drinks.

She said, 'I could only tell him what you told me, but he's right, that wasn't the half of it, was it? What else happened today?'

'Trish, I'm not like you, I can't remember every word of every conversation I've ever had. I gave you the concise version because that's all I retain.'

I hadn't told her about Paddy Barr, or Derek Beattie, or DI Springer and the teeth, I hadn't mentioned that Maxi was no longer protecting me or that I was now leader of the UVF and held sway over our government. There was no need to trouble her with such detail. It didn't matter anyway, because she had bigger fish to fry.

'Who is she?'

'Who is who?'

'The woman you have showers for in the afternoon.'

'That would be you.'

'Let me rephrase. Who is the woman you have sex with in the afternoon, so that you then have to have a shower to wash her fucking smell off you before you come to see me.'

'Trish, for fucksake, take a wild leap in the dark there.'

'Bobby told me there was a woman in your flat.'

'Did he really? I thought he was against squealers?'

'Who is she, Dan?'

'*She* is the manager of the apartment block. *She* came round because someone's been throwing pizza on to my veranda every night and I put a complaint in. Okay? All right? Am I not allowed to even talk to other women now?'

'Are you sleeping with her, Dan?'

'No, Jesus! How's that ever going to win you back?'

'Is that what you're trying to do, win me back?'

'Yes! Isn't it obvious?'

'Not really, no.'

'Aw, Trish.'

I moved closer. I opened my arms. She hesitated, and then stepped into them.

Her head rested against my chest. She said, 'This is all going to work out, with Bobby, isn't it?'

'Of course it is.'

'You wouldn't just say that to make me feel better, would you?'

'Of course I would.'

The shake of her shoulders told me she was laughing. She put a fist against my chest, right by her nose, and pushed a knuckle into me.

'We keep doing this, over, and over, and over again; it's like a roundabout we can't get off.'

'A magic roundabout,' I said.

Years ago we used to have what we called a

magic settee, because every time we sat on it we ended up making love. It had been reupholstered several times since, and finally thrown out as a potential fire hazard.

'If you say time for bed, Florence, you're getting a friggin' diggin',' she purred.

I stroked her hair with the back of my hand. I had taken the thick bandage off before my shower. I was, effectively, rubbing a soft scab up and down her locks.

'Now that you mention it . . .'

47

Obviously that didn't work. It *might* have if Bobby— miraculously recovered from his explosive upset over missing his mother's funeral—hadn't come downstairs to get a snack from the fridge, causing Trish to push me away so that we weren't caught in a compromising position. It might even have worked if she had managed to smother her suspicions about Lenny for a few moments longer, but she couldn't resist another poke, asking Bobby as he passed between us, a doughnut in each hand, if Lenny had acted anything remotely like an apartment block manager on her visit, and he'd just smirked and that was enough to send her flying off the handle and me out of the front door shouting abuse back at her.

A few days before, in the absence of anything as unlikely as a customer, I had been concentrating on my attempt to watch every single music video on YouTube when I came across a single by Jack Jones from the sixties called 'Wives and Lovers', which was so perfect for its time, and so perfectly out of step with our own. Its lyrics suggested that women should remember that just because they're married they shouldn't forget to wear make-up, that they should run into your arms when you come home from work, and that they should most definitely never send you off to work with their hair still in curlers, because you might never come home. For some inexplicable reason, the words came back to me as I stood screaming at her.

She was yelling something along the lines of me being a two-faced fuck-face, and I counter-attacked with, 'You should be fucking grateful for me coming round! And at least I wash my fucking hair!'

'What's that supposed to mean?'

'Whatever you want, but at least I make the effort! I don't remember you ever standing at the door with your make-up on and your arms open wide waiting for me! You never did that! Too much trouble! And you haven't even the wherewithal to make me a fucking rissole!'

I was kind of paraphrasing.

I stormed off, leaving her at least as perplexed as I was.

*   *   *

I sauntered through the dusk, quietly grateful that she'd picked the fight, because at least for a little while it shifted my focus off the Millers and what they might be up to, off Pike and whether he could be trusted, and squarely on Patricia and our marriage.

I returned to the *Bob Shaw*. I supped, sitting at a table, back to the wall, watching for trouble. Lenny

299

wasn't working, and it was a relief. I returned to the apartment pleasantly inebriated and went on to the veranda with a Bush and a couple of slices of reheated pizza. I wasn't hungry. I was lying in wait for my phantom attacker. He was going to get the surprise of his life. However, by two a.m., I'd eaten my ammunition. By three, I was asleep. At a quarter past, I was woken by a slice of Hawaiian frisbeeing out of the darkness to wrap itself around my face. I was on my feet *instantly*, but there was only hurried footsteps and laughter.

I retired to bed, but lay awake for a *long* time, plotting revenge.

*   *   *

In the morning, I showered first and then had a banana for breakfast. When you live by yourself, sometimes it's whatever takes the least effort. I was dressed by eight and out the door. First open shop I came to, I purchased a coffee and a box of Jaffa Cakes. A banana will only get you so far. As I continued to the office, I called Trish.

'Sorry about last night,' I said. 'It's just . . . everything.'

'I know. I'm sorry too. But one thing . . . ?'

'Yep.'

'Where the fuck did *rissoles* come from?'

'I honestly don't know. I don't even like them.'

'I think you're starting to lose the plot, Dan.'

'Honey, I could do with a little less plot.'

She said, 'It'll be fine.'

'Can I have that in writing?' I said. 'How is he this morning?'

'Sullen. He's going to have to start walking to

work; these early starts are killing me.'

I came to a junction. I stopped, waiting for the green man. 'You sound like he might be there for a while longer.'

She sighed. 'No, just until, you know.'

'Convincing.'

'He hardly says a word, and he's as moody as hell, but . . . there's something about him. Something in there.'

'Potential.'

'Aye. Maybe. He's smart, y'know? You can see it in his eyes. Do you ever notice that in people? There's a kind of brightness in the eyes of people who have a bit of wit about them. Does that make sense, or am I talking shite?'

'No, I know what you mean. I see it in the mirror every morning.'

'Yeah, you wish.' She hesitated. 'Sometimes I think . . . you know . . . ?'

'Our boy might have been like him.'

The lights changed. I crossed over.

'Is it wrong to think that?'

'No, it's natural. They're about the same age.'

'Sometimes I think they look a bit the same.'

'Yeah, I can see that.'

'I wonder all the time about how he would have turned out.'

'I know.'

'He'd have been just like you.'

'He had none of me in him.'

'It's nurture, Dan, not nature. He was a little you. Youse laughed together so much.'

'Aye, well.'

'And he sulked when he didn't get his own way. He was inconsolable whenever you left. I went out, he never noticed. You, he cried the place down. I miss him so much.'

'I know you do.'

'But I don't want to project *that* . . . on to Bobby.'

'You're not. You know what's real and what's not. There's not a problem with him staying longer as far as I'm concerned.'

'Really?'

'Really. Anyway, his family sound like a bunch of chickens. I think he'd be miles better off with you.'

'Well, it's just a mad thought. Nothing will come of it.'

'Let's see how this all plays out.'

'Yeah, yeah. You're right. Fingers crossed for you, anyway, today. You're very brave, my Dan, confronting bastards like that.'

'It's not bravery, it's foolishness.'

'Is that not what I said?'

I smiled. I told her I'd phone her as soon as I heard anything, and cut the line. It was a pleasant morning for walking. Having a good conversation with Trish always cheered me up.

Five minutes later, just as I neared the office, a Romanian approached.

'*Big Issue*?' she asked.

'Fuck off,' I replied.

The shutters were up on Joe's, but the meat hadn't yet made it to the trays in the window, and the front door was still closed. They were probably slicing and dicing out back. I placed the Jaffa box against my throat and jammed it there with my chin while I felt in my pockets for the keys. As I did, I glanced around at a bunch of kids in Methodist College uniforms gathered around something on the pavement that I couldn't quite see but which they evidently found hilarious. I located the keys and slipped the correct one into the lock. There was a mechanical wheeze from behind and I turned to see an Ulsterbus: its doors were open and the kids were hurrying towards it. Just as I turned the key and opened the door, my eyes fell on what they had been gathered around.

A leg.

A false leg.

Standing erect.

All by its lonesome.

Exccpt for a wire, leading away from it.

And in that very moment of jarring recognition, a huge force lifted me off my feet and hurled me into the air, and for what seemed like an eternity I was looking down on Belfast from above, at the traffic, and the smoke, and the flames, and glass, and the charging pedestrians, and I was wondering how come I was flying, and who'd turned the sound down and what had happened to the Jaffa Cakes, and I had the distinct impression that something wasn't quite right.

48

White sheets. Bed. Nurse. Hospital. Ringing. Ringing. Ear bleeding. Rain beating against the window, branches swaying in the wind.

'You have a perforated eardrum,' the nurse said.

'What?'

'You have a perforated eardrum.'

'What?'

'You have . . .'

She stopped. 'I'm glad to see you have retained your sense of—'

'What?'

'I'm glad . . .' She stopped. 'How are you feel—'

'What . . . ?'

'He can be very annoying.'

My eyes flitted left. Patricia was sitting there. Tear-stained. She sounded like she was about twenty miles away.

'I think I may have a perforated ear drum,' I said.

'Yes,' said Patricia, 'and three broken ribs, and concussion and some minor burns. The doctor said it was a miracle you weren't killed.'

'What?'

She looked at me.

The nurse said, 'He's disorientated, and the sedative, and the morphine for the pain . . . Will I tell them he's awake?'

Trish said, 'The police are waiting outside to interview you.'

My head felt like it was filled with cement. I said, 'Is the other guy okay?'

'What other guy?'

'In the other car.'

'What other car?'

I looked at her. 'The car I crashed into. I'm sorry about the drugs and the money, did it go everywhere?'

'Dan. It was a bomb. Or an IED, as they call it these days.'

'A bomb?'

'Bomb.'

'A *bomb* bomb? Oh yes. Now I remember. It was the IRA. Oh no, they're gone. It was the Diffident IRA, although they're too shy to claim

304

responsibility.'

'Dan . . .'

'No, in fact it was the Surreal IRA, though I'm surprised, they're usually all over the place . . .'

'Dan!'

I looked at her. 'What?'

'How are you feeling?'

'Fine,' I said.

I had not yet moved my head off the pillow. I tried.

And I wouldn't try that again in a hurry. Everything swam and I almost threw up.

The nurse said, 'Easy there.'

'You're lucky to be alive,' said Trish.

'A miracle,' said the nurse. 'You're lucky she was there.'

'Who was where?'

'You swallowed your tongue, nearly choked to death. Lucky there was a Romanian woman, gave you the kiss of life, got you into the recovery position.' She looked at Trish. 'So will I tell Detective Constable Hood it's okay to come in?'

'No,' I said.

'No?' said Trish. 'But—'

'No.'

There was a jug of water on the locker beside me. I tried to reach for it and nearly fell out of bed. The nurse came to my rescue. She poured, and held it up to my lips. I sipped greedily. She smelled of mandarin oranges and Dettol.

She said, 'The police officer is very keen to—'

'No.'

'All right, dearie, have it your way.' She set the cup down and turned for the door. When she opened it, I caught a glimpse of Hood, sitting on a chair against the corridor wall. He started to get up. The nurse closed the door behind her.

I closed my eyes. Trying to remember.

I said, 'Are they okay?'

'They?'

'I had Jaffa Cakes.'

'Dan . . .'

Coffee. Jaffa Cakes. *Big Issue*. School kids.

Leg.

I sat up again.

'Bobby?'

'He's gone . . .'

'Gone . . . What . . . ?'

'They took him . . .'

Dizzy. I slumped back down. It was flooding back. I held on to the side of the bed to stop it tipping up. I let go and waited for it to settle. I pinched my nose and closed my eyes and took big gulps of air in through my mouth. The Millers. They were not supposed to be able to do that. That wasn't the deal I had struck with Pike. He was supposed to have them arrested in the early hours of the morning. He was supposed to announce a new crackdown on organised crime and that the Millers were in custody and would be charged with terrorism, drug trafficking, murder, membership of a proscribed organisation and playing music in public without the proper licence. As part of the investigation, a number of police officers would also be arrested and charged with blackmail, extortion, murder and other offences related to collusion with paramilitaries.

But evidently not.

I suppose it did not surprise me.

Of course, I knew better than to put all my eggs

306

in one basket. I had a Plan B. I knew I had a Plan B. I was reasonably sure I had a Plan B. I just could not, at that moment, with my eggs scrambled, remember exactly or even vaguely what it was.

'Joe . . .' I said. 'What about . . . ?'

'He's down the corridor,' said Trish. 'Broke his jaw, knocked him out, fire bridgade found him just in time, the whole building has gone up.'

'My office?'

'Yep,' said Trish.

'The police know about Bobby?'

'Yes, of course, they're looking for him.'

'Him . . . out there?'

'Yes . . .'

I shook my head. I glanced at my watch. The face was cracked.

'What time is it?'

'What? Oh—three o'clock.'

'*Three?*'

'You were unconscious for . . .'

'It doesn't matter.'

I rubbed at my jaw. My teeth felt like they'd been yanked out, and then smacked back in with a toffee hammer.

The Millers had Bobby. On past form they would torture him until they learned the whereabouts of their missing cash and drugs, and then they would kill him. They were fearless. They had completely ignored my threat to release the evidence against them virally. The only reason I was alive was that traditionally Loyalist paramilitaries are a bit shite at making bombs.

There were raised voices in the corridor.

The door opened and Maxi was standing there, grim.

I managed a smile and said, 'Don't worry, I'm harder to kill than they think.'

But then I saw that he had blood on his shirt, and smudges of black on his face and hands. Hood was behind him, white-faced.

'Maxi?'

His voice was gravel-dry.

'They killed my wife,' he said.

49

Maxi sat crumpled in the chair by my bed, and he cried, and he cried, and he cried. He was a big man, hard but fair, and as far as I knew, he had spent a lifetime keeping his emotions in check. But now here he was, distraught. It was just plain wrong, like watching John Wayne having a breakdown. Trish had never met him, and knew little about him, but she still sat on the arm of his chair and put her arm around him and he cried even more, against her; and I lay there in bed, knowing, yet again, that I was the reason his wife was dead and his retirement home burned to a crisp. I had drawn him in and the Millers had punished him for it.

Hood stood awkwardly by the door. He said, 'I don't know what the hell is going on.'

And in an extraordinarily fluid movement, Maxi leapt from his chair and grabbed Hood by the throat and began to crack his head back against the door frame. With each bang he spat out:

'Ask . . . your . . . pal . . . Springer!'

'Please . . . *stop*.' Trish had a hand on his arm. Maxi's purple face turned to her, and he seemed to struggle to place her, and then he slowly nodded and let go of his former colleague, and Hood slid down, clawing at his throat and gasping for breath. There was blood on the door frame. Maxi backed away towards his chair. He tripped on the leg of the bed and stumbled and fell back on to the seat. Trish looked at me helplessly as he buried his head in his hands.

'I don't . . . understand,' Hood rasped. 'We'll be all over this. Why would Springer . . . ?'

Before, he had been full of the swagger of a young cop on the make, but I could now see the confused kid in him. He had had two mentors in Comanche Station—now one was in bits in front of him, the other was teetering on his pedestal.

Hood felt the back of his head, then examined the blood on his hand. Maxi saw it and wiped his sleeve across his own face. He shook his head.

'My wife, my girl . . .' he said. 'She was . . . unrecognisable.'

Trish stroked the top of his head. It was a soothing motion, but she said, 'Bastards.'

'I didn't know,' said Hood. 'I've heard nothing. I'm sorry, Maxi.'

Maxi let out a long, miserable groan. 'I drove up last night to surprise her,' he said, 'but they beat me to her. I was at my farewell party all afternoon; all the time youse were clapping and wishing me the best, and I was telling you all about my perfect wee cottage up the coast, someone was passing it on. Someone like Springer.'

Hood was shaking his head in disbelief. 'How do you know it was him?'

'Because he works for the Millers,' I said. 'He's their enforcer.'

'They shot her in the legs,' said Maxi. 'She couldn't move. Then they set fire to the cottage. The neighbours, they wouldn't let me near, but I could hear her, hear her screaming . . .'

'Jesus,' said Trish.

There was a knock on the door. Hood turned, raising his hand to stop whoever was coming in, but he was too late. It was Joe, a bandage on his head, the lower half of his jaw badly swollen.

'Sorry, mate . . .' Hood started.

'It's okay,' I said. Hood gave me and him a doubtful look each, but stood aside. 'Hi, Joe. How're you doing?'

'Okay.' His eyes met Maxi's.

'Hey, Joe,' said Maxi. 'Long time.'

'Sorry for your loss,' said Joe. When he spoke, his lips barely moved; and even that caused him to grimace.

Maxi nodded. He rubbed at his face as Joe came fully into the room and closed the door behind him.

'How do you two . . . ?' I asked.

'I told you where I'm from,' said Joe. 'It was Sergeant McDowell who put me inside, way back when.'

'Aye,' said Maxi, 'you were a hard wee nut.'

'Best thing that ever happened to me. They said down the hall what happened. I put two and two together.'

'Was it the Millers did you too?' Maxi asked, indicating his jaw.

'Some of their boys, aye.' Joe nodded at me. 'There was nothing I could do, I'm sorry. I was out at the wholesaler's early; when I came back, they were dragging Bobby out the door, jumped me before I could do anything. I was out for the count when the bomb went off, some fireman dragged me clear. Shop destroyed, my home gone, and my apprentice stolen. They just can't do that.'

Maxi was staring at the ground, but nodding in agreement.

'There has to be someone we can call,' said Trish. 'Someone who can save him.'

'There's no one,' I said. 'No one we can trust.'

'Of course there is,' said Hood. 'My God, we get back to the station, we get warrants . . . we go after them . . .'

'You think they're going to give you your head?' Maxi spat. 'They won't move against the Millers unless it comes down from on high. By the time they manage that, *if* they manage that, it'll be too late for the boy. He'll be floating gutted in the Lagan with the rest of them.'

'I know for a fact the government won't do anything,' I said.

It was clear in my head now. The Pikes as a couple were both under the sway of the Millers. The Millers could do whatever the hell they liked.

'We can't just leave him,' said Trish.

'No,' said Maxi.

'No,' said Joe.

It sat in the air. Eyes met, flitted.

'You get your hands on anything?' Joe asked.

'Sure,' said Maxi. 'You?'

'Our boys who did the decommissioning kept a few to one side for emergencies. I haven't been involved for years, but I've enough mates who are.'

'Wise,' said Maxi. 'They'll lend?'

'Sure. They've no love for the Millers.'

'This is all my fault,' I said.

They all looked at me.

311

'There's a first,' said Trish.

'It's not your fault,' said Maxi. 'That's like blaming an X-ray for the fact that you have a tumour. You've just drawn attention to the bleeding obvious. We have to cut the tumour out.'

'Cutting is my field of expertise,' said Joe.

'I know a thing or two about it myself,' said Maxi.

'At the risk of stating the bleeding obvious,' I said, 'are we talking about what I think we're talking about?'

Joe nodded at Maxi. Maxi nodded at me.

'If you want him back alive,' said Joe, 'it's the only way.'

'I'm going that way anyway,' said Maxi.

'I have to go with you,' I said.

'No you don't,' said Trish. 'But you will.'

'You'd be better off waiting here,' said Maxi.

'No,' I said.

'You've just been blown up,' said Joe.

'I'm going,' I said. 'I have my own gun and everything.'

Maxi looked to Joe. Joe shrugged. 'Well if you have your own gun . . .'

It even coaxed a smile out of Maxi.

'I just need to go and get it,' I said.

Patricia said: 'Right. Where is it? I'll drive you.'

'It's in your car,' I said.

'My . . . ?' She took a deep breath. 'Why am I not surprised?'

I threw back the blankets and moved my legs round. Patricia helped me up. I groaned. Things swam.

'I'm fine,' I said.

'You must be. When you get a sore throat, you're usually in bed for months.'

Maxi pushed himself up from his chair. Joe turned and put his hand on the doorknob, but he couldn't open it without Hood shifting. Hood had no intention of it.

'Just . . . just hold on to your horses there,' he said, looking around us. 'Youse can't be serious.'

'Move it,' said Joe. 'We're going to get the boy.'

'I can't allow it,' said Hood.

'You're not in a position to stop it,' said Joe.

Hood looked at Maxi. 'You . . . *can't* . . . You're one of us.'

'I was, I'm not now. And even if I was, with what's been going on, it's not a boast I'd care to make. Now get out of the way.'

'No . . . Maxi . . . Sergeant McDowell . . . listen to me. It's just . . . madness. Man, you're the cop everyone looks up to; don't throw that away. I'm sorry about your wife, it's a horrible, terrible thing, but they've gone too far now, you know we always get them when it's one of our own.'

'Well it shouldn't have to be,' said Maxi.

Hood drew himself up. He puffed his chest out, what there was of it. 'If you're knowingly going to commit an act of violence,' he said, 'then I'm going to place you under arrest for your own protection. It's nothing more than you've taught me to do.'

'Just move, son,' said Maxi.

'No.'

Hood was tall, but skinny as a rake. He had planted his feet at the optimum distance apart to give him both leverage and a base from which to resist an attack. He was armed, and could have gone for it. He chose not to.

Joe looked him up and down, and nodded admiringly. 'You've got balls, kid, I'll give you that.

But you should protect them at all times.'

'Excuse me?'

By way of response, Joe punched straight down, smacking Hood full in the groin, and he went down *instantly*.

In my head I was thinking: *this time all bets are off*.

50

I was doing a lot of groaning. I couldn't help it. Every time the car went over a speed bump, it was like getting a punch to my broken ribs. And Belfast is obsessed with speed bumps. The fresh air had cleared my head enough to be wondering how sore I would be feeling if I hadn't been shot full of morphine.

Trish drove, Joe was beside her, I was in the back. Maxi had gone off to retrieve his weapon. Hood was handcuffed to a radiator back in the hospital, with surgical tape over his mouth and, courtesy of our friendly neighbourhood nurse, an injection of something that had been intended to help me sleep in his arse. There was a hospital equivalent of a *Do not disturb* sign on the door.

Every time I moaned, Joe glanced back at me and rolled his eyes.

'A couple of broken ribs,' he said. 'You don't hear me complaining.'

'It's sore. I don't think they even X-rayed me. I probably have internal bleeding and ruptured kidneys.'

'You're fine,' said Joe.

'And you would know?'

'I'm a butcher. I know more about anatomy than any six trauma teams combined.'

'Yeah, *cow* anatomy. And dead ones at that.'

'They did X-ray you,' said Trish. She looked at Joe. 'Is this it?'

'Aye,' said Joe, 'pull up there on the left.'

We were just off the Shankill, on Crimea Street. Joe got out, then leaned back in and said he would only be a minute. He went up to a front door and knocked. It opened, and he disappeared inside. Trish glanced back at me.

'I'm scared.'

'I'll be fine.'

'For Bobby.'

She reached back and put her hand on my leg. I had the revolver resting in my hand on the other leg. I had managed to retrieve it from the glove compartment. The money and the drugs were still snug in the boot. As bargaining tools, they had proved worthless. When this was all over, I would have to find a charity to donate the money to. Or maybe charity would begin at home. I wasn't sure what to do with the coke. I could distribute it to the homeless. It wouldn't put a roof over their heads, but they probably wouldn't give a shit.

'I know you want to do this,' said Patricia, 'and I know in your head you blame yourself and you probably think you're the brains of this bunch, but if you've any sense left in you at all, you'll lead from the rear.'

'That was always my intention.'

'Good.' She stroked my leg. 'We've seen all shades of shit together, Dan Starkey, haven't we?'

'We have.'

'But no one has ever described you as a man of action.'

'Inaction is how I prefer it.'

'I know. It's how I like you.'

'It's how you love me.'

'Don't push it.'

She smiled. I put my hand over hers and squeezed gently.

'Trish. Don't get your hopes up. We'll do our best, but he might already—'

'*Don't*. This glass is half full.'

'Okay. Absolutely.'

The passenger door opened and Joe got in. He was carrying a Nike sports bag.

'It's always good to have a sponsor,' I said.

Joe ignored me. 'Let's go,' he said.

*   *   *

We parked initially about a hundred metres down from the old Methodist church, on the opposite side of the road. It gave us a decent view of it in between the steady rhythm of the wiper blades. After ten minutes, Maxi pulled in just in front of us. He opened the back door of his car and took out doubled-up Tesco bags containing something heavy. He walked up to our car and climbed in the back beside me. He placed the bag at his feet.

'Okay?' Joe asked.

'Okay.'

The snooker hall was open and appeared to be doing steady business. In the thirty minutes we waited there, there were always two guys in the doorway, smoking. Not always the same guys, but always two of them.

'Got to presume they're armed,' said Joe.

'They do about ten minutes each, then switch,' said Maxi.

'Be good not to get four at the same time.'

'Be good not to get any of them.'

'They need distracting,' said Joe.

We all nodded. With the exception of Trish, who said, 'I could do that.'

I said, 'No way.'

'I could, absolutely.'

'I mean, I don't want you involved.'

'Dan, I'm here, I'm here for Bobby, I will do what I have to do to get him back.'

'No.'

'Yes.'

'What sort of distraction?' asked Maxi.

'I could undo a couple of buttons, ask them to give me a terror tour of the Shankill.'

'No,' I said.

'Three, then.' She swivelled in her seat and undid them. I'd seen it all before, but I was still looking. Maxi was looking too, and nodding. Joe, who probably had a better view than either of us, glanced once, reddened slightly and then kept his eyes on the church. 'I'll go up and ask them to take me inside and show me the finer points of snooker.'

'No,' I said.

'It's not enough,' said Joe.

'I can't go topless,' said Trish, 'I need the support.'

'No,' said Joe, 'we need something to draw them out.'

'Three buttons and a flat tyre, then,' said Trish.

'Not enough,' said Joe.

'You need to crash it,' said Maxi, 'and get

317

hysterical.'

'Comes naturally,' I said.

She looked at me. 'You wish.'

Joe smirked and looked away.

Maxi had other things on his mind. He said, 'You up to it?'

Trish nodded.

'Okay. *We* transfer to my car. You take this one round the block. You see thon lamppost? You run her into that hard enough to set the alarm off and do some damage. They'll come running and we'll be in. Can you handle that?'

'Perfect,' said Trish.

He looked round us all. We were all in.

We took a few minutes to slip out, one by one, to reconvene in Maxi's car. I was the last to go. I said to Trish, 'This is mental.'

'It usually is,' she said.

I leaned across to kiss her. She kissed me back. It was passionate. We finished. We looked into each other's eyes.

'Love you,' I said.

'I know,' she said.

We left it with a smile, as it should be.

I got out and did my best to saunter casually to Maxi's Volvo. A brief glance towards the church, and I was in.

As I closed the door, Trish drove past.

Maxi started the engine and pulled out. We eased past the church and parked about fifteen metres beyond it, facing away but giving us a partial view of the doors and vestibule through the rain-speckled left-hand side mirror.

'Okay,' said Maxi. 'This is it. Dan, you've been here before, you know what the set-up is. Joe, we go right from the entrance, up a set of stairs. There's a hall with two guards at the end of it. Armed. Beyond is the Millers, don't know if they're carrying or not. Room behind them is where they'll have Bobby, if they have him. If they're having a go at him, and they run to form, Detective Inspector Springer, pride of the force, will be in there interviewing him with pliers.'

Joe nodded. 'And if they don't have him?'

'Then we'll have a lot of apologising to do to the dead folk.'

'You're *killing* them?' I asked.

Maxi looked at me. 'We're not a fucking debating society, Dan.'

'I know, but . . .'

'But nothing.'

Maxi lifted the Tesco bag from the passenger seat. From within he withdrew what appeared to be a sawn-off shotgun. He showed it to Joe.

'Twelve-gauge Beretta. Three in the magazine, one ready to pop.'

Joe unzipped his Nike bag. He withdrew a revolver not dissimilar to mine. He showed it to Maxi. 'Mateba semi-automatic, takes a .357 Magnum cartridge, six shots.'

I showed my weapon, and turned it over, looking for the maker's mark. I couldn't find one.

Maxi took it off me and examined it. 'Smith and Wesson,' he concluded. 'Replica.'

'Rep . . .'

'Exactly. If you pull the trigger, don't forget to say bang.'

'Fuck,' I said.

'Probably for the best,' said Maxi.

'You concentrate on the boy,' said Joe, 'we'll

worry about the rest.'

'Like a wide receiver,' I said.

'No,' said Joe, 'nothing like a wide receiver. You halfwit.'

Trish's car passed us.

'Ready,' said Joe.

'Ready,' said Maxi.

'Ready,' I said, though I was precisely the opposite.

'What the fuck is she doing?' asked Joe.

I turned. Trish had driven past the lamppost, and pulled one side of her car up on to the footpath, but facing away from her target.

'Did she just overshoot?' asked Maxi.

We were perplexed, and then the coin dropped.

'She's going to reverse into it,' I said.

'Why *the fuck* would she do that?'

I laughed. They looked at me.

'What's so funny?' Joe asked.

'*She* is. Even now, this traumatic time, she's thinking about her good looks. She's going to reverse in so she doesn't set the airbag off. She doesn't want it to break her nose.'

Maxi laughed too. 'Women,' he said.

'Women,' agreed Joe. 'I'm well rid.' He checked the mirror. He looked from Maxi to me, then said: 'Tell her.'

I called Trish. She answered on the first ring. 'Go for it, gorgeous,' I said.

'Yes, boss,' she replied. 'And good luck.'

She cut the line. My heart was thumping madly. I had been through a lot of strange, dangerous adventures in my time, but I had never purposely involved Patricia in them. It did not feel good. She was doing this for someone she hardly knew, a

320

tearaway, a dealer, and a snotty teenager to boot. She had a heart of gold, except when it came to me.

I turned in the back seat. Trish's reverse lights were on; even with the rain and the traffic, I could hear her revving the engine.

'Why is she revving the engine?' Maxi asked.

'Just floor the fucker,' said Joe.

And then she did.

The car leapt backwards with engine roaring and wheels spinning and whacked into the lamppost with a huge amount of force. The post remained standing, but the lamp at the top shattered. The car boot flew open. The rear window smashed, spraying glass everywhere. The alarm began to reverberate. Trish kept revving that engine. Passers-by lowered their umbrellas to watch, and then battled to stop them from being blown inside out. We turned to the church—the two hoods on duty were looking across. One took a step down on to the pavement. The other stayed where he was.

'Go on . . . move . . . move,' Maxi whispered.

Patricia was climbing out. She seemed to stumble, then fell to her knees. I couldn't be sure if she was hurt or acting. The alarm continued to sound. The rain was driving sideways, and the wind was whipping up bits of paper, which were swirling around her. There was an awful lot of it; the crash must have crushed the rubbish bin attached to the lamppost.

People began to rush towards her.

Towards her . . . and *past* her.

'What the fuck . . .' I said.

The people of the Shankill were literally dropping their umbrellas, and running *around* the car. Vehicles began to stop. Drivers jumped out and joined everyone else charging about like headless chickens. They were all ignoring Trish. They were jumping up and down, up and down, as if they were taking part in some bizarre flashmob dance extravaganza. They reached up into the air, grabbing, grabbing and grabbing.

And then a piece of the paper slapped into our back window. And the Queen's damp face on a twenty-pound note stared in at us.

'Oh, Christ,' I said.

Patricia's crash had been powerful enough to tear a gash in the boot, which also ripped open the bin bag full of cash, and the wind did the rest.

It was raining money.

Miller money.

'We're on,' said Maxi.

I turned to see the hoods darting through the abandoned cars to join in the paper chase. Snooker players were spilling out of the church after them and shops on either side of the road were emptying. It was turning into a huge scrum, a melee of greed and good fortune. Through it all Trish remained on her knees, completely ignored, and I had a desperate urge to run to her instead of into the church.

But I couldn't.

She would have killed me.

Maxi was out of the car. Joe followed. They paid no attention to the money. They held their guns at their sides, parallel to their legs. I scrambled out after them, my useless revolver held similarly and pointlessly.

I followed as they weaved effortlessly through the throng. Maxi stepped into the vestibule first, bringing his gun up as he did, and led the way up the stairs, which were only wide enough to go single file. Maxi went second, while I brought up the rear, bravely guarding for assault from behind. The steps were old-church wooden, and loud. Before we were a third of the way up, the guard who'd been reading the *Sun* on my last visit appeared at the top. He had a newspaper tucked under his elbow. I don't know if he was there because he'd heard us or because he'd been alerted to the commotion outside. Whatever—he was not expecting what he now encountered: he came to a dead stop, his mouth opened, and he began to paw at the interior of his zip black jacket.

And that was as far as he got.

Maxi fired once, straight into his chest, and the *Sun* man shot backwards, hitting the ground before the sound had finished reverberating in the confined space. Maxi stepped over him and continued on. As Joe passed, he leant down and punched him once, hard in the face, to make sure he didn't try to get up. I looked down at his fluttering eyes and his bubbled bloody breath and also swept past. The table at the end was abandoned and the door behind open. Maxi and Joe charged along and took up positions on either side of the entrance. As far as I knew, Joe had been in the UVF, which was hardly renowned for training its killers in the etiquette of storming enemy fortresses, or indeed anything beyond saluting the flag and kneecapping, but he seemed to know what he was doing. Two shots sounded through the open door, and I hit the deck.

'Stay there,' Maxi hissed. I did as I was told. Maxi looked at Joe, nodded, and they turned into the doorway at the same time, guns raised and

323

shooting. The noise was incredible, the air caustic; when there was a momentary lull, I scrambled forward on hands and knees and peered through the opening. The second of the guards was face down, his T-shirt a bloody mess. Rab was on his back; there was blood pumping out of his throat; his whole body was juddering. Maxi and Joe were already at the other door, in similar positions.

'Windy?' Maxi called out. 'You in there?'

'What's it to you?' Windy yelled back.

'It's Maxi McDowell. You killed my wife.'

'Prove it!'

'Don't need to.'

'Windy . . .' said Joe. 'It's Joe Martin. Joe the Butcher.'

'I know you, Joe. This is none of your business.'

'You have my boy.'

'Your boy?'

'He works for me. You let him go.'

'Yeah, balls I will.'

Maxi calmly began to reload his gun.

'Don't be stupid, Windy,' said Joe. 'Your brother needs help, he's not going to get it while you're in there.'

'My brother is dead, I saw him shot.'

'No he's not, but he soon will be.'

'Rab? Rab!' Windy called. 'Can you hear me?'

'He's shot in the throat,' said Joe. 'He can't talk, but he's still breathing, I can see it. C'mon, Windy, let the boy go.'

Joe began to reload as well. I moved up beside him at the door. Almost the only sound was the frantic gasping coming from Rab. Somewhere in the background there were sirens. Surprise and bravado had got us this far. Now Maxi and Joe were stuck with the knowledge that the first of them through the door would almost certainly be shot. But there was a cold determination about the both of them. Maxi had nothing left to lose. His wife was dead. The man in the next room was responsible for it. Joe's motives were obscure but possibly even more admirable. He was sacrificing his own life for a relative stranger, for nothing more than good.

And then there was a sound from the next room, a clump of something heavy falling.

Maxi looked at Joe, and Joe back at Maxi, and they both looked at me. I shrugged my classic shrug.

'Windy?' Joe called.

'Windy's dead,' came the response.

Unmistakably: Bobby.

I stepped around Maxi. He tried to stop me, but I walked straight through the door, and a fraction of a second later they came after me, one on either side, and there was a sight we would never forget.

Windy was face down on the floor, blood from three gaping wounds haemorrhaging out of his back and spraying the room like a garden sprinkler. Bobby was standing over him, in his gore-spattered stripy apron. He was grinning through swollen lips, three front teeth missing, and a butcher's knife dripping in his hand. His other hand was clutching a chair for support. At the base of the chair there were three teeth that very probably matched the gap in his frightening smile.

'I gutted the fucker!' Bobby cried. 'I gutted the fucker!'

51

'Poor wee skitter,' the doctor said. 'That must've hurt like hell.'

He was a burly man in his fifties; if he'd worked through the bad-olds, then a few missing teeth and an interesting pattern of cigarette burns on the palms of Bobby's hands hardly qualified as major trauma.

'Never mind him,' I said. 'Can you give me something? My head's busting.'

He declined.

Bobby had been shifted up from Casualty to the Royal Belfast Hospital for Sick Children, on the grounds of the RVH, for which he just about qualified. It was an open ward, and full; lots of baldy-headed kids insatiably curious about the new arrival and his connection to the police milling about wanting to ask him questions. They had a lot of questions. When they couldn't ask Bobby, they asked me. They might have asked Maxi, or Joe, if they'd been able to find them.

Maxi had been resigned to the fact that he would be arrested; he didn't care. It was Joe who persuaded, cajoled and finally dragged him away by arguing that they had to finish their work. Springer had fled down the fire escape. He had as much to do with Bobby's kidnapping and Maxi's wife's murder as the Millers. So they went looking for him, and that left me with toothless Bobby and four corpses for all of about five seconds, until the cops came storming up the stairs, armed to the teeth and screaming at us to put our hands up. So I did, but

Bobby said, 'I can't, I'll fall over,' and it was all the funnier because he was pasted in blood. We started giggling, and we could hardly stop, and the cops looked at us like we were mental.

The fact that they had then allowed me to accompany Bobby to the hospital—yes, *of course* I'm his legal guardian—meant that they at least partly believed that I was the innocent bystander I claimed to be. I had, of course, planted my useless replica gun on one of the corpses, and my pointing out towards the fire escape and proclaiming, 'They went thataway,' as the peelers entered also contributed to my pulling the wool over their eyes. It couldn't possibly last.

Once she was assured we were safe, via the expeditious method of spotting us being brought out by the cops and escorted to an ambulance, Patricia managed a quick smile and wave, but otherwise kept her head down. As more and more police arrived, she quietly got into her car, started the engine, and gently pulled its mangled rear end free of the lamppost with the minimum of screeching and drove away, completely unnoticed. The cops were too busy with the carnage in the church, while the people of the Shankill had no further use for her now that they had picked her car clean. Not only was every single twenty-pound note gone, but the cocaine with it; not content with that, they'd stolen a family bag of mini Mars bars from the dash, and rifled Trish's multi-CD player, removing Van, David Gates and Simon and Garfunkel's *Greatest Hits*. For some strange reason they left behind my sole contribution to her playlist, the Ramones' *It's Alive*, even though she pursued them up the street offering it to them for free.

When she was finally allowed in to see Bobby, Trish was all concern for him and daggers for me.

'My car . . . you used my *fucking* car . . .' she hissed, as he began to drift off. 'How *dare* you!'

'How dare I what? Come up with a plan that saved Bobby?'

'That . . . that . . . *that* was not part of the plan!'

'Sure about that?'

'You're a deceitful, untrustworthy, lying son of a—'

'Hold your horses, Trish,' I said, raising calming hands, which were guaranteed to inflame her further, and didn't disappoint. 'Didn't it all work? All's well that ends well?'

'Don't *fucking* give me that!' She leant across the bed, her elbow resting on the covers where one of Bobby's legs should have been. 'What if I'd been stopped by the peelers and they'd checked the boot and found all that money? How would I have explained that away?'

'You wouldn't,' I admitted. 'But look on the bright side, they mightn't even have noticed it. They would have been distracted by the cocaine.'

'The . . . Holy fuck . . . you *didn't*.'

'Holy fuck I did.'

She raged as only Trish can.

'You fucking big waste of space, you can't even look me in the eye, can you?'

I couldn't, but mainly because I'd spotted DS Hood coming towards us over her shoulder. His lips appeared red and swollen, probably from being taped shut. His demeanour was earnest and concerned. Not for me, obviously.

'What about Maxi?' he asked.

'What about him?'

He made an apologetic hand to Trish, and took me by the arm and led me off to one side. 'I'm talking to you now as a friend of Maxi's, not as a police officer.'

'Aye, right,' I said.

'I swear to God I didn't know Springer was . . . involved.'

'*Involved?*'

'I know, I *know*. I had no idea. Honestly. Just, just tell me what I can do to help Maxi.'

'Detective Sergeant Hood,' I began, 'forgive me, but I've forgotten your first name?'

'Gary.'

'Detective Sergeant Hood, Maxi's wife is dead, killed by your colleague and partner. His life is over, there's not a damn thing you can do to help him.'

'Then . . . save him. What can I do to save him?'

'From what?'

'I don't know. Himself. From doing anything worse.'

'I think that horse has bolted.'

He studied me. I studied him back. His demeanour changed.

He said, 'I'm going to have to take you in.'

'For why?'

'What do you think? We haven't even spoken to you about the bomb outside your office, about how you came into possession of an incriminating photo of the late Paddy Barr, what your connection to Malone Security is, what your connection to a serious assault on the head of that company is, why you accompanied two gunmen into the headquarters of the de facto leaders of the Ulster Volunteer Force, what you have to do with the

329

death of the Miller brothers, and why your wife's car, according to the CCTV footage I've just watched, appears to have disgorged several million pounds' worth of banknotes on to the Shankill Road.'

'You'd have to ask her about that,' I said.

*   *   *

Hood was no more Maxi's friend than I was, but I think he cared enough. However, he was still a cop, and had to do his business. Fortunately, there was enough going on, what with everything he'd just pointed out to me, plus the fact that there were two gunmen on the loose, and in pursuit of a rogue cop, that he didn't have to haul me down there and then. We came to a gentlemen's agreement that once we'd sorted Bobby out, then I would volunteer myself at Comanche Station. I would do my very best not to incriminate myself, and possibly not Patricia either, depending on her attitude.

We remained on the ward, either side of Bobby. After a while, the police disappeared. It should have been a depressing place. Sick kids, dying kids. But they were up to their necks in mischief. It was good to see, and might have brought a tear to the eye, if I'd been the type.

I looked at Trish across the bed. She was a brave, compassionate, funny, beautiful woman, and I'd loved her since the year dot. We were older now, but clearly less sensible.

I said, 'What do you want to do?'

'About?'

'The boy wonder.'

'Oh, I don't know.'

330

'He's a one-legged drug-dealing hoodlum who has just cut his mother's killer to ribbons with a butcher's knife.'

Trish smiled. 'I know. Every home should have one.'

I looked at her. 'Good one,' I said.

'Good one, what?'

'Every *home* should have one?'

'He has nowhere else to go.'

'Excuse me? The Millers are dead, the threat is lifted. He can go to his relatives.'

'Would you put him back into that environment, after what he's been through?'

'Absolutely.'

'Dan.'

'Patricia.'

'You know something? He reminds me of you.'

'Thanks a million.'

'I'm serious. I mean, his attitude. And he's funny, when you're not there.'

'Trish.'

'Dan.'

'He reminds you of me? Well if you want a *me*, you can have a me.'

'Darlin', I already have you.'

She smiled. It was warm.

'What's that supposed to mean?' I asked.

'Work it out,' said Trish.

*   *   *

She elected to stay by his side. I elected to leave. Elections are so divisive. It was early evening. It had been a busy day. I was exhausted. And confused. And exhilarated. I was in need of a drink.

331

There was a line of taxis outside the hospital.

I climbed into the first and said, 'The *Bob Shaw*.'

He caught my eye in the mirror.

'Kid sick?' he asked.

'Aye.'

He pulled out on to the Falls and headed for the West Link.

'It's not the answer, you know,' he said.

'I didn't even know there was a question,' I said.

'I was on the bottle for twenty years.'

'Really.'

'Nearly killed myself.'

Not nearly enough.

I enjoy the occasional pint or three. I'm not the worst at it. I'm not the worst at anything, unless you include marriage. I don't fall down drunk, I don't throw up over people, I don't annoy strangers, unless they're asking for it. I enjoy my own company, and thinking things through, like why or how or what the fuck Trish was thinking of wanting to take a waif and stray under her wing. She struggled to cope with me as it was. You couldn't adopt every sick puppy in the pound. Sometimes you had to just nod in sympathy and leave them to their fate.

The driver was yittering on about how he was saved, and his twelve-step programme. I grunted and nodded.

By way of distraction, I took out my mobile. I hadn't looked at it since giving Trish the okay to crash her car into the lamppost. If she'd showed a little more restraint, I would have been several million to the good, and a drug baron to boot. I sighed. I'd switched the phone off on entering the hospital, because there was a sign, and a nurse warned me. There was a voicemail waiting.

It was from Bobby's dad in England. He said he'd finally talked to his wife about it, and she was mad that he hadn't told her he had a son from a previous relationship, and absolutely he should get in touch with the boy. He said he wasn't promising anything, but, you know, he could maybe have a chat with the lad, see if he could start something with him, it might lead somewhere.

I deleted the message. If he wanted to make contact bad enough, he'd find a way. In the meantime, Trish could have a free run at Bobby. She needed it. She had been carrying a coal shed full of guilt about the death of our boy for nearly a decade; if it made her feel better offering Bobby a leg-up in life, even if it was just for a short while, then who was I to stand in her way? I've made her miserable and happy in equal measures, and one day we'll meet somewhere in the middle. I thought maybe that Bobby might help that process a little.

Or stab us to death in our beds.

I glanced at my watch, then leaned forward a little and said, 'You wouldn't stick the Jack Caramac show on the radio, mate, would you?'

'That mouthpiece?'

'Aye, him.'

He blew air out of his cheeks and switched it on.

I don't quite know what my expectations were. Jack is an odd mix of righteous indignation and rampant ego, but he does seem to care about this stupid place, about the concerns of the little man and the very simple but wilfully ignored importance of doing the right thing.

The first voice I heard was not Jack's, but a caller into his show. He was saying, 'Say what you want about the Millers, but at least the streets were safe to walk at night . . .'

'You're talking through your hat,' said Jack.

'Before they came along, there were gangs of kids terrorising us, and now they're not . . .'

'Because the Millers shot them!'

'Well the peelers weren't doin' nothing!'

'So you think anyone should be able to take the law into their own hands?'

'All I know is we were able to walk down our street without—'

'I hear what you're saying. Thank you for your call.' He cut the line. 'If you're just joining us, we're talking about the tragic death of the Miller brothers in a shoot-out on the Shankill Road earlier today. And when I say tragic, I'm only joking. Everybody is someone's son, someone's brother, someone's dad or daughter. But I'm sorry, Mrs Miller, if you're out there, your boys are gone, and I say good riddance to bad rubbish. We've been getting calls about this all afternoon and into this evening from concerned citizens hoping and praying that now that someone's done the decent thing and gotten rid of this . . . pestilence, maybe the forces of law and order will step in and *stop it happening again*. Am I being naïve? Am I being ridiculously optimistic? Let me know what you think. Call us up, go on to our website, Facebook, Twitter, open your front door and shout, get in touch whatever way you can.'

'He just likes stirring things up,' said my taxi man.

I grunted.

'Now,' said Jack, 'for something completely different—or is it? I have a book in front of me here, a book that might just strike terror into

334

many people across Belfast and further afield, and have many of the rest of you nodding your heads and saying, *I told you so*. I don't normally promote books on this show, apart from my own autobiography, because it's such an entertaining read—and which is, incidentally, still available from all good bookshops—but this isn't that kind of a book. It's what you might have called in the old days a ledger, that is, a book used in accounting. I'm sure it's all software programs these days, but this is just an old-fashioned book with names, and amounts, and dates. Do you remember the tick man, used to come round the doors collecting debts? That's what this is. Now why would I want to talk about a ledger live on national radio? Well, you see, this isn't a record of ordinary transactions. This isn't the milkman keeping tabs, it's not the *Belfast Telegraph* delivery boy; this is for a company called Malone Security, a company owned by . . . you guessed it, the Miller brothers. And what it shows, I kid you not, is a record of all the cocaine deliveries they were making to private addresses across our wonderful city. Yes, folks, cocaine! And huge amounts of it! Millions of pounds snorted up those nice middle-class noses in south Belfast!'

'Is he serious?' my driver asked.

'Who knows?' I said.

The fact was that I'd given Jack an iPhone, not some ancient ledger, but he was a showman, he knew how the story would play best. A ledger felt more real.

'Now, folks, I'm not saying these people are guilty of using drugs, I'm not saying this will stand up in a court of law, and I certainly hope I'm not libelling anyone or slandering anyone; all I'm going to do is read out a list of names and addresses I've found in a book belonging to two drug dealers who were just this morning killed in their gangster headquarters on the Shankill Road. You may draw whatever conclusions you want. Let's just flick randomly through it and see what name I come to first. Oh—that's interesting. Abagail Pike. Isn't that . . . no, that couldn't be . . . ? Abagail Pike, the Assembly member, wife of our Minister of . . . Surely not? And in debt for how much? Good Lord! Oh my goodness. Why, if this was true, she'd have to resign! And probably her husband, too! Okay, let's turn to the next page!'

The taxi man indicated and pulled in outside the *Bob Shaw*. He looked back at me and said, 'He shouldn't be allowed to say stuff like that.'

'Well switch him off, then,' I said.

'I will as soon as I hear what happens next,' said the driver, and then quickly added: 'Six fifty.'

I gave him the exact money and got out. He rolled down his window and said, 'What about the tip?'

'Don't sleep in the subway,' I said, and winked, and turned. I could hear him swearing after me as I pushed my way into the bar.

It was early yet, but busy. I took a seat and ordered a pint from Lenny. She was looking as lovely as ever. I scanned the clientele, looking for her husband or heavies in his employ. There appeared to be no immediate threat, and her welcoming smile seemed to confirm it. I was just lifting the glass to my lips when someone behind me said, 'Dan Starkey?'

My heart beat a little faster. I turned to find a small man with receding hair and wearing an unremarkable grey suit. His cheeks were flushed red, and his bottom lip was quivering nervously.

'Maybe,' I said.

'It is, isn't it? She said you'd be in.'

He nodded at Lenny. Lenny smiled encouragement to him.

I raised pacifist hands. 'Okay, you got me,' I said.

'I heard you were like a private investigator . . . ?'

I was about to laugh and say no, but instead, and it being easier than trying to explain about my bespoke service, I nodded and said, 'Uhuh?' like it was a perfectly normal thing to be asking.

'Just, my wife—I think she might be having an affair. She's a big woman, but not unattractive. Is there any chance you might look into it for me?'

I looked at him. I looked at Lenny. I looked at my pint.

I took a sip.

It was good.

I have long believed that in life, there are no happy endings, just happy beginnings, and that my own life has been a series of troughs, connected by creaking bridges.

But as I stood there, drink in hand, I had to admit that for once, things had turned out okay. The boy was safe, the bad guys were vanquished or in the process of being . . . vanked. Maxi and Joe, our unlikely saviours, were still somewhere out there in pursuit of Springer, but I did not doubt that they would find him and kill him. I was battle-scarred but otherwise in fairly good nick, considering what I'd been through. Patricia had made some optimistic noises about our relationship, and I would do my best to make things right there. But for the moment, there was a girl behind the bar making eyes at me, I'd a cold pint in my hand, and if the man in the grey suit was an indication of things to come, then my new career was beginning to show signs of life. I couldn't complain.

'Well?' the grey-suited man asked. 'Will you do it for me?'

'Absolutely,' I said, 'but first . . .' I held my hand up and turned back to the bar, 'let there be crisps.'